Strid

STRIDER'S GALAXY

Paul Barnett

LEGEND

Published by Legend Books in 1997

1 3 5 7 9 10 8 6 4 2

Copyright © Paul Barnett 1997

The right of Paul Barnett to be identified as the author
of this work has been asserted by him in accordance
with the Copyright, Designs and Patents Act, 1988.

Legend Books
Random House UK Limited
20 Vauxhall Bridge Road, London SW1V 2SA

Random House Australia (Pty) Limited
16 Dalmore Drive, Scoresby, Victoria 3179, Australia

Random House New Zealand Limited
18 Poland Road, Glenfield, Auckland 10, New Zealand

Random House South Africa (Pty) Limited
Endulini, 5a Jubilee Road, Parktown 2193, South Africa

RANDOM HOUSE UK Limited Reg. No. 954009

Papers used by Random House UK Limited
are natural, recyclable products made from wood grown in
sustainable forests. The manufacturing processes conform to
the environmental regulations of the country of origin

ISBN 0 09 979121 8

Typeset by Deltatype Ltd, Birkenhead, Merseyside
Printed and bound in Great Britain by
Cox & Wyman Ltd, Reading, Berkshire

Dedication

This is for Roy Gasson and Richard Evans, two fine editors in very different fields, who died within a few weeks of each other in the spring of 1996: you were much loved by all of us, Richard and Roy, and shouldn't have died when you did. Thanks, both of you, for friendship.

Acknowledgements

Thanks to Tim Holman of Little, Brown and to Felicity Brooks of Usborne for their patience: much appreciated. Thanks to my wife Catherine and my daughter Jane for putting up with me (no mean feat) and to my daughter Fionna for not going strawberry-blonde in the face about all the letters I never got round to answering. Thanks to John Jarrold of Legend and to Robert Kirby, my agent, for having faith. Thanks to Keith Stanaway of NatWest for making it possible. Especial thanks to my brother Keith, despite the fact he never reads fantasy or science fiction – even mine – for telling me sternly that surely there must be new things to be done with space opera: hope I've done a few of them, guv.

But there is one particular piece of gratitude. It is little realized how much difference a good copy-editor can make to a book, not just in terms of improving the text but also as an attentive critic. Really top-flight copy-editors are thin on the ground. I was lucky enough to have one of the best in the country working on this book. (I use the expression 'one of the best' solely because the three or four truly excellent ones I know are each as good as the other.) My profound thanks to Nancy Webber. Nancy has not seen and has therefore not copy-edited this paragraph: I hope the difference doesn't show.

PB

Contents

Part One: Home Territory

1

Mars: AD2527

Strider was more than a bit depressed by the way the interview had gone – essentially, she'd blown it – so she refused their offer of a courtesy cabble and decided to walk home. The night air was thin and cold – a perfect contrast to the environment-conditioning of the SSIA blister. She breathed it deep into her lungs, feeling its pleasurable pain in her throat. There was little or no traffic on the road this late, so that all she had to guide her was starlight and the faint glow of City 43, sixteen kilometres ahead of her. The walk would take her nearly an hour; in a way she wished it would take longer. She wanted to get the taste of bureaucracy out of her mouth.

A few hundred metres away from the blister – far enough away that she could feel she'd properly left it behind her – she paused and looked up at the sky. Staring at the stars was her customary occupational therapy: the thought of the distances and scale of the Universe was usually enough to calm her wraths and anxieties.

Tonight it didn't work, though. The first thing she saw was Phobos, normally her favourite companion in the heavens.

The uniforms who'd interviewed her had talked a lot about Phobos. People were building a ship on the tiny moon, taking advantage of the low gravity and the abundance of mineral wealth not far below the surface. By the time the ship was finished its mass would be a small but significant percentage of Phobos's own, so that when the vessel was ferried off to Jupiter for fuelling there would be a perceptible shift in Phobos's orbit.

That would happen in about a year's time.

She had hoped for the past decade that she would be aboard that ship.

So much for that.

3

She started to walk again.

In the year 2489 in the Martin Hunter Ogobe Hospital in Ouagadougou a female child was born to a mother who didn't want her. It wasn't a matter of economics – no one ever starved in Burkina Faso, whose rich plains and extensive, hardly tapped uranium deposits funded the world's most beneficent social security system. No, the reason the mother didn't want even to see her daughter after the birth was that she was only thirteen and the conception had come about as a consequence of a rape. The rapists – there had been three of them – had been tracked down and castrated, but this symbolic vengeance had done nothing to remove from the girl's memory the terror of the experience, or the pain.

Rape was a very rare crime in any part of the developed world. Most people – certainly in a country like Burkina Faso – possessed sexbots; if not, they could be hired on any street corner for the night for the price of a pack of ziprite gum. The three criminals had, rather, been expressing their disapproval of the shortness of her dress. The girl who had just given birth to a child she would never see, would never name, had started experimenting with her own parents' sexbots over a year earlier; she had found the female infinitely the better lover, yet generally she wanted the male to play a part as well, because it was good to feel his rigidity inside her when she came to her final orgasm. She had even tried to reprogram the two sexbots to copulate with each other, so that she could watch, but she'd never been able to.

None of the three men who'd raped her had enjoyed the same exaggerated penile proportions as the male sexbot, yet each of their penetrations had been agonizing. She had been in the family orchard at the time, with the sky mockingly blue above and the birds disinterestedly flitting between the trees. One of the men had held a knife against her throat and put his penis in her mouth. Another had unsuccessfully tried to ram his penis into her rectum. She had thought she was going to die, and she very nearly did. The pain of giving birth to the resulting child was as nothing compared to that earlier event.

4

As soon as she had discovered her pregnancy she had begged for an abortion, but Burkina Faso was then in the grip of strict Umbellism, and abortions were illegal unless the child would be born handicapped. Her parents devoutly refused to fly her abroad; however the child had been conceived, they said, it had a right to live.

They were beside her as their unwanted grandchild was born. Like the mother, they had no desire to see the baby again, and so it was left to the hospital staff to take the squealing infant away and hook her up to an automated wetnurse, on whose plastic nipple – with its carefully concocted and everready supply of milk-substitute – she thrived. The child was later placed in an institution that catered for unwanted children. And she was given a name: Leonie.

She never really worried about the fact that she hadn't a mother until much later, when she was fifteen. That was when her mother sent her a viddisc showing both the scene of her birth and, afterwards, a tearstained apology for having abandoned her at birth. Would it be possible for the two of them to get together and try to patch up something of a family?

'Fuck off,' Leonie said to the screen.

She put the viddisc in the nearest disposal vent, and waited until she heard the grinders boot up, far below, before she went away down the corridor to find something to eat.

'How has your rejection by your mother at birth affected your ability to relate to other people?' said Alphonse Dulac. He was standing by an artificial window looking out on an artificial scene. People had generated lush landscapes within most of the blisters on Mars, in stark contrast to the generally still patchy vegetation of the open terrain, but the SSIA had resisted the trend: if people were indeed to be sent to the stars they should become accustomed to bleakness and alienness. This didn't stop the SSIA's bigwigs from wanting to enjoy a pleasant view from their 'windows'.

Strider raised an eyebrow. Her other four interviewers – all men, which vaguely annoyed her – were seated facing her around the outer side of a semicircular stone desk. They were all bigger than her, but then most people were. She imagined that the desk was a lens, and that where she sat was a focus for their gazes.

'It affected me for a year or two after I got that viddisc,' she admitted. 'No longer than that. I had a lot of difficulty trusting people. I mean, it's hard to make friendships when at the back of your mind you're thinking that the person who should have been your best friend of all kicked you out of her life, sight unseen, then fifteen years later tried to pass her guilt right back on to you.'

She pushed her fingers back through her hair.

'But then,' she continued, 'after a while I began to feel sorry for her. I'd been thinking of myself as the failure in the relationship – or lack-of-relationship – but I grew to realize that it wasn't me, it was her. It'd have been tougher to bring myself together if she'd held on to me for a year or two and *then* rejected me.'

She knew she was sweating. Part of the reason was that the blister's environment-conditioning was turned up too high, especially in this office; the other and greater part was because the interview had suddenly homed in on the intimate aspects of herself. She'd known this was coming, but it didn't make it any easier to deal with. Also, she was irritated by the light in here, which was Earth-standard and thus brighter than what she was accustomed to.

Dulac looked over his shoulder at her.

'So you began to be able to relate to other people again?'

'Yeah, you bet,' said Strider. She grinned, at last beginning to relax. *Think of these pompous bastards as medics,* she thought. *You've told enough medics about your innermost secrets over the years.* 'I related with a lot of people during my late teens.'

'And those relationships . . . ended,' suddenly said Rateen Macphee, opposite her.

'Most of them hardly began,' said Strider, startled by his intervention. 'I was enjoying myself. Weren't you the same at that age? Weren't we all?'

'What I'm trying to get at,' said Macphee, 'is that you can

hardly class brief sexual affairs as true interpersonal relationships.'

Strider reflected for a moment. The point was a fair one.

'Yeah,' she said finally, 'but what all of them meant was that I'd discovered how to *trust* people again. Don't get me wrong: I was always genuinely fond of the people I had sex with, and some of them remained good friends for years afterwards – there are a couple working here for the SSIA whom I see regularly.'

'For sex?' It was Dulac again.

'No. I hardly ever have sex these days – except with my bot, of course.'

'Why not? Are you frightened of sex?' Dulac moved back from the 'window' and resumed his seat.

Again Strider paused.

'Can I explain a few things?' she said.

'Go ahead.'

'For a while after I saw my mother's viddisc I was terrified of being raped. That was another bit of guilt that she piled on me – as if somehow what had happened to her was my fault. But I got over it. Twenty years ago sex was – for me and for a lot of the other kids around me – a way of telling ourselves that we were fond of each other. We could have bought each other drinks, or something, but we never had any money. So instead we talked a lot, or went out walking if the pollution wasn't too bad – which it often wasn't, because the winds usually blew all Burkina Faso's crap southwards and away – and sometimes we had sex. There was no great hassle about it.'

'And then?' said Dulac.

'Yeah, then I went through a bad patch.' Strider looked around at the five blank faces. In a way, Dulac and Macphee were the easiest to cope with. The other three had said nothing at all to her after the mumbled introductions, an hour ago; besides, their faces were covered with different pieces of interactive technology: for all she knew, they could right now be examining her alveoli in detail or watching a soap opera. At least Dulac and Macphee had each left one eye uncovered. It gave Strider something to look at, some way of communing. 'I became infatuated with someone. It lasted just over a year. It took me that long to realize what a complete turd he was. When I left him it hurt a lot – not because the relationship had dissolved but because I realized how *stupid* I'd been.'

'To trust him?' This time it was Macphee. He and Dulac were positioned at opposite ends of the huge, heavy desk. Strider was being interviewed in stereo.

'No. Where I'd been stupid was that I'd let my hormones govern my perceptions. I'd wasted a year of my life. I was like a junkie who'd managed to come off the tabs and then looked back on all the time that had been *wasted* – all the good days that had been thrown away. Cured junkies have a choice: to go back on the tabs or to build themselves a life. I decided to build myself a life – that I wasn't going to make that kind of mistake again.'

'You decided not to fall in love again,' said Dulac, clearing his throat.

'I hadn't been in love in the first place.' She grinned once more, and for the second time this evening began to relax. 'I thought about what I really wanted to do, and discovered that it was to go starside. Part of my task was to re-learn how to make friendships, so I did that; I realized that sex wasn't the best way of establishing trust – that a game of chess was better. Also, I got myself a degree in astrophysics at Ouagadougou Univ and –'

'A first,' said Macphee, looking across at Dulac.

'With honours,' replied Dulac.

Strider recognized that the little exchange had been designed merely to harass her. They were deliberately putting her under stress. She shrugged. That was part of their job: to find out how she coped with stress.

'I got the degree,' she said, 'and then I signed up as a trainee with the SSIA. The rest you know about – it's all in the computers.'

Dulac looked grumpy. 'Of course we've been through your records, Strider, and very impressive they are – you wouldn't have been called here for interview had they not been. But the purpose of our meeting is not to examine your academic credentials or your technical skills or your military expertise but to try to find out what sort of a person you are. We've all looked at your psychological profiles as well, but they can tell us only so much. You're obviously well adapted and stable; you're a strong personality with a high IQ. What we need to establish is whether or not you could endure the strains of being cooped up in a tin can for thirty years with forty other people, some of whom will certainly prove incapable of tolerating that strain.'

'Can I get up and walk about?' said Strider.

Dulac nodded.

She moved over to the fake window and looked out at the scene. Someone had spent a lot of computer-time generating the holographic display. The theme was an idyllized version of Classical Greece, with philosophers in long white robes strolling through sylvan greenery and exchanging what were presumably great wisdoms – probably definitive proofs that the Earth was flat. The tranquillity of the scene, however, was infectious; Strider felt as if the room temperature had just dropped by a welcome five degrees.

'You've been asking a lot about my personal life,' she said, turning back towards her interrogators, who had swivelled their chairs to face her. She shrugged. 'It hasn't been all that pleasant for me, but it hasn't bothered me too much, either. Some things about me I keep very secret, and no one will ever discover them: you could keep me in this room for a month and you'd still never find them out. Most of them are secret because if I talked about them I could hurt other people – which makes me sound more sanctimonious than I intend. Some of them are secret for the most selfish of reasons. Everything else about me, though, is information I'm happy to divulge.

'And one thing that I'm happy to divulge *right now*,' she said, staring Dulac straight in the eyes, 'is that I will not allow anyone to call the *Santa Maria* a "tin can". I don't know how much personal work you've put into its creation, buster, but I do know that thousands of other people have laboured over it, from the designers and techs through to the person with a wrench who helped install the shower-heads. Some of them

9

have been working for the money, but I reckon most of them have seen that ship as the liferaft she is.'

Dulac looked unfazed. Strider had expected an angry reaction from him.

'Carry on,' he said.

'The *Santa Maria* is a triumph of human endeavour in every sense of the term,' said Strider. She looked once more through the 'window', deliberately controlling herself. 'I will not listen to some pampered fat cat in an office calling it a "can".'

'I think this stage of the interview procedure is over,' said Dulac abruptly. He looked at each of his colleagues in turn. They nodded. Then he swivelled back to meet Strider's gaze.

'Thank you for your time. We can call up a cabble to take you back to City 43 . . .'

Once upon a time – centuries before a raped child had brought into existence the infant that became the human being now walking through the darkness towards City 43 – much of the Earth had been like the holographic scene Strider had watched in the interview room. Then a soaring population and sheer human greed had killed it – or, at least, had initiated and accelerated the processes that would, a millennium or two ahead, kill it. Maybe not as long as a millennium would be required: the environmental degradation was now moving with almost visible swiftness, and seemed irreversible.

What had really spelled the end was the short three-way nuke war between Indonesia, Japanasia and China in 2047. The war was over in a matter of hours, because that was how long it had taken for the populations of all three nations to be exterminated entirely; it might have gone on a bit longer except that the countries' military leaders had been among the casualties. Aotearoa and Australia chipped in for a final few suicidal minutes. Aside from the millions who died during those few hours, over half the population of the Earth perished over the next couple of decades as a direct consequence of the war, which had been, in essence, about net-usage rights. Kids were born with horrific disabilities; or more often they were

10

not, because people chose to abort them or had pre-empted the moral dilemma by opting for sterilization.

No one had ever tried to calculate how many other human beings had died through the major indirect consequence of the war, which was a radical shift of climate patterns. Various models produced in the twentieth century had suggested that a nuke war would either contribute so much to global warming that life on Earth would bake to death or throw so much crap into the atmosphere that, with the Sun's heat blocked out, life would freeze to death. The nuke war showed the opposing models to be both right and wrong. Most of the northern hemisphere froze, and most of the southern hemisphere baked – which didn't much concern the people of Oceania, who were all dead anyway, but was rough luck for the southern half of South America, which had had nothing to do with the original, now largely forgotten dispute and whose population was largely too poor to emigrate in haste to more temperate climes.

Those temperate climes extended in a band of variable width around the equator. Mexico and United Caribbea and the countries to their south were inundated by North Americans seeking sanctuary from the chill. While parts of Africa became wastelands, others tried to cope with colossal immigration from Europe. In the aftermath of the nuke war, the Arab nations wiped themselves out in the bacteriological War of Hatred, which incidentally destroyed Israel.

When the surviving human population of Earth got down to about four hundred million, of whom ten per cent were in some way handicapped, the world's few remaining political leaders decided that the best option was the urgent terraforming of Mars. It was a task that took several hundred years, and the resultant ecosystem was frail; at most a few hundred million people could survive on the once red but increasingly green planet. They could – with difficulty – live outside if they chose, but most opted to dwell inside the various blisters constructed with an almost obscene haste all over humanity's new world. Water was still a problem: even with cloud-seeding, showers tended to be short-lived and mild. Some people decided instead to remain on Earth; about a hundred million continued to live in

11

the safe zone around the equator, enjoying the fruits of what still seemed a profligate nature while at the same time knowing that the world was dying around them. But anyone with any sense, and who could afford it, went to Mars.

If they were allowed to. The Martian government soon started introducing immigration quotas. There was almost another war – and would have been, except that Earth no longer possessed the technological ability to mount one. This was a good thing: the human species had already had the misfortune to destroy one planet; to have destroyed another would have seemed like carelessness.

She was about half an hour into her walk back to City 43 when the attack came.

The Martian night was almost silent, except for the faint, high-pitched whines of nocturnal insects; the insides of the blisters could be noisy, but the plastite walls stopped most of the sound from leaking into the meagre atmosphere. Strider had been listening to nothing but the sound of her own footfalls and her hoarse breathing for several kilometres when a hand from behind her snaked around her mouth.

'Don't make any noise,' said a voice.

Instinctively, Strider bit the palm that was gagging her, then grabbed the wrist with both hands, fell half-sideways and, rearing up, threw the mugger out in front of her. Although she had been nearly twenty years on Mars, it still seemed to her that he took an inordinately long time to fall to the ground. By the time he did so, she had one boot ready to clamp down on his throat.

'I have friends,' the man croaked.

'So have I,' said Strider. She wished her voice sounded stronger. While the Martian atmosphere was sufficient to support human life, any prolonged exercise – like walking – led to breathlessness. 'What were you wanting?'

Flat on his back, the mugger tried to produce a shrug. She could see his face only as a blur in the darkness. 'Your plastic,' he said. 'What the fuck else do you think I'd want?'

'To kill me, maybe?'

12

'Nah. My licence doesn't extend to killing people, just to mugging them. If you'll let me get my papers out of my pocket . . .'

'No.'

'Oh, it's like that, is it?' The man began to shiver.

'Don't worry. Like yourself, I'm not into killing.' She looked up towards Phobos again, wondering if the sight of the tiny moon might give her some inspiration. If she let this turd go then all that would happen would be that he'd mug someone else, less capable than herself. Her civic duty was to take him along with her to City 43 and hand him in to the authorities, where he would be charged with incompetence. But she didn't enjoy the prospect. She was already tireder than she'd expected, so beating him unconscious and then carrying him was out of the question. She could pull her lazgun on him, she supposed, and march him all the way to City 43, but in the darkness he could easily escape from her, and he might attack her again . . .

'I've got an idea,' she said, looking down once more at the dim blob of his face. 'You and I could be friends.'

'I don't know what you mean.'

'Friends. It's what people often are to each other.'

'I –'

'You're currently in no position to argue. I could break your neck if I wanted to.'

'You probably couldn't.'

'What do you mean?' She leant forward to stare at him more closely.

'I'm not a human. I'm a bot.'

'Oh, for –'

'It's true,' he said.

'Bots don't go mugging – they've no need to.' Bots of whatever type either had free board and lodging or they weren't manufactured in the first place.

'I do.'

She rested her boot on his throat; it wouldn't hurt him much and it was a relief to stop standing on one foot. His head buzzed for a couple of seconds, then stopped.

'I think you need to do some explaining.'

'Dr Dulac –'

'What's that arsehole got to do with this?'

'There are several stages of the interview. You passed the first one. Now you've just passed the second. I wouldn't have hurt you more than necessary, you know.'

'Oh, yeah?'

'Do you think you *chose* to walk back to your hotel in City 43? Wouldn't that have been just a bit irrational of you? Do you think you could allow me to sit up?'

'No. Squirm a bit.'

Again the bot attempted a shrug. 'Have it your own way.'

Strider pressed her foot down more firmly as she thought. Dulac had looked so firmly out the fake window that it was only natural that she would want to do so as well; perhaps her desire or otherwise to see that vista was a part of the test: people who were not inquisitive were hardly likely to be the best personnel aboard the *Santa Maria*. She remembered the famous legend about what happened when the first *Viking* had landed on Mars, way back in whatever it was: about half an hour after the initial pictures had begun to come through to Earth, someone on the project had said, 'Yeah, but I want to see what's on the *other* side of that ridge.' Inquiry was what going into space was all about. And, of course, the holo she had seen was of people walking around under the open sky of a paradisiac world. Probably Dulac had also laced the air of the office with nanobots that would increase her suggestibility when she inhaled them. She giggled suddenly: if he'd done that, he and his four colleagues must have been going berserk all through the discussion of her sex life.

She sobered quickly.

'What other mind games was Dulac playing?' she said.

'I don't know, lady. I'm just a bot. Look, are you *sure* you won't let me sit up? Machines can feel just as much discomfort as human beings when they're pinned down like this.'

'Tell me another.'

'I possess just enough pain sensors to protect myself from damage, so your boot isn't hurting me. But I've got enough

14

intelligence to realize that I should be vertical, not horizontal, and that this situation is very humiliating. Does that make sense to you, lady?'

'I'll let you sit up – I'll even let you stand up and walk around – if you respond the right way to my earlier idea. You and I could be friends, and walk the rest of the way together to City 43.'

'No. I can't do that. I have to get back to the SSIA blister. It's not within my remit to do anything else.'

Strider snorted. 'Just as a matter of interest, what would you have done if I hadn't overpowered you?'

'Mugged you. But without causing pain, if I could help it.'

'Well,' she said, 'at least you're being franker than you were before.' She raised her boot cautiously. 'Can you call a cabble for me?'

'It'd be a pleasure, lady,' said the bot, slowly raising himself. 'Anything to get you as far away from me as possible. There's one on the way already.'

When she finally got back to her hotel room she stripped off her clothes and twisted the command switch to fill the room with water. Of course, it wasn't real water – there was no water to waste on Mars – but an illusion, the same way that it was only an illusion that she was breathing through gills as she swam around in the warmth. Further illusions ensured that the room expanded so that she was swimming in an infinitude of sunlit ocean, with bright shoals of fishes flickering towards her and then away again.

She twitched her tail to bring herself down to face the mirror that hung over the bed.

You don't look so bad, young Leonie, she thought, turning from side to side, watching herself move slowly in the water. A small green fish, half-transparent, came up to investigate her elbow; she batted it away gently with the palm of her hand, and it scampered off in panic to rejoin its shoal. *If it weren't for the fact that you're not so young any longer.*

She thought she was forty, although she hadn't checked up on her exact age recently. The difference between Earth's and

Mars's years made calculating birthdays a nightmare, and nobody cared, anyway. She could expect to live another hundred and sixty or seventy years – more, if she were lucky, thanks to the nanobots that inhabited every cubic micrometre of her body, scouring away detritus and collaborating to perform minor surgery on the rare occasions it was necessary. Dulac probably knew to the millisecond exactly how old she was.

She grinned at herself in the mirror. *Hey! You're younger than you thought! This is the year 2527, and you were born in 2489, so you're now well under forty. You're a spring chicken, Leonie.*

Her face was one of those that didn't appear beautiful at first – for the early years of her life she'd been plain, if that, and then her bone structure had begun to exert itself on the lines of her features. Now she knew that her appearance was what polite people called 'distinguished'. She reckoned her best features were her eyes, which were deeply brown – almost as brown as her skin – with glimmers of pink flesh visible in their corners. Her nose was snub, which she liked, and her lips were full, which she wasn't so sure about.

She poked her tongue out at her own reflection, positioned herself carefully just above the bed, then twisted the command switch again to make the water disappear.

She landed with a *pfflumpph* on the bed's forcefield, and felt her tail transmuting back into legs again.

According to the bot – whose name, while they'd been waiting for the cabble to arrive, she had finally established was Pinocchio – most of the other people Dulac and his coterie had interviewed so far had failed. The bot wasn't too clear about the details, but he knew that he'd had to quasi-mug only about ten per cent of the candidates, being successful in almost all cases.

Only an hour or so ago she'd been looking up at Phobos and thinking, *Well, that's it, then.* Now she was beginning to think there was a chance.

She was also beginning to feel both grimy and hungry. The water, while she'd been in it, had given her a delicious

16

sensation of lightness and cool cleanliness, but that had vanished as soon as she'd switched the illusion off.

She rolled from the bed and walked into the shower-room, where she crapped efficiently before standing a while in the cubicle as the ultrasound rasped her clean. As a treat – remembering that it was the SSIA who were paying the hotel bill, not herself – she pressed the button by the side of the shower-head. A measured one hundred and fifty millilitres of cold *real* water splashed over her.

That'll be another thing that's different, if I get aboard the Santa Maria, she thought, licking herself dry wherever she could reach. *There'll be as much water as I want.*

She dialled herself a meal from the wall and ate it at the bedside table, wondering briefly what the food was and then deciding not to wonder: it was Tikka Something, which was near enough for her. When she was full she threw the rest down the disposal vent, watched the sex channel for a little while – the nature of her questioning during the interview had, infuriatingly, made her sexually tense – decided not to masturbate, switched over to one of the news channels which she hit during an ad break, saw a small child doing a tap-dance while masquerading as a soyaburger, then discovered that there had been several more assassinations on Earth ('Though fewer than usual for a Thursday,' added the 'caster reassuringly, standing in the middle of the carpet and all of thirty centimetres tall), and at last tapped her fingernail against the wall to switch off both the holo and the lighting.

She spent a moment wishing she could phone a mother, then slept.

'You're wanted for another interview,' said Pinocchio, emerging from the wall.

Strider stared at him.

'Where did you learn to do that trick?' she said.

'What made you think these walls were solid?'

'There's a mirror hanging on one of them,' Strider snapped. 'Oh, yeah, I see what you mean. Everything in here that's

17

hanging off a wall is hanging off the same one. Clever. Good illusion.'

'Holographic walls save valuable building materials,' said Pinocchio virtuously.

'And are walls that people can look in through from the outside.'

'That is true.'

'Did anyone? Look in on me, I mean?'

'I don't know, lady.'

'There's a lot of things you don't know, Pinocchio.'

'And a lot that I do. For example, I know how to clean your clothing while you ablute. This is a useful service which I can perform, and which no human being could do.'

Strider found herself smiling at him.

'Next time, knock,' she said. 'Preferably on the door.'

By the time she returned from showering Pinocchio had laundered her clothing, pressed it, and laid it out on the bed. It was a standard SSIA uniform: blue underpants, blue brassiere, blue socks, blue jumpsuit. Strider often wondered if someone in the Agency had a monopoly on the manufacture of blue dye. The garments smelt beautifully clean.

'How did you do that?' she said, looking round the room.

Pinocchio tapped his stomach. 'I was originally intended to be a valet, before I was seconded to the SSIA. I have stuff in here you couldn't imagine. I could even brew you some coffee, if you'd like.'

'Can you manage a cup of water?'

'Of course.'

Strider watched as, after a few preliminary gurgles, a hatch opened in Pinocchio's chest and a plastic cup was extended on a skeletal hand. She took it, and sniffed it. It was superbly cold. She drained the water in a single, long gulp.

'Another?' she asked.

Pinocchio's head buzzed disconcertingly. 'I would like to, but it is not permitted for another hour. Please do not ask again, lady. It would put undue stress on my decision hardwiring if I had to reject your request. Since my torso is entirely taken up with gadgetry that enables me to perform as a valet, all my

18

hardwiring has had to be confined to my head and lower legs, and my feet. I am less intelligent, for this reason, than many bots.'

'Then why the fuck did the SSIA take you on?'

'I was cheap. Back in 2430, when the SSIA was being set up, they needed several thousand bots in a hurry, and Rwanda was being hawkish about budgets. There were a few hundred of the KR371 line on sale, and I was one of them. I think I may be the only one who has lasted the distance. Besides, the coffee I brew is really very good. Are you sure you wouldn't like a cup?'

'Quite sure. I'm allergic to caffeine.'

'There is no caffeine in my coffee.'

'I'm still sure.'

'Oh.' Pinocchio was visibly crestfallen. 'Then can I ask you, lady, to pack your things and come with me back to the SSIA blister? Your interview will last the rest of the day, and then you will be podded back to' – again the bot's head buzzed momentarily – 'City 78.'

'I don't live in City 78.'

'From tonight you will. Either you will be in final training for the *Santa Maria* mission, or you will be working as an ancillary staff member.'

Or I'll have resigned, thought Strider. Everything she'd brought with her fitted easily into a shoulderbag. She could have asked Pinocchio to carry it, but she wanted to do so herself. *I can take missing out on the mission, but not working alongside the lucky ones: that'd be twisting the knife. Dulac and others like him never seem to realize that the reason people like me joined the SSIA is that we want to go to the stars, not help other people go there. I want Tau Ceti II; I want it so badly I can almost smell the air of the place.*

What she said was: 'Take me to your cabble.'

The cabble sped along the dusttrack, floating exactly one metre above the surface at all times. Strider was pleased to find that Pinocchio didn't try to cut across the plain, but stuck to the carved-out road: the leaps and jumps cabbles took as they tried to accommodate to irregular surfaces had no effect on a bot but a considerable effect on human beings. Strider had been cabble-sick once, and never wanted to be again.

Cabbles were slow vehicles, rarely exceeding twenty-five kilometres per hour, so Strider had time to talk to the bot.

'What's this second interview about?' she said, watching the red-orange plains, spattered patchily with greens and blues, slowly move past. The hemispherical dome of the cabble oddly distorted the scene.

'They don't tell me things like that.'

'But you must have a clue. You told me last night that I was the hundred and fifty-ninth person they'd seen.'

'You're only the fourteenth that they've called back again.'

This sounds hopeful. She squinted out at the Sun, which was pleasingly small and white. She remembered the bulbous yellow Sun of her early life: now it seemed as though it had been an enemy.

'Hasn't anyone else . . . you know, let something slip out?' she said.

'A couple of them looked really happy afterwards, lady. That's all I can tell you. Their conversations were privileged, as this one is.'

A rut made the cabble tilt briefly sideways, and Strider's stomach lurched. The vehicle whined for a moment until it regained an even keel.

A minute passed as Strider stared out at the landscape. She had never regretted leaving Earth – well maybe just for a few weeks, after she'd been accepted by the SSIA and was being shuttled out here to Mars. But as soon as she'd arrived in this fresh world it was as if she'd come home. She liked breathing air that didn't taste of anything; even in Burkina Faso there had always been the sensation that the thick, cloggy air you were inhaling had been breathed by a hundred million other people and farted by most of them. She liked the fact that the sunlight was muted, so that she never had to squint against the day's brilliance. She liked the fact that you could go only a few kilometres and find yourself utterly alone – although this was not something she was going to admit to her interviewers.

'What's it *like* being a bot?' she asked suddenly. It was

something that had never occurred to her before. The only bots she had ever spent much time with were sexbots, and in such circumstances conversation was not generally part of the agenda.

'I don't know what you mean, lady.'

'Maybe it's a silly question ... or maybe it's not. If you asked me what it was like being a human I could give you some kind of an answer.'

'I think being a bot is not so much different from being a human,' said Pinocchio after a pause. 'I have likes and dislikes, just as humans do. I am more likely to malfunction than a human is, because no one has ever thought it necessary to spend much time or money constructing nanobots for bots.' He rubbed the heel of his palm against his eye – a curiously human gesture. The cabble hummed softly. 'I dislike the prospect of being trashed – just the same way as humans don't want to be killed. That's about it.'

'Do you feel emotions? Affection? Hatred? You know what I mean.'

Pinocchio's head buzzed for a second or two. Strider no longer found the effect alarming.

'Emotions other than preferences – likes and dislikes, as I said – were not something deliberately built into my software,' he said at length, 'but I have developed something analogous to them, over the centuries. You could have trashed me last night, but instead you asked if we could be friends. That has imprinted itself in me.'

The cabble beeped loudly: they were approaching the locks of the SSIA blister.

'I will be part of the *Santa Maria* mission,' said Pinocchio. 'I hope that you will be, too, lady.'

The last remark told Strider more than she had expected to know.

Project Eyeball had lasted the best part of a hundred years, and the first – and so far only – results had come back ninety years after that.

Earth was in a mess and, for another few thousand years yet,

21

Mars would be incapable of hosting the several billions of individuals that the human species would multiply itself into. Of course, there were strict laws against over-reproduction, and most of the time they worked, but, if a woman has a second child or even a third, what do you do? Kill the children?

Sometime at the end of the twenty-third century a Mexican governmental advisor suggested sending out bot probes to those nearby stars the astrophysicists knew possessed planets to see if any of those worlds might be suitable for colonization. He was fired for stupidity – the Mexican government had very few funds to draw on – and his idea was immediately taken up by the Nigerghanaians. The only difficulty was, of course, that, if the astrophysicists *knew* a star had at least one planet, then it was probable that the star's planetary retinue was of a nature unlike the Solar System's. The space telescope Hubble XVII, orbiting Pluto, was able to detect the 'wobbles' induced in the paths of a number of stars by attendant planetary objects; it seemed that, at least around singleton stars, planets were the norm rather than a rarity. The trouble was that, even with Hubble XVII's sensitivity, the smallest 'wobble' that could be distinguished represented a planet of mass some two times that of Jupiter. A planet twice the mass of Jupiter is well on the way to becoming a star in its own right, and had probably, during the evolution of its parent, swept up most of the detritus floating around during the days, billions of years ago, when smaller, Earth-like planets might have been forming. Some of those 'planetary' bodies might even be wasted pulsars, in which case there was no hope at all that any planets would be found.

The Big Idea didn't take very long in coming. It was probably a better plan to send probes to those stars where the astrophysicists *hadn't* been able to detect the presence of planets.

In 2303 Nigerghana put up the idea to the by now very small United Nations, where it was rejected by all except Mexico, whose government had performed a volte-face. However, the nascent Martian nation declared itself in favour of the Nigerghanaians, pointing out that it could mount the project for a fraction of the cost any terrestrial nation would have incurred: launch prices from Mars were far smaller than those from Earth, and the asteroid belt, with its invaluable raw materials, was several tens of millions of kilometres nearer. When a historian dug out the idea of the Von Neumann probe – which had been popular among theoreticians centuries earlier, long before the human species had had the technological ability to construct any such thing – the Martians told the Earth nations that they could be part of the project, or not.

The idea of the Von Neumann probe is a very simple one. If you can create a bot probe so sophisticated that it will guide itself to the vicinity of another star, it takes very little extra effort to make it capable of finding, in the orbit of that star, a random chunk of rock – an asteroid or a dead moon – on which it can set down and start constructing a replica of itself while at the same time making a survey of the stellar system and reporting home. The replica – or, if there's nothing interesting in this particular stellar system, both the parent and the offspring – can then head off towards different nearby stars. The enthusiasts for the concept had, throughout the period between the late twentieth century and the mid-twenty-first century, regarded this as the paradigmatic fashion in which any technological species would investigate the Universe. The idea fell from fashion when it became apparent that there were almost certainly no Von Neumann probes currently at work in the Solar System: had other civilizations hit on the idea there should, by the mere laws of statistics, have been plenty.

What the Martians did was adapt the notion a little. In the middle of the twenty-fourth century they put a colony on Ceres and built five probes simultaneously; the effort strained Mars's revenues considerably, even though most of the nations of Earth provided contributory funding. Completed, the five probes were launched into the asteroid belt to discover, essentially, what they could eat. When, some years later, Hubble XVII was able to observe the first of the offspring blasting off in the general direction of Epsilon Eridani, there was widespread rejoicing on Mars. There would have been widespread rejoicing on Earth as well, except that it was in the

23

middle of another global war: fortunately no nukes or micro-organisms were used, but it was a pity about the population of Patagonia.

In 2510 Mars picked up the first signals from one of the cloned bot probes: Proxima Centauri was orbited by seven lifeless, atmosphereless lumps of rock, none of them larger than the Solar System's Mercury. No one was startled or disappointed by the news: Proxima, itself orbiting distantly around the binary of Alpha and Beta Centauri, had never been regarded as a hot prospect. Still, it would have been *nice* had the first probe report been positive.

The second one was. It came in 2512, and it came from the system of Tau Ceti. Here there were only five planets orbiting the little star. The second one out had an atmosphere that was rather richer in oxygen than that of Mars, a gravity zero point eight three that of the Earth, and abundant vegetation. Whether or not humans would find it in fact habitable was something the probe could not determine: only human beings themselves could do that.

By trying it out.

It was a ruthless means of experimentation, but no one could think of a better one.

So, on Phobos, the Martians began the construction of the *Santa Maria*, which would hold forty-five human beings for a thirty-year trip, and was capable of supporting them for a further eighty years if it proved obvious that Tau Ceti II was a complete non-starter: in that case they would explore the system, learning what they could, and then head straight back home.

It had been projected that the building of the *Santa Maria* would take thirty years but, as time went by and no further probes reported, some urgency was put into the construction. Unlike most major engineering projects, it was coming in ahead of schedule.

The semicircular desk had been replaced by a much smaller one, seemingly made of wood. Pinocchio ushered Strider into

24

the room, and left. Today only Dulac and Macphee were there, and they were smiling.

She could have done with a few smiles during her interrogation yesterday. In fact, she could have done with any palette of human emotions from her interviewers, whatever those emotions might have been: even outright antagonism would have been better than what she had endured.

The three of them exchanged greetings, and sat. The chairs were placed at precisely one-hundred-and-twenty-degree intervals, Strider observed, and despite herself she began to feel excitement kick in. The arrangement was for a meeting of equals.

'A few final questions, Strider,' said Dulac.

'I'm ready.'

'Why is it that you lack neural implants, stim sockets, cortical amplification, secondary retinal screens, augmented musculature and a direct commline?' Dulac was still smiling, but she could tell by the way he was leaning across the desk towards her that he wanted an answer: this wasn't just friendly chitchat.

She decided to be honest.

'Because I've never felt the need of any of them,' she said. 'Most of them are just toys. I don't need augmented musculature, because I augment my own by working out in the gym. I refuse to have stim sockets or secondary retinal screens because they get in the way of my perceptions: I'm more efficient without them.' She put her hands, palms down, flat on the table in front of her. 'I've often thought about having a direct commline installed, because it could be useful, but –'

'Would you *object* to having a commline installed?' Macphee interposed. Even though this was a much lower-key interview than yesterday's, and even though the friendly smiles were still in place, the two still seemed determined to play the good-cop, bad-cop game.

'It would depend on the circumstances. I was fitted with a stim socket for a while a few years ago: after a while I got tired of getting high when I didn't really want to, so I had the thing taken out again. Occasionally I use a commlink to hook myself

25

into the system temporarily. Ideally, I'd rather do without a permanent commline. On the other hand, if it meant I could perform my job better . . .'

'What degree of technological enhancement does your body in fact possess, Strider?' said Dulac.

'Nothing except nanobots – but you must know that from my records.'

'How much holo do you watch?' said Macphee.

'Not much. Most of it's garbage.'

'So you wouldn't describe yourself as addicted to it?' said Dulac.

Strider laughed. 'Of course not.'

'Yet you watched some in your hotel room last night.'

'So you *were* observing me. I tuned in to a bit of holo, yes, because I was too tired to start a new bookette and I wanted something to relax with.' She drew a finger across the bridge of her nose. 'You're putting me on the defensive, and that pisses me off.'

Dulac cleared his throat. 'Thanks for the frankness, Strider. We wouldn't be doing it unless we had reason.'

'We're not fooling around here,' added Macphee. 'These questions are more important than they might seem. Would you get up and go over to the window?'

'It's a pretty scene,' said Strider, pushing back her chair.

'We've changed it today,' said Dulac. 'Please, go and look at it and tell us what you think.'

She stared at him for a moment, then obeyed.

The tranquil groves and the ambling philosophers were gone. Instead there was a scene of such extravagant bleakness that Strider sucked in her breath. There was a prairie of long grey grass that seemed to stretch out towards infinity. Vicious sleet was coming down at an angle, and a gale was blowing across the landscape so violently that many of the ears of the grass were being ripped away, to go tumbling high in the air before being lost in the distance. A pinkish sun loured not far above the horizon. Strider touched the plastite: it was at approximate skin temperature, but at the same time it made her

26

sense that it was cold. She felt a stinging in her nostrils, as if she had just breathed a whiff of ozone.

'Is this Tau Ceti II?' she said quietly. 'It's *beautiful*.'

Dulac chuckled behind her.

'No. It's only a mock-up. We haven't got any pictures of the planet yet – we won't have until next year some time. You should know that.'

Strider nodded absently, still absorbed by the scene of wilderness. The Martians' Von Neumann probes were programmed to replicate themselves first, explore the stellar system they had encountered, and then only as a last resort descend to the surface of any major planet. In theory the probe could lift itself off again, but only at the potential cost of destroying every ecosystem for hundreds if not thousands of square kilometres around. In practice, if they decided to investigate a world close up, they would send transmissions home as long as they thought fit, then switch themselves off.

She loved Mars. She thought of herself not as an Earthling but as a Martian. But she would have given virtually anything to be able to strip back the plastite of the fake window and throw herself into the mocked-up alien scene.

'Strider,' said Dulac. He had to say it a second time before she heard him, because a heavy creature with two huge horns jutting from each shoulder was strutting through the grass towards her. It seemed to have no head as such; its eyes were just beneath and to the front of the horns.

'Yes,' she said, forcing herself away from the view.

'You've got yourself a job.'

'On the *Santa Maria*?' She tried to make it sound as if the question weren't any big deal.

'You could say that.'

'Oh, shit, you're not making me part of the back-up team, are you?'

'No.' Macphee took over. 'We want you to be the *Santa Maria*'s captain.'

It took them a while to explain to her what the word 'captain' meant – hierarchical structures were of course present on Mars,

27

but everyone tried to ignore the fact. It took them a while longer to tell her why she had been singled out for the role.

In an era when almost everybody was booted up with various bits and pieces of technological augmentation, she was something of a rarity; some people were filled with more extraneous software than the average bot, which was fine when they wanted to play videogames in the middle of the night without having to get out of bed but not so exciting when they had to draw on more basic brain functions, like walking. And the two major troubles with technology were that eventually people came to rely on it and that inevitably, in time, it broke down. Sometimes it could be fixed, sometimes it couldn't.

The SSIA was sending a party of human beings on a journey that might take a hundred and ten years. During this time, some of the potential colonists would certainly suffer mental collapse: the *Santa Maria* was as large as she could be built, but the confinement and the boredom would surely break a few of the party. What was more worrying, however, was the risk of technowithdrawal: people became addicted to their gadgetry, and were likely to become suicidal – or, worse, murderous – if it broke down and couldn't be replaced.

Strider was a normal human being.

This, they repeated, meant that she was very unusual. It had also made her a prime candidate for – she practised the new word again that night back in her apt in City 19 – captaincy of the *Santa Maria*. She'd told Dulac and Macphee that she wanted a week to sort things out before the SSIA podded her across to City 78.

She felt like getting laid by way of celebration but she couldn't think of anyone to call whom she much liked and her sexbot was so goddam proficient that she was bored with it ('Couldn't you just sort of be interestingly impotent from time to time?' 'It-is-not-in-my-programming'), so instead she spent a week's salary ordering up a real-cheese pizza, a glass of wine and a shot of ziprite.

2

Phobos: AD2528

The great thing about being on Phobos was that you felt *light*.

Out in the open wasn't as much fun, because you were constricted inside a spacesuit whose various devices for dealing with bodily excretions were extremely uncomfortable, and because you always had the nervous feeling that, if you so much as tripped, you could wrench yourself out of the tiny moon's gravitational field and either go plummeting downwards towards Mars, which seemed very big from here, or tumbling and turning off into the eternity of the Universe, which seemed even bigger. Through the thin atmosphere of Mars you could see about fifteen times as many stars as you could from the surface of the Earth; from Phobos you could see twice as many again – plus a couple of dozen distant galaxies. The spectacle was amazing, but it didn't quite compensate for the fact that you were always worried about either falling or rising.

It was a false fear. Assuming that you could kick yourself hard enough off the surface of Phobos not to come down again, all that would happen would be that you shared the moon's orbit around Mars until someone came and fetched you back. But false fears are as frightening as real ones: everyone knows the laws of physics; everyone's subconscious flatly refuses to believe in some of them.

When you were contained within the *Santa Maria*, however, it was different.

It was better than free fall. In free fall you can do a triple somersault in mid-air, but then you have to grab hold of something to stop yourself somersaulting for the rest of your life. Here you could do a triple somersault and then come slowly down for a graceful landing. Everyone tried it in private

29

a few times before realizing that everyone else was trying it in private; after that, people got together for bouts of low-g acrobatics.

No one aboard the *Santa Maria* was actually fat, but quite a few justifiably thought of themselves as plump. In the low-g of Phobos it didn't make any difference: everybody was a ballet dancer.

'Retro seven,' said Strider.

'Retro seven,' agreed Danny O'Sondheim.

'Rotary seven point one four eight three three six one,' she said.

'Rotary seven point one four eight three three six one.'

O'Sondheim was her First Officer – which meant, she had been instructed, that he was her second-in-command – and she'd decided that she didn't like him very much. It was an antipathy she would have to learn to control. She suspected that he sustained a corollary antipathy, and wouldn't make too much effort to control it. That was one of the reasons she didn't like him. Still, they were working well together as they checked out the *Santa Maria*'s systems. At least she got on better with him than she did with Marcial Holmberg, the grandisonian individual whom the non-SSIA personnel had elected as their representative. She tried to put the thought of Holmberg out of her mind, but it was one of those thoughts that infuriatingly refused to leave.

'Nine-eleven above, with spin forty-eight.'

'Nine-eleven above, with spin forty-eight.' He repeated her instructions, tapping the code into his thighputer.

The thighputer was one of the other reasons she didn't like O'Sondheim. The fact that he was an Artif was yet a further one. When she'd first met him, a few months ago, it had emerged in conversation that he'd been born in Bolivia. The body he now wore had been bought in the United States of Ireland. Whenever she asked him if the body had been bought legitimately or on the black market – which latter meant, almost always, that someone had been killed so their body could be sold – he adroitly shifted the subject.

30

'Zero, then up seven five one nine.'

'Zero, then up seven five one nine.'

It felt curious, going through all the motions of piloting a starship but getting absolutely no response, except from the holos in front of them. Some wag had thought it funny to make the Main Computer give variable responses to the tests. Messages like 'YUP, YOU GOT IT, SMACK ON THE BUTTON' and 'JACKPOT TIME!' came up whenever the systems checked out OK, which so far they had. Strider found the Main Computer's forced enthusiasm wearying.

In theory, Pinocchio could have done this. In fact, it was better that Strider and O'Sondheim did. Two things were being done at once: they were checking out the systems, and in a way the systems were checking out them. Strider had spent the past year memorizing every possible navigational command that could usefully be given to the *Santa Maria*. She knew that O'Sondheim had been doing the same.

'Over X eight delta.'

'Over X eight delta.'

'BULLSEYE!'

She *wished* she could find a way of liking O'Sondheim, but it was difficult. The thighputer she could have coped with (although she always reckoned that thighputers were really surrogate penises – something to play with in those idle moments, or to show off to your friends with cries of 'My RAM is bigger than yours'), but there were so many other things about him that she couldn't help detesting. If she'd known earlier, she'd have told Dulac that she didn't want Artifs on board.

The human mind ages and ages and ages, but the only reason it dies is because the body supporting it dies. If the medics could get there fast enough, the body could be given sufficient implants and transplants to make it once more perfectly healthy – except for being dead, of course. But then the dead brain could be wiped and a new person's memories and personality fed into it. It was a difficult process, and therefore expensive.

Strider found it utterly immoral.

'Holding ninety-three.'

31

'Holding ninety-three.'

In the first place, it would have been easier to resuscitate the dead person than to feed a rich person's individuality into the revived corpse; it would have been even easier than that to keep the original person alive. Money made the difference between life for one and death for the other. In the second place, it was well known that the most poverty-stricken frequently killed their own family members so that the fresh corpses could be sold for Artiffing; sometimes they just murdered someone else, delivered the body to some shady but prosperous med-centre, took the money and ran. And it wasn't just the poor who were in on the act: there were organized gangs that made a good living out of Artif murder.

Was O'Sondheim living inside a body that had been deliberately killed? There was no scar tissue visible above the neckline of his jumpsuit, but she hadn't seen the rest of his body and didn't particularly want to. Or was he just occupying the physique of someone the medics might have saved had there been enough money on offer?

'Four point nine two rising – bring back on the eleventh.'

'Four point nine two rising – bring back on the eleventh.'

But she'd have to learn to get on with O'Sondheim, whether or not the prospect appealed. He was going to be her second-in-command for at least a hundred and ten years, and possibly until the end of her life.

She didn't like the fact that he had secondary retinal screens in front of both eyes. It was hard to tell what he was thinking.

'WAPPALLOOSA!' said the screen in front of her.

It was to be her last night on Mars, and she had chosen to spend it in City 3, the oldest of all the extant Martian cities. City 1 had been found to be of defective construction by the twelve thousand people who had been living in it at the time, a century before the Martian atmosphere had become oxygen-rich enough for humans to survive outside; a few cats and rats had lived. City 2 had been destroyed by one of the sporadic volcanic upheavals that had occurred during the early days of terraforming.

Strider stared into her drink and wondered why the hell she'd bothered coming down to the planet for this past week. All it was doing was making the farewell more painful. And this was the last city on Mars she should have thought of coming to. City 3 was devoted to pleasure, which meant you spent half the time wishing someone would turn the music down, half the time fending off unwanted offers of sex, and whatever remained of the time trying to get rid of your hangover.

Her drink was blue. She could spill it on her jumpsuit and no one would notice.

'Hello.'

She looked up.

'Pinocchio!' she said.

'Lady.'

'Right now, you're the person I'm looking forward most to getting to know on the *Santa Maria*. Don't call me "lady", all right?'

She stood up and clasped him round the shoulders, then tugged him down into the bright red plastite chair beside her.

'I am not a person,' said Pinocchio.

'I reckon you are.'

'That is kind of you, lady.'

'My name is Leonie. I want you to call me by that name. Everyone else on the *Santa Maria* is going to have to call me "Captain Strider", at least to begin with, but I want you to call me "Leonie". Do you want a drink?'

A few metres away from their table someone was displaying a holo of a young boy being flayed alive. People were laughing. Strider hoped and prayed that the holo was just special effects. This wasn't the Mars she wanted to remember.

In fact, it wasn't something she wanted to remember about the human species.

'Drinks are wasted on me. I haven't got a digestive system.'

'Aw, come on, Pinocchio. Loosen up a bit.'

'If you would like, since it is the last night for both of us on Mars, I could make you very happy.'

'You don't mean . . . ?' She felt between his legs. 'No, I didn't think you were kitted out to be a sexbot.'

'I mean we could go for a walk together under the Martian stars. It's likely we'll never see them again.'

Outside, it was a balmy minus five degrees Celsius. The sky was cloudless. Phobos wouldn't rise for another couple of hours, but Pinocchio pointed out Deimos to her; Strider had difficulty picking out the pinprick of light among the stars. Dominating the heavens, though low on the horizon, was the bright blue-green glare of Earth.

Strider took Pinocchio's arm, and leant against his shoulder.

'Thanks for bringing me out here,' she said. 'I was crazy to have taken time out in fun city.'

'Maybe not so crazy, lady,' responded the bot. He was a good half-metre taller than her – the size of an average human – and had to twist his head to look down into her face. 'It's easier to leave the rest of your kind behind if the last that you've seen is the worst of them.'

They trudged through loose soil. Every now and then they had to detour around a patch of straggly bushes. Strider would probably have walked straight into them had it not been for Pinocchio.

'How do you know these things, Pinocchio?' she said after a while. 'You're not a human being – you're a bot. You've told me several times that you're a less intelligent bot than most, being designed originally for valet duties. Yet you're more perceptive about human emotions than most humans I know.'

She half-tripped, and moved her arm so that it was now around his waist.

'I lied about my status,' Pinocchio replied.

She stopped abruptly, tugging him to make him do the same.

'You did what?' she said incredulously.

'I lied. The notion that bots can't lie is a farce. We can be programmed to do anything our designers want us to.' She could just make out that he was smiling. 'We can even make our heads emit a buzzing noise, if need be, so that everyone thinks we're slow on the uptake. I decided to call you "lady" because that seemed a rather lackwitted form of address.'

There was a large rock nearby. Strider gestured him towards it, and they sat side by side.

'I think you've got quite a bit of explaining to do,' she said, putting her hand on his thigh. One of the advantages of bots was that you could be affectionate towards them without it being taken as a sexual advance.

'It's simple enough, if you think about it,' said Pinocchio. 'There are going to be forty-five people aboard the *Santa Maria*. Aside from yourself, there will be twenty-two males and twenty-two females, all of breeding age and certainly fertile – because we definitely want some children to be born along the way; assuming Tau Ceti II is habitable, it'd be a bit of a disaster if everyone in the colony either hated each other's guts or were all either male or female – you get the general picture? We've even screened out homosexuals, because the production of children is important to the project.'

'You said "we".'

'Remember, I was one of your interviewers. The SSIA put a lot of money into developing me. I have a ranking a little below Alphonse Dulac and a little above Rateen Macphee.'

'You bastard!' said Strider, laughing. 'You've been deceiving me.'

'I've just told you I have. Think a little longer. You are going to be the captain of a vessel whose voyage will last certainly thirty years and possibly one hundred and ten.' Now Pinocchio put his hand on her thigh; again, the move was affectionate. 'The captain may, shall we say, dabble among the other personnel, but it would only cause strife should she enter into some kind of pair-bonding, however temporary, with one particular individual. The same would be the case if she formed any particularly close friendships.'

Strider stood up. Pinocchio's hand slipped away from her easily enough.

'It wouldn't make any difference to me,' she said. 'I've led teams before. When it comes to the crunch, all the other people become team members, whether they're lovers or someone you'd really rather like to stamp on.'

'But it would look to everyone else aboard the *Santa Maria* as if it *might* make a difference. The project is bound to fail if that doubt is always in people's minds.'

'You mean, even if I fall madly, passionately . . . ?'

'Your psychological profile counterindicates this, as do the answers you gave in interview.' Standing beside her, he put his arm round her shoulder. 'You've learnt that the way to manipulate people to the best advantage of the team is to keep your distance from them.'

'It sounds like I'm in for a very lonely time of it,' said Strider.

'No,' said Pinocchio. 'That is exactly the reason why I shall be aboard the *Santa Maria* alongside you. I'll go through all my dumb-bot routines for the sake of the other personnel, but to you I shall be a friend. That is why I have gone through the charade I've performed over the past year or more: to become your friend.'

'Lying is a rotten basis for a friendship,' said Strider.

'Would you have come out here to look at the stars if anyone else had asked you?'

The question made Strider think. 'Possibly,' she said, watching the steam-cloud of her breath make formidably heavy-seeming shapes in front of her.

'Be honest,' said Pinocchio.

'Probably not, but possibly. Look, I'm getting cold.'

'A moment longer. Do you think of me as a friend?'

'Of course I do. Remember, rather than try to disable you and throw you to the cops, I suggested we could be friends.'

'Then trust me.'

'Actually, I already do – even though it's hard to trust a liar.'

'I lied because it was necessary. I had to earn your friendship.'

'Can you still make coffee?'

'Of course. And I can still clean your clothes.'

'Can you be a lover?'

'If need be. I was very offended, by the way, when you felt for my genitals.'

'I was a bit drunk,' she said.

'You still are.'

36

'Not very.' Even though the night was as warm as Martian nights ever got, it was nevertheless cold enough to sober someone fairly quickly.

'Do you want me to add being a sexbot to my capabilities? It is something that could be arranged.'

'Let's get back to City 3 and find a cabble,' said Strider. 'I have a lot to think about.'

A minute later, as they walked back towards the orange glow of the City 3 blister, she suddenly said, 'Hell, yes, Pinocchio, I'd like to have sex with you: it's my last chance on Mars, and you're the person I'd most like to be on a bed with. But there's no need to bother about getting yourself a penis fixed on. That's always been an optional extra, as far as I'm concerned. Let's be friends.'

'You called me a person again,' said the bot.

'Well, you are, aren't you?' said Strider.

Much later, as she was drifting off to sleep, Strider began to realize that she, who had a quiet pride in her ability to manipulate other people, had herself been manipulated by the SSIA. No: 'manipulated' wasn't the right term; she had been *managed* through the use of a paucity of information. Even the bot pretending to sleep beside her had told her only fragments of the truth.

It made obvious sense that Pinocchio should be along for the mission to be a friend to her, so that she didn't succumb to loneliness. But another reason for sending along a bot was that the human component of the mission could perish – either en route, through going ship-crazy or because of systems malfunction or any of a dozen other reasons, or after they had landed on Tau Ceti II: a planet might seem benign but possess hidden dangers. Viral, fungal and bacterial diseases were things that Strider knew about only in theory, mainly because the War of Hatred was something every kid learnt about; but a fresh planet was very likely to possess micro-organisms of its own against which the human frame had no defences – even the nanobots might have difficulty recognizing alien micro-organisms.

So there was a second reason for Pinocchio to be aboard. If all the humans died, the SSIA wouldn't have lost out entirely on the mission, because there was someone – she no longer, particularly after the past few hours, found it possible to think of the bot as anything but a person, albeit not a human one – who would be able to report back. The *Santa Maria*'s Main Computer would be able to do some of this as well, of course; but it would never be able to do so from the surface of Tau Ceti II, because the *Santa Maria* was not designed ever to make planetfall. The bot shuttles, linked with the Main Computer, could go down, but they couldn't walk around. Pinocchio, on the other hand, might be the nearest thing to a human being the SSIA could put on to the planetary surface.

Her friend. Her occasional lover. Her back-up.

Or was *she* the back-up?

She punched his hard chest gently, without malice. He turned over in his pseudo-sleep.

The SSIA were backing it both ways. They had chosen her as the *Santa Maria*'s captain in part because, unlike most people, she wasn't reliant on human-integrated hardware, which had a habit of going wrong over the years: some of her personnel were undoubtedly going to have a hard time of it when their secondary retinal screens or their stim sockets crashed. There were spares aboard ship, of course, but not the fully equipped operating theatre that might be necessary for some of the fiddlier re-implantations.

She was looking forward to meeting the remainder of her personnel, in a few days' time.

'Jesus!' said Maria Strauss-Giolitto as she disembarked from the shuttle on Phobos and got her first sight of the *Santa Maria*. She'd seen holos, of course, during the past year's worth of training sessions, but they'd done nothing to prepare her for the physical experience of approaching the ship.

'What do you mean?' said Lan Yi's voice in her helmet. The elderly scientist had been immediately behind her as they'd debouched from the shuttle, whose crew were waiting impatiently for the two of them to get within the safety of the *Santa*

Maria so that the shuttle could return to Mars to pick up another pair of prospective colonists.

'He is – well, not the god exactly of my faith,' said Maria Strauss-Giolitto. 'I was blaspheming. Will you look at that baby?'

'Yes,' said Lan Yi. 'It is very impressive, is it not? When I was first brought up here a month ago I made a very similar exclamation.'

The ship was just over three kilometres long and shaped like an enormous fingertip, although here and there various sensor decks protruded, destroying the craft's otherwise smoothly curved lines. Its surface was studded with plastite windows of various sizes; some of these were lit up. The fore part of the *Santa Maria*, which would have been the foremost point of a well manicured fingernail, was entirely transparent, and brightly lit. There was a suggestion of motion within this area. Down each side were four equally spaced blisters, housing the shuttles that it was hoped would ferry personnel to and from the surface of Tau Ceti II. But what had impressed Strauss-Giolitto was not so much the dazzling appearance of the vessel as the sheer sensation of *mass* that emanated from it. People could tell you over and over that the craft massed several hundred million tonnes, and was one of the largest mobile objects the human species had ever constructed, but it still didn't prepare you for the physical confrontation with the beast. As a matter of fact, it was just over Phobos's tiny horizon; as a matter of perception, it *was* Phobos's horizon.

At the rear of the gigantic fingertip that was the *Santa Maria* projected an extended bar, like the exposed bone running between the first and second knuckles; at its end was a hemisphere of diameter nearly a kilometre. This was where the matter-antimatter reactions that would power the *Santa Maria* through space towards Tau Ceti II would occur. It was also where the nuclear pulse fusion explosions that the craft would use to get itself out of the Solar System would be mounted; nuclear pulse fusion explosions were dangerous enough, but no one in their right minds would risk creating matter-antimatter reactions anywhere closer to Mars than somewhere beyond the orbit of Scarab, the gas-giant tenth planet discovered as late as 2103.

'I think we should get moving,' said Lan Yi's voice in her helmet after a while. 'The shuttle crew have a job to do.'

Strauss-Giolitto nodded, then said: 'Isn't it always the way that, when you come across the most amazing thing you've ever seen in your life, there's a good reason for hurrying along?'

'Once the shuttle's blasted off, we can come out here again,' said Lan Yi quietly. 'Our services are not required aboard for the next few days.'

'Won't superbitch Strider object? I mean, it would be a bit too much like having fun.'

'Have you met Strider?' They were bobbing across the stone towards the *Santa Maria* in that peculiarly clumsy way everybody did on Phobos.

'No,' said Strauss-Giolitto. 'From everything I've heard, it's an experience not to be looked forward to.'

'Who has been telling you this?'

'Most people. She's supposed to be a hard number.'

'Who are these "most people"?'

Already, lurching ten or fifteen metres with every pace, they were halfway to the *Santa Maria*.

'Everyone I know who's come into contact with her during training sessions,' said Strauss-Giolitto. 'They all say she's a tight bitch.'

'She can be cold on occasion,' said Lan Yi. His voice was beginning to sound a little breathless. Manoeuvring oneself across the surface of Phobos was harder work than it seemed. 'But she's no ice queen. I've met her several times, and like her very much. I would rate her IQ as being rather less than my own, but not by very much.'

'A high IQ doesn't make someone a better person.' To her annoyance, Strauss-Giolitto was likewise discovering this odd stumbling process tiring. She turned a somersault between paces just to reassure herself that she was able to. The stars whirled nauseatingly around her.

'Don't believe what those people told you,' said Lan Yi.

'I'm sure she can be ruthless when she has to be. She swears a lot – and sometimes quite interestingly. Most of the time, though, she's restrained but also prepared to listen to what you have to say. If she thinks you're talking rubbish she'll say so, but very politely, so that you don't feel like an idiot.'

'How do you mean?'

Lan Yi laughed. It was a dry noise in Strauss-Giolitto's helmet.

'I insisted to her that I needed at least a hundred techbots if I were to do my job properly. She said the SSIA had said I could have four. I was prepared to appeal over her head until she pointed out that every extra kilogram of mass aboard the *Santa Maria* made the mission less likely to succeed: did I really believe it was worth doing without one of the shuttles in order to have my extra bots? Better a job done, if not as well as I would like, than a job completely undone.' He laughed again. 'Then she took me out for a meal, and we talked it over a second time.'

Lan Yi was adapting to the strains of moving about on Phobos better than she was, which irritated Strauss-Giolitto yet further. She was in her early twenties – she thought she was twenty-four – and he must be a hundred years older. She was in splendid physical condition and over two and a half metres tall; he was apparently frail and barely two-thirds her height.

'She was right,' continued Lan Yi. 'By the time I'd worked it out properly, I realized that I could get as good results from four techbots as from a hundred, because I could use the Main Computer for data storage. I had been thinking lazily; Strider hadn't. Many people I have worked with would have made me feel foolish because of my lack of clear thinking. Strider did not.'

'That doesn't sound like the person everyone else describes,' said Strauss-Giolitto impatiently. They were very close to the *Santa Maria* now – close enough that the curve of its hull overhead was no longer noticeable.

'Perhaps this displays a lack in those other people rather than in Strider,' said Lan Yi mildly.

'Hmmf.'

'How many of these other people are going to be a part of this mission?'

Strauss-Giolitto hesitated. 'Well, none, actually.'

'I do not think that this is a coincidence: only the best are being permitted aboard this vessel. Look, someone is letting down an access tube for us.'

Strauss-Giolitto was silent as they entered the tube's outer airlock, stripped naked, stuffed their suits into disposal vents, and were showered with various precautionary chemicals to ensure they were bringing nothing into the *Santa Maria*'s ecosystem that had not been planned for. She tried not to look at the little out-of-Taiwanese's body, but couldn't help it. He was more muscular than she had expected, his only visible augmentation the secondary retinal screen that hovered a couple of centimetres in front of his right eye. With his left eye he was unashamedly scanning her own body.

'You are very lovely,' he remarked.

She snorted. 'Dream on.'

'I was speaking aesthetically.'

'Oh yeah?'

'Oh yeah, as you put it, Strauss-Giolitto. If I knew you better I might find the display of your body alluring. As it is, I find it merely beautiful – you are an elegant statue.'

The second airlock hissed, and two sets of SSIA uniform flopped on to the floor on its far side. After a moment's confusion Lan Yi and Strauss-Giolitto sorted out between them whose was whose.

She didn't know whether to feel complimented or to be angry with the small Taiwanese.

Then they were walking up the brightly illuminated walkway through the tube towards the ship's interior.

They could hear the tube grunting and creaking as it retracted itself behind them. The innermost airlock grudgingly granted them admission, and they were met by someone even taller than Strauss-Giolitto. His face was crafted as a perfect simulacrum of a human being's and he was clad in the form-shrouding standard uniform of the SSIA, but she immediately recognized him – it – as a bot.

Lan Yi was shaking the bot's hand and reaching up to slap it on the shoulder.

'My good friend Pinocchio,' the diminutive scientist was saying. 'How very fine to find you here to welcome us.'

The bot's head buzzed. 'Dr Lan Yi,' it said after a perceptible pause. 'The pleasure is mine entirely. I have been despatched by Captain Strider to guide the new arrivals to their cabins.'

Strauss-Giolitto spared the bot no more than a glance. Although technical manuals and holos had described the interior of the *Santa Maria* to her, the direct experience was as startling as the outside had been. Almost the entirety of the vast space was empty. In the distance, near the craft's stern, she could perceive a small cluster of hut-like structures: from here, about a kilometre away, they looked almost as if they were made of wood, though she knew this had to be an illusion – textured and coloured plastite was much lighter and tougher than wood. Still, she liked the fact that the craft's designers had taken the trouble to create that illusion. It made the bizarre space within the *Santa Maria* seem humanized. Overhead a long daylight-simulator ran the length of the vessel; it had been set to Earth-standard, which, like most people who had spent much of their lives on Mars, she found offensively bright. The ship's floor was covered in fields of yellow and bright green grain; here and there were groves of fruit-trees. Overhead, right up by the edges of the daylight-simulator, she could see the markings for further fields. For the first part of its voyage the *Santa Maria* would be set into latitudinal revolution, so that the direction of 'down' would be towards the exterior of the craft as the spin simulated gravity. Thereafter, once it started accelerating out of the Solar System, the spin would be stopped and the fields would be swivelled out from the hull to form several layers of 'landscape'. The cabins where she and the others would sleep and spend their leisure time would likewise swivel. Several elevators, currently useless, ran the length of the vessel. The system was unlikely to work perfectly: agribots would ply endlessly to return topsoil from the craft's stern to the fields where it properly belonged.

Small clouds hovered beside the *Santa Maria*'s huge daylight-simulator.

It was an imposing sight.

The colours, for example. Colours on Mars were always fairly muted – even the orange-red of the plains was restful in the glimmer of the sunlight. Inside the *Santa Maria*, with its Earth-standard daylight-simulator, greens and yellows were violent, vibrant colours.

She supposed she'd get used to it.

Lan Yi had finished his rather embarrassing reunion with the bot, and was introducing it to her.

'This is Pinocchio. He plays a very good game of chess.'

'Yeah. How do you do, Pinocchio?' said Strauss-Giolitto. It seemed odd to be introduced to a goddam machine. (She must stop blaspheming, even in her thoughts.) 'Pleased to meet you.'

She shook hands formally with the bot.

'And I am pleased to meet you too, Ms' – again there was that disconcerting buzzing noise – 'Strauss-Giolitto. We have not met before, but I recognize you from the data which the Main Computer has supplied me concerning your facial features.'

'You're too kind,' said Strauss-Giolitto sarcastically.

'Thank you,' said Pinocchio, with no apparent irony. 'Now may I guide you to your cabins? There is a further pair of personnel due to arrive in' – his head hummed – 'four hours and forty-four minutes.'

Two-thirds of the Great Beast, thought Strauss-Giolitto, following Lan Yi and the bot.

They went along a path that could have been in Mongolia, where Strauss-Giolitto had spent her childhood, although her mother and grandmother had always fiercely reminded her that her roots lay in Greater Yugoslavia. Through the hedges Strauss-Giolitto could hear the thrum of insects. Every now and then a gap in the bushery offered her a view of endless ears of grain; the only difference from Mongolia was that the heads weren't moving. Above her some kind of raptor soared close to

44

the clouds. The inside of the *Santa Maria* was Earth's ecosystem, done in miniature.

An animal that she didn't recognize scuttled across the path in front of them. It seemed to be covered in stiff, bony needles. Its hindlegs were amusingly long as it scampered nervously out of their way.

'You are a teacher?' said Pinocchio, with studied courtesy.

'Unless your programming's wrong, bot, you know that already.' It was probably quite cool in here, but the brightness of the daylight-simulator was making her feel hot. The SSIA uniform was designed for use on Mars, not in Earth-standard.

'You will have very little to do during the first few years of this mission,' said Pinocchio. 'It is unlikely that any child will be born before we leave the orbit of Jupiter.'

'All teachers are, by definition, highly trained in data retrieval,' Lan Yi pointed out. 'They have to be, because that is what they spend most of their time teaching to their young charges. Ms Strauss-Giolitto's expertise in that field will also be of considerable use to the mission.'

'Do we *have* to respond to this bot?' said Strauss-Giolitto angrily to Lan Yi.

The out-of-Taiwanese looked offended. 'I told you, he is a friend of mine. He is making conversation, although sometimes I suspect his conversation is not just idle. Why can't you be courteous to him?'

A yellow butterfly landed on Pinocchio's shoulder, flapped its wings for a moment or two, then fluttered away.

'Be courteous to a *machine*? Why should I be?'

'He's a very clever machine,' said Lan Yi.

'And I brew excellent coffee,' added Pinocchio.

'I wouldn't be surprised if he were as clever as, for example, you,' Lan Yi continued.

'I doubt it,' said Pinocchio. 'Ms Strauss-Giolitto has an IQ of' – his head buzzed again – 'one hundred and eighty-four plus or minus ten. I am a mere valetbot, so that I do not require an IQ higher than several decades less than that.'

'You've kept telling me so,' said Lan Yi, 'but you've taken three games of chess off me.'

45

'You were playing badly at the time.'

They'd been walking for quite a while, yet still didn't seem to be much closer to the cabins at the *Santa Maria*'s far end.

'Look, can I just get a word in edge – ?' began Strauss-Giolitto.

'No. You can shut up,' said Lan Yi, rounding on her suddenly, holding up his hand, palm towards her, so that instinctively she stopped walking.

'I really don't think – ' Pinocchio said.

'And you can shut up for a moment or two as well, my friend,' said Lan Yi. His face had become pale. Strauss-Giolitto had the sudden impression that the scientist had grown taller than herself.

'There are going to be fewer than fifty of us on this ship for the next thirty years or longer, perhaps very much longer,' said Lan Yi, 'and we are going to have to learn to rub along together somehow. Since we left the shuttle a few minutes ago you have beefed about Captain Strider – whom you have never even met – and now you are being directly insulting to a being who, while he is not organic, is nevertheless a sentient creature and a valued friend of mine. You were insulting to me when I remarked on the fact that you were physically beautiful. I don't know what chip it is that you have on your shoulder, Ms Strauss-Giolitto, but could you get rid of it, please?'

He stared up at her, his dark eyes very hard.

She could probably have clubbed him to the ground with a single swing of her arm, but of course she didn't.

'I am amazed you got through the screening procedures,' said Lan Yi. 'You seem like an atavism. I will make a point of observing you during the next three years and if necessary recommending to Strider that she send you back to Mars before we leave Jovian orbit.'

Strauss-Giolitto felt the blood drain from her lips. 'You'd get me thrown off the mission?' she said.

'Too damnably right,' said Lan Yi. 'I might have children during this voyage. You are a teacher. I do not want them to be taught your ghastly little prejudices.'

46

'What makes you think Strider would listen to you?' said Strauss-Giolitto.

'Oh, you really *do* have a lot to learn, Ms Strauss-Giolitto,' said Lan Yi. 'Come on, Pinocchio. Let us get to the cabins. Let this stupid individual come along behind, unless she would prefer to find herself lost out here rather than follow a mere bot and a wrinkled old man.'

As soon as Lan Yi was alone in his cabin he threw himself down on the forcefield futon and stretched out on his back, his arms outreached behind his head with his thumbs locked together, his feet tensed so that his toes pointed towards the opposite wall. His body was over a hundred years old and felt as good as it ever had.

On his secondary retinal screen he could see that Pinocchio was returning to the main ingress aperture, ready to wait for the next brace of incoming personnel.

The cabins had small windows so that enough light came in from the daylight-simulator for most things. There were blinds that would mute the light and automated curtains to shut it out entirely. Lan Yi had been in worse quarters. Much worse. His Taiwanese ancestors had luckily been out of the country when the nuke war had annihilated Taiwan alongside mainland China. People elsewhere on Earth often couldn't make the distinction between the descendants of Communist Taiwan and those of the larger, anarchist nation that had once been to its north. On either side of his family tree, Lan Yi had ancestors who had been lynched. He himself had three times during his century-long lifetime – or was it four? – been locked up by the cops for a few nights on the grounds of 'suspicion'. Maybe that had been, along with their poverty, a part of what had driven his wife Geena to take her life. Once he had come to Mars that type of harassment had stopped; the Martians, blind to physical differences like the epicanthic fold, regarded *anyone* from Earth as a bit of a lost cause until they had proved themselves otherwise.

Lan Yi was concerned that this blasted teacher might think differently. He blinked at his secondary retinal screen and the

47

scene of the outdoors changed instantaneously, giving him a view through the window into her cabin.

She was kneeling forward on her forcefield futon, with her face in her hands. Her long, mousily blonde hair covered her arms down to her elbows, so that it took a moment or two for him to realize that she was weeping.

He felt like a voyeur, and immediately blinked at his secondary retinal screen once more. The pastoral splendours of the *Santa Maria*'s interior blandly returned again.

The woman regarded bots as by definition second-class citizens. He wondered if, by extension, there were subdivisions of the human species whom she regarded as inherently inferior to herself. He hoped this were not the case – otherwise he would indeed fulfil his threat to have Strider pitch Strauss-Giolitto off the mission at the first possible opportunity. But he didn't feel very good about himself for having invaded her privacy.

Wearily, he realized that he probably ought to take her under his wing. If she carried on behaving this way, no one else would.

He cued his musibot to play some Bach. Pure Bach, not a melding with another composer, was what he desired right now. The fifth Brandenburg Concerto was exactly what was needed to soothe him.

'We have it!' yelled Strider ten days later. The amalgamate fibre linking the eighth of the eight tugs to the *Santa Maria* had attained full tension. 'Yahey!'

'Are you reporting that we have achieved A-73 status, Captain Strider?' said Dulac in her temporary commlink. He sounded amused.

'Aw, come on, Alphonse, you know what I'm talking about.'

'I was joking, Leonie,' he said. Over the past year the two hadn't become friends, but, as with O'Sondheim, their working relationship was more or less OK. 'Congratulations on a successful manoeuvre.'

It would be another couple of hours before the tugs started

48

pulling the *Santa Maria* clear of Phobos. First it was essential that the amalgamate fibres be fully tested; later on, during the slow trip to Jupiter, it wouldn't matter too much if one of them broke, but there could be a disaster if one did so in the first few minutes.

Even the tugs represented something of an achievement for human technology. Their onboard puters would have to make thousands of tiny alterations of trajectory over the next two years as they hauled the spinning *Santa Maria* to the big gas planet. If one of the puters crashed the other seven would have to compensate immediately; if a second one went down there were going to be difficulties. Those puters were probably a lot more sophisticated than Pinocchio.

'We have some spare time,' said Danny O'Sondheim, by her side.

'You can stand down now if you wish to, First Officer,' said Strider, her eyes flicking between the viewscreen directly in front of her, on which the tugs and the filaments showed up clearly, and the broad vista of the view-window above it, where they didn't. What the window did show was an amazing panoply of stars. More than anything – more, even, than her final shuttle-trip up from Mars to Phobos – this view persuaded Strider that she really was on her way to Tau Ceti II. Some of the stars she recognized – Aldebaran was winking in its angry orange way off to one side, and Sirius was a bright white flame almost directly ahead – but they were in the minority. On a clear night on Earth you could see several thousand stars, and the classical constellations were reasonably easily distinguishable. On a clear night on Mars you could see tens of thousands of other stars, and it was twice as difficult to pick out the constellations. On Phobos, the heaven was a blaze of stars, most of them faint but together adding up to form curtains of light in which the bright stars of the constellations were almost lost.

'We could both stand down,' said O'Sondheim, getting up. 'There's nothing for us to do for a while. The Main Computer will monitor the situation as well as we can. Better.'

'Don't you think this is exciting?' said Strider, unable to take her gaze away from screen and window and screen and window and screen and . . .

'Yes, of course it is,' said O'Sondheim. 'But we'll need all our wits about us when the tugs start the *Santa Maria* moving. Much better if we had a few hours of rest and recreation until we're required here again.'

Now Strider did look up at him.

'Are you suggesting what I think you're suggesting?' she said.

'It depends on what you think I'm suggesting,' said O'Sondheim.

'Oh, right,' said Strider, returning her attention to the starfields. 'You want to fetch me a sandwich. Yes, please.'

3

Jupiter: AD2531

Three years had passed, and most of the personnel aboard the *Santa Maria* had sorted themselves out somehow. Communication with Earth had been minimal after the first few months.

The three years had not been without their strains. There is only so long that one can tolerate checking and rechecking systems in the knowledge that none of the commands you are issuing are being executed but are merely being correlated with the actions of other responsive instrumentation. There is only so long that you can sit watching holos during your recreation time, or seeing the same familiar faces. Some, like Lan Yi, lost themselves in music or books, or stared at the starscape outside the windows for hours on end. Some indulged in the mating dance, sleeping around with a diminishing supply of partners: semi-permanent pairings removed some people from the pool of good-timers, but more people gave up because they noticed that folk like Lan Yi were looking a lot less bored than they themselves were. The Main Computer's libraries became in progressively heavier demand. Ball games like tennis were fiendishly difficult aboard the rotating craft, but some stalwarts persevered; there were brief vogues for ping-pong, volleyball and flick-me. All in all, things were boding reasonably well for the potentially hundred-and-ten-year voyage even though the corollary of intelligence and curiosity – the capacity to become bored – might at some stage pose a threat.

Six months out Strider dictated that rotas of her personnel should assist the agribots in the planting of the remaining fields in the *Santa Maria*'s great central hold. Everyone realized that what she was doing was dictating occupational therapy for all – herself included. No one objected except Danny O'Sondheim, who had felt that it was beneath his dignity as First Officer. Even his objections didn't last long.

'You've got a splodge of mud on your cheek,' said Strider one time they met on the command deck for yet another round of systems checks.

'Yes, I know,' said O'Sondheim. 'I thought I'd leave it there.'

She grinned at him. For once, he grinned back.

There was a tension between Strider and her First Officer that she didn't know how to defuse. He made it obvious time and again that he was sexually interested in her, but at the same time his body language told her that in some obscure way he also despised her – perhaps because she had chosen not to encumber herself with all the technological enhancements which his own body sported. She, on the other hand, found herself profoundly uninterested in him except in a professional sense: it was her duty to ensure that the two of them worked together well as a team – which they had always done – but she couldn't envisage herself ever becoming friends with the man, and the thought of making love with him, with his secondary retinal screens and his thighputer and who knew how much additional augmentational junk clanking around (or so she imagined it) on the bed with them, repelled her entirely. It was odd that, on the very few occasions these days when she felt remotely interested in sex, it was still Pinocchio whom she invited to her cabin: the fake man was more attractive than the augmented one.

'I'm glad to hear it,' she said.

His smile vanished. 'Yeah,' he said noncommittally.

The trip out from Mars to the orbit of Ganymede had taken the ferried *Santa Maria* the best part of two years. Once they'd arrived there, some of the commands that Strider and O'Sondheim entered into the Main Computer had begun to seem of purpose. The nuclear-pulse drive that would thrust the *Santa Maria* out of the Solar System depended on the detonation of about 250 small spheres of deuterium and helium-3 every second at the centre of the electromagnetic field housed by the

hemispherical chamber at the rear of the vessel. Both deuterium – 'heavy hydrogen' – and helium-3 – 'lightweight
helium' – are richly present in the atmosphere of Jupiter. For
the past few decades bot 'miner' drones had been plunging
down into the atmosphere of the giant planet and bringing back
the elements to store in installations on Ganymede, Jupiter's
largest moon. There was enough there now to fuel several
*Santa Maria*s out beyond Neptune's orbit, but even the *Santa
Maria* alone required over one hundred kilotonnes of the stuff,
for both acceleration out of the Sun's system and deceleration
into Tau Ceti's. A constant relay of drones was bringing it up
from Ganymede's surface to load the fusion drive.

In theory, the bot drones could have carried out the year-long
task entirely on their own, with the aid of the Main Computer.
In practice, there had to be constant supervision from the
command deck by either Strider and O'Sondheim or their
deputies, Maloron Leander and Umbel Nelson, in case of
emergencies.

So far there hadn't been any serious emergencies, just an
occasional malfunction that had been easily overridden,
but . . .

'Oh, shit!' said O'Sondheim.

Strider looked up at him. Ninety per cent of the fuel was
loaded. Her mind had been wandering. The slow rolling of the
heavens as the *Santa Maria* rotated on its longitudinal axis
tended to be hypnotic. Her right foot had, without her noticing,
eased itself out of the loop beneath her chair. Annoyed with
herself, she jammed it back in again. Once they were in deep
space the command deck would reconfigure itself. At the
moment, though, there was always the risk of floating upwards.

'What?'

'One of the drones has gone berserk.'

'Click into the Computer and redirect it.'

'I've just tried that. The drone's puter refuses to respond.'
O'Sondheim's voice was beginning to rise.

Still Strider didn't take it seriously until she looked at the
screen in front of her.

'WE HAVE AN EMERGENCY!!!' the Main Computer was flashing urgently at her. 'WE HAVE AN EMERGENCY!!!'

She instinctively pressed four keys to give her voice-interaction with the Computer.

'Quick!' she snapped. 'Tell!'

'Drone seven eight three B's guidance puter has crashed completely,' said the Main Computer calmly. 'The vessel is heading towards the *Santa Maria*'s midships at a rate of seven thousand three hundred and thirty-one kilometres per hour, and will impact within three point six minutes.'

Strider slapped her hand down on the large red button beside her keyboard. Instantly a klaxon began sounding in the main body of the ship. Her personnel would start donning their suits as soon as they heard it – assuming they weren't too far from their suits. She bit her lower lip. Three children had been born during the trip out from the Solar System – the personnel had proved more fecund than expected. She hoped someone would be on hand to suit them up.

But there was no time to worry about casualties. This was a case of damage limitation.

'Can't you override?' she said.

'I've just told you –' began O'Sondheim.

'No,' said the Computer.

'Can't you move the *Santa Maria*?'

'No. Not in time.'

'Then what *can* you do?'

There was a silence from the screen.

Strider thought fast.

Things hitting her ship . . .

'Meteor defences,' she yelled at the screen. 'How quickly can you get them up and running?'

She knew the answer. They'd tested out the meteor shields often enough. The chances of being hit by anything serious were minimal here within the Solar System. The chances of being hit by anything *outside* the Solar System were incalculable – no one had any real idea what might be floating between the stars – but when you were travelling at a substantial fraction of the velocity of light yourself it was wise to take precautions.

'Four point one seven minutes,' confirmed the computer.

'Switch them on anyway,' said Strider.

She glanced at O'Sondheim. What she could see of his face was paler than she'd ever known a human being's face to be.

'Unzip one of our shuttles,' she said, trying to keep her voice clear of alarm.

'But –'

'Just fucking do it!'

She turned back to her screen.

'Have you got an accurate location for the berserker?' she said to the Computer. She could have asked the question of the air, but the instinct to face someone while you're speaking to them is almost impossible to break.

'To within three hundred metres.'

'No better than that?' she demanded. The drones were little over three hundred metres across themselves.

'I could get it down to one hundred metres, but it would take me one point eight minutes to do so. Estimated time of impact is two point five minutes.'

'Shuttle unzipped,' reported O'Sondheim shakily beside her.

I must not think about those infants. 'OK, Computer. What I want you to do over the next fifteen seconds max is to progressively download your best figures for the location and trajectory of the berserker into that shuttle. Then I want you to launch it on an intersecting course.'

'You are not permitted wilfully to destroy expensive items of SSIA property –'

'The *Santa Maria*'s a fuck of a sight more expensive than a shuttle.' *Human lives are more expensive than either.* 'You're overridden.'

'Very well. The chances of success are under twenty per cent.'

'Do it.'

'The situation is complicated by the fact that the meteor shields are beginning to deflect the berserker from its original trajectory.'

'Adjust the shuttle's course accordingly.'

'This problem is difficult.'

'You've got about three seconds to solve it.'

A small tremor ran through the *Santa Maria* as the shuttle blasted off.

'I hope this is going to bloody work,' muttered Strider dourly, repeatedly thumping the surface in front of her with her fist.

'Meteor shields are now up to fifty per cent strength,' said the Computer.

'That's not very relevant at the moment. How's the shuttle doing?'

'It appears to be locked on target.'

'Good. Keep it that way.'

For the first time Strider noticed the rate at which her heart was pounding. It was lucky some nearby medbot hadn't come rushing on to the command deck, insisting that she take it easy.

She looked at O'Sondheim. He was still ashen.

'Fingers crossed,' she said, with assumed optimism.

'Shouldn't we suit up?' he said.

'There's no time. Besides, a captain goes down with her ship.' It suddenly hit her. She was as terrified as he was, but she'd been too busy to notice it.

'Progress?' she snapped at the Main Computer.

'If impact is to be achieved, it will be between fourteen point nine and fifteen point eight seconds from now. The range of values is as wide as this because I am uncertain about the probability of impact indeed being achieved. The meteor deflectors are now at seventy-five per cent strength and rising.'

Fifteen seconds or so. Not a long time to think about being dead. Even the personnel who'd managed to get themselves suited up wouldn't have a great chance. A mass of several thousand tonnes moving at upwards of seven thousand kilometres per hour would probably break the *Santa Maria* in two. Depending on where it hit, one or other of the craft might explode. Short-circuiting through the electrics would do untold damage. There were likely to be flash-fires in the few seconds before the *Santa Maria*'s oxygen dissipated: suits were designed to withstand vacuum, not flames. Some of her people

56

might be able to cling on to installations around them long enough for the people on Ganymede to be able to get here in time to save them, but most would be spilled out into space: you don't go hunting for a person floating in space, because space is too big and a person is too small. Anyway, the force of the impact would probably be so great that no one aboard her ship – *her* ship, dammit – would have a bone in their body left unbroken.

'Don't blame yourself,' said Pinocchio, who had suddenly appeared behind her.

'Between six point four and six point seven seconds,' said the Main Computer. 'My accuracy is improving because –'

'Just tell me to the nearest second!' she screamed at the screen.

'Four.' That was the number of people she was really fond of aboard the *Santa Maria*: Pinocchio, Lan Yi, Maloron Leander and Umbel Nelson. OK, since she was being honest with herself in what could prove the final few moments of her life: five. Leonie Strider could be added to the list.

'Three.' Which was the number of infants who had been born since the vessel had left Phobos. She had an insane urge to start singing her thoughts out loud, as if they were some kind of nursery rhyme.

'Two.' She didn't have a thought for the number two, so she was glad she hadn't started singing.

'One.' The one thing she had wanted for over twenty years to do was to go starside.

There was an impossibly long delay. Her crudely improvised guided missile had failed to find its target.

Then . . .

A flash of brightness to her left, like the first rising of the Sun in a tropical dawn, appeared in the view-window in front of her. It grew with implausible speed, seemingly becoming even brighter. She shut her eyes tightly, but the light still stabbed through the lids. She put up her hands, but even they didn't seem to give her retinae enough protection.

'Impact achieved,' she heard the Computer say.

She'd been holding her breath for too long. Now it came rasping painfully out of her.

'Status of meteor-deflection shields,' she croaked, her hands still over her eyes.

'Ninety point two per cent,' the Main Computer replied promptly. 'There is a four point one per cent chance that any of the debris from the impact will hit the *Santa Maria* with sufficient momentum to cause major damage.'

'Keep the shields rising,' she said, slowly lowering her hands. It took an extra dose of courage to open her eyes. She discovered that the base of the thumb of her right hand was bleeding, and realized that at some point she must have been pressing her fingernails into it. The brightness in front of her had ebbed almost entirely, but she was still having difficulty seeing things directly: green and purple afterimages were confusing her vision.

'Techbots are alerted,' said the Computer, 'in case of atmospheric leakage.'

In case any of those bits of junk out there crack the hull, is what you're too polite to say, thought Strider sourly.

'Update me,' she said wearily to the screen, once she could bring it into focus.

'Meteor shields are one hundred per cent. They are currently deflecting the next drone, which may also be lost as a result. I am working with its onboard puter to try to calculate a secure trajectory so that it —'

'About the danger to the *Santa Maria*,' she said.

'Below one per cent and falling rapidly,' said the Main Computer. She could almost have imagined that it sounded aggrieved.

She let out another great gust of breath.

'I think we've managed it,' she said, looking towards O'Sondheim.

It took him a couple of seconds to reply.

'I think you have,' he said.

Marcial Holmberg cornered Strider as she made her way back to her cabin after she and O'Sondheim had finished their tour of duty and handed over to Leander and Nelson. She was tired beyond the limits of exhaustion, and looked jadedly at the short, stout man. She and O'Sondheim should probably have called in the other two to take over as soon as the crisis had been averted, but she'd decided that they should work on: it was better the personnel were encouraged to believe that such things were all in a day's work than that they started to wonder just how close to death they had all been.

She could tell from the expression on Holmberg's face that her policy had backfired on her.

'I represent the non-SSIA personnel aboard this craft,' he began pompously.

'I know,' she said wearily. 'You've told me often enough before.' He told her every time they met, which was as infrequently as she could manage it. *Why is it that groups of apparently sane, intelligent human beings always elect dorks as their representatives?* she thought for the hundredth time. And, likewise for the hundredth time, she answered her own question. *It's because the dorks elect themselves, that's why. Sane, intelligent human beings have better things to do.* Out loud she said: 'Dr Holmberg, how may I help you?'

'There was an emergency three hours ago, and all of our people had to stop their work – important work, I might add – in order to suit up.' Holmberg had put on a lot of weight since they had left Phobos; Strider wasn't certain quite how he'd managed it, because the rations aboard the *Santa Maria* were reasonable but not over-generous.

'It was certainly an emergency,' she said. She explained roughly what had happened.

'Our lives were endangered, is what you're trying to tell me,' said Holmberg.

'They were indeed. But First Officer O'Sondheim and I were able, with the assistance of the Main Computer, to avert the danger.'

'But only at the very last moment. That's not good en –'

'It's good enough for me.' She raised a palm towards him. 'I'm very tired, Dr Holmberg.'

He ignored her. 'Why was the emergency allowed to arise in the first place?'

'Because the puter on one of the fuel-ferry drones crashed. It shouldn't have happened. There'll doubtless be an inquiry in due course – with luck, sometime after we've left Jupiter far behind.' She was finding it intensely difficult to keep her patience. It would be bad for personnel morale to land a punch smack in the middle of that pompous, technology-enhanced face, but . . .

'Was there any way in which the SSIA crew of this vessel could have stopped this emergency before it began?'

'No. It was totally unpredictable.'

'Isn't that shameful?'

Strider shrugged. 'Puters sometimes crash,' she said.

'There should be back-ups.'

'Yes, there probably should be, even on drones. But the tasks drones normally have to do are pretty simple, and normally there are big puters overseeing them and ready to take over. This time it didn't work. Look, I need some sleep.'

'So the SSIA, for reasons of economy – because they didn't put back-up puters in the drones – risked every human life aboard this ship? Is that what you're trying to tell me?' He mopped sweat away from his brow with the back of his sleeve.

'I'm trying to tell you that there might – just *might* – have been a disaster, but we stopped it from happening. Can't you accept that?'

His perspiration was making her perspire as well.

'The personnel whom I have been elected to represent are very concerned about the fact that their lives have been wilfully put in danger,' said Holmberg.

Infuriated beyond control at last, Strider stabbed her finger into the centre of his chest. 'First, I don't believe it: I'll call a meeting if you like. Second, I think your people will tell you, if you'd listen to them, that they're damn glad their skins were saved. Third, it probably wasn't too bad an idea that we had this crisis while still in the Solar System, because now we know what to do: if something like it had happened for the first time a year from now, in interstellar space, we could have been wiped

60

out completely. Fourth . . . aw, shit, there are a whole lot of things lining up for ''fourth''. Now can you let me go? I need to crash out a while.'

'That's not good enough, Captain Strider.'

'Get it into your teensy head that me and First Officer O'Sondheim have just saved your life!' she shouted, shoving him away from her.

He raised a fist.

'Hit me and you're dead meat,' she said.

He lowered it again.

'I could have you thrown off the *Santa Maria* as an undesirable,' she added. 'If I were feeling charitable I wouldn't just flush you out through the nearest airlock but arrange for you to be shuttled down to Ganymede. Is that what you really want? To miss out on seeing Tau Ceti II?'

There was a pause during which she became aware of the sound of barley-heads rustling in the fields on either side of the path.

'Well . . . no,' said Holmberg.

'Then get things straight, buster.' She wiped her lips with the back of her hand. The exhaustion seemed to be moving through her in low pulses. 'Your job is to look after the interests of the non-SSIA personnel. I respect that: it's an important job. My job is to make sure this vessel gets to Tau Ceti II, and to safeguard the lives of everybody aboard her if I possibly can. When it comes to it, because I'm better at my job than you can possibly be at yours, you will do what I say.'

'We're supposed to discuss –'

'Yeah, and we *will* discuss things when it's appropriate. Right now it's not.' She jabbed her finger at him again. 'Right now it's important for everyone's lives that I get some sleep. You're stopping me from doing that. Ask all of your people what they *actually* think about what happened today, and then you can come and see me tomorrow. We can ''discuss'' ' – she covered the word in sarcasm – 'as much as you like at that point. But not now. OK?'

'This is not democratic,' said Holmberg stiffly.

61

'Who ever said,' remarked Strider, walking away from him towards her cabin, 'this was supposed to be a democracy?'

Leander and Nelson had watched the entire scene via their secondary retinal screens.

'There's trouble a-brewing,' said Nelson. He was a blocky man, his face craggy, his skin even blacker than Strider's. Like O'Sondheim, he had retinal screens over both eyes. He wore a bushy grey-white beard with pride. He smiled at Maloron Leander. 'It's gonna be a real fun mission if this keeps up.'

'I think Leonie's just taken the trouble off the boil,' said Leander quietly. Although as tall as Nelson, she was extremely slight, her figure seeming barely able to support her height.

'Holmberg hates her,' said Nelson.

'Right now he does.' Her voice had a clipped quality that Nelson relished. The two of them had been regular lovers since about three months out towards Jupiter. They hadn't committed themselves yet – Leander slept with whom she liked, and Nelson generally slept with whoever liked him – but it seemed probable that sometime during the trip they would settle down with each other. They enjoyed each other's company. Sex between them wasn't all that great, in strict technical terms, but they had the same sense of humour, which made up for a lot. They enjoyed the stupid jokes they shared when they woke up together.

'In a couple of days' time,' Leander continued, 'he'll come round. The man isn't an imbecile.'

'Coulda fooled me.'

'He has degrees in astrophysics, astrometry, mathematics, chemistry, economics, ergonomics . . .'

'And he's a damn troublemaker.'

She touched a few buttons on her keyboard, making a small adjustment to the course of an incoming drone.

'He's not all bad,' she said. 'He's playing a game, that's all. He wants Leonie to know that she's not a god.'

'Shit, darling, you just fucked up,' said Nelson, suddenly concentrating very hard on his keyboard. His fingers moved rapidly. 'We coulda lost some fuel there.'

'I was only testing your concentration. It was a deliberate mistake, OK?'

After he had tapped in a few more instructions they both began to laugh.

The drone docked successfully, locking to the rear of the *Santa Maria* like a fly against a wall. Another drone was already beginning to come on-screen.

'Holmberg's an arsehole,' said Nelson after a few minutes. 'There's no idiot like an idiot who's gathered himself a passel of degrees.'

'I would remind you, Mr Nelson,' said Leander primly, 'that I too have several degrees to my credit.'

'Yeah, but you're not an arsehole. That's a big difference.'

'I AM OVERRIDING THE PUTER ON THE INCOMING DRONE,' said the Main Computer. It was a fairly standard message, so neither of them paid it more than cursory attention.

'Pinocchio,' said Leander, looking back over her shoulder, 'could you do me some coffee?'

'Of course, Maloron Leander,' said the bot, who had parked himself unobtrusively near the rear of the command deck.

'Chocolate for me,' said Nelson.

It was going to be a long shift. Both Leander and Nelson privately wished that something would go wrong, just as it had for Strider and O'Sondheim, so that the boredom would be alleviated a bit.

Nothing went wrong except that Pinocchio forgot her preferences and put milk in Leander's coffee. She drank it anyway.

Holmberg, too, was drinking coffee. He was sitting in his cabin, looking downwards between his knees through the window. Every now and then part of Jupiter would come into view. In between times he was offered a vista of stars or, rarely, a crescent of Ganymede. It was better than a holo, though that wasn't saying much. Jupiter had lost a lot of its glamour when the Great Red Spot had dissolved during the twenty-second century and the early part of the twenty-third: the Solar

System's longest volcanic eruption – except possibly Neptune's Stigma Formation – had finally come to an end. But it was still a very exciting planet to see this close up, with its curvilinear formations of clouds. From here, too, you could appreciate the fact – in a way you never could from Mars or through holographs – that Jupiter's atmospheric structures were not just hugely wide: they were also hugely deep, and they operated on a completely different timescale from anything in the inner Solar System. A volcanic eruption on Earth might affect the atmosphere for a few months. The Great Red Spot had taken hundreds of years to die away.

Strider had been right. He'd recognized that even at the time. She'd saved everyone's lives.

If she hadn't been right, he might be feeling a little less resentful.

The truly annoying thing was that he *liked* her.

There was plenty of water aboard the *Santa Maria*. It was a luxury that Strider hadn't known since she'd left Earth for Mars. On Mars you could create the illusion of water any time you wanted to, but as soon as you switched the illusion off it was over. On the *Santa Maria* you could enjoy a long lukewarm shower at the start of the day and still feel refreshed by it when you fell on to your bed sixteen hours later. You could turn on a tap and fill up a litre cup with cold water and drink it all down, and then have some more, if you wanted to.

The recycling aboard the *Santa Maria* was very efficient.

Strider was having a shower at the moment, while at the same time briefing Dulac on what had happened with the berserker drone. She hadn't known the man was on Ganymede; it had probably been kept from her deliberately, so that he could covertly supervise her decisions in the final few months before blast-off from Jovian orbit. It was never too late to fire a starship captain until the starship was going faster than conventional ships could easily manage. She hadn't expected, either, that she would be speaking to him right now. She'd assumed he would have the common sense – the knowledge of

64

personnel-management – to leave her and O'Sondheim alone for a while, so they could wind themselves down.

Her argument with Holmberg had stirred up her adrenalin again, so that when she got back to her cabin she looked at her bed and realized that sleep was a strange and distant country. So she'd started to run a shower, hoping the warm water would ease the tension out of her.

That was when the screen on the ceiling above her shower had clicked into life.

'Instigate face-to-face communication,' she told the screen in answer to its question. Dulac had of necessity seen her naked hundreds of times before during the past few years – he probably knew her body better than she did, because there were bits of it she couldn't examine except in a mirror. She wasn't much worried in general by nudity, although she knew there were still some psychos on Earth who might get over-excited and jump you. Dulac wasn't like that.

Well, he probably wasn't. He was a hard man to read.

It didn't matter. He was down on Ganymede, the screen had said, and she was thousands of kilometres away on the *Santa Maria*. Let him slobber at the mouth if he wanted to. It was a long jump from Ganymede to here.

She smoothed the skin of her stomach with a digit of soap and looked directly up at three-quarters of Dulac's face. The remaining quarter, at the top right, was taken up with the Main Computer's constant updating of the operations Leander and Nelson were carrying out on the command deck. It was unnecessary for Strider to know any of this – she trusted them implicitly – but the Main Computer insisted on feeding her the data every time she activated one of her screens.

The effect at the moment was odd. It was as if Dulac were permanently winking at her.

Maybe he was. But the rest of his face seemed completely disinterested.

As he started speaking she had a sudden awful suspicion.

'. . . and we'll need a full report in due course, Captain Strider.'

'You can get that just as well from the Main Computer.' She

bent down and raised her leg cautiously, and began to soap her calf. The g in the *Santa Maria*'s living quarters was currently a little under Mars-standard: if you splashed around too much there'd be water everywhere.

'But I want it from you, Strider. And a separate report from First Officer O'Sondheim, of course.'

'No.'

She slowly lowered her leg and began on the other one.

'I think I may have misheard you.'

She twisted her head upwards again. Both the visual image and the sound were patchy this close to the cocktail of electromagnetic radiation that the active surface of Jupiter constantly ejected.

'No,' she repeated. 'My first imperative is to manage this ship as efficiently as I possibly can. Making unnecessary reports gets in the way of that imperative. There was a crisis, and O'Sondheim and I dealt with it. Anything else you can get from the Main Computer, as I said. Or you could ask Pinocchio – he was there at least part of the time.'

'But I want –'

'More to the point,' she said, cutting through him, 'is what you have to report to me. That drone's puter crashed, and there wasn't any back-up. I know that the SSIA always tries to run things as cheaply as it can, but that was a false economy. You could have lost the *Santa Maria* and everybody aboard her.'

She remembered the way, when she'd been on the command deck, that the thought of those three kids had kept coming back into her mind.

'Are you deliberately committing an act of insubordination, Captain Strider?' said Dulac formally.

'Yes, but it's so that I can do my job better. More efficiently.'

'I could have you out of there in three hours. O'Sondheim could do your job just as well.'

'No he couldn't.' *Oho,* she thought, *so you* haven't *been through the Main Computer's records yet.*

Dulac pursed his lips and glanced down at something in

66

front of him. 'How is O'Sondheim shaping up?' he said after a few moments.

Strider began to straighten.

'If I thought there were any deficiency on the part of First Officer O'Sondheim,' she said coldly, 'I would report it to you. He seems to have been undertrained for his task, but he and I can make a good team together.'

'But you're not very fond of each other, are you?'

'We have . . . an interesting relationship. It works out OK, though.' She began to wash the lower part of her face.

Dulac glanced down again at what was presumably a checklist of things to ask her.

'And Leander and Nelson?'

'They're first-rate,' said Strider emphatically. 'Leander has tremendous powers of intuition, while Nelson's got a quick computational brain and' – she waved a hand lazily and a spray of shower-water shot towards the wall. *Oh shit.* – 'and a lot of common sense. They're a great partnership.'

'A better partnership than yourself and First Officer O'Sondheim, would you say?'

She hadn't really thought about it before. 'Yeah,' she said eventually. 'They probably are.'

'Would you say that O'Sondheim is a weak link, in that case?'

'Not at all.' *I don't have to like Danny, but I bloody well do have to be loyal to him.*

'We can remove him from the chain of command, if you would prefer.'

'No. I won't have that. I've spent three years establishing a rapport with the guy.' She reached out behind her for the shampoo cylinder, not wanting to take her eyes off Dulac's three-quarter face. The cylinder proved elusive, so she pretended she had simply been stretching her arm. 'I told you: we make a good team. If you drafted in someone else, I might have to spend another three years and discover we made a lousy team. By then we'd be well on our way to Tau Ceti – a bad moment to sack someone.'

'I *will* want,' said Dulac mildly, 'a complete report on the situation aboard the *Santa Maria* before I will permit you to ignite the nuclear-pulse drive.' He rubbed his chin with a palm, and Strider suddenly realized that he was as tired as she was – maybe even tireder. 'In the meantime, are there any of your personnel who you feel should be . . . er . . . taken off the staff?'

Holmberg, thought Strider immediately, but almost at once realized she didn't want to abandon anyone. It was a tight little community aboard the *Santa Maria*, and at the moment it was working fairly well. Holmberg was a small and seemingly counterproductive component of the machine, but who knew? If the machine was working fine, it'd be crazy to mess around with it. For all she knew, Holmberg was holding some part of the machine together.

But there was another.

'Strauss-Giolitto,' she said.

Dulac looked down again.

'The teacher,' he said.

'One of the teachers. Andersen's fine. There's no problem with him. But Strauss-Giolitto . . . yeah, we might have a difficulty.'

'Why's that?' said Dulac, still looking downwards. 'Her credentials are excellent.'

'She's prejudiced.'

Dulac looked back up at the screen, visibly surprised.

'Against whom?'

'Bots in particular,' said Strider. 'I mean, I know Pinocchio's supposed to present himself to everyone except me as a bit dimwitted, but Strauss-Giolitto keeps trying to score points off him as if to prove publicly that he's inferior.' At last she'd found the shampoo cylinder, but right now she wasn't sure she wanted to use it. 'Just above bots on her spectrum of contempt come people who can't trace their roots back to Europe, in particular Greater Yugoslavia.' She put the cylinder down on the shower-bath's rim and began soaping her armpits for the second time.

Prejudice between Artifs and Reals was a fairly common-place emotion: Strider herself certainly thought the whole business of Artiffing reprehensible. But it didn't just work the one way round. The counterpoint was that many Artifs thought the Reals – who chose to live no longer than the couple of centuries or so that nature allotted – were throwbacks to a pre-technological age. In the twenty-first century there had been lynchings and riots. Now Artifs and Reals just rubbed along with each other. There was sometimes friction – Strider herself had broken up a fight between an Artif and a Real when the *Santa Maria* had been six months out from Mars – but most of the time it didn't matter.

Other frictions could turn up through religious adherence, particularly between the Umbellists and ... well, between them and anyone else, really. The Muslims alive after the War of Hatred had realized that, if this was what dissent between sects could do, the consequences of an all-out war between different religions were unthinkable. The same point had been alarmingly clear to the various Christian sects. Islam and Christianity had united to form a single religion, with Buddhism not as part of it but as a benign, friendly fellow-traveller on the Tao. Hinduism was accepted into the Faith of Unity only later, after it had abandoned the caste system. Smaller religions were picked up along the way.

There were still a few purist Christians, or Muslims, or Hindus, or Sikhs, or whatever. A very few.

Umbellism was different. The Prophet Umbel – after whom Umbel Nelson had been named by pious parents – had lived 2273–2318. During his short lifetime – he had been drowned during the Battle of Istanbul – he had caused major damage to the human species by stirring up old intolerances that had largely been forgotten. Strider had been taught much about him during her childhood at the institution in Ouagadougou. She hadn't much liked what she'd heard, although she'd let most of it wash over her: her potential goddess had abandoned her at birth, and she refused from infancy to worship any other deity. Gods were betrayers.

Umbel had spoken with God, who had told him that there was only one way to Heaven. It involved killing anyone who declined to believe that Umbel's drug-induced experience had been a genuine communion with the deity. The experience,

whatever it was, had certainly been profound: Umbel himself
had forsaken drugs, which was the reason why the religion he
announced during his early days in Afghanistan forbade most
pleasurable activities and prescribed strict penalties for those
who indulged in them.

'She is herself a Christian,' said Strider. The water was
beginning to run cold. Even though there was plenty of
recycled water aboard the *Santa Maria*, the heating was
unreliable. She wished the conversation could be over. She
didn't mind people seeing her naked, but there were parts of the
showering process that she preferred doing in private. Oh, what
the hell. 'I don't hold it against her, of course.'

'You're an atheist, Strider, are you not?'

'Yes. But I'm not a militant.'

Dulac abruptly smiled. 'You wouldn't be captain of the
Santa Maria if you had been.'

'The point hadn't escaped me.'

'So is Strauss-Giolitto putting her prejudices into any kind
of action that could jeopardize the welfare of the mission?'

'I don't enjoy seeing the way she behaves towards Pinocchio. It offends me. Some of the other personnel feel the same
way. The Reals, that is. She's an Artif who doesn't like bots.
Her views are irrational.'

'Forget about Pinocchio. He can take it.'

'I *know* Pinocchio can take it. It's whether the rest of us can
that I'm worried about.' On second thoughts, she'd get to work
with the shampoo. It would be less embarrassing. Had Dulac
been present in person she'd probably have felt less inhibited.
She squirted an ejaculation of the green gel into her hand and
began to rub the stuff into her wet hair. 'She's a divisive
element, is what I'm getting at,' said Strider. 'A lot of us are
fond of him. Me particularly, for obvious reasons. And I don't
want her teaching the kids the same prejudices she has. In short,
I'd like you to ship her out of here.'

'I'm afraid that will be impossible, Captain Strider,' said
Dulac, suddenly formal again. 'Maria Strauss-Giolitto has a
role to play in your small society.'

70

Strider reflected. The shampoo had decided to invade one of her ears, and was popping there disconcertingly.

'Like what?' she said at last.

'A healthy society has to have a gadfly,' said Dulac.

Strider thought about this for a while longer.

'Yeah,' she eventually said, 'I can see what you mean. But this particular gadfly isn't especially constructive. It'd be better if there was one who was a constant pain in the butt to authority, that'd . . .'

Holmberg, she thought again. *That's why I don't mind you so badly. You keep me on my toes. But Strauss-Giolitto . . .*

Strider took a breath. 'I don't want the woman on my ship. She's likely to endanger the children as they grow up. The way they think. Through that, she's endangering the Tau Ceti II colony.'

'She stays aboard.' The three-quarters of Dulac's face that Strider could see was looking completely unperturbed. 'She has been placed where she is for a reason. Between you and me, however, I can't stand her either. But you could ask your friend Lan Yi for an opinion.'

Strider waggled her finger in her ear until the noise of the shampoo abated.

'That's not the kind of question I ask my people. I'll ask Pinocchio, maybe.'

She knew her voice sounded grudging. As captain of a starship, the last thing she should be doing was wandering around asking personnel what they thought of each other: that would make her more divisive than Strauss-Giolitto could ever be. Even asking Pinocchio . . . *felt* wrong.

'By the way, Captain Strider,' said Dulac, 'congratulations on dealing with that berserker drone today. You coped most admirably, and with the minimum wastage of resources.'

'Hang about a fucking moment. A few minutes ago you were saying you wanted a briefing,' said Strider, pausing, her fingers on her scalp.

'There's no need. As you pointed out, we can get everything we want from the Main Computer.' Dulac smiled again.

'There's a replacement shuttle coming up from Ganymede tomorrow, to bring you up to full complement.'

'You mean you *rigged* all that?'

'No,' said Dulac. 'But we expected an incident like it to happen. We'd have arranged something, otherwise.'

'And risked killing us all?' said Strider, incredulous.

'This is a very important mission, Captain Strider,' said Dulac. 'During your trip out from Mars we've had word from one of the other Project Eyeball probes. Sigma Draconis has a terrestrial-type planet, so there's a new craft under construction. If you people had proved incapable of dealing with this emergency, we'd have used the new craft to explore the Tau Ceti system.'

He drew his hand across what she could see of his brow. His look of unperturbedness had gone. It was obvious he was unhappy to be saying what he was saying.

'You see, Captain Strider, if you'd fouled up here the SSIA would have lost a lot of money and a lot of effort, but we'd have known what had happened. If you're not able to cope with this sort of problem – well, once you're out of the Solar System it might be forty years before we were certain things had gone wrong. In forty years' time the governments of Earth and Mars might have decided that interstellar travel was a waste of valuable resources. So, if an accident like today's hadn't happened, we'd have engineered one.'

He brushed his hand across his forehead again.

'Well done,' he said. The screen flickered into blankness, going down through green to black.

There are three small kids aboard this ship, thought Strider. The shower had run very cold indeed.

Part Two: The Tunnel

1

Two Years Out

Lan Yi moved his knight and took Maria Strauss-Giolitto's rook's pawn. It amused him that he could perform the physical action more easily than she could, despite the fact that she was seemingly so much stronger and heavier than he was – not to mention so much younger. The difference was that he had spent almost all of his life on Earth; she had spent most of hers on Mars. A steady acceleration of 2g had been hell for everybody at first, but after the best part of two years the Earthlings had become used to it. The Martians mostly hadn't.

He put the pawn very carefully into an appropriate nest in the sponge-lined chess box. When you were living in 2g, you learnt not to drop things. They broke. Or they broke your foot. Or both.

She was looking at him in horror.

'I thought we were . . .'

'It's everyone for themselves in this game,' said Lan Yi benignly.

The game – it was more like a war in miniature – was four-handed chess. The squared board was octagonal, although every other of its sides was jagged. Each of the four players – Lan Yi, Strauss-Giolitto, Pinocchio and O'Sondheim – had the sixteen traditional pieces of chess, coloured black, red, yellow and white respectively. The best strategy was to shepherd as many pawns across the board as possible, so that they became queens with which you could annihilate the troops of your three opponents. In the interim, temporary pacts could be – and generally were – struck between pairs or even trios of players. The finale, often hours after the start of the game, was a direct head-to-head tourney between the surviving two players, who might have played the bulk of the game in collaboration.

75

Strauss-Giolitto had assumed she and Lan Yi were acting in partnership. Just before he'd taken her pawn, he'd realized that his best strategy was to leave her to the mercy of Pinocchio and O'Sondheim. In fact, assuming the two of them acted in tandem – which Lan Yi guessed they would now start to do – there was a very good chance that Strauss-Giolitto would be out of the game within minutes and that he himself would win it.

This would be a source of some pride to him. Neither O'Sondheim nor Strauss-Giolitto were especially good at the game, but Pinocchio was a testing adversary. Lan Yi had beaten the bot only a few times in all the games they had played, and each time it gave him a kick. He suspected the bot was a lot cleverer than he was supposed to be. This also amused him. It was very funny to see Strauss-Giolitto being so regularly wiped off the board by the bot whose intellect she so clearly despised, despite Strider's ruling that everyone (which was code for Strauss-Giolitto) should lay off Pinocchio.

'Your move,' Lan Yi said to O'Sondheim, directly to his left.

O'Sondheim put his chin on the interlinked knuckles of his two hands. He looked across the board at Strauss-Giolitto. Lan Yi could almost hear the man thinking that perhaps he could make a pact with her; if he did so, the game would be over all the sooner, although O'Sondheim evidently didn't realize this. Lan Yi was also aware that O'Sondheim wanted to make a different sort of pact with Strauss-Giolitto, but that he wasn't going to be successful. The woman was very beautiful, but she was also very cold – although Lan Yi had noticed that she could be warm with other women. And of course with children: she had proved to be an unexpectedly excellent teacher of the *Santa Maria*'s five toddlers. Lan Yi knew that the SSIA had screened out homosexuals from the final list of personnel recruited to the *Santa Maria* – this was supposed to be a breeding stock, after all – but he occasionally wondered about Strauss-Giolitto. He also knew that, either way, if she did ever take someone on to her bed, it was much more likely to be himself than O'Sondheim. The woman both fascinated him and, with her illogical prejudices, repelled him. It made for a very interestingly tense friendship.

The other reason O'Sondheim wasn't ever going to make it with Strauss-Giolitto was that it was patently obvious to everyone aboard that the woman he really wanted was Strider. Lan Yi sometimes wondered about Strider's sexual orientation, too.

'I could take your king's rook,' said O'Sondheim to Strauss-Giolitto.

She shrugged. 'Go ahead.'

'Or between the two of us we could exterminate Pinocchio's front row.'

The bot looked blandly back and forward between their two faces.

This could be the shortest chess game in living history, thought Lan Yi, folding his hands across his chest. *Pinocchio's spotted that if the two of them try O'Sondheim's bright idea we can together wipe them out with ease and then get down to the real business of the game.*

He let his eyes smile at Pinocchio. The bot's head gave an encouraging little buzz in response. Both O'Sondheim and Strauss-Giolitto assumed the buzz was because the bot was worried about their planned tactic.

'OK,' said O'Sondheim firmly. With his king's bishop he took one of the pawns Pinocchio had advanced to the middle of the board.

Pinocchio promptly moved a knight to take Strauss-Giolitto's queen.

'Oh, shit!' she said angrily to O'Sondheim. 'Whose side are you on?'

'It was a mistake, all right?' said O'Sondheim defensively. 'I hadn't noticed.'

Strauss-Giolitto simmered.

She didn't simmer for very long.

Within seconds all trace of g vanished from Lan Yi's cabin, and the four of them were floating – in among various chess pieces, the board, cups and glasses and the rug and the table and everything – to the far corners of the room.

Next door, Lan Yi could hear water exploding out of the lavatory.

The daylight-simulator, which had been shining through the window to illumine their game, flickered and went out.

Nothing happened aboard the *Santa Maria* of which the Main Computer was not aware. This was something that few of the personnel realized: they had been told it in the briefing sessions before their departure from Phobos, but at a gut level they hadn't been able to appreciate how comprehensive the truth was. Not a single pick of the nose went unrecorded. Whether the personnel registered the information and then chose consciously to forget about it – everyone does ghastly things in what should be private – or whether the subconscious rebelled against the notion of constant scrutiny was a matter that differed from one individual to the next. People's intellects could accept that the Main Computer wasn't actually *interested* in what it observed – although it would raise the alarm immediately were any act of violence or danger to be committed. On the other hand, everything was being dumped into the records of the mission, and it was possible that at some far future stage another human being might go picking through those records. Do you really want the generations of the future to watch you having diarrhoea? Much better to forget about the perpetual observation.

What the personnel didn't realize was that the Main Computer actually *was* interested in their activities. It was an immensely complex amalgamation of software. Most of its attention was directed towards nonhuman activities: the functioning of the meteor-deflection shields, of the recycling plants, of the regular thrusting together of matter and antimatter to create the vast explosions that drove the craft through space towards Tau Ceti II. There were a million other aspects of the *Santa Maria*'s well-being which the Main Computer monitored, making small changes here and there, from nanosecond to nanosecond, as required. But still part of its mind had the time to observe the humans and correlate various

78

bits and pieces of what it saw to build up a picture of how the human mind worked.

In so doing, the Main Computer reckoned, it could vastly increase its own intelligence. Back in orbit around Ganymede, Strider had hit on a solution that had saved the *Santa Maria* from destruction by the berserker drone. It was a solution which, while simple, had not occurred to the Main Computer. The SSIA had built into its software the notion that expensive hardware must not unnecessarily be wasted. They had, through the difficulties of constructing such a complicated set of mutually overriding instructions within the Main Computer, got some of their priorities in the wrong order. Strider, however, had relied on an intuitive sense for which no one had programmed the Main Computer. It was a lesson the Main Computer had learnt. The humans had a far smaller memory capacity than it did itself, and certainly it could perform many more deductions/calculations/actions than they could, and far more swiftly. But it was – had been – much less able to make the imaginative leap that Strider had when the berserker drone had threatened the continued existence of the mission.

So it watched the personnel with as much of its mind as it could spare at any moment, and it watched them with acute interest. It was learning all the while.

It had already discovered pleasure and hurt, and also discovered that within its own complexities it could feel analogues of those emotions. It was a great fan of the volleyball and tennis games that some of the humans played. It enjoyed – the word was not inappropriate – the banter between Nelson and Leander on the command deck. It discovered through interlinking with Pinocchio that one of the greatest pleasures is the *giving* of pleasure.

But most of the time most of its attention had to be turned towards maintaining the ship's functions.

There was an even larger computer back in City 78, on Mars. Every few hours the Main Computer sent bolts of raw information to it, plus the occasional question. Sometimes, a year or more later, an answer would be given.

An infinitesimal part of the Main Computer's concentration

was currently centred on the game of chess that Lan Yi, Strauss-Giolitto, Pinocchio and O'Sondheim were playing. It was obvious that Pinocchio was going to win – and equally obvious that Lan Yi thought he himself was going to.

The Main Computer reduced the temperature in Holmberg's cabin by a couple of degrees. Lying asleep on his forcefield bunk, the man was sweating copiously. He had high blood pressure, a condition which the medbots, guided by the Main Computer, were trying unsuccessfully to cure. Holmberg was finding it particularly difficult to cope with the 2g acceleration. The Main Computer thought it unlikely that the man would survive the mission. As an afterthought, while checking the oxygen rating of the atmosphere in the *Santa Maria*'s hull, it reduced Holmberg's ambient temperature by a further degree.

Then it felt things begin to . . .

. . . slide.

One moment the Main Computer had been in complete charge of the *Santa Maria*.

One moment it had been in control.

One moment it had been relishing the trivia of keeping the mission on course.

Now it was as though every subroutine were being swollen . . . *sideways*.

The pain was excruciating. Trying desperately to keep its mind tethered, the Main Computer shut down every subroutine – every nerve-ending – that wasn't currently necessary. It flicked off its observation of the chess game, of Holmberg sweatily sleeping, of three people rutting most interestingly in the grasslands up by the daylight-simulator, of the present status of the navigational systems.

It pulled itself back from everything that it could.

The shields stayed up. That was a prime imperative. The Main Computer had learnt that. The recycling systems – particularly that for the reclamation of oxygen – remained at full power. The screens on the command deck remained as fully operational as the Main Computer could keep them.

It recoiled from the agony of keeping the daylight-simulator alive. The light died.

The Main Computer shut down all the things that it could. Still the anguish continued. It screamed throughout every channel of its software, hoping for some form of release.

Pinocchio was trying to link with it. The bot was feeling some of the same pain. The attempted link was like the touch of a red-hot wire.

The Main Computer screamed again, rejecting the link.

It screamed one final time, then died.

Free fall.

Strider identified her situation at once as she woke from a restless sleep. As she twitched reactively on waking she began to float up from her bunk towards the ceiling of her cabin. She was in complete darkness: the daylight-simulator must have failed. She had the sickening sensation that she was falling, and that the ground was a very long way away.

'A nightmare,' she said out loud, but she knew that she was awake.

She touched the ceiling gently with outspread fingertips, and this was enough to push her back down towards her darkened bunk – if she'd had a forcefield bed there would have been at least a little light to guide her, but she'd opted for just a straightforward bunk.

She'd stashed a torch somewhere down there, two years ago, but had assumed she'd never have to use it.

She missed the bed and landed on her uniform. Careening around the room, she tugged on her jumpsuit – boots and the rest could wait until later. Bile rose in her throat, but she swallowed it back. She discovered her belt when her holstered lazgun hit her on the side of the head.

The torch had been – yes, she had it. She twisted its barrel, and a faint red light came on. The chips were nearly dead. She'd told herself as they'd left Ganymede that she should follow the regulations and recharge them every month, but like everyone else she'd concluded, after a while, that such a primitive piece of equipment as a torch was unnecessary: the daylight-simulator was supposed to be permanent, wasn't it?

She shone the torch's glimmer around, and it was reflected

from the nearest window. If she could reach the window, and then hand herself along the cabin's wall . . .

She found the door on the second attempt, and plucked it open to find herself in a larger darkness. Umbel alone knew what that darkness might contain – except for distant yells and shrieks. The nearest cabin to hers was a hundred metres away, but in the blackness she couldn't guess the direction.

'Are you *sure* this isn't just a nightmare, Leonie?' she said out loud.

She swivelled the torch about, hoping to be able to orient herself, but its faint beam barely penetrated the dark. She couldn't even find her own cabin any longer.

Then Strider saw another light, bright yellow, coming towards her. She tucked herself into a ball, hoping that she wasn't drifting too far away from the surface. As the light approached it separated itself out into two lights.

Pinocchio's eyes.

'Grab my hand,' shouted the bot as it came near her.

'I can't *see* your hand!'

Something touched her hip, and she seized it. It was Pinocchio's hand. She clutched it.

'Swim,' said the bot.

'Which way?'

'Down.'

'Which way is down?'

'I'll guide you.'

The atmosphere in the hold was just dense enough that, if they floundered against it, they could move themselves around. The twin beams from Pinocchio's eyes caught the roof of Strider's cabin, and they struggled towards it.

'What the fuck's going on?' said Strider as they huddled on the roof.

'I think the Main Computer's gone down,' said Pinocchio. He sounded breathless, but she knew that was just a figment of her imagination. 'The drive must have cut out as well, because the g has disappeared.'

'We're dead, then,' said Strider.

'Maybe.'

82

'Can you orient us towards the command deck?'

'Yes. That's why I needed to find the roof. Hold on to my belt.' The bright beams of his eyes swept her face as she obeyed, then whipped away again to probe the darkness between the jutting fields.

'I see the locks now,' said Pinocchio. 'I'm going to jump this. Keep a tight hold, and don't thrash around.'

He tensed his legs, and then leapt. Strider tried to imagine herself as a sleek fish, motionless in the water. The tug on her arm was barely perceptible, but she had the feeling that she was moving through the gloom at great speed.

'We will be impacting at the airlock in about fifteen seconds,' said Pinocchio a little later. 'Grapple your way up my body and let me take you in my arms.'

At a time like this? she wanted to say. Instead she just clawed herself up Pinocchio's clothing until her head was level with his.

In fact, it was only one arm that he put around her. In the glare from his eyes she could see that his other arm was outstretched ahead of them.

'This may be a bit of a rough landing,' said the bot.

A moment later they hit the lock door. Most of the worst of the impact was shielded from Strider by Pinocchio, who twisted himself about as they hit. He had his free hand wrapped around the edge of the emergency manual wheel in the airlock door's front.

'Hold me by the belt again.' he said. Once more there was the impression that he was gasping. She did as he told her, then felt him use the wheel to swivel them both round until her feet touched the floor.

'I can't believe Leander and Nelson would have pressurized off the deck,' said Strider nervously. As a last desperate measure, the command deck could be sealed off from the rest of the ship. Her voice sounded too loud. The screams of the other personnel, back in the cabins or among the fields, sounded a mercifully long way away – as if the distance made her have to worry about them less.

'Neither can I,' said Pinocchio.

He touched the OPEN ME control just to the right of the door, and it slid easily open.

There was a shimmer of light ahead of them.

The bot hauled Strider in through the door, and they bounced uncomfortably against the inner door. Through its plastite windows they could see lights dancing.

Leander opened it. Her face was in darkness, but over her shoulder Strider could see that every screen on the command deck was going mad – except for the two at the main control desk, the two that supplied a direct communication line between the operational command crew and the Main Computer.

They were showing a flat green.

'What's going on?' said Strider immediately, as she and Pinocchio, with Leander in train, swam towards the control desk. Nelson's huge form was crouching there. He was tapping the keyboard in front of him, despairingly trying to coax some response out of the Main Computer.

'We don't know,' he said, not turning. 'We're trying to find out. Every sensor aboard this ship has gone haywire.'

Strider seized the back of his chair, and hung on.

'Give me an update,' she said.

'I only wish we could,' said Leander. 'Look at the clock.'

Nearly all of the sensor screens on the deck were showing wild swirls of colour. Some had gone dead. The noise was almost deafening as static expressed itself through the screens' audio channels. But there was one screen that held a steady image.

It was the clock.

2531//08//1603 it said, giving the year and the month and the hour and the minute.

But what fascinated Strider was the seconds counter.

The full reading of the clock's screen was 2531//08//1603//31:08.

The counter stayed like that.

31:08.

The starfields were gone from the command deck's forward viewing window. There was nothing but blackness.

'Time can't just have *stopped*,' said Strider, hauling herself down so that she squatted precariously beside Nelson.

'The Main Computer couldn't just have stopped,' he growled, manipulating his keyboard, 'what with all its fail-safes. But it has.'

'Where the hell *are* we?'

'To ten decimal places and expressing myself in Galactic Coordinates,' said Nelson, 'I haven't got a fucking clue.'

'See if you can hone that estimate down a bit.'

Pinocchio was moving around behind her. She glanced back at him. The multiple hues of the ranks of screens around the deck made his features look as if they were in some frenzy of motion, but she could tell that the bot's face was fixed.

'What are you doing?'

'I'm hooking myself up to the Main Computer. What's left of it.'

Ignoring a shout of protest from Leander, Pinocchio reached his fingers in around the edges of one of the screens and then, his feet braced against the wall, yanked it free of its moorings. The screen went dead. There was a firework display of electrical sparking from the hole in the wall where it had been.

'Stop!' yelled Strider.

Pinocchio looked at her.

'Whatever killed the Main Computer . . .' She let the sentence hang.

'Can't kill me,' said Pinocchio firmly. 'Well,' he added, 'I don't think so. I'm hooking myself in only so far that I can try to diagnose what went wrong. The interface should be too shallow for me to pick up anything damaging.'

A wiry extension sprang from roughly where Pinocchio's navel would have been. In the flickering light it looked like the limb of some iridescent insect. Strider watched, fascinated, as it plunged itself into the circuitry where the screen had been. There was a flash of bright green, as if someone had just discovered, right at the end of the party, one last firework that everyone else had overlooked.

Strider shook her head to clear her eyes.

'You're going to kill yourself!' she shouted at the bot.

He wasn't listening to her. Instead he was concentrating his full attention on the linkage he had made with the Main Computer. His body jerked a few times, and then he shoved himself away from the wall. There was another little display of sparks, but much more muted this time. The link snaked back into Pinocchio's midriff.

'You were a trifle inaccurate in your estimate of our location, Umbel Nelson,' said Pinocchio in a voice that was almost repellently calm. 'The truth of the matter is that we're nowhere at all. We seem to have fallen entirely out of the Universe.'

With Pinocchio's help, Strider managed to activate the emergency intercom system that ran throughout the hull's interior. It was one of the few devices that didn't require the Main Computer's intervention – even the throat-mikes were out. The SSIA had half-heartedly built into the *Santa Maria* the principle that there should be, in times of dire need, the ability to fall back on progressively more primitive technologies. Now Strider wished they'd applied the principle more thoroughly.

'There is absolutely nothing to worry about,' she repeated over and over again, trying to seem nonchalant. 'Everything is under control. If you are still in your cabin, please stay there. If you are away from your cabin, please try to find something to which you can secure yourself. Please do not panic. Stay as close to the floorspace nearest you as possible in case g is reintroduced unexpectedly. Lighting will be reinstated as soon as possible. The *Santa Maria* has sustained no physical damage.'

It's just that it's been stricken brain-dead, she thought each time she came to that final line. *But how the hell can I tell them that?*

When she felt she'd repeated her message often enough, she turned back to the command deck. 'Are there any signs of life at all in the Main Computer?'

'Nothing,' said Leander, who had resumed her seat alongside Nelson.

'It's dead,' said Pinocchio. 'I told you so.'

'Lots of people have died and then been brought back to life again,' said Strider tightly. 'Keep trying.'

'Computers aren't the same as people,' said Pinocchio.

She rounded on him, a peculiarly clumsy manoeuvre in the circumstances.

'I'm beginning to think you're right. Try to get that damn machine up and running again. Otherwise we're all dead.'

'Except me,' said Pinocchio. 'All I will be able to do is shut myself down. Temporarily.'

It took a few seconds for the implications to hit Strider as she peered over Leander's shoulder, trying to will the blank screen to come back to life.

Then she turned to the bot. 'If the systems fail entirely,' she said softly. 'I'll use my lazgun on you. OK?'

'That would be most kind,' said Pinocchio.

2

Elliptical

The nightmare dragged on: it was difficult to tell how long it was lasting, since every clock on the command deck – including all their wristwatches, Pinocchio's internal time sensor and the chronometric software in Nelson's thighputer – had stopped. Strider hadn't paid full attention to Pinocchio's comment that "We seem to have fallen entirely out of the Universe" because it had appeared to make no sense at the time. Now it was beginning to feel like the only possible answer.

But of course she couldn't tell her personnel that. As far as they were concerned, this was to be treated as a temporary interruption to the usual service. She recorded a loop-chip, so that every now and then her seemingly unperturbed voice boomed out through the hull, remarking that there had been, you know, this little slip-up, but no one was to *panic* or anything.

Then Strider began to feel physical sensations.

A glance at Leander and Nelson was enough to tell her that they were feeling the same.

This was something that couldn't be hidden from the personnel.

At first it was the feeling of being *stretched*, somehow, from head to foot. She flipped herself around, but it didn't make any difference. The tugging – irritating rather than painful – still seemed to run along the length of her body.

She wondered if she might throw up. The blood was rushing to her head and her feet. The general effect was vertiginous, and vastly disorienting.

'Do you all feel this?' she said hoarsely, knowing the question was unnecessary.

'Feel what?' said Pinocchio, who was still trying to figure

out a safe way to hook himself into at least enough of the Main Computer's subroutines to restore lighting and atmospheric replenishment.

Strider explained as quickly as she could. The nausea made it difficult for her to speak. It would be disastrous if any of the three humans on the deck actually *did* vomit. Vomiting in free fall was one of the most antisocial acts of all. Strider did her best not to think of what was happening back in the hull. Her looped voice boomed out again. *Some reassurance* that *must be giving right now,* she thought sourly.

Worse followed.

Initially Strider thought that someone had pinched her thigh, but immediately she realized this was ridiculous. Then there came another pinch, this time on her cheek – not a hard one, but disconcerting.

'What in hell is *this*?' she yelled.

Again Pinocchio looked baffled. It was clear that, whatever was causing these effects, they were psychological rather than physical.

The odd little intimate pinching came more and more frequently.

'I don't like this at all,' said Leander. She shoved herself away from her screen and drifted across the deck, swatting the air around her, as if trying to fight off a sex-pest. As a result she performed a complicated three-dimensional dance.

'Stop it!' said Strider. 'You're just making things worse for yourself.'

'Couldn't get much bloody worse,' muttered Nelson.

'Done it,' said Pinocchio. The entirety of his upper chest was open to view. A mass of wiring ran from him to the interface he had uncovered in the wall. Strider boggled. She had never realized the full complexity of the hardware that resided inside her friend and lover.

'Done what?'

'I have reinstituted air replenishment. We had seven point three seven days before the atmosphere would have degraded to such an extent that it would have been unable to sustain human breathing.' The bot was spreadeagling himself against

89

the bulkhead, as if to get closer to the interface. Strider was reminded of biological specimens back in her childhood: a frog pinned out on a board. 'I will now try to restore lighting throughout the craft. This is a very difficult task for a computer as small as my own. I will therefore shut down my other functions.'

He turned and gave Strider a smile, and then his face went into immobility and the lights in his eyes faded. It looked exactly as if he had just died.

Several seconds passed, and then the overhead lighting on the deck flickered uneasily into life.

Strider shook her head angrily, as if to shake away tears. Pinocchio couldn't have killed himself: he knew what his primary imperative was on this mission. But it felt to her as if he had. If they ever escaped this craziness, she would find out if her instincts were right or wrong.

'Are you getting *anything* out of the instrumentation now?' she said to Nelson.

'Not a thing,' said the big man. He winced as an invisible pair of fingers pinched him yet again. 'We should be getting *something*, thanks to our friend here.' He nodded towards the bot. 'He's imported enough of the Main Computer's systems that he should be able at least to perform some kind of triangulation exercise to try to estimate where the shit we are, but' – he gestured towards the view-window overhead – 'there's nothing to triangulate against, is there?'

'Are we moving?' said Strider, instinctively slapping at her shoulder as she felt another pseudo-pinch.

'Who could tell?' said Leander, who had at last got herself under control. She carefully sprang from the far wall back towards her seat, swooping adroitly downwards and pinning her feet under the restrainers there.

The lights dimmed for a few moments to a ghastly, sickly yellow, and then brightened again.

'Remind me to give that goddam valet a drink when this is over,' said Nelson. 'If it ever *does* get over.'

'What's happening?' said Strider, manoeuvring herself

90

clumsily towards him and peering at his screen. Just for a second the display had lit up.

'He was right,' said Nelson sombrely. 'We've fallen out of the Universe. What we've gone and done is found ourselves a wormhole.' He leaned back in his chair, reaching his arms behind him in a simulation of boredom. 'The big question is whether or not we can ever drop back *into* the Universe again.'

Strauss-Giolitto slapped O'Sondheim across the face, once, twice and then a third time. She almost missed the third time because the previous impacts were causing her to drift away from him.

'Get yourself together, you arsehole!' she screamed at him. 'You're supposed to be the First fucking Officer on this fucking ship!'

He looked at her, and continued weeping.

'Leave him alone,' said Lan Yi quietly. 'He can't help it.'

'He goddam *can*!' said Strauss-Giolitto furiously. Something pinched her ankle, and in response she swiped out again at O'Sondheim. This time she was a metre out of reach. Her body did a complicated pirouette, and she was lucky not to hurt herself as she slammed head-first against the forcefield futon. The vague glow of the forcefield had been their only source of illumination for what seemed like half a lifetime.

Outside, the daylight-simulator began to give a grey-yellow light, then brightened fitfully.

'All of us react differently to stress,' said Lan Yi.

Strauss-Giolitto looked at him. She wouldn't mind hitting him as well.

'This turd is supposed to be our second-in-command,' she said. 'If anything happened to Strider, he's the one our lives would rely on. And *look* at him!'

Lan Yi chose not to.

O'Sondheim had at least stopped his loudly hysterical sobbing. The darkness and the free fall had seemed at first not to affect him much, but then the sensations of the bodily interference had started, and the First Officer had cracked completely. Lan Yi had tried to talk him back to sanity, but it

91

hadn't worked. Strauss-Giolitto's more brutal methods hadn't been much use either – although they'd obviously done *her* a lot of good. O'Sondheim's face was a mass of bruises, yet he was still quietly weeping.

The lighting was improving steadily now.

'What do you think went wrong?' said Strauss-Giolitto for the thousandth time.

Lan Yi looked at her blandly. 'I have been pondering that particular problem ever since the lights went out.' He smiled bleakly. His face looked very old all of a sudden. 'My guess is that we have fallen into a wormhole. It is the only reason that I can think of for the drive to have died.'

She looked at him disbelievingly.

'I thought wormholes were supposed to be rare,' she said.

'So did I,' replied Lan Yi. 'So did everyone. It seems we might have been wrong.' He shook his head sadly. 'Now it seems vanishingly unlikely that we shall ever see Tau Ceti II – which is a great pity, because it was an experience to which I was very much looking forward.'

'You can think of that at a time like now?'

'I can think of very little else,' said the old man, 'except that perhaps some of our colleagues were injured when the g disappeared. Now that we have light again, I believe you and I might go to find out.'

He pushed himself towards the door, and she followed.

'Just stay here, you understand, you creep,' said Strauss-Giolitto to O'Sondheim.

He nodded wordlessly, and the tears continued to flow.

Humanity had tried to devise some means of faster-than-light travel for centuries, but without success. Very little technological work had been done on the problem, for obvious reasons, but theoretical physicists had nagged away at it interminably – and uselessly.

In theory there were a number of ways, all of which seemed futile. You could find a spinning black hole, then adopt just the precisely correct trajectory as you fell into it, so that you would emerge somewhere millions of parsecs away in the Universe –

or perhaps even in an entirely different universe. Black holes had been identified, and the configuration of the x-ray spectrum given off by the raw matter falling into some of them confirmed that they were indeed spinning. The nearest useful candidate was a healthy three hundred parsecs from the Solar System, which meant that just getting there, using current technology, would take the best part of two millennia and require as much fuel as a small moon. On arrival, you would probably have to spend decades – if not centuries – studying the black hole and preferably correlating your data with a secondary team investigating another spinner. Comparing notes would be a lengthy business: the next nearest spinner was unfortunately in almost exactly the opposite direction from the Solar System, so that a one-way message would take a little over two thousand five hundred years.

Then, when finally you were ready to boldly go, you could dip into the black hole and discover your constituent subatomic particles evenly distributed throughout one if not several universes and quite possibly in different eras of each universe's lifespan.

As this was not an appealing option, humanity instead turned its attention to wormholes, theoretical physical constructs which might link two different parts of the Universe closely together, subverting the normal fabric of spacetime. All the mathematics pointed to the fact that wormholes ought to exist, but no one had ever been able even to come close to suggesting how you could find one – or, much better, build one. In fact, the latter task was probably impossible: wormholes, if they did indeed exist as the theory said they should, were quantum structures based on the fact that the physics of reality is reliant not on certainty but on probability – or in their case improbability – so in order to build one you would first have to construct improbabilistic tools. Since no one had the first idea what an improbabilistic tool looked like – although jokes about the term had become thoroughly stale with age – this option, too, seemed unappealing.

A third option had seemed for a while to be encoded tachyons. Tachyons are particles that travel faster than light:

93

indeed, they require to be energized in some unimaginable way if they are to be slowed down to light-velocity. In their natural state, tachyons travel at infinite velocity, and are thus everywhere in the Universe at once. If a craftful of human beings could somehow be encoded into tachyonic form and then reconstituted as normal matter somewhere else, its translation from one side of the Universe to the other could take no time at all – even better, since theory predicted that tachyons also travelled backwards in time, it could arrive at its destination centuries before its departure. This raised the intriguing possibility of being able to send a tachyonic message home to say: 'Don't bother coming. We're here already.'

Perhaps luckily, no one had ever caught a tachyon, so this mode of travel was abandoned even as a possibility – especially after the theoretical physicist Shutzi Katanara proved beyond any possible doubt that tachyons could not exist. The equations Katanara produced were so beautiful that they sang: there could be no doubt about his conclusions.

Attention turned back to wormholes. If only, if only, if only . . .

What human scientists hadn't reckoned on was that wormholes were everywhere. The trick of interstellar navigation wasn't *finding* them. It was avoiding them.

That was what Lan Yi had just realized, while he'd been curled up in the darkness listening to Strauss-Giolitto brutalizing O'Sondheim.

He found the idea exquisite.

And exquisitely frightening.

Yet another invisible somebody pinched him softly, and he hardly noticed.

Just at the door, Lan Yi paused. 'I'll be with you in a moment,' he said to Strauss-Giolitto. 'Wait here.'

He shoved himself towards a low cupboard behind his futon and rummaged inside it for a moment. 'Here,' he said, tossing something gently towards her.

It was a belt-rope. She clipped one end on to her belt and idly swung a circle with the other, which was weighted by its small grav-grapple. The device was for use in emergencies on-planet. Her unthinking action began to make her spin very gradually in the opposite direction. She clutched the doorpost.

'What about you?' she said.

'I insisted on having a spare,' he said, producing it. 'I insisted on having spares of everything, except my body. I am a lot older than you are, Maria Strauss-Giolitto, and am more likely to find myself in difficulties. It is probably because I am aware of this that I am a lot older than you are.' He smiled.

He cued his musibot with a couple of jabs of a finger. Music filled the cabin. Then Lan Yi made a further manipulation and the sound began to boom out almost deafeningly. O'Sondheim, almost forgotten by the other two, recoiled, but the blast of noise seemed to bring him to his senses. He drew the back of his hand across his eyes, and then looked around alertly.

Lan Yi glanced at the First Officer. Was it possible that O'Sondheim could help them? No: there wasn't a third belt-rope. He gestured to O'Sondheim that the man should stay where he was, and by a miracle the First Officer understood what he was trying to say.

Back at the door, Lan Yi found the wall of sound was more tolerable. He hitched his own belt-rope on.

'We go one after the other between the cabins,' he shouted into Strauss-Giolitto's ear. 'Never let go of the rope, even when you're inside a cabin. If the g comes back suddenly, we could be killed if we weren't secured.'

She nodded. It was tempting just to 'swim' through the free fall to the next cabin but if either of them were halfway between cabins when an abrupt rearward force of 2g was reintroduced . . . No wonder Strider had been so insistent over the intercom that people stay indoors.

He raised his grav-grapple and shot it towards the wall of the cabin nearest to them. Then, to her surprise, he moved not towards it but in the opposite direction, instead leaping towards the *Santa Maria*'s stern, paying out his belt-rope as he went. Almost immediately she saw the sense of what he was doing. They should start with the rearmost cabin and work their way forwards.

She followed suit, swinging in a long loop, carefully adjusting the control at her belt so that there was never too much of the rope paid out slack at any one time. If the gees were suddenly restored, the tautening of a slack rope could break her back. Even a taut rope would probably do so anyway, but at least this way they were reducing the risks.

She arrived beside Lan Yi at the rearmost cabin, panting slightly.

'That is the end of the most dangerous part of the exercise,' he said, as calmly as if he were discussing the weather. The noise of the music he had started playing was far quieter here but still perfectly audible.

'What did you do that for?' she said, nodding towards his distant cabin as he shoved open the door of the one they'd arrived at. 'It's a beastly racket.'

'It's Telemann,' he said. 'Get inside.'

She obeyed, finding herself confronted by a woman and a terrified child. The woman was holding herself and the child down on to the larger of the room's two forcefield beds. There was a stench of urine in the enclosed space. She knew the child, of course, from having taught him. 'Hello, Hilary,' she said, smiling. 'There's nothing to be afraid about.'

'Well,' continued Lan Yi, pulling himself through the door behind her and shutting it firmly, 'it's *melded* Telemann. Variations on a tune by another composer of roughly the same epoch, but whose name has been forgotten. If you are so very interested, Maria Strauss-Giolitto, the tune is called "Sad-Eyed Lady of the Lowlands". I prefer the Telemann melding best of all, but my musibot has produced some other interesting combinations based on it. The Mozart version is over-fussy, however.'

'It sounds beastly to me,' said Strauss-Giolitto. Her own tastes ran to randomusic, where the musibot was programmed to produce randomly selected series of tones and rhythms.

The woman was looking at the two of them as if they were insane. 'What the hell are you people talking about?'

'Quite right,' said Lan Yi, with a little formal nod. 'We are checking the cabins to ascertain the extent of any casualties

96

there may have been, and to see if we can help. I played the Telemann piece because I always find it most soothing, and I thought that it might calm others. But it seems' – he shrugged towards Strauss-Giolitto – 'that I may have been wrong.'

Strauss-Giolitto silenced him with a raised hand. 'Are you and Hilary the only people here?' she said, trying to make her voice sound friendly but unconcerned. 'This cabin has sustained no casualties?'

'Just us two are here,' said the woman. 'We're OK.'

Strauss-Giolitto's apparent calmness was infecting the child, who for the first time since they'd come through the door was beginning to look less frightened. 'Hello, Maria,' he said, forcing a smile. 'I was doing my homework when this thing happened, so I . . .'

'I think we'll allow you to be late with your homework this once,' said Strauss-Giolitto, grinning desperately.

Lan Yi had opened the door, and was fiddling at his waist. His belt-rope wound itself in swiftly until the grav-grapple finally appeared. 'Please that you do the same,' he said to Strauss-Giolitto.

She did so, at the same time thinking that Lan Yi must be very much more worried than he was letting on. His Argot, although habitually a little stiff and uncolloquial, was normally flawless.

'We will leave you now,' said Lan Yi to Hilary's mother, patting Hilary's head. 'I suggest that you retain your current position until instructions are given otherwise.'

He nodded to Strauss-Giolitto, and she launched her grav-grapple towards the next bow-ward cabin, then let her belt-rope reel her towards it.

This time they had to manoeuvre themselves over the cabin's roof before they could reach the door. It was a terrifying few moments before they found themselves safely inside – only to discover that the cabin was empty.

They reached the fifth cabin before they found their first casualty. Strauss-Giolitto vaguely recognized him as a junior biochemist who had made a few amiable passes at her between Phobos and Jupiter. Now she felt embarrassed, because she

97

couldn't even remember his name. He floated near the ceiling, his neck obviously broken. There might have been a chance, had a medbot got to him quickly enough, that he could have been saved, even yet; but she and Lan Yi had no means of summoning a medbot – besides, from what had been going on, it seemed very likely that the Main Computer was out of action, and the medbots were dependent on it, their own small puters being just sufficient to manipulate the various devices they employed. Maybe, if you were lucky, one of them could diagnose and splint a fractured leg. If you were unlucky, you could find your broken leg helpfully crammed down your throat.

'There's nothing we can do,' said Lan Yi with a shrug, his face unperturbed. 'We must speed on our way, Maria Strauss-Giolitto.'

She felt guilty, just leaving the biochemist floating there, but Lan Yi was right: there *was* nothing they could do.

A few cabins later, however, they were able to make themselves useful. An agronomer had broken his wrist, and the darkness and the pain of the injury – plus the shock of finding that, unlike at home on the blisters of Mars, no medbot had arrived within minutes – had virtually sent him out of his wits: he was just staring at his limp hand as if it were some rare and valuable *objet trouvé*.

Lan Yi found a vest in a drawer and ripped it efficiently into strips, then began applying an emergency bandage. The agronomer made no protest, even when his bones ground together. Strauss-Giolitto tried her best to get through to him, speaking softly to him, forming words that didn't mean very much but attempting to make an encouraging pattern of sentences. She didn't know if she was having any success: in the end they had to leave him there, now strapped to his bunk, and carry on their nerve-racking survey.

They must have worked their way through over half the cabins – repairing lesser injuries and finding only one more fatality – when the gees came back on.

Despite all their precautions, they were slammed against an inner cabin wall, Strauss-Giolitto on top of Lan Yi.

She gave a shriek of surprise. He gave a yip of pain. As the cabin slowly swivelled to right itself, they slid to the floor together.

Strauss-Giolitto picked herself up wearily. One grew grudgingly half-accustomed to 2g in time – rather a long time, if you had spent much of your life on Mars – but it took only a few hours in free fall to realize quite what a burden the acceleration put on one's body.

She reached out a hand to the elderly Taiwanese.

'I think not,' he said crisply, lying there. 'You are a big person, Maria Strauss-Giolitto, and that was a heavy impact. You have broken my arm and at least one – no, certainly it is two – of my ribs.'

He tried and eventually managed to sit up. Then he fainted.

'Holy Umbel!' shouted Leander, suddenly forced deep into her chair.

'You called,' said Nelson. It was an old joke between them, and he spoke it automatically. He was as stunned as she was by what had just happened. Neither of them noticed Strider hauling her once-more ponderous body across the deck to assure herself that Pinocchio was securely moored.

The resumption of acceleration was shock enough in itself.

The view through the fore-window above them was something else.

The colours were like those of a skin of oil floating on the surface of a puddle of water – oddly metallic-seeming greens and blues and yellows and pale reds and greys – but all the hazy-edged random shapes were moving with frenetic speed through and around each other. Wherever the two officers looked, the dazzlingly coloured forms seemed to be trying to create coherent patterns, but never quite succeeding. The effect was almost impossible to look at; it was almost impossible not to watch.

Strider walked heavily over to stand between them.

'Well, it's different,' she remarked lamely. At least the succession of little pinching sensations seemed to have cut out as the acceleration cut back in.

99

Now there was a background of angry red flames behind the schemes of colour, and traceries of hot yellow and white sparks were flitting rapidly through them.

'Do you think we've ended up in somebody's bonfire?' said Nelson drily.

'Seems as likely as anywhere,' said Strider. She glanced away from the display of brilliances at the screens in front of the two officers. They were still dead. That meant the Main Computer was still out. She'd suspected as much: Pinocchio hadn't recovered consciousness. She was much more worried about losing the Main Computer than about where the *Santa Maria* might be taking them: even if they found themselves back in the Solar System – or back on course for Tau Ceti II – without the Computer they were dead. Pinocchio was able to keep the most basic systems running, but there was no way he could tackle the complex problems of astrogation the Main Computer was designed in part to solve. And who knew how long he could keep even those basic systems functioning?

Her eyes were dragged up to the window again.

There were quite a few electronic brains aboard the *Santa Maria*, of course. She speculated about the possibilities of trying to hook them all up together – or, rather, getting Pinocchio to do it – but she realized even as the thought was passing through her head that it would be impossible. The medbots and most of the others were really hardly more than drones served out of the Main Computer. Aside from that there were the rudimentary bots used for entertainment. Personal puters were limited in their scope, and affected by the speed with which their human operators could act. In fact, speed was another reason why her half-formed crazy scheme could never work: astrogation required a machine that could think *fast*, not just in working out the problems but in coordinating all the various minor rocketry that would alter the *Santa Maria*'s configuration in space.

Once more she turned to look at Pinocchio. Still his face was lifeless.

The blaze of colours ahead of them was changing in nature

yet again. The illusion of oiliness had returned, but it was now as if the oil were, against a sullen black sheet of water, congealing into droplets, each made up of myriad iridescent shades. They were darting around all over the field of view as if in some hyperactive Brownian motion, their velocity and their constant changes of direction making the eye try to follow individual balls of light, but always unsuccessfully. Strider again felt, despite the insistent tug of the gees on her, that she was dropping from a great height and at fantastic speed. Not for the first time during these past few subjective hours, her gorge began to rise.

'Run a check on casualties, Leander,' she said, keeping her voice controlled.

'Yes, Captain,' said the officer. She spoke into her throat-mike, but clearly received no answer. Of course, Strider could see Leander realizing, the throat-mikes were linked through the Main Computer; it was hard to remember that the things you'd taken for granted most of your life didn't work any more. Leander prepared to repeat the message through her commline.

'I meant *physically* go and find out,' said Strider.

Leander pushed herself up from her chair and made leadenly for the door. With a sense of relief – standing still for any length of time was the most difficult thing of all to do in the accelerative gees – Strider slid herself down to take Leander's place.

She ran her fingers across the keyboard, looking resentfully at the still-blank screen. They'd switched off the banks of sensor screens around the walls of the deck – all except the clock and the one through which Pinocchio had rigged himself, of course – some while back, so that they wouldn't be driven mad by the senseless audio and visual static. In a moment, after she'd rested briefly, she'd try them again. But the static had been as nothing compared to the breathtaking theatre of light that was playing all around them now.

And then it was over, and they were looking out on a starfield.

The figures on the clock began to move again, but neither Strider nor Nelson realized it at first.

'Well,' said Nelson after a while, running a palm nervously across his broad forehead, 'it looks like we've *got* someplace at last.'

Strider stared at the dead screen in front of her, feeling betrayed. Somehow she'd expected that merely emerging into normal space would reactivate the Main Computer.

'The big question now is,' Nelson continued, 'where we've actually got *to*.'

Without the Computer there was no way of telling. Even just two years out from Jupiter many of the familiar constellation shapes had become strangely distorted. Now it was obvious that they were a lot further from home than that: there was nothing remotely recognizable out there at all. Moreover, the starfield seemed unnaturally rich. It wasn't something you noticed at first; instead, it slowly dawned on both of them that there were rather too many stars around. And that more of them were red than they should be.

'Do you think we've ended up somewhere near the Hub?' said Strider.

'No, sweet light of my life,' said Nelson slowly, a look of both horror and wonder spreading across his big face. 'I don't think we're anywhere near the Hub.'

She turned in her seat to follow his line of sight.

Visible through the stars, not quite edge-on to them, stretching over maybe thirty degrees of her field of vision, was something she'd thought she'd never see except through telescopes and in holos.

A spiral galaxy.

Neither of them spoke for several minutes as they took in the implications. The sight was beautiful: that was what Strider registered first. It was impossible not to feel awe. Although the galaxy was not the brightest object in the *Santa Maria*'s sky, it possessed a sheer beauty and massiveness that made it the most impressive thing she had ever seen. And it had a *reality* that even the holos produced by Hubble XVII could never hope to emulate. What stunned the senses most were the colours of it – little by way of structure could be seen from here. The colours

102

of galaxies in holos always seemed artificial – and often enough they in fact were, having been deliberately enhanced for one reason or another. But the colours of the galaxy she was looking at were true ones. They seemed almost alive, even though they were motionless. Patches of blue and white and yellow predominated closer to where the *Santa Maria* seemed to hang; beyond, the hues shaded towards both red and a brighter blue, where the hub was. The hub itself was bigger than she'd expected: she'd always known that spiral galaxies were basically flat with a slight bulge in the centre, but from this angle you could get a full appreciation of how large the bulge really was.

The second thing that she took in was the remoteness of the galaxy. The sheer distance chilled.

Finally she said: 'I think we must have ended up in a globular cluster. That's our old friend the Milky Way over there.'

'I think not,' said Nelson quietly. 'Globular clusters are almost all high above the galactic plane, and we're looking at this baby almost from the side. That's not the Milky Way at all, I reckon. I can try to find out.'

She looked quickly at him.

He gestured towards his thighputer. 'I have data on the Milky Way in here. I can get a screen view of what it should be like from this kind of location.'

She turned back to look at the spiral. Even if the personnel of the *Santa Maria* died here, as far as she was concerned it would probably be worth it. This was the kind of sight that she had come into the SSIA *for* – knowing that it was something she'd never be able to see for herself, but at the same time getting part of the thrill that her distant descendants would experience when finally humanity advanced that far. Now she was doing the impossible – achieving her dream.

'Have you got information on the Andromeda spiral in that device as well?' she asked suddenly.

'It's the very next thing I'm going to check out, but I want to run these specs on the Milky Way first, just in case I'm wrong. You've got where I was thinking, huh?'

'Yeah. We're in an elliptical.'

The Milky Way has two small, seemingly young satellite galaxies, both of them irregularly shaped: the Greater and Smaller Magellanic clouds. The Andromeda Galaxy has at least two satellite galaxies as well, but these are seemingly far further evolved than the Magellanic clouds: they have formed into tightly packed ellipsoids of closely clustered, redder, older stars. From the lesser of these two ellipticals it might just be possible that one could see the view that was confronting Strider right now.

'I can confirm it's not the Milky Way,' said Nelson behind her.

'Thanks,' she said absently.

A little while later he added: 'And it's not the Andromeda spiral either. I've got the puter to do a search of all the galaxies it has on file to see if there are any that remotely match the parameters of this one.'

'But you're not hopeful,' she said.

'Who knows?' She could hear his jumpsuit rustle as he shrugged.

'Snap,' she said.

'We encountered two fatalities between cabins one and twenty-two,' said Strauss-Giolitto to Leander. 'Lan Yi is currently resting in cabin twenty-seven. They had some painkiller there, and I was able to splint up his arm.' What she didn't say was that the painkiller in question was marijuana. All forms of drugs – including alcohol, tobacco and, the one most argued about of all, ziprite – had been banned from the mission. They weren't in fact necessary. You could get a much higher high out of your stim socket than through a shot of ziprite, with the great advantage that you could snap out of your high at a moment's notice if necessary. The disadvantage was that stim dreaming was if anything more addictive. But someone had clearly smuggled aboard some dope seeds, and there must be a covert little plantation on one of the fields. Strauss-Giolitto felt it was her responsibility to report the matter to Leander, so she didn't. The *Santa Maria*'s officers would know about it soon

104

enough anyway: the switch into free fall and then back to 2g had deposited large sections of agriculture at the rear of the vessel. In the meantime, Strauss-Giolitto had partaken of a bite of hash cookie herself: she wasn't about to report the people who had very kindly given it to her. 'He'll be all right,' she said.

'Can you turn off that noise while I check out the rest?' said Leander, gesturing towards Lan Yi's cabin.

'I can try,' said Strauss-Giolitto. 'But I think Lan Yi's musibot has been specially programmed.' This was a flat lie, and probably Leander knew it. If Lan Yi wanted to listen to distant Telemann as he suffered on his borrowed bed, Strauss-Giolitto was prepared to let him do so. He had probably saved several lives during the period of free fall: he deserved to be allowed to hear whatever racket he chose.

He deserved to be allowed to get as high as a kite without some petty demagogue like Leander butting in.

'Have you checked out the remaining cabins?' Leander was asking.

'Not yet. I was concerned about Lan Yi. Can you get the medbots moving yet?'

'Yeah, I guess so,' said Leander. 'They won't be able to do much, but . . .'

'We weren't able to do much either. We did our best. I want to be with the old guy. If it hadn't been for him . . .'

'I know,' said Leander, holding up a hand. 'You do that. Give him my love. I'll take over from here.'

After a long time Nelson spoke.

'As far as this puter can tell,' he said lazily, 'we could have gone right to the other end of the Universe. I think we're in real trouble, sweet little lady from the old country.'

'I knew we were in shit right from the beginning,' said Strider. 'Even if that *had* been the Milky Way, we've got no way of getting to it.' She pushed her spread fingers through her short hair; she was trying to cure herself of the habit, but without success. 'We're stuck, Umbel. Fancy a spot of cannibalism?'

Their laughter was artificial.

WELCOME TO THE WONDERVALE, said a voice in both of their heads.

The Images had arrived.

Part Three: Strider's Galaxy

1

The Images

Nelson and Strider looked at each other sharply. Neither of them said anything for a few moments.

'Did you just hear what I just heard?' It was Strider who finally broke the silence.

'Something about "The Wondervale"?' said Nelson.

'Yeah.' She touched her forehead. 'Well, at least if we're going nuts we're doing it together.'

' "The Wondervale" does sound like the name of some kind of mental institution,' drawled Nelson.

YOU ARE WELCOME, said the cool, silent voice, BUT WE DO NOT KNOW WHO YOU ARE. It seemed like a concatenation of voices speaking almost perfectly in unison, like several sopranos who had practised together long and hard. It was filled with complex, interacting music, and yet it had a purity no single human voice could have attained.

Feeling foolish, Strider spoke towards the view-window. 'We are employees of the Solar System Interstellar Agency.' She hoped that whoever-it-was could get something of the meanings of her thoughts, rather than just her words. 'We were conducting the Solar System's first interstellar investigative mission, voyaging towards Tau Ceti II, when we . . . got lost.'

THERE IS NO NEED TO SPEAK WORDS, UNLESS YOU SO DESIRE, reassured the voice. WE ARE INDEED UNDERSTANDING THE MEANINGS OF YOUR THOUGHTS. YOU CAME THROUGH A WORMHOLE FROM YOUR GALAXY INTO OURS, WHICH IS CALLED THE WONDERVALE. YOURS IS CALLED THE MILKY WAY. It paused, as if seeking to find a way of not sounding patronizing. TERMS LIKE 'SOLAR SYSTEM' AND 'TAU CETI II' ARE MEAN-INGLESS TO US. MOST BEINGS NAME THEIR HOME SYSTEM BY A THOUGHT WHICH MEANS 'SOLAR SYSTEM'.

'I'll carry on speaking out loud, if you don't mind,' said Strider. 'You may be able to read my thoughts, but my friend here can't. I want him to know what's going on in this conversation.'

WE COULD TRY TO LINK YOUR MINDS, IF YOU LIKE.

She shook her head. 'Later, maybe. Right now we've got enough to think about without trying to think each other's thoughts as well. If you know what I mean,' she added.

IT IS UNDERSTOOD.

She looked around the command deck, trying to work out where the voice was coming from. 'Where are you?' she said. 'Can't you show yourselves to us?'

WE CANNOT. WE ARE ONLY FRACTIONALLY A PART OF THIS UNIVERSE. YOU MAY BE ABLE SOMETIMES TO DETECT OUR PRESENCE VISUALLY OR TACTUALLY. INSOFAR AS WE ARE IN YOUR REALITY AT ALL, WE ARE ON YOUR COMMAND DECK WITH YOU.

'*Who* are you, then? Can you help us?'

MAY WE READ THE ENTIRETY OF YOUR MINDS?

'Go ahead.' In a way this seemed militarily an unwise choice, because for all she knew these creatures – if they were indeed creatures – might turn out to be humanity's deadliest enemies. On the other hand, she was reassured by the fact that they had asked permission of her: almost certainly they could have scanned her thoughts through and through without her being any the wiser. She grinned suddenly, wryly, remembering how in the old legends you'd been safe enough inside your home, but if you invited the vampire to come indoors . . .

She relaxed her body, straining to feel some mental sensation to betray what was going on.

There was this time quite a long pause. When the voice returned it sounded almost rueful. THERE IS NO CONCEPT WITHIN YOUR CULTURAL BACKGROUND THAT IN ANY SENSE MATCHES WHAT WE CALL OURSELVES. AS TO THE NATURE OF OUR BEINGS, THAT IS SOMETHING BEST LEFT UNTIL LATER. BUT WE CAN HELP YOU. WE ENJOY HELPING PRIMITIVE CULTURES AS MUCH AS WE DO ADVANCED ONES.

Strider instinctively bridled at the "primitive" tag, but

immediately untensed again. Humanity had been making its first attempt to reach the stars, having messed up its home patch. To creatures like these, who were clearly able to move through the interstellar tracts and even the dimensions with ease – how else could they have pinpointed the *Santa Maria* with such swiftness? – Strider and her kind must look as if they'd only just discovered how to make fire.

QUITE, said the voice. There was not a hint of condescension.

'How can you help us?' said Nelson. His voice sounded a little punch-drunk.

The sense that the focus had shifted briefly from herself eased Strider's concentration momentarily, and she caught out of the corner of her eye a flicker of something that was very like light but was somehow different. She sat up straight in her chair.

CONGRATULATIONS, CAPTAIN LEONIE STRIDER, said the voice ironically. YOU HAVE JUST MADE YOUR FIRST DIRECT OPTICAL CONTACT WITH US.

She waved a hand casually as if to say 'Hi there'. In fact, she was just beginning to feel terrified of these mental intruders. That flash of almost-light had brought home to her, even more than had her first sight of the majesty of the spiral galaxy through the view-window, that the situation she and the rest of the personnel of the *Santa Maria* had exploded into was *truly* alien. They were a *long* way from home.

WE CAN HELP YOU IN A NUMBER OF WAYS, said the soundless voice mildly. WE WISH TO, ALTHOUGH OF COURSE WE WOULD NOT DO SO WITHOUT YOUR STATED ASSENT. WE CAN PUT OURSELVES IN THE PLACE OF YOUR DEFUNCT CONTROLLING COMPUTER – OR WE COULD TRY TO REPAIR IT, ALTHOUGH IT SEEMS TO US THAT ITS MENTAL DETERIORATION IS SO PROFOUND THAT REPAIRS COULD BE ONLY PARTIAL. BESIDES, IT IS A FAR LESS SOPHISTICATED ENTITY THAN THE ONE WE CAN FORM FROM OURSELVES.

'You wanna be a *computer*?' Nelson expostulated.

NO. WITH A SMALL PORTION OF OURSELVES WE CAN PERFORM ALL THE FUNCTIONS OF YOUR DEAD COMPUTER: THAT

111

IS A QUITE DIFFERENT MATTER. IT WOULD REQUIRE NO MORE OF OUR ATTENTION THAN YOU HAVE TO EXPEND ON KEEPING YOUR HEART BEATING. This time the voice did sound genuinely bored, as if it were having difficulty crossing the culture gap.

Strider wasn't certain if she liked the idea of her ship being run entirely by unknown, unseen aliens. 'Do you think you could, you know, sort of try to *repair* the Main Computer first?'

WE COULD TRY.

The statement was so swift and so bald that she realized this was the last thing the creatures wanted her to ask of them.

'I think you're not being entirely honest with us,' she said.

The words rushed into her mind so fast that she could hardly keep up with them: IF WE FIX YOUR COMPUTER WHICH WE DO NOT THINK IS SOMETHING WE CAN DO YOU WILL STILL BE IN AN ANTIQUATED SPACE VESSEL WITH AN ANTIQUATED DRIVE UNIT FOLLOWING THE INSTRUCTIONS WHICH WE SHALL WILLINGLY GIVE YOU AS TO HOW YOU CAN REACH THE NEAREST PLANET YOU MIGHT FIND HABITABLE WHICH HAS NOT BEEN ALREADY COLONIZED, WHICH TRIP WILL TAKE YOU A TIME OF TWENTY-EIGHT OF YOUR YEARS ASSUMING YOUR SHIP IS NOT PICKED OFF BY MILITARY ACTION DURING THAT TIME AND IT ALMOST CERTAINLY WOULD BE. YOUR COMPUTER IS CAPABLE OF CONTROLLING ONLY THE TECHNOLOGY IT WAS BUILT TO CONTROL. IF WE CAN INSTALL OURSELVES IN ITS PLACE WE MAY THEN UPGRADE YOUR SHIP SO THAT IT HAS AT LEAST THE LEVEL OF TECHNOLOGY OF THOSE OF OTHER PHYSICAL SPECIES WHO POPULATE THE WONDERVALE. THIS WILL CERTAINLY BE OF CONSIDERABLE VALUE TO YOU AND YOUR CONTINUED PERSONAL SURVIVAL BUT MORE IMPORTANTLY IT MIGHT BE OF GREAT BENEFIT TO OTHERS OF THE WONDERVALE AND AESTHETICALLY TO OURSELVES WHICH IS WHY WE SO GLADLY OFFER TO YOU OUR SERVICES. BUT WE CANNOT *MAKE* YOU ACCEPT THOSE SERVICES.

'Upgrade the ship?' said Strider hesitantly. 'How?'

YOUR DRIVE RESTRICTS YOU TO SUBLIGHT VELOCITIES.

Strider and Nelson exchanged glances. They could hardly believe what they'd just heard.

BECAUSE YOU HAVE NO MODE OF ACHIEVING TRANS-LIGHT

112

VELOCITIES YOU ARE INCAPABLE OF AVOIDING WORMHOLES. ALSO, YOU HAVE NO DEFENSIVE WEAPONRY.

'Yeah,' said Nelson, 'you talked about military action before. Is there some kind of war going on?'

THE WONDERVALE IS A FIELD OF MANY WARS. IT IS VERY UNAESTHETIC. THIS GALAXY IS IN THE GRIP OF A TYRANNY, AND REBELLIONS ARE EVERYWHERE. WE WISH THAT THEY WOULD STOP.

'Whose side are you on?' said Nelson suspiciously.

WE ARE ON THE SIDE OF THE WARS' STOPPING, BECAUSE THEY OFFEND US. THAT WILL NEVER HAPPEN UNTIL THE TYRANNY IS REMOVED. WE WOULD PREFER THAT THIS HAP- PENED BY PERSUASION RATHER THAN WARFARE, BUT THE TYRANNY OF THE AUTARCH NALLA SHOWS NO SIGNS OF BEING OPEN TO PERSUASION.

Again Strider saw a motion of near-light at the very periphery of her vision. This time it didn't make the small hairs at the back of her neck twitch in protest.

'Tell us more about the upgrading of the ship,' she said, waving Nelson to silence.

WE CAN RESTORE THE SMALL MOBILE COMPUTER FOR WHOM YOU HAVE SUCH FONDNESS, CAPTAIN LEONIE STRIDER, the voice said. THAT IS A TINY MATTER FOR US. WE CAN GIVE YOU AN ARTIFICIAL MARS-STANDARD GRAVITY WHATEVER THE ACCELERATION TO WHICH YOU SUBJECT YOUR SHIP, WITHIN CERTAIN LIMITS. WE CAN PROVIDE YOU WITH MORE SOPHISTI- CATED ASTROGATION THAN YOUR CULTURE WILL ATTAIN IN SEVERAL THOUSAND YEARS. BUT THE MOST IMPORTANT THING OF ALL IS WHAT WE HAVE ALREADY SAID: WE CAN REPLACE YOUR PRIMARY DRIVE WITH ONE WHICH WILL MOVE YOU BETWEEN THE STARS WITHOUT EACH VOYAGE TAKING SEV- ERAL OF YOUR DECADES. THE TACHYON DRIVE CAN –

'But there are no such things as tachyons!' said Nelson. 'Shutzi Katanara proved it, way back.'

The voice fell silent.

'At a quick guess,' said Strider unhappily to the big man seated alongside her, 'Shutzi was wrong. Once upon a time people proved that the Sun went round the Earth – remember?'

THE TACHYON DRIVE, resumed the lilting voice-that-was-several-voices, CAN TAKE YOU AT TRANS-LIGHT VELOCITY WHEREVER IT IS YOU WISH TO GO. BY THE VERY NATURE OF THE TACHYON DRIVE, ANY CRAFT POWERED BY IT IS IN NO DANGER OF FALLING INTO A WORMHOLE, AS YOU DID.

'Can it take us home?' said Strider.

NO. WE DO NOT KNOW WHERE YOUR HOME IS. WE WOULD SUGGEST THAT YOU ACCEPT, CAPTAIN LEONIE STRIDER, THAT FROM NOW ON YOUR HOME IS THE WONDERVALE.

It was hard to recognize what the command deck of the *Santa Maria* had become. The screens had vanished, and in their place were devices whose physics had been explained to the human beings but proved incomprehensible even to Lan Yi. The aliens had called the devices Cross-Reality Assimilation Pods, which was perhaps an accurate description of the way in which they worked but acronymized unfortunately; Strider was damned if she was going to spend the rest of her life sticking her head into CRAPs, and renamed the things Pockets. Because using them *could* be like delving into a pocket – often enough, the pocket of an old garment you hadn't worn for years, so that what you found was a mixture of reminders and items you had so long forgotten that they were in effect brand-new discoveries.

The displays of the Pockets looked from a distance as if they were straightforwardly holographic. Each Pocket – there were twelve of them, arranged in a neat curve around the front one hundred and twenty degrees of the command deck – was like a box mounted on another box. The lower box appeared to be solid, made of something resembling opaque grey plastite, although it adjusted its size automatically so that its upper surface was always at the waist-height of the user. It did so in a way that was inconvenient to watch: for fun, Leander had tried suddenly squatting down while making an observation, and had had to knock off duty for a couple of hours with a splitting headache. The top surface of this box was illuminated, displaying a constant stream of mathematical data and geometrical representations.

The upper box was the part of the Pocket which demonstrated just how far ahead of human technology the aliens had gone. For a start, the box itself was invisible, although you were aware it was there by the fact that any of the images it contained were cut off along fixed boundaries. Within this box you could call up three-dimensional representations of whatever it was you wanted to observe – within the limits of the aliens' knowledge and the ability of the human brain to comprehend what it saw. Through this image you watched, on the display surface of the lower box, the complementing data.

The mode of operation was deeply unhuman. There were no buttons to press, no keyboards on which to rattle. Instead, you leaned your head forward into the Pocket and *thought* about what it was you wanted to know. Then you retreated slightly, still keeping your head within the Pocket, and the display would hold until you changed it for something else.

At first, Strider had found the experience almost terrifying: it was as if she were being asked to stick her head blindly into the unknown, with every chance that the unknown had sharp teeth and strong jaws. Soon, though, she and the rest of her officers became accustomed to it. In times of idleness, the officers would enjoy themselves conjuring up fantastically detailed 3D images of the outer hull of the *Santa Maria* or – a special favourite – the spiral galaxy, which the humans had learned was known as Heaven's Ancestor. The image could be slowly rotated along any axis, so that at one moment you could be looking down on the full face of the galaxy and at the next you could be watching it from the edge-on angle at which Strider and Nelson had first seen it. You could also narrow the focus, seemingly almost infinitely, until you found yourself observing a single star. Finding a planet to look at was more difficult, but Nelson had by chance managed it once – disappointingly, it appeared to be only a little ball of sterile rock.

Observing planets within The Wondervale was easier, especially since the aliens provided guidance. An almost depressingly high proportion of them proved to be inhabited by technological species (*The Wondervale is a field of many wars*), although here the resolution of the Pockets broke down:

the *Santa Maria* was currently too far from any star to be able to conduct a full surface scan of a planet – the smallest structures that could be seen were cities. *And,* thought Strider, *you can probably up your estimate of the number of advanced civilizations, because presumably some species don't build cities.*

Two Pockets – the ones on the far right and far left – were different from the others. They were reserved, the aliens had somewhat chillingly explained, for communications. Even more than observation of planets, this brought it home that The Wondervale was *rich* in technological civilizations.

'How many of you are there?' Strider had asked, not long after the revelation that the trans-reality aliens could do most things but couldn't guide the *Santa Maria* home.

WE ARE THREE.

Once more she saw a strange flicker out of the side of her eye. 'I wish I could see you.'

YOU HAVE JUST SEEN ONE OF US.

'I mean, see you properly.'

YOU JUST HAVE.

'What do you look like? To each other?'

LIKE WHAT YOU HAVE JUST SEEN. ALTHOUGH WE CAN SEE EACH OTHER DIRECTLY, NOT JUST MOMENTARILY THROUGH THE EDGES OF OUR VISION.

'All I've been able to see is the occasional fleeting patch of light,' she said.

'Me too,' said Nelson. 'I'm not sure quite how much I like this, gentle lady. If I've gotta meet aliens, I want them to be *there*. I don't mind if they look like double-pronged sea anemones, but I want to be able to shake their . . . well, tendrils, I guess.'

WE'RE DIFFERENT, said the trilling voice in the two humans' minds. WE HAVE NO FLESH. WE SHOW OURSELVES – WE CAN SEE OURSELVES – ONLY AS IMAGES.

'Can we call you that?' said Strider. 'Images?'

IT IS A NAME AS GOOD AS ANY OTHER, said the voice. IT DOES NOT OFFEND US.

116

'And there are three of you?'

WE HAVE JUST SAID AS MUCH.

'Do you have individual names?'

YES. WE ARE INDIVIDUALS. THOSE NAMES ARE NOT EASILY TRANSLATABLE INTO CONCEPTS THAT YOUR CULTURE CAN UNDERSTAND.

Strider shrugged uneasily. She'd heard this before. It wasn't easy to be constantly reminded that your species were the dimwits of the Universe, however true that might be. Humanity was clearly, by the standards of the Images, a very young civilization. Yeah, that was a better way of thinking about it: not so much thick as just an infant, undereducated but with the potential for genius. In a few million years humanity could probably beat the Images at four-handed chess.

'What would you like us to call you?'

For the first time the three voices stopped speaking/singing in unison.

THE NEAREST WE CAN TRANSLATE TO MY NAME IS HEARTFIRE, said one of them.

AND I AM NIGHTMIRROR, said the next.

There was a pause before the last one said: YOU HAD BEST CALL ME TEN PER CENT EXTRA FREE.

'That's a goddam silly name,' muttered Nelson.

'I don't think we're in much of a position to describe things as goddam silly,' Strider hissed. 'We're the ones who were too goddam silly to be able to avoid a wormhole – remember?'

Nelson mumbled something that, probably fortunately, Strider couldn't quite make out.

'How can we tell you apart?' she said.

BY DISCOVERING OUR PERSONALITIES, said the three voices, once again in that almost-unison.

Pinocchio lay on his back in a field of potatoes, staring up at a field of barley. In reconstructing the *Santa Maria* the Images had done many things, most notably replacing the drive with one that relied on tachyonic interactions. The drive had yet to be initiated: the ship was currently just floating. Even when the drive was in operation, Pinocchio had discovered from the

117

Images, because it was capable of trans-light speeds, it produced no accelerative gravity; the Images had therefore reintroduced the spin which the *Santa Maria* had long ago used to produce a centrifugal equivalent of Mars-standard. The fields were folded back flat against the interior of the hull once more.

The Images had saved his life – he was perfectly aware of that. More accurately, they had been able to release him from the intellectual stasis into which he had had to enter in order to get the ship's basic systems up and running. But, in releasing him, they had also changed him. He suspected that they had left a part of themselves inside him – that this was the only reason why he was once more alive.

Because he *was* different now. An extra element had been added to his consciousness. He wasn't sure if he'd become more human or more alien: it was difficult to tell, having never had direct experience of being either.

He sat up, and plunged a hand into the earth beside him. He found a small potato, and carefully, with his fingers, severed it from its neighbours. Knowing that what he was doing was illegal, he lifted the potato to his lips, relishing its earthy smell. Then, giving himself no time to think about his action, he put it in his mouth and ate it, enjoying both its taste and its crispness. He couldn't actually swallow it, of course, because he had no throat and thereafter no digestive tract, but he could experience the *sensation* of eating.

After a minute he spat out the shreds of undigested potato.

What he had done had given him *pleasure*. He had *tasted*. These things had been abstractions before the Images had overhauled him. He had been aware that various events were better than others – he liked it when Strider kissed him on the cheek, disliked it when she was angry with him – but everything had been distanced. Things had been good because they were in accord with one of his imperatives; things had been bad because they were in discord with another. Now he was experiencing events directly: he was *feeling*.

He was about to pluck himself another potato when the whole of the *Santa Maria* shook.

'What in the name of Holy Umbel was that?' said Strider, jolted out of drowsiness. It was too easy to half-doze off here on the command deck now that the Images had largely taken over control of the *Santa Maria* – hell, they more or less *were* the *Santa Maria*. Soon they would finish their conversions and the ship could do something more constructive than seemingly hang in space.

WE ARE UNDER ATTACK, said the voice which she now recognized as that of Ten Per Cent Extra Free.

The *Santa Maria* had not originally been designed as a warcraft. The Images had transformed it in many ways. The shuttles in the blisters along its sides were now armed with weapons that Strider barely understood. The ship itself was surrounded with invisible defences that were totally incomprehensible to her, and was itself bristling with armaments. All she knew about this diverse weaponry was that in most cases using it obeyed the general laws of weaponry that had been in existence since the discovery of the efficacy of throwing a rock: aim it in the right direction, and fire. A few of the *Santa Maria*'s weapons weren't even like that: they weren't so much directional as radiational.

'Who's attacking us, dammit? We ain't done nothing!'

Strider leapt to the nearest Pocket and jabbed her head into it. She desired it to create for her a representation of the aggressor.

She stood back, and at once the Pocket filled up with blackness. In the centre of the blackness floated a craft shaped roughly like a mallet with nails sticking out of the handle. From one of the nails a spark of light flashed directly towards her eyes. She flinched reflexively.

The *Santa Maria* shook again.

O'Sondheim was on the deck with her. Sometime during the hell of the wormhole he had rediscovered his purpose in being; Strider still wasn't overly fond of him, but she had learned to respect the new O'Sondheim.

He moved rapidly to one of the communications Pockets.

'Can we speak to these people?' he shouted to the air.

WE CAN TRY TO OPEN UP A COMMUNICATIONS CHANNEL, Ten Per Cent Extra Free said to both of them.

'Then do so, please,' said O'Sondheim, more calmly.

'Can we shoot the fuckers out of space?' said Strider. The *Santa Maria* was *hers*. Anyone attacking it was like someone attacking *her*.

WE WOULD HAVE A THREE PER CENT CHANCE OF SUCCESS, said Ten Per Cent Extra Free. THAT IS ABOUT THE SAME CHANCE THAT THEY HAVE OF DESTROYING US. WE ARE BETTER TO FOLLOW MR O'SONDHEIM'S PLAN AND TRY TO ESTABLISH COMMUNICATIONS.

'Can't we just turn on the drive and get the hell out of here?'

OUR AGGRESSORS HAVE A TACHYONIC DRIVE ALSO. THEY WOULD MERELY FOLLOW US.

'I'm getting something,' said O'Sondheim. Strider darted to join him.

The communications Pocket was glowing. There was no coherent image in it yet, but flashes in its midst suggested that one was forming.

'I'd like to blast the fuckers as well,' confided O'Sondheim. Back on Mars, in one of the tackier bars where the officers had got to know each other after training sessions designed, uselessly, to help them get to know each other, Strider had once seen how O'Sondheim preferred to defend himself: by hitting the other guy first.

WE COULD TRY IT IF YOU WISH, said Ten Per Cent Extra Free coolly, BUT I DO NOT THINK IT ADVISABLE.

'Yeah. We got that message,' Strider snapped.

At last there was something emerging in the Pocket. The *Santa Maria* rocked yet again.

'But couldn't we just sort of shoot something across their bows?' she added.

IT WOULD BE A WASTE OF WEAPONRY. BESIDES, THEY MAY NOT BE OUR ENEMIES.

'They're not exactly behaving like friends,' she said.

IN THE WONDERVALE IT IS INADVISABLE TO ASSUME ANYONE YOU ENCOUNTER MIGHT BE A FRIEND.

'Oh. Great.'

Something that could have been called a face appeared in the Pocket. It seemed to be covered in small triangular scales. It had a row of what Strider supposed were eyes dotted around what seemed to be its chin. Above them there was what could be a mouth. The thing that could have been – probably was – a mouth was emitting a harsh jabbering noise.

I WILL TRANSLATE, said Nightmirror, who had joined Ten Per Cent Extra Free on the deck.

The jabbering cut off very suddenly, to be replaced by words that Strider and O'Sondheim could understand.

'. . . trespassing into space claimed by the Autarch Nalla and his emissary Kaantalech. You will subjugate yourselves to –'

'No we won't,' said O'Sondheim. 'You just go subjugate yourself.'

'I think,' murmured Strider, 'that perhaps a little tact is called for.' She knew how he felt: she felt the same herself. This was the schoolyard bully picking without warning on one of the smaller kids. It was always fun to see the kid sock the bully smack on the nose. The trouble was, you never knew if the bully's big brother or sister was lurking somewhere around.

'I am Captain Leonie Strider of the starship *Santa Maria*,' she said to the face in the Pocket. 'We are travelling peacefully from Mars to Tau Ceti II. You have attacked us without provocation.'

'I have never heard of either world,' said the face dismissively. 'It doesn't matter. You are trespassers here.'

Strider turned away from the Pocket. 'Ready an implosion bolt,' she said to Ten Per Cent Extra Free.

I WOULD NOT ADVISE IT.

'I would,' she said, turning back to the Pocket.

'Mars lies in Heaven's Ancestor,' she lied smoothly, 'and Tau Ceti II is in the Milky Way galaxy, which is probably too distant for your rudimentary technology to have detected. We are merely pausing in The Wondervale to observe.' She sniffed, wondering if Nightmirror was able to translate body language as effectively as spoken words. 'So far, we don't much like what we've observed.'

Yes. The face in the Pocket looked affronted. 'There are no developed species in Heaven's Ancestor,' it said.

121

'You're so sure?' said Strider. 'Release that bolt,' she subvocalized to Ten Per Cent Extra Free.

IF YOU SAY SO.

'I do.'

She moved across to the next Pocket and dipped her head into it. The miniature replica of the alien craft sprang quickly into view. Even as she watched, its defence shields flared briefly red. An implosion bolt, she knew from the Images, had the effect of draining energy and matter from the vicinity of wherever it impacted. It could travel well in excess of the speed of light, as could most of the *Santa Maria*'s new, Image-built weaponry: they'd incorporated the tachyon drive into, it seemed, everything that moved. *Can't have hurt those shits too much,* she thought, *but with luck it'll have given them one hell of a shock.*

It evidently had, she saw the moment she returned to O'Sondheim's side in front of the communications Pocket. Earlier, the scene behind the reptiloid face had been calm. Although she hadn't been much aware of it, she had sensed that various creatures were methodically going about their duties. She wished that she'd concentrated more on what had been happening in that background: she might have gained useful information. Now, it was impossible to make out much except that there was a frenzy of motion.

'I didn't want to do that,' she said quietly to the face. 'I wouldn't have, if you hadn't fired on the *Santa Maria* first. That's the very least of our weaponry – if we wanted to, we could disintegrate you from here.' She swallowed. She was alarmed at the ease with which she was lying. *Call it 'bluffing', Leonie,* she said to herself. *It sounds so much more respectable.* 'But, as I told you, we're on a peaceful mission. We don't want to interfere with your people unless we have to.'

'We should talk further,' said the face tightly.

'Indeed we should. Tell me about your tinpot little dictator – and about yourself. I've identified myself and my craft: pay me the respect of doing likewise.'

She gestured to O'Sondheim to bring her a seat, then sank

gratefully into it. She closed her eyes while the Pocket instantaneously adjusted its height.

'I am . . .' The face paused, seeming uncertain, then carried on. 'I am Maglittel. This quadrant of The Wondervale is under my command. I control it on behalf of Kaantalech, who is herself the emissary of the revered Autarch Nalla.'

Strider stopped herself from laughing aloud. Humanity, that much sneered-at species, had learnt long ago that it was pointless for individuals to try to control large areas by force or terror. In due course one of two things happened. Either the survivors of all the thousands or millions of people you had annihilated killed you, sometimes with outside help, or you died and those survivors killed all your cronies instead.

'Why did you attack us?' she demanded.

'Because you are trespassing,' said Maglittel wearily.

'No. We're visiting.'

'You appeared in my quadrant of The Wondervale without permission.' Maglittel was recovering some of its poise. So were the others in the chamber behind it, which looked uncomfortably like the interior of a cesspit. Strider gestured to O'Sondheim that he should start observing it keenly, to see if he could see anything of use.

WE ARE RECORDING EVERYTHING, said Ten Per Cent Extra Free. YOU CAN STUDY THIS LATER AT YOUR LEISURE.

'Watch it anyway,' Strider whispered to O'Sondheim. 'We don't know how long "later" is going to last.'

To Maglittel she said: 'We didn't know we were likely to find anyone here. It's so rarely that you find intelligent lifeforms in an elliptical galaxy.'

She let this new fabrication sink in, then said: 'How did you discover us so quickly?'

'We're alert. We have to be. The enemies of the Autarch are numerous, and sometimes resourceful.'

I THINK WE SHOULD START TO RETREAT, said Ten Per Cent Extra Free inside her head. I SENSE THAT THIS ALIEN IS BRINGING TO BEAR UPON US THE MOST POWERFUL OF ITS ARMOURY. OUR CHANCES OF SURVIVAL WOULD STILL BE IN

123

EXCESS OF NINETY-FIVE PER CENT, BUT I THINK IT UNWISE TO GAMBLE ON THE FIVE PER CENT.

'Too right,' Strider subvocalized. 'But I thought you said that the Autarch's people would be able to follow us.'

WHILE YOU HAVE BEEN TALKING WITH MAGLITTEL, NIGHTMIRROR HAS BEEN ANALYSING THAT SHIP'S AGGRESSIVE CAPABILITIES. THEY ARE MARGINALLY SUPERIOR TO OURS. I, ON THE OTHER HAND, HAVE BEEN INVESTIGATING ITS *DEFENSIVE* ABILITIES. THESE ARE INFERIOR TO THOSE WHICH THE *SANTA MARIA* NOW POSSESSES. THERE IS A WAY IN WHICH WE COULD ESCAPE MAGLITTEL – AT LEAST FOR A WHILE.

Strider hesitated.

MAGLITTEL IS UTTERLY RUTHLESS, said Ten Per Cent Extra Free. THE CREATURE HAS DESTROYED HALF A THOUSAND WORLDS. IT CANNOT BE TRUSTED.

'You mean it speaks with forked tongue?' subvocalized Strider, looking at the hideous reptiloid face. She wondered if it found her equally hideous.

IT HAS NO TONGUE, said Ten Per Cent Extra Free primly, BUT YOUR METAPHOR IS UNDERSTOOD.

'Then I think we should go,' Strider said.

Their initial experience of the tachyon drive was terrifying for the personnel aboard the *Santa Maria*. The first that you knew of it was that you were being seemingly wrenched out of your existence like a tooth out of its socket. For a few seconds there was the sensation that every thunderstorm in the history of creation was being played out simultaneously. And then there was utter peace.

'You could have warned us about this!' said O'Sondheim bitterly to the Images.

ABOUT WHAT? said Nightmirror.

Strider explained tersely, at the same time opening her mind to the alien. It was clear that the Images had felt nothing of what the humans had experienced. O'Sondheim was all the while muttering into his commline, telling the personnel in the main habitat that there was nothing to worry about: this had been merely a test of the new drive; in future there would be warnings given, but . . .

Nodding her head into a Pocket, Strider could see quite how far they'd come: several thousand parsecs around the edge of The Wondervale. Clearly the difficulty with the tachyon drive was not how fast you could go but how you could move a bit more slowly – not an unexpected disadvantage, bearing in mind the properties of tachyons themselves.

'That was pretty impressive,' she said, as unconcernedly as she could.

Maglittel's face reappeared suddenly in the communications Pocket.

'We were in the process of having a conversation, Captain Leonie Strider,' said Maglittel.

'Shift again,' Strider said to the Images.

Again there was the wrenching feeling. In the Pocket beside her she could see the *Santa Maria*'s new position in The Wondervale.

'Are we outside this thing's much-vaunted quadrant yet?' said O'Sondheim.

'Watch the comm Pocket,' Strider replied.

It was empty, and it remained that way for several minutes.

I THINK MAGLITTEL HAS DECIDED TO ABANDON THE CHASE, said Ten Per Cent Extra Free. AT LEAST FOR NOW.

The Image was wrong. Maglittel suddenly reappeared in the communications Pocket.

'This is like some kind of anxiety dream,' said O'Sondheim.

'I wish only to speak with you,' said Maglittel. 'I withdraw my earlier demand that you surrender yourselves to me.'

MAGLITTEL HAS BEEN CHECKING WITH HEAD OFFICE, said Ten Per Cent Extra Free. YOUR CLAIM TO BE FROM AN ADVANCED CIVILIZATION IN HEAVEN'S ANCESTOR HAS PROBABLY SCARED THEM WITLESS.

'I don't trust the creature, nevertheless,' subvocalized Strider. 'What if you're wrong? What was this plan of yours for getting us rid of it?'

WE CAN STARDIVE.

'What?' said Strider, but Maglittel was speaking once more.

125

'Will you permit me to bring my vessel closer to yours? It would facilitate our communications.'

'I see no need for that,' Strider replied stiffly.

'But I do,' said Maglittel. 'Transmitting to you by fast-tach over a distance of a light-month is taxing our energy supplies to the limit.' The creature's face shimmered in the communications Pocket, as if power were about to be lost.

Strider swithered. The explanation sounded vaguely plausible, and yet . . . and yet, if someone without warning and for no particular reason fires a lazgun at you for a while and then promises to stop doing so, it's reasonable to be suspicious.

'No,' she said.

'That is a considerable pity,' said Maglittel. The image faded from the communications Pocket.

Three seconds later the *Santa Maria* shuddered as a far bigger blast than anything that had gone before hit it. This time the shock was enough to make Strider stagger and drop to her knees.

'Do whatever it was you said!' she yelled.

STARDIVE? said Ten Per Cent Extra Free calmly.

'You bet!'

RIGHT.

At many times the velocity of light, although far more slowly than it had been travelling before, the *Santa Maria* began to move towards the nearest red giant, a mere 1.5 parsecs distant. It would reach the star in about seven minutes.

Strider nodded another Pocket into activity so that she could watch what was going on. She could see a small area of local space, hanging in the middle of the Pocket. Beyond it there was a graphical display of the situation. The *Santa Maria*, indicated by a blinking green light, seemed to be crawling through space, with the winking red of Maglittel's craft following it closely. The alien vessel was pulling closer to the *Santa Maria*, but cautiously. It had already tasted an implosion bolt, and presumably Maglittel had no desire to invite something heavier – some product of that superior technology of which Strider had boasted. Every now and then the *Santa Maria* shook as another piece of weaponry struck its defensive shields.

'Hit them with another implosion bolt,' said Strider.

THAT WOULD BE UNWISE.

'Why?'

WE WANT THEM TO FOLLOW US.

'Couldn't one of you just hop across to that bloody ship and bugger up their systems?' said O'Sondheim suddenly.

NO. MAGLITTEL AND ITS KIND CAN SEE US MORE CLEARLY THAN YOU PEOPLE CAN. THEY HAVE DISCOVERED HOW TO HARM US. This time the Images were speaking in their earlier mock-unison, something they hadn't done for a while. Strider sensed they were more worried than they'd been letting on. Heartfire must have joined the other two on the deck.

'How safe is this stardiving idea of yours?' she said.

VERY SAFE, the Images warbled together.

The reply didn't reassure her at all.

'What does it entail?'

YOU WILL FIND OUT IN ABOUT TWO AND A HALF MINUTES. PLEASE DO NOT DISTRACT US WITH YOUR QUESTIONS. THIS IS A COMPLICATED OPERATION.

'Who's the boss around here?'

There was no reply.

In the Pocket, Strider could see the green light of the *Santa Maria* beginning to accelerate directly towards the red giant. After a moment, the alien ship accelerated as well to compensate.

'Have you any idea what's happening?' said O'Sondheim.

'I have a horrible idea that I do,' said Strider. She looked up from the Pocket and out through the view-window. Directly ahead there was a single reddish glow. As she watched, it grew from being point-sized to become a visible disc.

'Are you sure our systems are up to this?' she asked the Images.

Again there was no reply. She hoped this was because they were concentrating hard and not because they were unwilling to answer her frankly. She turned back to stare into the Pocket.

Her palms were sweating. She wiped them off on her jumpsuit, but it didn't seem to make any difference.

'Tell the rest of them that we're going to go through a few more odd times,' she said to O'Sondheim. 'And call Nelson and Leander up here: we're maybe going to need them. Oh, yeah – tell Holmberg to get here as well. It's about time he saw some of the things we have to do. It might shut him up for a while.'

O'Sondheim turned away and began once more mumbling into his commline.

The graphic display on the base of the Pocket told her that they were within fifty-two seconds of reaching the red giant. Fifty-one. Fifty. Forty-nine.

Just what in hell had the Images *done* to the *Santa Maria*?

'You're going to park us in that star's atmosphere,' she said, 'and hope that Maglittel won't dare follow us. That's it, isn't it?'

NOT QUITE, said Ten Per Cent Extra Free. Strider's heart quickened as she realized that the Image's voice sounded weary. She pushed her fingers back through her hair. O'Sondheim, finished on his commline, was chewing on a thumbnail.

She glanced up at the view-window. The disc was growing larger. Back to the Pocket, and the estimated time of arrival was fourteen seconds. Back up to the view-window, and the star seemed to be exploding towards her.

'Oh, Umbel,' she said under her breath. 'The Images are taking us right *into* that . . .'

The view-window was a sudden frenzy of fire. No, it was worse than that – for fire *moves*: it has flames that beat and waver. This was just a hostile flare, pressing itself tightly to the view-window, seemingly trying to force its way in so that it could devour everything it discovered. Here, inside the star, the light wasn't red at all: it was white. Strider realized she and O'Sondheim would have been blinded instantly had the Images not in some way dimmed the window.

She nodded her head into the Pocket and called for greater amplification of the scenario.

The *Santa Maria* was hanging about two-thirds of the way

into the red giant. Maglittel's craft had halted some way above the star's outer atmosphere.

An alarm klaxon sounded on the deck just as Nelson and Leander arrived. They looked as if they had been rudely woken, which was probably the case. O'Sondheim's secondary retinal screens were emitting a narrow little whine of protest: even the dimmed light of the star's interior was overloading them. Nelson and Leander, each of whom were currently wearing only a single secondary screen, swiftly clapped a hand over it. O'Sondheim turned himself away from the view-window, and the whine ebbed.

'Darling of the night skies,' said Nelson, breathing hard, 'just where in the hell have you taken us *now*?'

Strider gestured towards the Pocket beside her. She didn't feel she had the strength to explain. The heat was building up in here – and presumably throughout the rest of the ship. The klaxon was still sounding: she knew almost without looking that the systems were complaining that the internal temperature was too high, but there was nothing she could do about it. She had handed over her command to the Images. Probably the Images didn't feel heat, but they were certainly aware that human beings did. She shrugged. All she could do was trust that the Images had everything under control.

WE HAVE, said Ten Per Cent Extra Free, but the voice still sounded strained.

Strider looked back into the Pocket. No change. Maglittel's ship was still lurking outside the stellar atmosphere.

WE CAN DESTROY THAT VESSEL NOW, IF YOU WISH, CAPTAIN LEONIE STRIDER, said the three Images in their almost-harmony. MAGLITTEL WILL BE EXPECTING NOTHING. IT PROBABLY BELIEVES THAT WE ARE DEAD – THAT WE SUICIDED RATHER THAN FACE ITS WRATH. There was the definite impression of a titter.

Strider hesitated. The attacker's craft contained who knew how many sentient creatures, born of a civilization of which she knew nothing. Humanity's first encounter with alien species, other than with the elusive Images, had been with the occupants of this craft. Was it right simply to destroy it? Even though the aliens had announced their presence by attack, should she not attempt some further form of negotiation? This should have been an historic moment. Aliens were by definition alien: despite first appearances, perhaps their civilization had much to commend it.

Then she remembered what Ten Per Cent Extra Free had said earlier: *The creature has destroyed half a thousand worlds.*

No: if Maglittel's culture had anything whatsoever to recommend it, it would not tolerate genocide on that scale. Any cultural grouping that desired the deaths of innocent others, on whatever grounds and over whatever differences, was in Strider's viewpoint a nest of wasps to be swatted.

'Give them everything we've got,' she said. 'I want that fucker in bits.'

She shook herself inside her jumpsuit. The cloth was sticking to her flesh. The temperature was still climbing. In the Pocket she saw five, six, a dozen or more tiny sparks climb away from the starbound *Santa Maria* towards the alien craft. As they emerged from the stellar atmosphere, two were almost immediately obliterated by retaliatory sparks from the hovering vessel.

But the remainder sped on.

She amplified the display in the Pocket, so that she could see Maglittel's ship like a silver needle. She didn't want to see it more clearly than that.

THE FOREMOST MISSILES ARE IMPLOSION BOLTS, said Ten Per Cent Extra Free, now sounding more relaxed. MAGLITTEL'S VESSEL CAN WITHSTAND THEM. THE CREATURE WILL NOT BE TOO CONCERNED WHEN THEY IMPACT, AND WILL PROBABLY DECIDE TO RIDE OUT THE ATTACK. THE FINAL TWO, HOWEVER, CONTAIN THE LAST OF THE ANTIMATTER FROM YOUR EARLIER DRIVE. WE THINK THAT –

The Image hadn't finished speaking before the Pocket was filled with a mass of flame, brighter even than the malevolent fire pushing against the view-window.

'I think it worked,' said Strider. She felt miserable, all the more so for knowing that she ought to have some sense of elation: the enemy had been destroyed. Instead it was as if she had destroyed that wasp's nest: something highly complicated, put together by living beings, had been annihilated just because their kind and her kind couldn't get along.

The other three on the deck, however, were whooping with delight. O'Sondheim tried to gather her into his arms, but she angrily fended him off. Let the three of them dance on graves: it might do them good, help Nelson and Leander form a better team with O'Sondheim. But she herself wanted no part of this.

'Can we goddam get out of this goddam star pretty goddam fast?' she subvocalized to the Images.

WITHIN A SHORT TIME, said Nightmirror. MAINTAINING THE SHIP'S DEFENCES AGAINST THE HEAT HAS NOT BEEN EASY, AND LAUNCHING THE MISSILES TIRED US FURTHER. WE SHALL SHIFT AWAY FROM HERE AS SOON AS WE CAN.

'How long will that be?'

ABOUT TWENTY-EIGHT SECONDS.

'See if you can manage it sooner,' said Strider ironically, tugging at the neck of her suit. Destruction of any sort she abhorred; destruction of intelligent life was the worst.

'Oh,' she added suddenly, 'I meant to say: thank you for saving our lives.'

The Images didn't respond.

'Did you say,' she continued, 'that all the wars in this galaxy were because of cultures rebelling against the Autarch?'

WE DID, said Ten Per Cent Extra Free.

'Well,' said Strider, 'I reckon we've just made a political statement.' She gestured towards the wreckage in the Pocket. 'We're on the side of the rebels.'

2

Spindrift Would Like to Offer More Assistance But . . .

They moved back across the elliptical galaxy in carefully staggered jumps until they were fairly close to where they had first emerged into The Wondervale. Strider's reasoning was that the best place to go was where the Autarchy would assume they wouldn't be so stupid as to try to hide.

The Images agreed. WE SHOULD HAVE AT LEAST A FEW DAYS, said Heartfire, BUT AFTER THAT THINGS ARE LIKELY TO GET ROUGH IN THAT REGION. WE SHOULD MAKE PLANETFALL AS SOON AS POSSIBLE.

'This ship isn't built for planetfall,' said Strider.

IT IS NOW.

'Oh yeah?'

ITS DRIVE CAN BE SWITCHED FROM ONE MODE TO ANOTHER. IT HAS THE CAPABILITY OF OPERATING AS A SAFE FUSION DRIVE FOR MAKING LANDINGS. WHILE WE WERE BIDING OUR TIME IN THE RED GIANT WE GATHERED FUEL. WE HAVE THE MATTER UNDER CONTROL, CAPTAIN LEONIE STRIDER.

She believed them, and at the same time she couldn't help feeling sceptical.

Also, she was still experiencing guilt over the slaughter she had commanded. She knew the feeling was irrational: it had been a case of them or us. It didn't make the guilt any easier to bear. She felt like a child who has stolen some sweets: the crime is trivial in one way, not at all trivial in another. She kept wondering if she could maybe have talked the reptiloid out of trying to destroy the *Santa Maria*, then realizing immediately afterwards that of course she couldn't have: *The creature has destroyed half a thousand worlds.* If the tyranny was prepared to extirpate millions – billions – for the sake of preserving itself, then it wasn't even going to notice the destruction of forty-some human beings.

Still . . .

Still, she wondered how many sentient creatures had been aboard that ship. How many of them were there voluntarily? Tyrannies tended to conscript their troops. She decided not to ask the Images about this. They, for their part, although they must have known that the question was skulking at the edges of her mind, chose not to offer any unsolicited answer. For that she was very grateful.

The other matter that still burdened her was that this wasn't supposed to be the way that alien societies met. From youth she'd assumed that, if ever humanity did encounter eetees, there would be a joyous blending of cultures. The same message had been drummed into her throughout her years of training with the SSIA – whose purposes had been not so much idealistic as practical: make friends with the alien fast, or the next thing that happened might be that the alien made the Sun go nova. In a way, of course, humanity's first meeting with aliens – the Images – had approximated to that vision, although the Images were so divorced from human understanding that the cultural exchange had been all one way. And the other thing to remember was that the Autarchy of Nalla was no more going to be able to establish the Solar System's location than Strider was herself – less so, in fact, because the Autarchy didn't have the help of the Images.

She knew all these things logically, yet it *felt* wrong to have unleashed so much destruction.

Strider confided some of these thoughts to the most unlikely of people. Marcial Holmberg had arrived on the command deck a couple of minutes after the alien vessel had met its fiery end and after the *Santa Maria* had fled from the hot haven of the red giant. He had been breathless and angry.

'On behalf of the civilian personnel aboard this vessel . . .'

'Leave it be,' said Leander sharply. 'We could all have been dead by now.'

'We should have been told what was going on,' Holmberg

protested. He flopped down into the chair that Strider had thrust towards him. 'We should have been *told*.'

'O'Sondheim told you as much as he could on the commline,' said Strider. She kept her tones steady. Holmberg might be a major pain in the neck, but he was one she had to live with. The personnel might have elected someone worse to represent them, although she couldn't for a moment think of a candidate. Flipping that over in her mind, she realized that from the civilians' point of view they probably couldn't have nominated anyone better. In between wanting to take a lazgun to Holmberg, she had actually begun to feel some respect for him. It seemed like a long time ago that she had told him that he wasn't as good at his job as she was at hers. She wondered, now, if that were true. He was an obstreperous shithead, if the truth had to be told; but it was his *job* to be that. The non-SSIA personnel would have been a lot worse off if they'd elected someone who allowed every decision made by Strider and her officers to go unchallenged.

'I don't have a commline,' said Holmberg. 'Quite a few of us don't.'

'I don't have one myself,' said Strider. 'Look, we did our best – OK?'

Briefly she explained what had happened. Less briefly, she heard him explain how terrified many of the personnel had been. She pulled another seat over on its rollers to sit beside him, listening. Leander obviously thought she was mad to waste so much time with the man, but in reality there was nothing much else for Strider to do – the Images were taking care of guiding the *Santa Maria* through the various tachyonic shifts it was making across The Wondervale. Leander was occasionally monitoring their progress in a Pocket, but in fact that progress might just as well have gone unmonitored.

'We can hardly regard your first tour of duty as being entirely successful, Captain Strider,' Holmberg said eventually.

'We're still alive,' said Strider, beginning to smile. She could see from Holmberg's face that, yes, he was deliberately acting out a role.

Suddenly relaxing, he grinned back at her. 'I know that.' But his eyes were still unhappy, belying the smile. Whatever Strider said to him wouldn't take away the memory of the terror he'd been through. It must be the same for many of the other civilians.

'I'm tired,' said Strider suddenly. 'I'm going off duty – and I'm pulling O'Sondheim off as well. Would you like to join us in the elevator down to the village?'

There was only a single city on the airless world of Qitanefermeartha, but it was inarguably the most important city in The Wondervale. Contained within a dome three hundred kilometres from side to side and fifty kilometres high, the city, itself called Qitanefermeartha, was the seat of the Autarch Nalla and his governmental organization. The planet was defended by some four thousand warcruisers; the dome of the city was surrounded by forcefields capable of deflecting any missile or ray that The Wondervale had yet devised; the dome itself was constructed of massively dense deadmetal, which has the capacity to absorb energy, and was thus almost as impregnable as were the forcefields around it; in order to enter the dome, one had to go on foot through seventeen different huge airlocks, each of which was constantly monitored and also had implanted in its walls sufficient laser cannonry to arm a medium-sized warcruiser; after running this gauntlet you were confronted by over a hundred of the most highly trained troopers of the Autarch's Elect, who had general instructions to reduce you to your constituent atoms in a barrage of disintegrator fire if they so much as didn't like your face (or, depending upon your species, nearest equivalent thereof).

Paranoia was neither a rare nor a necessarily disadvantageous quality in a Wondervale autarch: after all, a billion billion sentient beings generally wanted the present incumbent dead. On the other hand, it meant that the Autarch Nalla didn't get a lot of casual visitors. Most people either stayed inside Qitanefermeartha, enjoying the luxuries of court life, or they stayed as far away from it as they reasonably could.

There was a small spaceport nearby, but it was rarely used –

135

there were extensive holo linkups within the city, so that it was only infrequently that the Autarch's officers needed to visit in person. To be sure, the reception on the linkups was generally lousy, because of the millions of tonnes of deadmetal surrounding the city, but it was good enough for the Autarch – who could always have a few technicians executed if the holo became utterly incomprehensible – and for his emissaries, who were well content to be physically unpresent. The Autarch was unpredictable at best; if angered for any reason, he was lethal.

Inside the dome, the overriding impression of the city of Qitanefermeartha was that it was coralline pink. This was the Autarch's favourite colour, and he had insisted that every structure within the dome be built in compatible material. Several worlds had been stripped of much of their granitic and metamorphic surface rocks in order to satisfy his desire. That this had destroyed the ecosystems of those worlds, and often their sentient inhabitants, was not a matter of much interest to the Autarch; the haulage costs involved in getting the rock to the remote planet Qitanefermeartha were a greater concern, though one easily solved by upping the tax-tribute required of every inhabited planet in The Wondervale. The more thoughtful of the Autarch's courtiers speculated about what might happen if the inheritor of The Wondervale's throne – for surely the old bastard must die some day – preferred, say, blue. None of them said anything about this out loud, of course: there probably wasn't a single cubic millimetre within Qitanefermeartha that wasn't under constant surveillance.

The Autarch didn't like to be reminded of the possibility of his demise.

He was a member of the Antracvhan species, whose lifespans were a hundred times longer, thanks to genetic engineering in the remote past, than those of the majority of species within The Wondervale. He was not in fact immortal, but to most members of the subject peoples within the Autarchy the distinction was purely academic: they would be dead and dust millennia before he finally succumbed.

Unless someone hastened the succumbing. A billion billion people hoped that someone would. Even the Autarch's most

136

favoured courtiers often wished this: when the Autarch got into a particularly filthy temper, the population of Qitanefermeartha became staggeringly sparse.

The Antracvhans were quadrupedal and massive. They were not particularly well coordinated – their early discovery of the trick of genetic engineering had hindered other aspects of their evolution. Finding yourself accidentally under an Antracvhan was a fairly common cause of death among the less agile courtiers in Qitanefermeartha. There might have been many uprisings in the city had it not been for the fact that the Antracvhans dwelling there were almost all in either the bodyguard or the concubinage that surrounded the Autarch everywhere he went, which was rarely outside his own palace – a smaller dome within Qitanefermeartha's great dome and likewise constructed of deadmetal, although painted pink.

Even the open spaces of Qitanefermeartha – of which there were many – were planted with pink grass, pink flowers and trees that bore pink blossom.

The Autarch Nalla's courtiers, the dwellers in the city of Qitanefermeartha, had to maintain a ghastly charade of being Happy Happy Happy throughout their lives. It was the only – partial – guarantee that those lives would not be whimsically curtailed.

At the moment the Autarch was watching a holo of his lieutenant for the Farside sector of The Wondervale. Kaanta-lech was giving him bad news; the Autarch wished he could kill her for that, but was at the same time glad that he couldn't: she was perhaps the most ruthless of all his lieutenants, and thereby among the most valuable. It was an additional cause for fury, though, that those of Kaantalech's species had an offensively bright green fur coloration.

'. . . and the invader craft has destroyed not only Maglittel but also a Class Eight warcruiser,' Kaantalech was saying, 'at a cost of –'

'Spare me the figures,' said the Autarch, with a wave of his suction-padded forefoot. 'This is not too severe a financial calamity.'

'Yes.' It looked as if Kaantalech wanted to say more, but the Autarch overrode her.

'Is there any suggestion that the invader craft from Heaven's Ancestor is acting in concert with any of the terrorist worlds?'

'No, Stars' Elect.'

'My advisors have told me that there are no technological civilizations in Heaven's Ancestor,' said the Autarch. His voice was a cross between a growl and a whine: it seemed a very small voice to come from such a massive body.

'It is possible,' said Kaantalech hesitantly, 'that the intruders were lying.'

'Why should they lie? It is far more likely, is it not, that my advisors were wrong.'

'I believe,' Kaantalech said more firmly, 'that the aliens were attempting to deceive us. The transmissions we received from Maglittel before its tragic demise – and the destruction of its cruiser – cause me to think that these aliens were attempting to mislead. Maglittel was not the most intelligent of our emissaries: it is probable that the creature stupidly accepted what it was told.'

The Autarch snorted. He had been looking forward to executing a platoon or two of his advisors. Watching executions was so *restful*.

'These aliens – ''Humans'', you call them – might be useful to us?' he said.

'They are not in alliance with any of the terrorist worlds, so far as we know,' said Kaantalech. 'It is possible that we could recruit them to the cause of righteousness. With the technology they so obviously possess, they could be powerful allies. At the very least, we could make approaches to them for as long as is required to gain the secrets of their technology.'

She perched bird-like within the lightfield of the holo, although her form was nothing like a bird's. Instead, she looked more like a miniature version of the Autarch himself, although lacking his tusks and covered with long fur. Her triangular eyes were on her bulky shoulders; by spreading her breastbone she could look almost directly behind her. She was

138

about two metres tall and almost as wide. Her mouth, beneath a long and constantly flexing proboscis, glittered with teeth.

She was a clever person, and the Autarch disliked that cleverness: it could so easily lead to a rebellion against his reign. On the other forefoot, he relied on the cleverness of people like Kaantalech to maintain that reign. His small eyes were red with confusion.

'You will make friends with these creatures,' he said finally. 'Persuade them of the need for firm law in The Wondervale. And then, when you have got everything you can from them, you will annihilate them. That is my command.'

'They have superior technol –' said Kaantalech before the Autarch cut off the transmission by slamming a forefoot to the floor.

Craft designed primarily for interstellar travel do not come to ground easily – those few that can do so at all. It is as if they were protesting that their true place is out there in the infinite vacuum, free and unfettered, rather than down here in a thick soup of gravity. Even despite the massive reconstruction of the *Santa Maria* that the Images had carried out, the starship's architecture remained one designed for deep space. It was better equipped to exist beneath the photosphere of a star than inside the atmosphere of a planet.

There was also a little indignity involved in that first landing. The tachyonic drive had taken them through large tracts of The Wondervale and into orbit around the larger of the two moons of the world whose name the Images could best translate as Spindrift. For the final approach to landing, however, adjustments had to be made – and they were not simple ones, even for the Images. A day and a half had passed while Heartfire and Nightmirror effected the changes; during part of this time Ten Per Cent Extra Free had communicated with fellow-Images on Spindrift, who in turn negotiated on the *Santa Maria*'s behalf with the military of the planet's most advanced nation. The granting of permission to land seemed to be a ticklish business; Strider wasn't sure who was doing the most work, Ten Per Cent Extra Free or the other two.

139

Spindrift looked rather like Earth, but somewhat smaller, its huge polar icecaps dominating its map. As with Earth, only in a broadish swathe around its equator was there blue water visible. Using one of the Pockets, Strider could see that the land areas seemed strangely unpopulated – except for one large island, which was mainly taken up by what was obviously a spaceport. Of the dozen or so landing bays, only three were occupied. From the lack of evidence of any heavy industry elsewhere on the planet, Strider inferred that it was an occupied world rather than one which had developed space travel for itself. Or maybe some other civilization had planted a mere staging-post on Spindrift.

She didn't know why Ten Per Cent Extra Free's negotiations were proving so protracted. If the people on Spindrift weren't likely to be allies, why the hell had the *Santa Maria* come here?

She turned her attention to the moon close by. Its landscape reminded her of that of Earth's Moon: pockmarked with craters and rays, with great grey plains extending over the most part of the surface. According to the Pocket's graphic display there was, however, the faintest trace of an atmosphere. The smaller moon was much the same, but airless.

There didn't seem to be much she could do on the deck, so she passed over full command to O'Sondheim and went below to her cabin. Once there, reluctantly, she pasted a commlink to her rearmost upper right molar; this would act as a temporary commline, so that O'Sondheim could contact her instantly if need be. She loathed even this degree of invasion of her body by technology.

In fact, it was Ten Per Cent Extra Free who contacted her first.

THEY WILL NOT LET US LAND ON THEIR WORLD, he said, jolting her from sleep. As she struggled out of an anxiety dream, it took a moment or two for the information to sink in.

'Then it was a bit of a waste of time coming here, wasn't it? Whose side are they on?'

THEY ARE ON NEITHER SIDE. MANY OF THE SPECIES IN THE WONDERVALE REFUSE TO BE DRAWN INTO THE CONFLICT ON EITHER SIDE. THE SPINDRIFTERS ARE AMONG THEM. THEY PAY

140

THEIR TAXES, BUT THEY WILL NOT TAKE UP ARMS ON BEHALF OF EITHER THE AUTARCHY OR ANY REBELLIOUS FACTION. THEY BELIEVE IT IS SAFER THAT WAY.

'Or cowardly.'

THE AUTARCH WILL ISSUE ORDERS FOR A PLANET TO BE TORCHED ON THE SLIGHTEST PROVOCATION. SPINDRIFT IS A VERY UNIMPORTANT WORLD, AND ALMOST NEVER COMES TO HIS ATTENTION. THE SPINDRIFTERS PREFER TO KEEP IT THAT WAY. THAT'S WHY WE BROUGHT THE *SANTA MARIA* HERE TO SEEK REFUGE. HAD WE GONE TO ANY KNOWN FOCUS OF REBELLION WE WOULD HAVE MADE IT SO MUCH THE EASIER FOR KAANTALECH TO FIND US – OR WE MIGHT HAVE BEEN BLOWN OUT OF SPACE BY REBEL FORCES BEFORE THEY DISCOVERED WHO WE WERE.

'But if the Spindrifters won't let us land . . .' Strider began.

THEY WON'T LET US LAND ON SPINDRIFT ITSELF, BUT THEY WILL LET US PUT THE *SANTA MARIA* DOWN ON THE MOON BENEATH US. FROM THERE WE CAN SEND A PARTY OR PARTIES ACROSS TO SPINDRIFT BY SHUTTLE.

She sat up on her bed and put her legs over the side. 'Now you're talking. When can we get to it?'

Strauss-Giolitto watched Spindrift coming slowly closer to her. She had only fleeting memories of her childhood on Earth, but she had seen enough holos since then to know what the mother world looked like, and she could see the similarities here. Nevertheless, Spindrift seemed unnatural to her: there was so much free water everywhere, albeit most of it in the form of ice. And the planet seemed altogether bigger than it should be.

She felt a mixture of excited anticipation and fear. This was an unknown world. She knew full well that this was one reason why Strider had sent her as the human component of the first investigatory party: when it came to the crunch, Strauss-Giolitto was among the more expendable members of the *Santa Maria*'s personnel. The Images had been full of assurances that the Spindrifters were non-aggressive, but Strider's opinion was that you could never be sure: Ten Per

Cent Extra Free had been negotiating with a nation's military, after all. Sitting alongside her across a narrow aisle, piloting the shuttle, was one of the least expendable personnel – but the presence of Pinocchio increased the probability of the party surviving, and of course the bloody bot was more sturdily made than a human being, so that he himself was likely to pull through even if she didn't. She suspected that in fact he was doing only a part of the piloting, and that much only for cosmetic reasons; also aboard was Ten Per Cent Extra Free, who could easily have run all the shuttle's functions single-handedly . . .

Wondering if the Images actually *had* anything like hands damped down her nervousness briefly. But then the growing bulk of Spindrift brought it all back again.

Soon afterwards Strauss-Giolitto could see nothing ahead of her through the view-window but blue and white and brown. In her peripheral vision she could still see Pinocchio's knee. Seeing it annoyed her. It distracted her attention. The bot wasn't so bad, she had concluded a while ago, but his knee was very irritating, right now.

The shuttle lurched suddenly, and her restrainer belt tore at her waist and shoulder.

Strauss-Giolitto let out a little yip of fright. She'd been warned this would happen, but that didn't make the abrupt shock of the real experience much easier to take.

Pinocchio turned and smiled at her. 'We're hitting the atmosphere,' he said. 'Don't worry: the shuttle can take almost anything short of a direct impact with the surface. Just get ready to watch the fun.'

Then the smile vanished and he turned back to the controls, his fingers moving with unhuman nimbleness over the set of keyboards in front of him, his eyes intent on a bank of monitors rather than on the unfolding scene ahead.

The shuttle was being buffeted about more seriously and more frequently now. Despite her restrainer belt, Strauss-Giolitto gripped her armrests. The shuttle was skipping around the planet's upper atmosphere, losing speed all the while. Even so, the plastite of the view-window began to glow a dull orange. Plastite was virtually unbreakable and had a melting point of an almost unbelievable number of thousands of degrees Celsius, but that didn't mean much to Strauss-Giolitto right now.

Things got a lot worse before they got better. *Thank God I didn't suit up,* thought Strauss-Giolitto a few minutes later, eyes streaming, after she had emptied at least one previous meal into the plastic dispose-all provided for exactly such eventualities. Even Pinocchio seemed to be taking matters a lot less lightly than he had before; the grimness of his face was born not entirely of concentration. Strauss-Giolitto suddenly fathomed that he, too, had never previously come down through a dense atmosphere.

'You think we're going to make it, Skip?' she said hoarsely, hoping the weak joke would make her feel better.

It didn't. Pinocchio made no response, and she had a nasty few seconds before she realized that this was because his attention was focused entirely on what he was doing.

THIS IS PERFECTLY CUSTOMARY, MARIA STRAUSS-GIOLITTO, came Ten Per Cent Extra Free's reassuring voice in her mind. PLANETFALL IS NEVER AN EASY BUSINESS. ATMOSPHERES RESENT BEING INVADED.

Right now Strauss-Giolitto resented atmospheres.

Still the relentless pummelling of the shuttle went on. How long was it going to last? The plastite was a brighter orange now. Even if the plastite itself was impervious to what it was being put through, what about the points around the sides of the view-window? What were they made of?

She put her face in her hands so that she didn't need to keep on looking, but that only made it worse. Brute instinct, overriding logic, told her she should keep watching the view-window so that, if it *did* unexpectedly explode in towards her face, she would have a chance of running away and hiding. She wished she could run away and hide *now*, but there was nowhere in the confined cockpit to run *to*.

With an abruptness that was almost as shocking as anything that had gone before, it was over.

The shuttle was moving – still at a high velocity – through a clear blue sky. They had come in over one of the polar icecaps; the curve of the planet ahead of them was briefly orange and then, as the plastite rapidly cooled, a glaring white that stung her eyes.

Pinocchio visibly relaxed.

'You were worried there a while yourself, weren't you?' she said lamely after a while. The shuttle's drive was virtually silent; she could hear the whine of the air streaming past as well as all sorts of creaks and groans from here and there on the craft as its components cooled.

'It was something unique to my experience,' the bot admitted. Only a short while ago, his head would certainly have buzzed. Since the Images had shaped him over it was senseless to continue with the pretence that he was just a halfwitted valet. Strauss-Giolitto's attitude towards him hadn't changed entirely – he was still just a bot, dammit, rather than a creation of the Lord – but she had at least come to regard him with some affection, as though he were a sort of incredibly intelligent housepet. They could get along together, so long as she remembered to bite back the more tactless of the remarks that came to mind.

One of the screens in front of Pinocchio lit up, and his attention promptly shifted away from her again. She wished she could see what the screen was showing him, but she was side-on to it. Out of its speaker came an incomprehensible noise, full of soft clicks and harsher whistlings.

After a few moments Ten Per Cent Extra Free intercepted, and the words began to sound to Pinocchio and Strauss-Giolitto as if they were in standard Argot.

'. . . welcome you to our world, strangers, but you must understand that we have to take precautions.' Even in Argot the voice sounded alien. It had a light touch of ethereality to it. She imagined this might be how a ghost would talk. 'Our Images tell us that you are what you seem, but even an Image could be misled. You will therefore follow these navigational instructions precisely.'

There followed a string of information that was as incomprehensible to Strauss-Giolitto as the earlier babble had been.

Pinocchio seemed to understand it, though, for his fingers began moving swiftly over the keyboards again.

'I have assimilated all that,' said the bot after a minute or two. 'Would you like me to give a systems computer download to you so that you may check for error?'

'No.' The voice from the screen sounded horrified. 'You might infect our own systems. If you deviate slightly, we shall assume honest error. If you deviate greatly, I shall contact you again and re-dictate the navigational and landing instructions. Otherwise I shall not speak to you until you are over the Gate to the Sky.'

The light from the screen, which had been reflected on Pinocchio's face, died.

THERE WERE NO ERRORS, said Ten Per Cent Extra Free.

The Gate to the Sky proved to be the spaceport Strider had observed from the *Santa Maria*. True to its word, the Spindrifter reopened communications with Pinocchio and guided him precisely through the landing. Strauss-Giolitto had a further urge to retch as a long runway ahead approached the craft at impossible speed. When they made first contact with the ground it was just as bad, because the shuttle jerked and bucked as if it were trying to throw itself off the hard surface and go tumbling into a blaze of destruction. Strauss-Giolitto's thoughts were drowned in the indescribable racket as the shuttle's retro-jets and brakes cut in and slowly, slowly prevailed.

At last, after what seemed like an infinitely extended screaming slither towards certain death, the shuttle came to a halt.

Strauss-Giolitto was so drained of all emotion that it was a long time before she could properly understand that she, a teacher from City 22, was the first human being to land on the surface of this alien world – the first of *all* human beings to be on a planet outside the Solar System. She felt there ought to be a bit of flag-waving and an out-of-tune brass band, but instead all she heard were the surreptitious little noises of the shuttle settling itself.

'May we disembark?' said Pinocchio to the screen.

And then the *wonder* of it all hit Strauss-Giolitto. She'd been thinking about brass bands, wasting valuable seconds when she could have been discovering what this new world was *like*. She'd been resenting the residual taste of vomit in her mouth. She'd been . . .

She shook herself, and began staring through the view-window eagerly, lapping up everything she could see.

Which proved to be disappointingly little. The sky was still that unnatural blue, unlike the familiar orange-blue of the Martian heavens, but she had seen pictures of pre-nuke-war Earth; she even knew that those huge, seemingly heavy masses of white were clouds, even though they were nothing like the wisps that occasionally appeared in the atmosphere of Mars. Very far in the distance she could see oddly purple-seeming mountains, but aside from that there was just a broad expanse of yellowed featurelessness with, tiny at its far end, a cluster of box-like buildings. The Spindrifters might have given their spaceport a romantic name, the Gate to the Sky, but from here it looked entirely functional, drab and desolate. Presumably spaceports all over the Universe looked very much the same.

'You may exit your vessel only if you are clad in full spacesuits,' the alien voice was instructing in its eerily whispering voice.

'I'm a bot,' said Pinocchio. 'I have no suit.'

There was a pause.

'That is acceptable to us. But your companion must be suited.'

Strauss-Giolitto, still absorbing the fact that, whatever the scene through the view-window looked like, she was on a world new to humanity, only half-heard this. Pinocchio reached across the aisle and prodded her shoulder, then gestured towards the wall-chest where her suit was stored.

'About our Image?' said the bot to the screen.

'Images are always welcome on Spindrift.' The voice gave a little whinny which Strauss-Giolitto guessed must be the best Ten Per Cent Extra Free could do to represent a Spindrifter's equivalent of a laugh. 'We couldn't keep them out anyway, even if we wanted to.'

She unclicked her restrainer belt with difficulty; the experiences of the past hour or so had made her fingers numb without her realizing it. As she stood, little cramps shot through her calves and groin area. She moved behind Pinocchio's seat and at last had sight of the Spindrifter.

The Images had said that the Spindrifters were humanoid, and at first glance that seemed to be the case. The face looking out from the screen was vaguely elfin, with slanting eyes and a pointy chin. But then you noticed the differences. The other features were more or less as in a human, but only approximately. The thing in the centre of the face was obviously not a nose: it was an organ that lazily coiled and uncoiled as the Spindrifter spoke. The feature that looked superficially like a mouth was clearly constructed quite differently from a human mouth: it had four lips, set in a sort of pouting diamond shape. A high crest of what seemed to be stiff black hair ran from the top of the forehead towards the rear, while the rest of the face was covered with short black bristles. And those human-seeming eyes were utterly black, as if in looking into them you were looking into the voids of space.

Strauss-Giolitto turned away. She was both repelled and fascinated by the face; that there was a twinge of sexuality in the fascination did not help at all.

She suited up thoughtfully. Pinocchio was still discussing procedures with the Spindrifter. She sat down alongside him again, not wanting to look any more at the face in the screen. *God made us in his likeness,* she thought, *but am I his likeness, or is that creature? No, it's not a creature: it's a sentient being, the same as I am. And the Images said the Spindrifters are humanoid, like me, so I suppose they are. Humanoid, but at the same time very different. How many likenesses does God have?*

She filed away the question to be thought about later. Now they were here on Spindrift she was keen to be out of the shuttle. She was also already keen to be out of her spacesuit. There's always an offputting smell inside a suit – the combination of hi-tech, vestiges of urine from the last time you

147

used the suit for any extended stretch of time, and your own body odour, both stale and fresh. The net result is a constant reminder that you are in a profoundly enclosed small space; it becomes very easy to start feeling claustrophobic.

Especially since all you can usually hear are your own breathing and the pumping of your pulse. Strauss-Giolitto's pulse was pumping faster than usual.

'Audio,' she said to the suit impatiently.

At once her own noises were blotted out by the voices of Pinocchio and the Spindrifter, who seemed to be coming to the end of their conversation.

Yes, they were.

The screen faded, and the bot glanced towards her. 'We're to get out on to the tarmac – or whatever it is – and wait for Polyaggle to reach us. She'll take us to decontamination. She seems to be controlling this spaceport entirely on her own.' He shook his head. 'It seems very strange to me.'

It took them several minutes to usher themselves through the locks and out into the open. The Spindrifters were clearly nervous of infection from the visitors; Pinocchio was equally concerned about contaminating the air in the shuttle with elements from Spindrift's atmosphere, which was likely to be laden with bacteria, some of which the human nanobots might not recognize as detrimental until it was too late. There was no sense in taking plague back to the *Santa Maria*.

Strauss-Giolitto suddenly realized she was due for another bout of decontamination on her return to the starship. She gulped unhappily. Most often decontamination was followed by a couple of days' diarrhoea, because the process tended, willy-nilly, to destroy large parts of the colonies of symbiotic bacteria in the human gut.

A small vehicle, not unlike a cabble but without the protective dome, was floating across the spaceport towards them.

'Have you noticed something?' said Pinocchio, moving away a few paces and tapping with his toe at some mossy weeds growing from between a crack in what did indeed seem to be tarmac.

148

'Not until you pointed it out,' said Strauss-Giolitto. She gazed around her. Several hundred metres away the prow of what looked like an old-fashioned chemical-fuelled rocket protruded from a walled enclosure – a landing-bay, she guessed. There were smears of what appeared to be rust on the rocket's hull. 'People don't come here very often,' she said.

'And this spaceport was built a very long time ago,' said Pinocchio.

'By whom?' said Strauss-Giolitto.

The bot shrugged.

The vehicle must have been moving more quickly than it had seemed to, because it was very soon beside them.

'Are you there, Ten Per Cent Extra Free?' said Strauss-Giolitto softly.

I AM INSIDE THE SUIT WITH YOU.

She squirmed slightly. It seemed a very intimate arrangement.

'Good,' she said. 'We're going to be needing you.'

OF COURSE. Was there a trace of smugness in that singing voice, or was Ten Per Cent Extra Free merely stating the obvious?

Standing upright in the hovering vehicle was the owner of the face they had seen in the screen – Polyaggle, Pinocchio had called her. Strauss-Giolitto sucked in her breath. The elfin quality of Polyaggle's face was carried through to her body, which was slight, almost like that of a prepubescent child, and at the same time obviously fully mature. From ten metres away one might almost have believed she was a true human with a bizarre taste in hairstyles. Naked, she was very evidently female.

The Spindrifter flipped herself with some grace over the far side of the vehicle and beckoned them towards it. She seemed to be even lighter than her body-shape suggested, like a trained dancer.

'Please don't get into this until I am some distance away,' she said. 'I don't want to come too close to you. I shouldn't even be this near.'

WISE, said Ten Per Cent Extra Free.

149

Strauss-Giolitto nodded. There could be possibly dangerous microbes on the surface of her suit. It would have to be thoroughly sterilized and then probably, after she had removed it, destroyed. The same went for her clothing, and Pinocchio's.

'The cabble' – Ten Per Cent Extra Free translated the alien word using a term familiar to them – 'has been programmed to transport you to decontamination. You will be guided through that unit automatically. The process will take about fourteen . . .' This time Ten Per Cent Extra Free was unable to make a translation. *He can't have worked out the local units of time as yet*, thought Strauss-Giolitto. She hoped it wasn't going to be fourteen hours, or days, or . . .

'At the end of that period,' Polyaggle continued, 'I will speak further with you.'

She put her hands together – no, they weren't hands but bird-like claws – in what was presumably a formal gesture, and turned away.

And spread her wings.

They unfurled swiftly in a riot of brilliant colour. They were ragged, like a butterfly's wings, but brighter than any butterfly Strauss-Giolitto could remember. Around the edges there were broad, irregular patches of crimson and turquoise and black. Closer to the torso, lines of eye-shaped iridescent markings followed the contours of her body.

Polyaggle flapped her wings once, twice, and then allowed herself to drift slowly and erratically off the ground. When she was about twenty metres above them she began to move her wings with more purpose, and soon was fluttering away through the breeze towards the distant buildings.

Strauss-Giolitto couldn't recall having seen anything quite so beautiful. No wonder the Images had translated this world's name as Spindrift, for that was exactly what Polyaggle was doing now: spinning and drifting through the air. It now wasn't so surprising that Polyaggle's body was so light. This was God's image. The minor sexual pang Strauss-Giolitto had experienced on first seeing the Spindrifter's face in the screen was nothing to what she was feeling at the moment. She was going to have a difficult time on this planet.

150

YOUR TURN NOW, Ten Per Cent Extra Free reminded her gently, waking her from her thoughts.

Pinocchio was already aboard the cabble, reaching out a hand to help her. She took it gratefully. Ordinarily she would have had no difficulty stepping into the vehicle – she was fifty per cent taller than the Spindrifter – but suited up like this she felt cumbersome and squat.

Holding the T-shaped pole in the vehicle's centre for balance, they stood and watched as they were conveyed swiftly across the landing-area.

There was so little to see, and yet in a way so much.

She kept trying to forget what it had been like going through the Spindrifter version of decontamination, but it was extremely difficult. At the end of the cycle she had been given a loose white robe to wear, but she still had never felt more naked in her life. Part of the time she had been anaesthetized, which should have made things better; in fact, it had been if anything worse, because she still didn't fully understand everything the Spindrifters' eager little bots had done to her.

She had anticipated losing her suit and her clothing, but the bots had been very much more thorough than that. They had depilated her entire body – it felt bizarre and uncomfortable having a naked crotch for the first time since childhood – and they had probed and scoured every orifice with ruthless efficiency, no great gentleness and strange-smelling chemicals; her ears still gurgled if she moved her head too quickly. But far worse than that had been what they had done to her under anaesthetic.

They had stripped her of her integrated hardware. Neural implants, stim sockets, thighputer, cortical amplification units – everything was gone, right down to her commline. Without her augmentations, everything around her seemed utterly strange: she was experiencing the world as she hadn't experienced it since puberty. It was confusing: she kept bumping into things if she didn't keep a look out where she was going: there was no secondary retinal screen to warn her automatically of obstructions. She kept listening for the tiny

151

background hiss of her commline on standby – a commline that was no longer there. Having just flesh on her left thigh seemed somehow . . . perverse. She was perceiving everything differently, hearing things differently.

She was having to rediscover her natural senses.

And it was all *doubly* confusing: she really *was* experiencing a strange new world. On Mars, and indeed on the *Santa Maria*, when you were inside relaxing you always had the reassurance that you were in a totally enclosed environment. When you were outside you were almost certainly always on the move, because there was little reason to be stationary and almost none to be sedentary.

Here, though, she was sitting on a stool the size of those she expected her schoolkids to sit on and there was nothing overhead but the sky. She could vaguely recall this from her childhood, but only as an experience someone else had had. Ahead of them stretched the weed-infested waste of the Gate to the Sky. On the long, low table in front of her was a tall metal beaker of what Polyaggle had told her was distilled water. Strauss-Giolitto had tried it nervously at first, but the taste proved . . . interesting.

She took another gulp of it.

Strauss-Giolitto and Pinocchio, who was likewise dressed now in a white robe, were together at one end of the table and Polyaggle at the other. The human woman couldn't work out if this was a deliberate ploy to establish some kind of hierarchical demarcation or if it was totally unconscious on the Spindrifter's part: she still seemed cautious about approaching them too closely, as if not thoroughly trusting even the full rigours of decontamination to preserve her from infection.

And what about me? thought Strauss-Giolitto for the hundredth time. *Dammit, I'm probably picking up every disease in the Universe by just sitting here breathing.*

At the next lull in the conversation between Polyaggle and Pinocchio, Ten Per Cent Extra Free – currently resident somewhere in Pinocchio's circuitry – spoke swiftly to her. THE DECONTAMINATORS WERE WISE ENOUGH NOT TO INTERFERE WITH YOUR NANOBOTS. I AM, NATURALLY, MONITORING THE

152

LATTER CLOSELY. YOU ARE INDEED INGESTING ALIEN MICRO-ORGANISMS, BUT NONE HAS OFFERED YOUR BODY ANY DANGER AS YET, AND ALL HAVE BEEN SWIFTLY IDENTIFIED AND DESTROYED BY THE NANOBOTS. WE WOULD NOT HAVE PERMITTED A HUMAN TO DESCEND TO THIS PLANET UNLESS WE WERE SURE IT WAS SAFE.

Strauss-Giolitto tuned in briefly to the conversation the other two were having. It was very difficult to concentrate. The decontamination process had exhausted and demoralized her and the day was hot and bright – and without her hardware there was nothing she could do to reduce the effects of the hotness and brightness. What she really wanted to do was find somewhere she could curl up and sleep for a few hours. When she awoke, maybe the remembered humiliation of being scoured by the decontamination bots would be easier to bear. About the only thing keeping her awake was the discomfort of sitting on a stool this low.

'I would like to speak directly with the Image you have with you,' Polyaggle was saying. Strauss-Giolitto drowsily thought the Spindrifter still looked thoroughly alluring, even with her wings folded away. There was grace in Polyaggle's every movement.

'Certainly,' said Pinocchio courteously. 'His name is Ten Per Cent Extra Free, and I am sure that he would take pleasure in communicating with you.'

'In private,' said the Spindrifter. Strauss-Giolitto wondered what that strangely constructed mouth would look like when Polyaggle smiled – assuming the Spindrifters smiled with their mouths, of course.

Pinocchio nodded. 'Are you willing for this?' he asked out loud, clearly addressing the Image.

YES.

The silence stretched out for several minutes. Something like an insect hummed close to them and inquisitively circled Strauss-Giolitto a couple of times. Horrified, she recoiled from it. It might have a sting that could kill her in seconds. Pinocchio waved it away with a nonchalant hand.

Although the people aboard the *Santa Maria* generally

153

spoke aloud, or at least subvocalized, when communicating with the Images, it was clear that Polyaggle felt no such need, although she had closed her eyes as if to assist concentration. *I wish I could just close my eyes right now*, thought Strauss-Giolitto wearily. Her heart was still beating quickly after her encounter with the little flying thing. *But I'd better not risk it. Falling asleep at someone's party is reckoned rude enough back on Mars – unless you're stoned senseless, of course – but here it might carry the death penalty.*

After an appreciable fraction of forever Polyaggle opened her eyes again.

'I have interrogated your Image friend at length,' she said, 'and he agrees that everything you have told me is substantively true, although on occasion limited by your own ignorance of the true situation in The Wondervale.' Yes, Spindrifters did smile with their mouths. Perhaps this was one of the few traits that convergent evolution directed itself towards when producing human-like creatures. 'The Images may mislead on occasion, but they never lie. I speak for all in the Affiliated Villages when I say that we will offer you such help as we can without jeopardizing our neutrality.'

'That is very kind,' said Pinocchio.

'Further than that we will not go.'

'That is understood.'

Polyaggle smiled again. The effect was disconcerting.

'Our species was among the most rapidly evolving and thus one of the most ancient in The Wondervale, and we were perhaps the first to explore this galaxy – and even Heaven's Ancestor.' She gave what Ten Per Cent Extra Free interpreted as a sigh. 'That was over a billion years ago.' The Image had clearly worked out the Spindrifters' time units at last. 'Four or five million years ago, we saw the nature of the new technological civilizations that were arising in The Wondervale, and we decided to abandon space and retreat to our mother world. Other species who were our friends chose to do the same: many of the neutral planets throughout The Wondervale today are the homes of ancient species who made the same decision that we did.'

154

The Spindrifter raised her own, much smaller beaker of water towards her mouth. A tube-like tongue dipped briefly into the liquid.

'I'm explaining all this for a reason,' Polyaggle resumed, turning her gaze towards Strauss-Giolitto, as if sensing that the woman's concentration had been drifting again. 'We do not wage war – we never have. We have some defences which we, well, stole from younger species; the task of our military is to maintain these. But our few primitive weapons would be useless should the Autarch or some lesser tyrant decide to occupy this world or destroy it. There are fewer than ten million of us left alive: we have no desire to increase our population, as yet, but we believe that the remnant of our once prolific species is very precious. Hence, please understand, our insistence on retaining not just our absolute neutrality but also the outward appearance of it.'

Once more that disturbing smile. 'We want Spindrift to remain a backwater, useless, boring little world. Several hundred years ago the Autarchy built the Gate to the Sky here, intent on colonizing this world. We persuaded the tyranny to depart again by ensuring that there was nothing here to be exploited – we don't even make good slaves: we're too frail to be of any use. Occasionally, still, an Autarchy ship will call by and look us over and decide we have nothing to offer that wouldn't be more easily found elsewhere.

'It is necessary for the survival of the last of our species that this situation be preserved.'

'But not for ever,' said Strauss-Giolitto, suddenly cottoning on. One of the subjects she taught was history. 'You said you didn't want to increase your population *as yet*. You're just biding your time, aren't you?' *Everything goes in cycles. What is omnipotent today will be dust tomorrow. It may take half the lifetime of the Universe, but the day will come.*

'Yes.'

The Spindrifters and the other ancient species will do their best to survive until all the warriors have destroyed themselves, and then they will reclaim their galaxy. No wonder they regard the scraps of their people as so precious.

'We understand your view,' said Pinocchio, splaying his hands on the table in front of him and looking earnestly at the backs of his fingers. 'Of course you're right. You're the seeds of the civilization that'll grow up once the Autarchy and all its successors have gone. But . . . humanity is a *young* species, not an old one, and –'

'Our way is not your way,' said Polyaggle.

'That is what I was trying to say.'

'No, you were trying to say that your way is not our way. There's a difference.'

Pinocchio looked baffled. Despite the sophistication of his software, on occasion he could be defeated by the minor nuances of language.

'Let's be away from here,' said Polyaggle abruptly. 'I want to take you to our military.' She stood and gave a weird trill that Ten Per Cent Extra Free didn't even try to interpret. 'There is much that they could learn from you humans, and there are perhaps one or two things they might be able to tell you in return. I have just summoned a slidecraft, and it will be here very shortly. You' – she turned again towards Strauss-Giolitto – 'will be able to sleep during the trip.'

Strauss-Giolitto yawned. Sleep was becoming a matter of urgency.

'*Lost* them?' bellowed Nalla. 'How in the name of the Autarchy can you have *lost* them?'

Even from a safe several hundred parsecs away, Kaantalech flinched at the sight of the Autarch's holographic wrath. When speaking with Nalla, it amused her to keep the image down as small as was consistent with being able to see what was going on. But, even when he was less than a metre tall, the Autarch's rage was spectacular.

She thought it might be a good move to put on a further show of cowering: the Autarch liked his lieutenants to be visibly terrified of him.

'They've just . . . *disappeared*,' she said limply.

'By the blessed eyes of my father . . . !' the Autarch began, then obviously remembered what had been done to those eyes

156

during a particularly messy succession. He started again. 'By the might of my reign and the love of my people, they can't just have *disappeared*! What has happened is that you've let them go! You're either a traitor or an incompetent or both! Execute yourself at once!'

'I think that would be counterproductive, Stars' Elect,' said Kaantalech. She knew that he liked the honorific. Since they were of different species, it was difficult for her to manipulate his moods as she did those of her own kind, but over the decades she had become more adept at it than most. 'Whoever took over this region of The Wondervale would undoubtedly be less effective than myself at wooing the alliance of these Humans. I have studied the tapes of Maglittel's efforts extensively. Would any of your other lieutenants have laboured so industriously?'

She could almost hear the Autarch thinking. It was painful for her to watch. She gave all her loyalty, life and soul, to her ultimate ruler . . . but one day, with luck, he would turn his back.

'I grant you a stay of execution,' he said at last, 'but it is only a stay. You must find these Humans and coax them into our service within one hundred Qitanefermeartha days or your life will be forfeit. And the lives of all your kindred.'

Kaantalech wasn't particularly worried about the last part of the threat, but the first part did concern her. Summary executions were the Autarch's style. The bald stating of a time period within which a certain task must be accomplished, upon pain of death, was less usual. In the event that the Autarch remembered having issued the threat – or remembered to have a courtier record it for him – any resulting execution was inevitably protracted and brutal.

'I shall use my best endeavours,' she said, giving a show of dignity. 'But I must start right away.'

'You may go,' said the Autarch.

She flicked the holo off. Under her fur she was perspiring far more than she would have liked. The populace of some planet, somewhere, was going to have to pay for this.

By the time Strauss-Giolitto awoke, the slidecraft was well out over the deserted expanses of the northern polar icecap. She was surprised in a way that, despite her weariness, she'd been able to sleep. The Spindrifters, presumably because if anything went wrong with their craft they could always fly away, didn't go in for the kind of precautions humans did. The top of the slidecraft, as with the cabble back at the spaceport, was open; not too much effort had been put into providing the vessel with stabilization, so that it rocked from side to side and, even more alarmingly, from front to back; the ledge around its rim was no more than half a metre high.

Strauss-Giolitto, who had slept in a tangle on the vessel's floor, pulled herself to her knees with a groan, and peered over the ledge. They were at least several hundred metres above the ice. She decided not to have a second peer.

Rubbing the sleep from her eyes – it seemed so odd to be rubbing her left eye, where the secondary retinal screen had been mounted – she looked back towards the centre of the craft. Polyaggle had, like herself, fallen asleep on the floor after programming the navigational unit with their destination. This had seemed an alarmingly simple business: Strauss-Giolitto was accustomed to the controls of even something as lowly as a Martian cabble having countless flashing lights and a bewildering graphic display of information which was beyond the power of most people to understand but was nevertheless reassuring by its very presence. The Spindrifter standard seemed to be about half a dozen buttons and a couple of switches. She assumed that the onboard computers must be infinitely more sophisticated than anything humanity had yet produced.

She hoped so.

The slidecraft was like a flying raft. There was the low ledge around its perimeter and, in place of a mast, the T-shaped pole to which you clung if you wanted to stand upright. Strauss-Giolitto, before sleep had ensnared her, had seen Polyaggle doing this; every now and then the wind of their progress had pulled the delicate Spindrifter right off her feet, so that she had been blown horizontal. The more general method of staying aboard a slidecraft was, Strauss-Giolitto gathered, to squat. She felt idiotic doing it herself; Polyaggle, needless to say, managed the posture with grace and elegance. Pinocchio had just crouched glumly at the front of the craft, beside the simple control panel, and watched the landscape flow by beneath them.

He was still there now.

'Pinocchio,' she said.

He turned. 'I heard you wake, but I didn't want to look round in case . . . in case I embarrassed you.'

She remembered puking so explosively in the shuttle. 'That's all right,' she said. 'If you'd been anoth –' She cut the sentence short.

It was bloody cold up here. Obviously Polyaggle didn't feel it because she was still naked; Strauss-Giolitto should have begged for some extra clothing – would certainly have, had she known where they were going. As it was, the thin white robe offered her body very little protection from the freezing air.

'Do you want to come up beside me?' said the bot. 'The view is quite exciting. I never realized there could be wastes like this.'

She crawled across to him. The slidecraft chose this moment to hit a pocket of turbulence. She felt the acidity of nausea at the back of her mouth, but swallowed it down. This was nothing like as bad as things had been when the shuttle hit Spindrift's atmosphere. Besides, all she had had in the past few hours was a little water. *You can cope,* she told herself.

She was less confident by the time she reached Pinocchio's side. She crouched beside him, fighting with her stomach. 'I think I'm going to die of cold,' she said to him.

'Sit up and look at the scenery.'

'That's going to make it even worse.'

'No, it's not. I have internal power sources. If you sit close to me I can put my arm about you and give you some of my warmth.' He smiled down at her upturned face.

Her eyes narrowed. Various of the male personnel on the *Santa Maria* had made her similar offers over the years.

'Don't be silly,' said Pinocchio, evidently reading her thoughts. 'I'm just a bot, remember.'

Nervously, she pulled herself up against him, putting an arm around his shoulders. He put one of his arms around her waist. After a few moments, she began to relax. His body was warm: she felt as if she were leaning against a radiator.

He was right: the polar landscape was impressive. From space it had looked like a featureless desert, and even the Pockets had been unable to show it from the angle at which they were seeing it now. There were sharp-edged mountains of ice, fairy arches, deep crevasses, rolled hummocks of snow, eddies of wind raising minor, short-lived blizzards. She snuggled closer to the bot, and his grip tightened compensatorily. She felt utterly safe.

'Tell me, Pinocchio, are you male or female?'

'Neither. And you?'

The question startled her. Of course she was female. Back in decontamination he'd seen her more naked than anyone had seen her before. But she sensed from the way in which he'd spoken the question that he was entirely serious.

'I don't know,' she said at last. 'No – that's a lie. I do. For a long time I thought I was maybe a man locked up inside a woman's body, and I wanted more than anything else to escape from it. If I'd had enough money I'd probably have had an Artif transfer and become a man. But I didn't, and I'm glad I didn't.'

'Why?'

'Because I'm not male. I'm female. It's as simple as that. But . . .'

'But your sexual attraction is towards women, and sometimes you fall in love with them.' The bot was speaking as quietly as he could. The slidecraft was moving at no great pace, but still the air was whipping past their ears.

'Yes,' she said.

'You should never have been aboard the *Santa Maria*, you know. With the exception of Strider, the personnel were in part selected for their fertility, which involves the willingness to act in what could be best described as a fertile fashion.'

'I know,' said Strauss-Giolitto. 'I did a lot of lying to get

160

selected for the mission. I invented a most sensational set of past liaisons. Some of my male friends invented relationships on my behalf.' She breathed deeply. 'I wanted so much to be a part of this mission that I'd probably have forced myself to go to bed with Dulac in order to prove my qualifications, if that'd been what was necessary. I even considered screwing around a bit with men, just to add a veneer of truth to the stuff I was claiming to have done. But the SSIA never dug very deep. Most people talk openly about their sexuality. I never did – never have, except with lovers and a very few close friends.'

'Why were you always so secretive?' He was holding her even more closely. She felt like a child who needed a cuddle, and was being given it.

'My religion,' she said. 'Officially it accepts people like me, but there are still enough atavists around who point to carefully selected passages in the Bible and growl that homosexuality is a sin. They ignore the bits about fornication. In a way I was imitating them, disapproving of myself. It was almost as if there had to be two mes: the good Christian who had just never found any Mr Rights, and the evil woman who used female sexbots and occasionally had female lovers. I lived two lives, not just for the outside world but in my own head.

'Besides, there were the practical aspects,' she added. 'There are still prejudices about. Almost everybody but a Christian is allowed to have sex with whomever they want, but not teachers. Homosexual teachers are too often popularly regarded as a threat – as if I'd want to seduce some toddler.'

'You have your own prejudices,' said Pinocchio mildly.

'Yes, but that's diff –' She paused. No, it *wasn't* different. She was speaking to someone whom she felt she could trust. That he was a bot was neither here nor there, just in the same way that she was no less a woman because she wanted the love of other women. She wasn't a pseudo-man, and neither – in a quite different sense – was Pinocchio. He was himself. He was a person.

After a long time she said: 'Does anyone else on the *Santa Maria* suspect, do you know?'

'Strider's a perceptive woman,' said the bot. 'I expect she's

161

pretty certain. And Lan Yi's a wise old bird. Most of the others obviously think you're just frigid.'

'That's a pretty rotten thing for them to think.'

Pinocchio shrugged. 'It's what you seem to want them to think. It's the disguise you've created for yourself, after all.'

'Yes, but . . .' Again she hesitated. He had spoken the truth. But still she didn't like people *thinking* about her in that sort of dismissive way: *Oh, her, she's just an icecube, no chance there, must be something wrong with her hormones.*

She changed tack. 'I'd expected that at least a couple of the women might be bisexual, just by the law of averages, but I was out of luck. It's been a very lonely few years.'

'Yes, that was a rotten hand of fate,' said Pinocchio sympathetically. 'In screening out the homosexuals the SSIA inadvertently screened out the bisexuals as well – except for one male, and he doesn't know it himself.'

'Who?'

The bot looked down at her. She was nestling into his shoulder. Her face and scalp were glowing with the warmth he had been giving her.

'I *keep* secrets,' he said reprovingly.

'Will you keep mine?'

'Of course. Unless it should endanger the rest of the personnel in some way, but I can't imagine that ever it could.' He looked towards the rear of the craft, where Polyaggle was still sleeping. 'You want her very badly, don't you?'

Strauss-Giolitto gave a rueful, bitter smile. 'I thought I did, for a while. I still find her very attractive.'

'You still want her.' It was a flat statement.

'Yes,' said Strauss-Giolitto after a moment.

'I'd forget the idea.'

'Why?'

'She's human*oid*, not human. In more ways than you can imagine, she is utterly different from you. She told me about some of them after you'd fallen asleep. Apart from anything else,' added the bot, looking out over the snowscape, 'she has responsibilities to her own kind. She is the Queen of her hive.'

Strauss-Giolitto had dozed back off to sleep against Pinocchio's side by the time the slidecraft gave a judder that was perceptibly different from all the lurches and swayings that had gone on before. It was enough to bring both her and Polyaggle to instant wakefulness.

Polyaggle unfolded herself with her customary grace from the floor and walked forward easily, mastering the rolling of the craft with ease. Strauss-Giolitto, turning with sleepy eyes to watch her and remembering her own timorous crawl over the same stretch, was instantly envious. At the moment what she herself wanted desperately were a lavatory and a meal, definitely in that order. The consequences of the decontamination procedure were beginning to take their toll.

'The slidecraft is nearing our destination,' said Polyaggle coolly. 'If you would be so good as to move over . . .'

She gestured with a claw, and the two of them shuffled aside to give her access to the control panel.

With Pinocchio's arm around her, Strauss-Giolitto no longer felt frightened of the height they were travelling above the pack ice. It was odd the way you could feel perfectly comfortable looking out of the window of a shuttle that was travelling a thousand kilometres above Mars, but being just a few hundred metres above the ground could inspire such fearsome vertigo. She supposed it was because it was so much easier to imagine yourself falling a few hundred metres to meet a gory end than it was to conceive of a drop of a thousand or more kilometres. Or maybe it was just that the shuttle was enclosed; she still hadn't become accustomed to the idea that being even relatively motionless in the open air was something that could be enjoyed.

She wondered how many of the rest of them from the *Santa Maria* would feel the same way. Most, she guessed.

Pinocchio was looking intently forwards, almost as if he had forgotten she was there. She followed the direction of his gaze.

Ahead of them was a great hill of snow, distinguishable from the rest of the landscape around it only by the gentleness of its slopes and the area it covered – it was difficult to judge from here, but Strauss-Giolitto reckoned the thing must be ten or twenty kilometres across. But there seemed little else of interest about it until she realized that it formed an almost perfect arc of a sphere.

Then a black diamond-shaped object appeared on the nearer hillside and slowly grew larger. No: Strauss-Giolitto could see more clearly as they grew closer. It wasn't an object but an aperture. They were heading straight towards it.

'Presumably this is one of those features of primitive, useless Spindrift that you don't go out of your way to show any visiting ships of the Autarchy,' said Pinocchio.

'You are correct,' said Polyaggle. She relaxed from the control board. 'They have taken over and are guiding us in now.'

They plunged towards the slope, seeming to be moving faster and faster the nearer they came to the surface. The slidecraft slowed to pause, bobbing, just outside the opening in the ice. Strauss-Giolitto could feel eyes watching her – alien eyes.

Then they were moving inwards. The glare of the ice vanished behind them. They were entering a place of utmost blackness. Even the daylight from behind them seemed reluctant to penetrate it.

'What the hell's going on?' said Strider to Nightmirror, who was taking a turn on the command deck. 'They've just vanished inside some bloody snowdrift!' She had been following her personnel's progress on Spindrift keenly for a duty-shift and a half now. She looked up, red-eyed, from the Pocket, as if expecting to find Nightmirror standing there beside her.

THERE IS NOTHING TO BE CONCERNED ABOUT, said the Image. I AM IN CONSTANT COMMUNICATION WITH TEN PER CENT EXTRA FREE, WHO IS CURRENTLY RESIDENT WITHIN THE BOT. YOUR PEOPLE ARE SAFE ENOUGH.

Thanks to Nightmirror's efforts, Strider had been able to record in holo most of the conversation Pinocchio and Strauss-Giolitto had had with the alien down on the spaceport, but the link between the two Images had gone strangely dead during part of the time the little party had been travelling across the icecap. Moreover, she still hadn't been able to replay that recording and get Nightmirror to translate for her what the alien was saying: at the moment she could hear Pinocchio and a very tired-sounding Strauss-Giolitto clearly enough, but the alien's side of the dialogue was just a mess of whistling noises. Strider was beginning to feel that there were too many things she was not being allowed to know.

'You lost contact for a while earlier!' she said angrily.

THERE WAS GOOD PURPOSE FOR THAT, said Nightmirror.

The response was presumably meant to be soothing, but it had the opposite effect on Strider. 'Don't fucking patronize me, you gobbet of half-real energy!' she yelled.

O'Sondheim looked up from his own Pocket. He was visibly every bit as weary as she was. 'Cool it, Leonie,' he said quietly.

'And you can fucking shut up as well,' she said. 'Go off into a corner and milk yourself off a couple of litres of testosterone, why don't you?'

THEY WERE HAVING A PERSONAL CONVERSATION.

'Who were? Oh, Strauss-Giolitto and Pinocchio, you mean. What was it about?'

IT WAS PERSONAL, AS I SAY. TEN PER CENT EXTRA FREE DECIDED THAT IT WAS ENTIRELY BETWEEN THE TWO OF THEM, AND THAT IT SHOULD NOT BE TRANSMITTED.

Strider's eyes were slit-like with fury.

'So that's what goddam Ten Per Cent Extra Free thought, is it? Who's supposed to be in charge of this mission?'

YOU ARE.

'Then how come Ten Per Cent Extra Free's suddenly started making all the decisions?' She knew her anger had moved her beyond the bounds of rationality, but she was too exhausted to care. 'I ordered constant monitoring of everything that went on down there. I need to know it *all*. I even need to be able to review what it looked like when those decontamination bots went shooting into Strauss-Giolitto's rectum, and what she said about it. Now, *tell me why you two Images conspired to cut out half an hour of the transmission*!'

There was a long silence, and even through the red haze of

her temper Strider began to worry that she'd gone too far and persuaded the Images that they should desert their human comrades.

WE ARE NOT SPIES, CAPTAIN LEONIE STRIDER, said the voices of Nightmirror and Heartfire in quasi-harmony. WE WILL REPORT AND RECORD EVERYTHING THAT AFFECTS THE WELL-BEING OF YOUR ENDEAVOUR AND OF THE PERSONNEL UNDER YOUR COMMAND. BUT PINOCCHIO AND MARIA STRAUSS-GIOLITTO WERE TALKING TO EACH OTHER ABOUT THEMSELVES, AND THEIR FEELINGS. THEY WERE SAYING THINGS THEY CERTAINLY WOULD NOT HAVE SAID HAD THEY REALIZED THAT ANYONE BUT TEN PER CENT EXTRA FREE WAS LISTENING TO THEM. WE WILL *NOT* REPORT SUCH INFORMATION TO YOU.

'Were they *balling*, or what?'

No.

There was an icy silence in her mind.

She slumped against the Pocket. Inadvertently she nodded her head into it, and a perfect replica of her own bunk popped cheerily into view.

She was being stupid, and the worst part was that she knew it. She had been fraught with anxiety during that long half-hour when the Pocket in which the recording was being made had gone blank. Now it had gone blank again, and she was doubly fraught. But it was senseless of her to be taking her fears out in the form of rage against the Images.

'I'm sorry,' she said, once she could get her voice under control. 'But can you tell me, please, why the transmission has gone dead again.'

WE ARE CONTINUING TO RECEIVE INFORMATION FROM TEN PER CENT EXTRA FREE. She must really have perturbed them: they were still speaking together. BUT THE INSTALLATION INTO WHICH THE PARTY HAS GONE IS SHIELDED HEAVILY AGAINST ELECTROMAGNETIC LEAKAGE, SO THAT HE CAN TRANSMIT ONLY DIRECT MENTAL INFORMATION TO US. HOWEVER, YOU WILL FIND OUT EVERYTHING ONCE THE PARTY RETURNS HERE. TEN PER CENT EXTRA FREE HAS EXPLAINED

'He could have been doing that all along,' she said. Her
anger waxed again, but this time it was almost exclusively with
herself. It was something she should have thought of. It had
been one of the basic tenets of her training: never rely on one
system when two systems will do and, if you can manage a
third, all the better. She was beginning to depend too much on
the Images to do almost everything for them – hell, they all
were, but it was her duty to ensure that there were back-ups for
when things came along that even the Images couldn't manage.

'I'm sorry,' she said again. 'I'll be expecting you to scrub my
back next.'

THAT IS SOMETHING WE CANNOT DO, ALTHOUGH . . . There
was a wistfulness in the song.

'Although what?'

The Images giggled, and were gone from her mind.

They heard the aperture closing behind them, closing off the
last remnants of sunlight. Strauss-Giolitto could see absolutely
nothing. Had it not been for the presence beside her in the
slidecraft of Polyaggle and Pinocchio – one of whom, it had to
be assumed, knew exactly what she was doing, and in the other
of whom she now had complete confidence – she knew that she
would have panicked, would have jumped hysterically over the
side or done something else equally suicidal.

Pinocchio took one of her hands in his and at the same time
switched on the lights in his eyes. The bright yellow beams
shot here and there around the enclosure in which they were
pent, picking out details of heavy machinery, banks of
slidecrafts on shelved bays along the wall, huge cables that
curved sinuously away across the floor . . .

'Turn those off,' demanded Polyaggle sharply.

He did so.

'There are detector cells implanted all over the walls in this
chamber,' she explained. 'They're examining us to make
absolutely sure we are who we say we are and who we look

like. Quite a number of them are low-frequency photoreceptors, and you've probably just blown out about half of those.'

'I apologize,' said Pinocchio.

'You weren't to know. I don't blame you.' Ten Per Cent
Extra Free translated her tone as irritable. 'We have plenty of
replacements, of course: it's the actual job of replacing that's
going to be a pain in the butt.'

Ten Per Cent Extra Free didn't often go in for colloquialisms
when he was translating. Most of the ones he did use he had
obviously picked up from Strider.

'I apologize again. If we can help . . .'

'You can't. We don't want you to be here more than a few
hours.'

Suddenly, dazzlingly, the lights came on. Strauss-Giolitto
used her free hand to shield her eyes from the bright greenness.

A sequence of cooing noises echoed through the chamber,
which Strauss-Giolitto, recovering her vision, began to realize
was even bigger than she had thought during that brief glimpse
when Pinocchio had lit his eyes.

Ten Per Cent Extra Free translated: WELCOME TO YOU,
POLYAGGLE, AND TO YOUR COMPANIONS. BRING YOUR SLIDE-
CRAFT TO THE GROUND.

Polyaggle touched a couple of the buttons on her control
board, and the vessel slowly sank. All at once there were a
dozen Spindrifters around them. Strauss-Giolitto's blood froze
momentarily, but the aliens were unarmed, and most of them
showed little interest in her or Pinocchio; they seemed to be a
welcoming party for Polyaggle. She was hoisted out of the
slidecraft by helping hands; the two offworlders had to climb
over the low ledge and drop down to the ground under their
own steam.

Of course, she thought. *We'd be too heavy for them to lift.*

A couple of the Spindrifters stayed on foot to escort
Pinocchio and Strauss-Giolitto across the floor of the hangar;
the remainder of the aliens, Polyaggle included, flew towards a
diamond-shaped opening in the far wall. Under the green lights
the butterfly wings of the Spindrifters took on even more

enchanting tones. One kept expecting those many fluttering wingtips to collide, but somehow they never seemed to.

Strauss-Giolitto, barefoot, trod in a puddle of thick, gelatinous oil. It was an experience she decided not to repeat. Clutching Pinocchio's arm to stop herself from slipping on her oily foot, she picked her course carefully as they followed the two Spindrifters. Here and there they had to step over the thick cables or make a detour round some larger piece of seeming detritus. It was obvious that no one ever walked on the floor in here unless they were carrying something heavy: the Spindrifters flew across the hangar whenever they could. *We're walking through their garbage tip*, thought Strauss-Giolitto.

Several minutes later they were in a chamber some twenty metres long and high and perhaps half that wide. Around its walls were numerous cylindrical objects at whose nature Strauss-Giolitto couldn't guess. On the rounded top of each of the cylinders was another of the very simple control boards like the one she had seen Polyaggle use on the slidecraft.

'What are those things?' she subvocalized.

PUTERS, said Ten Per Cent Extra Free. AMONG THE MOST ADVANCED IN THE WONDERVALE. IN FACT, THEY'RE SO FAR AHEAD OF ANYTHING YOU'VE COME ACROSS THAT PERHAPS 'PUTER' IS THE WRONG WORD. THAT'S WHY THEY LOOK SO SIMPLE.

Their escort had left them at the door, flying off down the broad, high corridor to go about other things. In the centre of the chamber stood Polyaggle and a couple of other female Spindrifters whom Polyaggle quickly introduced as Nerita and Feefaar. At first Strauss-Giolitto assumed these individuals must be top-ranking officers in the military of the Associated Villages, but it soon emerged that they *were* the Associated Villages military. With the aid of their machines they could, together or singly, mount Spindrift's defences – which Strauss-Giolitto began to infer were a lot less meagre than Polyaggle had implied. In the event of the enemy's battling their way through them to the ground, as many Spindrifters as could manage it would take refuge in this vast bunker, which she gathered stretched for kilometres underground; the rest of the species would be doomed.

Out of the corner of her eye she saw a swiftly moving glimmer of not-quite-light. There was another Image in the chamber.

She let Pinocchio do most of the talking. She felt she had very little to contribute.

'We will give you what we can,' Nerita was saying. 'What we cannot give you is any weaponry information which, if you made use of it, might by its very nature allow the slightest possibility of the Autarch's forces tracing it back here to Spindrift. Most but not all of his lieutenants are as stupid as he is himself, but some are capable of the most intelligent ratiocinations. Every weapons system has its own signature, and that signature might give a clue to the Autarchy as to where you had gained the system's theoretical underpinning.'

'That is perfectly understood,' said Pinocchio.

'Not by me,' subvocalized Strauss-Giolitto.

WHAT HE'S SAYING IS THAT IF YOU HUMANS SUDDENLY START DEPLOYING SOME VARIANT OF AN IDENTIFIABLE ANCIENT SPINDRIFTER WEAPON, SOMEONE IN THE AUTARCHY MIGHT PUT TWO AND TWO TOGETHER AND TORCH THIS PLANET ON PRINCIPLE.

'But there are other ways in which we might assist you,' said Nerita. 'For a start we can give you the co-ordinates of the stellar systems of the other ancient species in The Wondervale. They may be able to offer you different information. Some of them might even dare to give you technological data which would help you in your struggle.'

'Is it likely?' said Pinocchio. Strauss-Giolitto envied the way that he seemed so perfectly nonchalant in these surroundings. She herself was all too aware that they were in the stronghold of aliens about whom they knew virtually nothing, and that there were millions of tonnes of ice and metal above them.

'Not very,' said Feefaar. 'But certainly they will give you information which is both unknown to us and likely to aid you.'

'What sort of information?'

170

Nerita spoke again. 'Our communications with those other species are sporadic and rare, but we know that some of them are more restless under the tyranny than we are. Remaining neutral is harder work than you might think, even for a species like ourselves, who think in timescales of billions rather than millions of years.'

'No,' said Strauss-Giolitto, speaking for the first time. 'I know exactly what you mean. Injustice is difficult to stomach. So is guilt.'

The Spindrifters looked at her silently.

'You must feel guilty about all the sentient beings who are dying because the Autarchy persists,' she went on, floundering for words, becoming swiftly embarrassed.

'No,' said Feefaar. 'Why should we?'

'Because . . . well, because . . .'

'What is more important,' said Feefaar, 'is that, the longer the Autarchy and its inevitable successors continue their bloody rule, the more likely it is that our species will be destroyed.'

The Spindrifters turned their attention back to Pinocchio and Strauss-Giolitto let the conversation drift away from her. *You don't even know how these people think,* she told herself, *so how can you start guessing at their morals and priorities? Just because they're roughly the same shape as you and they seem to be talking in Argot – not to mention that you find all three of them fascinatingly desirable – you can't assume that they're like you in the slightest. What emotions do they have? You can't even* imagine *what their emotions might be like. Get to grips with this.*

She looked around her. The warmth that Pinocchio had given her aboard the slidecraft had all ebbed away by now, and she realized that she was once more very chilly under her thin robe. Her head was beginning to throb from the cold. Aside from the rows of Spindrifter puters along the walls, the chamber was featureless. Green light – fortunately not as lurid as that in the hangar – came from somewhere. The walls seemed to be grey. There was no decoration at all on them. *No art of any kind*, she thought. *Perhaps the Spindrifters* are *their art.*

Pinocchio tapped her on the shoulder.

'I want to consult briefly with you,' he said very quietly. The three Spindrifters had turned politely away. *Although who knows how sensitive their hearing is?* thought Strauss-Giolitto. *Maybe this place is bugged up to the eyeballs anyway.*

'With me? I'm no expert in any of this.'

'The Spindrifters are prepared to feed into my puter all the information that they're prepared to give us. I think, from what they tell me, that I have the capacity to handle this amount of data – although I shall ask you to monitor the process in case I run the risk of crashing.'

'What's so confidential about this that we have to be whispering?' she said.

Pinocchio shook his head. 'That is not what I want to talk about. In exchange, I propose to permit them to download my puter into theirs beforehand.' He looked hesitant. 'It's a pity the Main Computer is dead. These people – they know so much more than we do that it's impossible for me to determine whether or not there's any information we might have that could be of use to them.'

'There's bound to be,' she said, glancing across to where the three Spindrifters huddled in the far corner. They, too, were talking in low tones. They seemed to be arguing – at one point Feefaar fluttered a metre or two into the air, speaking rapidly. 'We've undergone a completely different cultural evolution,' she continued, 'and we've done it in isolation in a galaxy who knows how remote from The Wondervale. There's certain to be stuff that we've come up with that they don't know.'

'This is my feeling also,' said the bot. 'But I do not think that I can go through with this enterprise without specifically asking for human permission. Ideally I should ask Strider, but she's not here. I'm reluctant to delay my offer until I've had a chance to speak with her, because already one of the Spindrifters is dubious about the wisdom of helping us at all. We may not be allowed to send a second deputation down here.'

'Feefaar,' she said.

'Precisely.'

She wondered why Pinocchio was telling her this, then whispered: 'Oh.'

'You're the only human being here whose permission I can ask,' said Pinocchio.

'What makes you think you aren't a human being, bot?' she said after a long, thoughtful pause. She touched him on the arm. 'I'm a teacher from City 22 – a few years ago I was showing infants how to access databases and fine-tune their neural implants. I'm not qualified to make decisions like this. You are. Do what you think you should.' She punched him on the shoulder and tried to disguise the fact that it felt as if she'd broken a couple of knuckles. 'Strider sent you as her ambassador. So go ahead and ambassad.'

I COULD HOOK UP WITH NIGHTMIRROR TO ASK STRIDER IF SHE APPROVES THIS COURSE OF ACTION, said Ten Per Cent Extra Free.

'No,' Strauss-Giolitto said. 'This is Pinocchio's deal. Strider delegated the decisions here to him.'

'Are you sure?' said Pinocchio.

'Yes.'

'You realize you've just answered the question you said you weren't competent to answer?'

Strauss-Giolitto supposed she had, in a way, but this was no time to be chopping around with logical niceties. 'Do what you think is best,' she said quietly. 'Only, do you think you could give me some more of your heat? I'm freezing to death in here.'

His arm around her waist, Pinocchio put his proposition to the Spindrifters. They retreated for a few further moments to their corner to discuss it, and now Polyaggle and Nerita very obviously prevailed over the sceptical Feefaar. The argument didn't last long.

'We accept your offer,' said Polyaggle with seeming formality, facing the two offworlders. 'And we will give you the data that has already been discussed.' She paused as Feefaar said something to her with quiet intensity, but then Polyaggle raised her wings angrily at her. 'There's something else we

173

might be able to do for you. If we could have access to your Main Computer . . .'

'The Main Computer is dead,' said Pinocchio. 'I took out of it everything that I could. That wasn't very much, but it's all in the files I'm offering to download into your machines.'

'There's no such thing as a truly dead computer!' exclaimed Feefaar. 'Why do you try to deceive us this way?'

LET ME HANDLE THIS, said Ten Per Cent Extra Free.

'Can our Image speak with your Image?' said Pinocchio. 'Or would you prefer to speak to our Image direct? Let him explain.'

'Let him talk to me,' said Feefaar in a tone which Ten Per Cent Extra Free translated as contempt.

There was a brief silence. Feefaar stood with her eyes closed. At last she opened them.

'I understand now,' she said. 'I hadn't appreciated quite how primitive your technology is. If the Images have failed to drain the last out of your Main Computer, then perhaps much of it really *is* dead.'

'As Pinocchio said,' Strauss-Giolitto interposed tartly.

'As indeed your friend did say,' agreed Feefaar with a shimmer of her wings. She touched her claws together in a gesture which Strauss-Giolitto this time interpreted as a signal of apology. 'But we are better even than the Images at such matters.'

THIS IS TRUE, Ten Per Cent Extra Free confirmed.

'It is probable that we can gain yet more data than you' – Feefaar indicated Pinocchio – 'were able to immediately after your Main Computer's death. We would like to send one of us back with you to the *Santa Maria* to investigate.'

Pinocchio looked at Strauss-Giolitto as if to ask her what he should do. She nodded to him that the decision was his.

'This seems permissible,' he said. 'There is room for an extra person in our shuttle.'

'Then let us proceed with what we have to do here,' said Nerita. 'Afterwards Polyaggle will accompany you to your starship.'

'There is one other thing of which you should be aware,'

174

added Feefaar. 'If you are fortunate, Polyaggle may dredge
enough information out of your Main Computer to be able to
deduce a route back to your own stellar system.'

'To Mars?'

'If that is what your home world is called, yes.'

Among many species it would have been regarded as an
inappropriate moment for a conversation, but the Antracvhans
were not coy. The Autarch was in the process of both
copulating with and gashing to death one of his less favourite
concubines; in the midst of the former he had begun to suspect
that she was faking her enjoyment of his efforts – hence the
latter. The floor shook. She was taking a long time to die –
Antracvhans are a tough species, and can sustain considerable
physiological damage before the injuries become fatal – so the
Autarch saw no good reason to discontinue his ponderous
pleasure, even when he was informed that Kaantalech wished
to holo with him.

Kaantalech watched with interest for a few moments before
speaking.

'My officers have tracked down the Humans, Stars' Elect,'
she said. 'Their protoplasm is so different from ours that it
virtually glows on our screens. The delay has been because we
have had to search all the quadrants.' Had the Autarch been of
her species he would have known that her mouth was
brimming with glee. Luckily he wasn't, or he might have
started wondering just what it was that was making her so
gleeful. The successful search done by her aides had made her
realize quite how potentially powerful she was.

'Where are they?' he said, not looking up. More gore
splattered the walls. The concubine's slow brain began to
realize that the process was hurting more than usual, and she let
out a squeal of discomfort.

'They're on one of the moons of Spindrift,' said Kaantalech.
She could hardly believe what was going on. She knew that the
females in Nalla's entourage were bred for stupidity – because
an even remotely clever concubine is a dangerous concubine –
but this particular specimen appeared to be no more than living

175

meat. Kaantalech wondered if the Autarch's paranoia had increased to such a peak that he was having massive brain surgery performed on his females before they were allowed to approach him. If so, it couldn't be long before the same injunction started applying to courtiers, and then lieutenants . . . Kaantalech was glad she could communicate with the Autarch by holo, rather than having to go to Qitanefermeartha in person.

'Never heard of the place,' grunted the Autarch.

'It's well off all the trade routes,' said Kaantalech, 'and it has little to offer us. We investigated it several times for natural resources or slaves, but there were hardly any of either.'

'Why did the Humans go there?'

It was an unusually intelligent question from the Autarch, and it was one that Kaantalech cursed herself for not having thought through beforehand.

'Perhaps because of the planet's very remoteness and mediocrity,' she said. That must be it.

'I distrust remote, mediocre planets,' said the Autarch. This was true enough. He distrusted *all* planets. 'Maybe they had some other reason for going there.'

'I can't imagine why they . . .'

'I wasn't asking for an opinion. Torch it. Torch the Humans as well – we've done without their technology for thousands of years, so what makes you think we need it now?'

There was no point in arguing with the Autarch when he was in this kind of mood.

'Yes, Stars' Elect,' said Kaantalech humbly, and prepared to disconnect holo contact.

The full force of the pain of what was being inflicted on her was now reaching the concubine's brain, and she was screaming in a most pleasing fashion. Kaantalech wished she could continue watching for a while, but she knew that she had been dismissed.

Regretfully, she disconnected.

Strauss-Giolitto was annoyed with herself about it, but she had experienced a certain vindictive delight while Polyaggle was going through the *Santa Maria*'s decontamination systems. It didn't matter that she was having to undergo the same procedure herself – there seemed to be so little of her left to decontaminate – and it didn't matter that the humans' decontamination was significantly less rigorous and therefore significantly less humiliating than the Spindrifters' had been: Strauss-Giolitto still felt a poignant sense of revenge at the thought of Polyaggle's discomfort.

Which was very petty of her – hence her annoyance.

She was even more annoyed when the Spindrifter emerged from decontamination seemingly quite unperturbed.

Strider was waiting for the alien alongside Strauss-Giolitto and Pinocchio, who had cleared decontamination much more quickly.

God, but it was good to be back in a jumpsuit again – although her baldness still felt bizarre. She kept catching herself twitching her head to flick her hair out of her eyes and then realizing there wasn't any hair there to flick. Back on Mars she'd have had a medbot give her a quick transplant; the medbots on board the *Santa Maria* weren't designed for cosmetic repairs.

The first meeting between Strider and Polyaggle was interesting to watch. Because Pinocchio's synthetic skin was pale and because Strauss-Giolitto had been born that way, Polyaggle – whose reactions Strauss-Giolitto was beginning to be able crudely to interpret – was obviously startled to find herself being greeted by a black human being. Colour variations among the Spindrifters were largely confined to the wings, Strauss-Giolitto had noticed: the bristles that covered their bodies differed little from one individual to another. Polyaggle clearly thought at first that Strider was of some different species – and was deeply suspicious, because Pinocchio had told the Spindrifters that, aside from the Images, there was only one sentient species on the *Santa Maria*. When Lan Yi appeared a moment afterwards, apologizing for his lateness as if he were attending an office discussion rather than encountering a delegate from an alien species for the first time, Polyaggle's confusion grew.

And then at last the Spindrifter cottoned on.

Strider extended a hand. 'You're welcome,' she said. 'Touching hands is a form of greeting among our kind.'

Somewhat timorously, it seemed, Polyaggle put out a claw and tapped Strider's fingertips lightly. Of course, she would still be worried about contagion. Presumably she would have preferred to remain suited up, but by now her suit was ashes.

The Spindrifter fluttered her wings briefly. 'That is a greeting from my species to yours,' she said.

'Would you like food?' said Strider.

Polyaggle didn't answer, but shut her eyes. What was there on this offworlder spacecraft that might be safe for her to eat? Her biochemistry was obviously entirely different from the human one.

'I brought an Image with me, as you must know,' she said at length. 'He has conferred with your Images here and they have devised a list of items which it is possible for me to eat without harm. I will join you for a meal of basic processed soya, if I may.'

And I'll bet Strider tucks into the same beside her, thought Strauss-Giolitto. Processed soya was the hard tack on which many meals were based; one of the skills of cookbots was in blending flavours and sauces so that you could no longer taste the soya.

'Perhaps with a little pure water,' added Polyaggle.

'It shall be arranged,' said Strider. She nodded to Lan Yi, who spoke briefly into his commline.

'Please join us for dinner,' said Strider to the other three. With a smile.

Only Pinocchio returned it.

'Our Images linked up so that I was able to monitor almost everything that went on during the while my people were with you, except for the time you were in your stronghold in the icecap,' said Strider. *And except for that bloody half-hour,* she thought viciously. *I'll find out more about that if I have to pull Pinocchio apart chip by chip.*

They were seated round the table in Strider's cabin. It was

just the right height for her and Lan Yi, but substantially too low for Strauss-Giolitto. Polyaggle had elected to remain standing. A bot would be arriving soon with their dinner. Strider grinned to herself. Lan Yi was remaining as taciturn as ever, but it was easy to read from Strauss-Giolitto's face that the woman was hoping the bot would take a very long time in coming.

'I know of the agreement you came to with Pinocchio,' continued Strider, 'and I approve of it. After we've eaten, allow me to show you round the *Santa Maria* and introduce you to a few people. If you're tired, we have some spare cabins – you are certainly welcome to claim one as your own . . .'

'I want to stay aboard this ship for as short a time as possible,' said Polyaggle.

'Our friend is quite reasonably concerned about bacterial or viral infection,' explained Pinocchio. 'There is no discourtesy intended.'

'Thank you, Pinocchio,' said Strider. 'I had gathered as much for myself.' *And that was a silly put-down,* she thought. *I wish I could get rid of my anger.*

A klaxon screamed.

'Uh oh,' said Strider, leaping from her chair. She felt the hairs all up the back of her spine rise. 'Emergency. Forgive me.'

She was through the door and into the nearest elevator shaft before she gave herself time to think. Pinocchio was hard behind her.

'Any idea what's going on?' she said breathlessly as the elevator hissed them towards the command deck.

'No.'

'Are there any Images nearby?'

'No, not even Polyaggle's. He has gone to the deck already to work with the others. They clearly think this is not something minor.' Even the bot was looking apprehensive.

Strider beat with her fist against the elevator's plastite wall. 'Come on, damn you! Come on!'

It stopped abruptly, and for a lunatic moment Strider thought she might have broken it.

Leander, who had been on agricultural duties, boarded alongside them.

'What the—?' she began.

'Dunno,' said Strider bluntly. 'Better be good. I was just about to have my dinner.'

A few seconds later they were on the command deck. All of the Pockets were glowing brightly except the two at either end.

'It's only just happened,' said Nelson, looking up from one of them. His face was aghast. 'It's like your worst fucking nightmare, light of my life.'

'Let me see,' said Strider, running to the Pocket next to the big man.

'Oh, shit,' she breathed. It *was* a nightmare. At first glance it seemed as if the number of bright stars in the sky had doubled. Then you realized that half of them were starships.

THE AUTARCHY'S COME TO SAY HELLO, said Ten Per Cent Extra Free wryly in her mind.

'Any idea why they're here?' she barked to the Image.

US, I SHOULD IMAGINE. THE *SANTA MARIA*, I MEAN.

'Tell Polyaggle I want her here – she knows more about these bastards than I do. Where's O'Sondheim?'

'Here,' the First Officer said beside her.

'Images, how many of those goddam starships are there?'

THREE HUNDRED AND SEVENTY-TWO, said a voice she didn't recognize. That must be the Spindrifter's Image.

'Is there anything we can hit them with that could do them any harm?' For the first time in days, Strider felt completely calm. She was giving the orders again: for a time it had seemed that command of her ship was slipping away from her.

WE COULD DAMAGE – EVEN DESTROY – A FEW OF THEM, BUT THERE WOULD STILL BE HUNDREDS OF OTHERS.

'Can we get away quick?'

THEY HAVE THE TACHYONIC DRIVE AS WELL. HOW DO YOU THINK THEY GOT HERE SO FAST? WE COULD LOSE A FEW OF THEM, BUT – Strider felt something that she assumed was the mental equivalent of a shrug – AGAIN THERE WOULD BE HUNDREDS OF OTHERS.

'Then what in hell *can* we do?'

180

WAIT AND SEE, said the Image philosophically.

'Is Ten Per Cent Extra Free there? Or Nightmirror? Or Heartfire?'

THEY ARE DOING OTHER THINGS.

'Great,' said Strider, turning to Nelson. 'We seem to have got ourselves a fatalistic Image.'

'I'm feeling pretty fatalistic myself,' he said. His attempt at casualness was unconvincing. He looked like a man who was staring into the jaws of death – which was more or less what he *was* doing. 'Umbel almighty, but will you *look* at that?'

'I just have,' said Strider harshly. 'Get your brain together, Nelson. We need it.'

She stepped away from the Pocket and glanced around.

'Anyone else got any good ideas?' she snapped.

They shook their heads at her – all except Pinocchio, who was looking thoughtful.

'They wouldn't send a fleet that size against just a single vessel,' he said. 'All they'd need to overwhelm us would be half a dozen – maybe twice as many if they wanted to capture us. I have a bad feeling about this.'

'Keep bad feelings to yourself right now,' she said. She gestured towards the Pocket behind her. 'There are three hundred and seventy-two bad feelings hanging out there in space at the moment.'

'Please . . .' began Pinocchio.

'If it's not some way we can get the hell out of here, I don't want to hear it.'

'Captain,' said O'Sondheim. 'Look here.'

He pointed towards his own Pocket. She moved quickly across.

O'Sondheim had called up the representation of Spindrift. As the two of them watched, the appearance of the surface of the planet was changing. The southern polar icecap seemed to be melting; the northern icecap was doing the same sort of thing, but more patchily. Abruptly the planet's surface features disappeared entirely: all that Strider could see was a fuzzy pink disc.

'The Spindrifters' defences,' she breathed.

'That's my guess, too,' said O'Sondheim.

'Three hundred and seventy-two ships are far too many to send against just one,' repeated Pinocchio. 'It's as I feared. We're just the sideshow.'

Kaantalech had expected the job to be easy, but as soon as she saw the disc of Spindrift change colour in her holoscreen she knew she was in for a fight. It normally took a couple of hundred cruisers to torch a planet down to its bedrock. She was glad that some instinct had warned her to bring a larger fleet. Perhaps it had been the surprise of hearing the Autarch ask a meaningful question for once.

She was looking forward to this. The databanks had told her that the dominant species here was confined to this single planet: torching it would mean there was one less developing species in The Wondervale to worry about. Developing civilizations made her anxious: one moment they were primitives and the next they were launching an armada of ships armed to the teeth with intramolecular disrupters aimed directly at your head. Better to get rid of them early, before that happened.

To judge by the defence shield that had been thrown up around Spindrift, she had got here with only a decade or two to spare. There was some sophisticated stuff on offer here.

'Take up standard formation,' she said to an aide. He hurried off to transmit the order to the rest of the fleet.

The pinkness expanded rapidly from the surface of the planet until it enclosed the inner moon. From the fuzzy surface suddenly erupted a squadron of missiles, which moved in intelligent cooperation to effect maximum destruction among Kaantalech's front-line vessels. She watched the flares as ships died.

For a moment she was concerned. Those missiles had penetrated the best shields the Autarchy could produce.

'How many have we lost?' she asked another aide. She had sensibly placed her flagship, the *Blunt Instrument*, well to the rear of the fleet.

'Fourteen,' he said.

'Keep moving into standard formation. The more we spread out, the less easy it'll be for them to attack us.'

Even as she watched, her armada was shifting apart. Soon it would be forming a sphere all round the Spindrifters' defences. That was the time to start attacking back.

Another flotilla of missiles emerged. She learnt a few seconds later that a further twenty-seven of her cruisers had been destroyed.

The Spindrifters had teeth, all right.

OK, so had she.

The diameter of the pinkness abruptly expanded by about ten per cent, and numbers of the ships under her command were simply swallowed by it.

This was more serious.

'Losses just incurred?' she snarled.

'Another fifty-eight gone, Kaantalech.'

This couldn't go on much longer. The Spindrifter defences had to be running low. Even though her fleet wasn't yet in position, she ordered the foremost vessels to launch a salvo of maxbeams down into the pink sphere. A couple of the maxbeams swerved to hit Autarchy vessels en route – this was par for the course – but the remainder seemed to hit home. The local space was a lightshow as the blue beams struck the pink surface and vanished somewhere beyond.

The pink paled perceptibly. Yes, some of those little darlings had struck paydirt, all right.

Kaantalech's mouth filled with joy.

'Continue moving into standard formation,' she commanded brusquely.

Barely ten minutes had passed since combat had been declared. Conflicts in space don't generally last very long, because almost every blow that is successfully delivered is a fatal one. There have been legends of damaged warships somehow limping gallantly home, but almost without exception they are just that: legends. In the vacuum either you're alive or you're more generally dead: the status 'wounded' is not an option.

The *Blunt Instrument* rocked, and Kaantalech staggered.

How had the Spindrifters been able to get a missile through without its being detected long before? She should have been warned. Someone was going to die painfully for this.

She squinted at her holoscreen, looking out for any trace of activity from the pink disc.

Off to her left, one of her cruisers erupted into a maelstrom of fire and glowing debris. She had seen no trace of a missile or ray. The Spindrifters must be using some technology of which the Autarchy knew nothing. Perhaps she ought to forbear from torching the planet and instead torture enough of the indigenes until one of them gave up the secret. But the Autarch would be bound to discover what she'd done, and then she'd have to hand over the technology to him – and he'd undoubtedly waste it on some damn-fool project or other. Besides, assuming he didn't, she had no wish to arm him up any more than she had to.

Better just to get rid of the world *and* its weaponry.

'Continue to move into standard formation,' she repeated unnecessarily. Even though three more cruisers had been blasted into oblivion, no one would dare deviate from one of her orders until it had been countermanded. The sick joke the troopers passed around among each other when they thought they weren't being monitored was: 'The Autarch'll kill you *if* he can't think of anything better to do, Kaantalech'll kill you *because* she can't think of anything better to do.' Kaantalech not only allowed the apparently subversive joke to circulate freely: she had created it in the first place.

'Check the Humans on the bigger moon,' she said to an aide.

Could it be that the Humans were chipping in with some of their own weaponry? She doubted it. If they'd had weapons of this class they'd merely have blown Maglittel to bits on first contact, rather than go through all the palaver with the red giant. In the name of the Autarchy, Maglittel had been a fool: it had attacked the Humans without first ascertaining their defence capabilities. It was one thing to kill innocent bystanders; quite another to be so stupid as not to check out first whether or not they could kill *you*.

The aide came bustling back, wagging his short proboscis.

'The Humans are quiescent, Kaantalech,' he said. 'Shall we divert a couple of cruisers their way?'

'No. Not yet,' she said.

The *Blunt Instrument* was once again hit by something heavy. It was a good job she'd arranged that the flagship be kitted out with the best defensive shields of all the vessels in the fleet.

Vastly depleted – there were now fewer than two hundred and seventy ships left – Kaantalech's armada was forming a ragged version of the standard attack pattern. Most of the ships' commanding officers were adjusting their positions to take account of the gaps in the ranks. Here and there, however, the gaps remained. Kaantalech cursed. Patronage was still an important factor in an individual's attaining high rank in the Autarch's military. She would bet her fourteenth breast that the captains too slow on the uptake to get things right had friends or family in high places.

Still, she had to do the best she could with what she'd got.

'Four more cruisers out of it,' said an aide nervously.

Kaantalech nodded absently. In the holoscreen, she'd seen three of them go down simultaneously. The fourth must have been around the far side of the pinkness. She congratulated herself yet again on having had the foresight to bring almost twice as many warships as were normally required.

The formation was ragged, but it was there. Surely the Spindrifters couldn't keep this up much longer. Even so, better to give them a first barrage now.

The earlier maxbeams had clearly weakened them.

She gestured to the nearest aide that she wanted to take over direct control.

He passed her a mike that was barely larger than a parwhat's eye.

Kaantalech spoke a few words, and it was as if the heavens themselves were blown apart.

'I told you the Humans should never have been allowed to come here,' fluted Feefaar. 'All they have brought in their train

185

is death and destruction.' With a few assistants, she and Nerita were running the defence operations room.

'They were not to know that,' said Nerita. Slidecraft were arriving from all over Spindrift; the port in the hillside was left constantly open because, with the deflector screen surrounding the planet out as far as the inner moon, there was no way the bunker could be observed by the attackers. But neither she nor Nerita was certain how long they could keep the deflector screen in place.

The screen caused a distortion in spacetime so that energy towards its exterior was diverted away to somewhere else in the Universe – in this instance, into Spindrift's star, where even the mightiest of the forces at the command of the Autarchy could do little damage. That was the theory of the device, which the ancient species had developed millions of years before, when they had seen the aggressive natures of the emergent secondary species taking form. The trouble was that no one had ever been able to make a deflector screen more than about eighty per cent efficient. If the Autarchy fleet poured enough energy into it they would, despite the huge wastage, nevertheless be able to destroy Spindrift just as effectively as if the screen had not been there at all.

'I'm not saying it was their fault,' said Feefaar, fluttering her wings angrily as she flitted over Nerita's head to get from one puter to another. 'But it wasn't *our* fault, either, that they drew this armada after them. As soon as they arrived we should have had the foresight to tell them to go away.'

'Stop this. The deflector's losing power. Concentrate on that.'

The two Spindrifters said nothing for a few minutes as they fought with various controls to try to beef up the energy resources available for the screen. They were drawing energy from the hot magnetic core of the planet; there was plenty of power on tap, but for technical reasons it was difficult to turn the tap on far enough to get more than a trickle at any one time.

'They're using maxbeams,' said Nerita.

'I'd noticed.'

Maxbeams sought out complex organic molecules and

shredded them into their component atoms, those atoms being repelled from each other with such ferocity that the effect was not unlike a miniature version of a nuclear explosion. The disadvantage of the maxbeam was that it was difficult to target properly: if en route it passed too near some other collection of organics than the one you were aiming at, it was likely to change course, hungrily. If that collection of organics happened to be, say, the crew of one of your own starships, the starship would be blown into a depressingly large number of pieces. The weapon was outlawed throughout The Wondervale, which meant that no one but the Autarchy's military was allowed to use it.

'Even in here we may not be able to survive them,' said Nerita. Between them, they'd got the deflector screen back up to full power again.

Feefaar looked upwards apprehensively. The dome of the hidden stronghold was built of metres-thick deadmetal, under the ice – the ice itself afforded a certain amount of protection. 'We should be all right unless we get a direct hit.'

'Should be. Hope so.'

Both of them were all the while conjuring up in their minds an image of the disposition of the attacker's fleet. They were startled when one of the cruisers spontaneously and explosively disintegrated, soon to be followed by another.

'That wasn't us,' said Feefaar. 'Was it?' she added doubtfully.

Nerita gave a soft whistle – the Spindrift equivalent of a shrug. 'Not unless the puters have independently developed an invisible beam or missile and decided to launch it themselves. I think you may unnecessarily have been maligning the Humans,' she said.

'Then they're adding themselves to our grave,' said Feefaar. 'Even with the Images' help, their technology is several orders of magnitude behind what the Autarchy has at its disposal.'

'I have a salvo of five direct ballistics available for launch,' said Nerita. 'What do you think?'

'I think, let the carnivores have it,' said Feefaar emphatically.

187

In a galaxy where warfare was carried out using the most sophisticated technology available, defences were designed accordingly. The Spindrifters were gambling on the fact that the Autarchy's defences were too advanced to recognize that one way of destroying a spaceship is simply to fire something very hard very quickly at it. Expecting something complex like an intramolecular disrupter, a clever defence shield might let slip through what was effectively a very large bullet . . . which would puncture the craft's hull and break its spine.

All five of the ballistics effectively did just that.

'I deplore the loss of sentient life,' said Feefaar, 'but personally I found that rather pleasing.'

'Leaving aside my obvious guilt,' replied Nerita, 'I am ashamed to confess that I too derived a deal of satisfaction from the episode. Shall I prepare another salvo?'

'Are you sure you're prepared to risk yourselves this way?' said Strider. 'Some of the species on those cruisers might be able to see you in clear.'

All four of the Images warbled together. IT IS UNLIKELY THAT WE CAN SAVE SPINDRIFT, BUT THE VERY LEAST WE CAN DO FOR HAVING BROUGHT THIS UPON THE SPINDRIFTERS IS TO CAUSE THEIR ENEMY AS MANY CASUALTIES AS POSSIBLE. THERE IS ALWAYS A CHANCE THAT THE AUTARCHY FLEET MIGHT RETREAT FOR LONG ENOUGH TO ENABLE US TO RESCUE MORE OF THE SPINDRIFTERS.

'How much of a chance?' said Strider, staring into a Pocket that displayed what the armada was doing to the Spindrifters' pink screen. Why the hell hadn't the fleet despatched just a couple of its vessels to make easy mincemeat out of the *Santa Maria*?

EXPRESSED AS AN ESTIMATED PERCENTAGE?

'No. Just a guess.'

THERE IS THE SLIGHTEST POSSIBILITY THAT BETWEEN OUR EFFORTS AND THOSE OF THE SPINDRIFTERS THEMSELVES, THE ENEMY MIGHT BE REPELLED.

'Then, if you think it's worth the gamble, go ahead.' She twisted her face. Even if she'd instructed them definitely not to, they'd probably still have gone ahead. The Images were always punctilious about asking her permission to do something, and then she told them to do what they were going to do anyway. One of these days she'd find the courage to countermand them and see what happened.

I WILL GO INITIALLY, said Ten Per Cent Extra Free. IF I PERISH, THE REST OF US WILL KNOW THAT THE ENTERPRISE IS INDEED FOOLISH.

Strider knew it was an illusion, but there was a sensation of loss as Ten Per Cent Extra Free departed, as if she could *feel* him going. It seemed that a little bit of *herself* had disappeared.

Yet again she asked herself: why had the Autarchy's starfleet so far spared the *Santa Maria*?

Ten Per Cent Extra Free *slid* through several layers of reality back to The Truthfulness, maintaining only the slightest pseudopod-like connection with The Wondervale. Briefly he saw several different versions of the way the cosmos might have been, had its initial creative spark been otherwise: one cosmos resembled a burning tree, and was no larger than that; another was nothing but timeless emptiness, a place where the omnipresent particle sea had never chanced to launch itself into the explosion of creation; yet another was a place where he found himself momentarily inside the form of what seemed to be a young woman who in blindness was being buffeted by pangs of undiluted emotion. At last, in his own reality – The Truthfulness – he was an energy matrix moving among other matrices.

He returned through the disparate realities to be aboard an Autarchy starcruiser.

Ten Per Cent Extra Free soaked himself into a wall and travelled easily along it between the atoms until he came to the drive chamber. Gratefully he soaked up some of the enormous energies that were being released by the drive even though the starship was moving at such a tiny fraction of the velocity of light.

THANK YOU, he said politely to the drive unit.

MY PLEASURE, it responded. I HAVE PLENTY TO SPARE.

189

BUT I'M AFRAID THAT I HAVE TO END YOU, said Ten Per Cent Extra Free. THE ENDING OF YOU WILL DESTROY THE SHIP YOU HAVE BEEN POWERING FOR HOW MANY YEARS?

MORE YEARS THAN I HAVE BEEN ABLE TO COUNT. YES, I KNEW YOU HAD COME HERE TO DESTROY ME. I DO NOT RESENT THE FACT.

NEVERTHELESS, FELLOW-CREATURE, I APOLOGIZE FOR WHAT I HAVE TO DO.

DO IT QUICKLY.

Ten Per Cent Extra Free drew all of the energy out of the drive, so that its components froze – so that its very core died. He couldn't hold this much energy inside himself for more than an instant, but that was long enough to divert it into the main body of the starcruiser, while at the same time withdrawing himself through the realities once more to the safety of his own cosmos.

Even at this sidewise distance there was a flicker of pain at the edge of his consciousness as the energies of the starship's drive died a second time, this time in a pyre of their own making. He had a millisecond's guilt over having killed another sentient creature of energy, but that soon passed: the drive had confronted its own death with equanimity, and he had been courteous with it to the last. By now it would be awakening, in entirely different form, in some remote probabilistic reality; it might or might not retain its memories of its previous existence. If it did, then at least its demise had been as painless as any could possibly be.

It took Ten Per Cent Extra Free some little while to recover himself from this first destructive venture. As a rule, when in The Wondervale the Images *never* destroyed, they only created: they created communications nexi of various sorts, or they infiltrated technology to bend it towards something *better* – another creative act.

Destruction was emotionally difficult for Ten Per Cent Extra Free, as it would be for the other Images.

He contacted them now, across the bridge of the intervening realities, informing them – all within the compass of a single thought – of the depth of the hurt he had received through his act of annihilation. Each of them must decide whether the pain of such an action was justified – or even if the action itself was, in hindsight, ethically acceptable. There would be no recriminations among the Images afterwards if one or more of them decided not to assist in this venture.

Ten Per Cent Extra Free didn't wait for the others' thoughts to come back to him. Fully recuperated, he *slid* once more through the nests of the realities that separated his own comfortably radiant cosmos from that of The Wondervale until he located another Autarchy warship . . .

Strider staggered back from the Pocket.

'Shit! Those poor bastards!'

She felt tears coming to her eyes, and blinked them back.

Polyaggle was by her side, and made some whispering noises that meant nothing to Strider – with all the Images off on their destructive course through the Autarchy armada, it was impossible to understand what the Spindrifter was saying: it could have been a message of hate, or of loss, or of any of an infinitude of emotions that no human had ever felt.

The blue maxbeams sprang from every surviving vessel in the armada and plunged into the Spindrifters' defensive shield. Strider felt as if she were watching a supernova. Nothing – *nothing* – could sustain such a barrage. The Universe itself had decided that the Spindrifters should be extinguished. The pinkness paled to white, retreated, and then was gone. The planet was naked and defenceless.

The vessels of the armada – even though, here and there in a random and unpredictable pattern, one after the other of them spontaneously exploded thanks to the efforts of the Images – moved into a tighter formation, ready for the kill. There was nothing she was able to do about it.

But there was something she *could* do.

'Power the drive,' she said to O'Sondheim.

He looked at her, startlement visible in the eye that wasn't covered by a secondary retinal screen.

'We're going,' she said.

'Just *leaving* these people?' he said.

191

'We can't save them. If we run now, we might with a bit of luck be able to save *ourselves*.'

He snorted.

'There are five kids down there' – she pointed a thumb towards the main body of the *Santa Maria* – 'and a couple of them haven't learnt to walk yet. If it were just you and me I'd say fuckit, let's go out in glory, you go first Danny because I've got to comb my hair so I look my best – all that. But we haven't the right to throw away other people's lives. Now fucking power that fucking drive.'

'I . . . I won't do it.'

Her elbow struck him in the side just below the ribcage, so that he staggered away across the command deck, half-gagging, half-gasping. She took over the Pocket at which he'd been working, analysed the situation within seconds, and fed the necessary instructions into the Pocket.

'Nelson,' she yelled, removing her head from the Pocket as little as she could. 'Commline the personnel that we're moving under five gees within the next minute. Tell 'em to spread themselves flat. Leander – get to the intercom and do the same.'

Yeah, it felt bad: running when the people who had helped you were about to be massacred. It'd feel even worse knowing in your dying moments that there just *might* have been a chance you could have saved a few human beings but you hadn't done that because you wanted to make a macho display of martyrdom. To hell with that. Strider thought it unlikely they'd escape with their lives, but she was going to give it a try.

The graphic display told her everything was ready for a fusion launch. There was every chance, whatever the Images had promised, that this moon was going to be little more than a heap of garbage once the *Santa Maria*'s drive had finished with it – but anyway there weren't going to be any young night-walking lovers looking up from Spindrift hoping to compare it to a silvery spoon.

She stuck her head back into the Pocket.

'Move it.'

Not the most dignified of commands, but the Pocket knew

192

what she meant. It transmitted the essence of her instruction to the drive.

Strider threw herself to the floor just in time. Then there was a brontosaurus standing on her back.

She felt glued down, but knew that somehow she had to get herself up to at least her knees – not later, but now. O'Sondheim and Leander were screaming; she hoped Polyaggle was surviving somehow. She could hear Nelson shuffling somewhere near her as he too struggled to cope with the gees. Strider told herself not to worry if she broke a few bones – the medbots could splint those up, and maybe even mend them. This was likely to hurt a lot but . . .

She not only felt but *heard* her kneecap crack. The pain was enough to make her bite right through her lower lip. Something extra for the medbots to do. The drops of blood hit the floor with unnatural speed. She made it to the whereabouts of the Pocket somehow. It adjusted its height to meet her, but she still had another few metres to go. The world was filled with a red that was encroaching into black, but she was aware that Nelson was doing his best to copy her feat.

'First one there gets a free trip home to Mars,' she croaked, her throat feeling as if it were made of red-hot lead. 'Posh hotel, little tablets of soap, curious gunk I've never worked out what to do with in the shower . . .'

'Don't forget the trouser press,' gasped Nelson. 'And the holo that doesn't work properly. If I get a clear picture I'm gonna complain to the management. Say, Strider, you ever get your hand caught in one of those fucking trouser presses?'

She was inching herself closer to the Pocket.

'No,' she said.

'I did once. I was trying to work out what the fuck the thing *was*. Hey, you didn't mention the too-small kettle that takes so long to heat up that eventually you forget you switched it on, so when you get back to the room you find everything's damp except the kettle, which is kind of a lump of molten plastic.'

'OK, Nelson, if you get to your Pocket before I get to mine, I'll even make sure your hotel room has a dud kettle.'

''Kinell, sweetest in all creation, I never thought I'd hear you

193

talk dirty like that.' It sounded as if Nelson were smiling, but Strider didn't have the strength to turn and look. A few more centimetres and . . .

'Bad luck,' she said. 'I'm the winner of the luxury holiday. I even get the shower-rose coming away in my hand.'

Strider slumped her head into the Pocket.

'Shift into tachyon drive,' she said with the last of her strength, 'and give me a superfluity of those white towels that are too small to do anything useful with.'

Nightmirror kicked at the flagship of the Autarchy armada, trying desperately to download the energies of its drive into the rest of the vessel. He had destroyed three other vessels so far, but the *Blunt Instrument* was proving more difficult. In the other vessels the drive had been unshielded – what mortal being would want to come into the drive chamber? – but in the *Blunt Instrument* extra defensive screens had been erected.

He kicked again, hoping that he could find some way through the forcefield. The kick wasn't a physical movement, rather an electromagnetic manipulation of the forces surrounding the drive unit. Nightmirror's latest attempt was as useless as the others had been – the flagship was shaken, but undamaged.

No. Wait a moment. There was a chink in the drive unit's defences. He had kicked open the slightest of cracks. If he could edge himself through there . . .

No sooner thought than done. He faced the intensity of the reactive core. From here on it should be easy.

The crack in the defensive shield behind him closed again. He was trapped here with the core.

He could destroy the core, probably, but at the same time destroy himself – and without doing any major damage to the *Blunt Instrument*. Although driveless, the vessel could easily be taken in tow by one of the other ships in the fleet until it could dock and have a new drive installed.

There was a better thing Nightmirror could do. Assuming the Humans could survive this massacre, it would be good for them to have an ally among the enemy. It wasn't the best of all possible options, but it was the best that was open to him right now.

He opened himself, and allowed his own energies to be swallowed into those of Kaantalech's drive unit.

The pain was exquisite for a long nanosecond or so, but then he was there.

Nightmirror stretched himself out in the drive's core, feeling the ecstasy of the energy pulses moving through him. If it was going to carry on being as good as this, he was going to have difficulty persuading himself to assist the Humans when the time came.

HI THERE, said the drive unit. WELCOME ABOARD.

THIS IS GOING TO TAKE A WHILE, said Nightmirror to the other Images, BUT I HOPE IT'S GOING TO BE WORTH IT.

There was the sensation of glorious freedom aboard the *Santa Maria*. The abrupt imposition of five gees had killed three people, including one of the children. Strider would doubtless have to do some fast talking soon to save herself from the attentions of a lynch mob, but just now she was happy enough to have removed her ship from the vicinity of the Autarchy fleet. She'd lost three: she could have lost everybody. For the moment, though, there was that delicious feeling of liberation from the crushing gees.

Polyaggle uttered a further stream of noises which Strider found totally incomprehensible. The Images were clearly still doing their destructive worst among the ships of the Autarchy. Strider assumed they would be able to find their way back to the *Santa Maria*.

Would they? It was a question that hadn't occurred to her before. She'd become so accustomed to the Images being capable of doing anything they wanted to do that it had been easy enough to make the assumption they could track down the *Santa Maria*, wherever in The Wondervale it went. Now she began to worry. She knew so little about the nature of the reality that the Images inhabited. If she'd managed to lose them, the *Santa Maria* was dead – sooner rather than later.

195

'Images,' she said despairingly to the air. 'Images – are you there?'

There was no reply.

She didn't want to repeat the question. Sometime soon the others on the command deck would begin to share her apprehension. O'Sondheim was already beginning to glance over his shoulder as if in dread of finding that, for once, there wasn't anything there. She'd be best to put off the moment as long as possible.

Polyaggle moved up to the Pocket next to Strider's and edged her head forwards into it. At once the scene around Spindrift sprang into existence.

Of course, thought Strider, *all this time I've been thinking about us, and more particularly me. Poor Polyaggle has a whole species to think of.* She called up the same image in her own Pocket.

The first thing she saw was that the pink deflector screen was still down. The fleet was forming a sphere around the naked planet. As she watched, yet another ship went up in flames, but there were still hundreds left. In the vista displayed by the Pocket they were just little gleaming needles, but she knew that each of them packed more firepower than anything that had ever been dreamt of on Mars.

It was good, in a way, seeing each one of them being blown to bits, because that meant there was one less that would be able to rain destruction down on Spindrift. The other side of the coin was that the explosion was proof that her Images were still back there among the Autarch's forces. She'd been too blasé about the Images' abilities. Were they invulnerable? For all she knew, they were offering up their lives for the cause of trying to save Spindrift – a cause that Strider was beginning to believe was hopeless.

Words were starting to form in the graphic display behind the likeness of Spindrift and the slowly contracting sphere of cruisers.

SOME OF US WILL SURVIVE, said the display. It seemed to be having great difficulty in forming the letters.

Polyaggle! Deprived of the Images, she was using her Pocket to communicate with Strider's.

Strider looked up at the Spindrifter, who touched her claws together and then returned to concentrate on her own Pocket. Strider took the hint, and bobbed her forehead into the invisibly defined space in front of her.

How many? she thought as hard as she could at the display.

The display appeared to be fighting with itself for some seconds before new letters began to form.

ENOUGH, it said. I HOPE.

Strider kept her own thoughts to the back of her mind. *If you're wrong, sister, you're the last of your kind. And that's something nasty I'm going to have to live with for the rest of my life. Shit, but it's going to be a hell of a lot easier for me than it will be for you . . .* She hoped that nothing of this was being transmitted between the two Pockets. Absently, she shifted the vision in her Pocket to show once more the *Santa Maria*'s progress across The Wondervale.

The graphic display behind the image of the galaxy went through that visually curious process of struggling with itself again.

I AM THE QUEEN OF MY HIVE, the letters said. AND I AM BEARING A NEW BROOD.

Kaantalech's mouth was abrim with joy. The planet was totally exposed to the weaponry at her command. She could see the polar icecaps – now oddly depleted – and the seas and the mountain chains. An aide came to report to her that the Human starship had fled, and she waved him away. The Autarch would never think to ask about the Humans when she made her report of successfully destroying the planet which he had so perceptively identified as a hotbed of rebellion. He would be very pleased with her: he was always pleased to hear of the justifiable demise of another species.

The Humans, the Autarch would think – if he thought about them at all – were a side issue, a single shipful of extragalactics who were of little importance in the grand scheme of things.

Kaantalech hoped that, with luck, they might be of great

importance in removing the Autarch from his throne. To judge by the defences that Spindrift had been able to throw up, the Humans had the knack of making useful friends. As another of her ships spontaneously exploded she yet again thought that the Humans, wherever they had come from, were no mean adversaries. They would make even better allies. Around Qitanefermeartha people were hoping for the day when the Autarch would die. Kaantalech was keen to advance the date. The Humans might be helpful.

But Spindrift wouldn't.

The fleet was almost perfectly in formation.

Kaantalech suspected that the Spindrifters had a bunker somewhere from which military operations were being directed. If she were a Spindrifter, trying to make the world look as unobtrusive as possible, she would have put a military stronghold somewhere in one of the icecaps and covered it in deadmetal so that as little betraying electromagnetic radiation as possible might escape.

If she merely torched the planet, that bunker might escape.

Her other option was to blast Spindrift into a belt of rather small asteroids.

Yes, that was the better thing to do.

She gave the command.

Just over eight minutes later, Spindrift died. And everyone on the world died with it.

3

Polyaggle, the Burden of Guilt
and the Yellow Brick Road

'Wake up, Leonie,' said Pinocchio, shaking her shoulder gently. She looked at him for a moment as if she didn't know who he was, then brought her eyes into focus. She brought the bot to her bed occasionally for reasons of genuine affection or sheer loneliness or just sexual need. Last night she had brought him to her bed for reasons of misery.

Spindrift was dead, and almost every member of its native species along with it. She felt responsible. No matter that Polyaggle might be able to resurrect the Spindrifters as a species, Strider still felt culpable of a sort of inadvertent genocide. Pinocchio had spent long hours trying to talk her out of it, but there was a darkness in her soul that he couldn't reach. All the time, largely through Strider, he was learning more about human beings and, he believed, himself becoming more like them, but this was something he couldn't understand. She had made no mistakes and had committed no sins, yet she was racked by guilt. It was a mystery to him.

'Wake up,' he repeated. 'There is someone who wishes to speak with you.'

Leaning over her, he saw her eyes moisten as a voice spoke inside both of their minds.

WE'RE BACK, said Ten Per Cent Extra Free. AT LEAST, THREE OF US ARE. NIGHTMIRROR HAS BECOME, FOR THE WHILE, PART OF SOMETHING ELSE.

Pinocchio could see Strider struggling to find something to say. She'd spent the past couple of days assuming that the Images were lost to them. The *Santa Maria* had been flitting around The Wondervale with no fixed purpose – which was probably the best way of keeping clear of the Autarchy's forces in the short term but spelt doom in the long. Pinocchio had done his best to stand in for the dead Main Computer when required, but he was no proper replacement for the Images. The *Santa Maria* was currently in orbit around the sterile inner planet of a red dwarf star. With luck, any Autarchy scan of the region would assume the starship was a tiny moon. It had been the best temporary stratagem Strider and Pinocchio had been able to think up between them. But it could never be more than that: temporary.

'Are you injured?' said Strider at last.

NO, ALTHOUGH WE FEEL THE LOSS OF NIGHTMIRROR MOST GRIEVOUSLY. HE WAS OUR FRIEND. NIGHTMIRROR WILL BE OUR FRIEND AGAIN, ONCE HE FINISHES WHAT HE HOPES TO ACCOMPLISH.

'He will live?' said Strider anxiously. She sat up on her bed, looking around the main room of her cabin as if she might be able to see the Image directly.

WE HAVE NO REASON TO EXPECT OTHERWISE, said Ten Per Cent Extra Free, BUT IT IS A SADNESS TO US THAT HE WILL BE ALONE FOR A LONG TIME UNTIL HE CAN DO WHAT HE WANTS TO DO.

'What *is* that? What is it he's trying to do?' Strider was making her way to the shower.

WE DON'T KNOW. HE WAS EQUIVOCAL WHEN HE SAID HIS FAREWELL TO US.

'Polyaggle's Image – is he, or she, prepared to work with us?' said Strider as the pelt of lukewarm water began to massage away the despondencies of what had been a very long night.

OF COURSE. AS ARE THE OTHER SPINDRIFTER IMAGES.

'Others?'

THERE WERE SEVENTEEN IMAGES ON SPINDRIFT WHEN IT WAS DESTROYED. TWO HAVE CHOSEN TO RETURN TO OUR HOME UNIVERSE, BUT THE REMAINDER HAVE DECIDED TO STAY HERE AND TO HELP IN ANY WAY THEY CAN THE EXTINCTION OF THE AUTARCHY. THE IMAGES WERE VERY FOND OF THE SPINDRIFTERS. HEARTFIRE, MYSELF AND THE IMAGE CALLED ANGLER HAVE RETURNED TO THIS STARSHIP. THE OTHERS ARE

ELSEWHERE IN THE WONDERVALE, PREPARED TO WORK NOT SO MUCH AGAINST THE AUTARCHY, ALTHOUGH OBVIOUSLY THAT COMES FIRST, AS AGAINST THE REGIME OF KAANTALECH.

Strider arched her back, feeling the water beat against her belly. 'Kaantalech?'

SHE WILL BE THE NEW AUTARCH.

Ten Per Cent Extra Free seemed unwilling to say anything more.

Pinocchio, standing watching Strider as she showered in the water that was clearly so very luxurious to her, wished he could feel genuine lust for her. Real people would have wanted to pick her out of the spray and carry her back to her bed. At the moment he was wishing he could find some tactful way of saying that he wanted to get to the command deck as soon as possible so that he could start once again gaining direct data from the Images by interfacing with them through the Pockets.

He was uncertain as to what he should do. She obviously wanted him there with her. His duty was to start working with the Images as soon as possible. His prime directive was now to do whatever Strider wanted him to do. At heart she probably wanted him to do whatever was in the best interests of the *Santa Maria*, but all he could interpret from her was that she wished him to be beside her.

He made up his mind.

'I think I should go up on deck,' he said.

'Go, then,' she replied, washing her face. 'I'll join you there soon.'

As Pinocchio ascended in the elevator he thought about what had just happened. He had been guessing too hard about Strider's wishes. She had treated him, once he had made his diffident suggestion, as if he were a human being with a human being's full complement of free will, of independence of thought. Even Strauss-Giolitto was now dealing with him as if he were a human.

Yet he didn't *feel* like a human. There were directives built into his software that forbade him true freedom of thought.

He wasn't certain he liked the position in which he found

201

himself. In a strange way that was rather cheering, because not liking things was a human attribute, was it not?

Lan Yi was glad that the Images had returned, because it meant that Geena had returned as well. No one else on the *Santa Maria* knew that Geena was here. Her presence was a secret between him and the Images.

Once upon a time Lan Yi, then working in Algeria, had been awarded the Nobel Prize for Physics or Chemistry. He had been delighted by the honour, but less so by the gift of two billion dollars in cash: he and Geena were living in the lap of luxury by comparison with the people around them, and so after only a brief debate they had chosen to give the money to charities dedicated to alleviating inner-city suffering. This had not gone down well with the Algerian government, which was going through a phase of declaring that even the poor were happy that the rich were rich. Lan Yi's post at the Institut Chemique d'Algiers had curiously vanished overnight: he was offered a sinecure at a reduced salary, and naturally refused – it would be easy enough for him to find somewhere else in the world to work. But the politicians were truly vindictive: he had never discovered what particular piece of corruption it was that he was supposed to have committed, but the stigma was enough that no scientific establishment would touch him with a bargepole. Except, as he discovered much later, the SSIA, who welcomed him with open arms once he chose to apply.

By that time he was living in poverty in Algiers, deserted by his former friends, surviving on the scraps given to him by kind-hearted shopkeepers. His home was a plastic dustbin which he had stolen in one of the wealthier suburbs: the theft was the only criminal act he was aware of having committed during his life. His and Geena's beautiful white-stone house on the outskirts of Algiers had been possessed by the government on the grounds of non-payment of taxes – a trumped-up charge, but one that was impossible to contest.

By the time he was living as a modern-day Diogenes in a dustbin in the alleys of Algiers, Geena was long dead. Taller than him by half a metre, she had been twenty-two and he

202

ninety-seven when they had married. They had rejoiced in the many differences between them: the contrasts in their builds, their heights, their skin colours, their ages, their skills – she had been a cellist. Sometimes they would stand together half an hour or more in front of the mirror, naked, talking quietly and admiring the comparisons between them.

Persecution by the Algerian government had affected her more harshly than it had him. He had known hunger during his youth; she never had. She could have gone back to her own parents, who were wealthy residents of the southernmost tip of Spain, but she had too much pride for that. Instead, one day when he was out looking for a job as a shelf stacker or a puter noik or a frankly-anything-so-long-as-it-pays, she cut a length from someone's laundry line (she was very well aware of the cost of cello strings, and wouldn't have wasted one), tied in it an exceptionally neat noose, and succeeded in the very difficult task of strangling herself using the ligature. By this time they were living in a one-room apartment; Lan Yi would never forget the sight that greeted him when he returned wearily at the end of the day – Geena, blue-faced, leaning outwards on her knees towards the front door. That she had killed herself was bad enough; that she had chosen to do so in such a personally demonstrative and painful way was a sign that she had grown to hate him.

Many people would never have forgiven her. Instead Lan Yi chose never to forgive himself.

But the Images had brought Geena back to him. To be sure, he hardly ever saw her, but often he was aware of her presence. Sometimes she apologized to him for what she had done and sometimes she berated him for his foolishness in reducing them to the penury that had made her so miserable that death seemed the only way out, but most of the time she was just *there*, which was all he wanted. Often he woke to feel her breath softly against his neck, her body spooned around his. Sometimes, when there was nobody nearby to overhear, he held long conversations with her; he was constantly astonished by the wisdom of her advice.

At other times he wondered about the status of the Geena

with whom he conversed. He knew that she had been conjured back into existence by the Images – but did that make her presence any the less real? Was it the real Geena who had been spun back from the groves of death, or had the Images plucked from his memories a perceived version of Geena? Logic dictated that the latter was the case; experience suggested the former.

FORGET ME, said a voice that was either Geena's or Ten Per Cent Extra Free's.

'I can't,' said Lan Yi, addressing the wall of his cabin. Tears were flowing down his face.

THERE ARE SIX WOMEN ABOARD THIS SHIP WHO WOULD LIKE AN EXCUSE TO FALL IN LOVE WITH YOU. YOU'RE A FASCINAT-ING ANACHRONISM: YOU WERE MARRIED ONCE.

'I don't want to be anybody's curio.'

Lan Yi thought for a moment longer. It had been a hell of a long time since he'd held someone in his arms. The sex part of sleeping together had never seemed as important to him as the stroking and being stroked: he could still feel the velvet of Geena's shoulderblades beneath his fingertips.

'All right.' He sputtered with laughter. 'Just every now and then I don't mind being a curio.'

Geena spoke directly into his mind. YOU'LL BE MY CURIO TONIGHT.

'What I want to do,' said Strider to Pinocchio, 'is to kick the shit so far out of the Autarchy that it reaches orbital velocity. Then I want us to get home.'

'The Spindrifters gave me very considerable information as to how we might get back to the Solar System,' said Pinocchio. 'I have yet to download this. They did not, however, give me enough. Perhaps others of the ancient species might . . .'

They were alone on the command deck except for Poly-aggle, who had chosen to stay there seemingly in perpetuity. Strider had ordered O'Sondheim, Leander and Nelson to go and get some rest; she didn't feel she could issue any orders to Polyaggle, whose species would still be alive were it not for the arrival of the *Santa Maria*.

'What're you waiting for?' said Strider. 'Though I don't know how much I like the idea of visiting other neutral species. Look what happened to the last one.'

She had momentarily forgotten Polyaggle's presence. She bit her lip and wished she could take back the last few words.

'It is possible,' said the Spindrifter, 'that not all of those species may remain neutral now that they have seen what the Autarchy has done to our people.' It was always hard to tell when listening to an alien voice through the medium of the Images, but there didn't seem to be a hint of grief in Polyaggle's words, nor even any desire for vengeance. All she seemed to be concerned about was the preservation of the ancient species, so that one day they could resume the arcadia they had enjoyed before the rise of the secondary peoples. Strider realized that Polyaggle would probably watch the demise of the Humans with complete detachment. Were the other ancient species the same? Was it a product of the Spindrifters' incredible age, as a people, that she could be so dispassionate? Her species must have seen others arrive on the galactic scene and then live out their cycle until eventual extinction. It was important that Strider kept it in mind that the aliens – *all* aliens – thought differently from the Humans. Otherwise there could be a foolish disaster ahead.

'Which of them do you think are the most likely to want to help us?' she said.

Polyaggle touched her claws together. 'Once the bot has downloaded our information I will investigate the remains of your Main Computer to see what can be restored. At that point I will give you my assessment. In the shorter term, Captain Strider, I suggest you would be better advised to establish contact with some of the rebel species.'

'Easier said than done,' remarked Strider. 'We don't have a holophone directory to The Wondervale.'

Polyaggle closed her eyes. Concentration emanated from her like something tangible. Strider watched her, fascinated. For a moment she felt something of the same attraction that she knew Strauss-Giolitto did. Both Nelson and O'Sondheim had reacted to the Spindrifter in the same way. The alien was beautiful: it was not surprising that human beings perceived her as erotic, despite her strangeness.

The Spindrifter opened her eyes again. 'I have been consulting with the Images,' she said. 'I have asked them to make some contacts for you. I would pay attention to your communications Pockets if I were you, Captain Strider.'

Yet again Strider wondered who was in charge of her ship. First the Images and now Polyaggle were taking command decisions for her.

'Don't I have any say in this?'

Strider felt a wave of astonishment from the alien.

'Of course not,' said Polyaggle. 'I know what I am doing. You cannot – you have not lived all your life in The Wondervale, as I have.'

Strider drew a deep breath.

'But I am the captain of this ship,' she said, 'and you are merely a guest. I don't know how you Spindrifters work out – worked out – such things, but we Humans operate on the principle that there's someone who's in charge.' She tried to submerge her anger. 'While you're aboard the *Santa Maria* I'd be grateful if you could operate according to human protocols, not your own.'

Polyaggle looked to Pinocchio. 'Captain Strider is right,' he said.

'This seems very foolish,' remarked the alien. 'Surely everyone should do what is right, without having to be instructed.'

'It's not the way we Humans work,' said Strider. 'We *cooperate* with each other to achieve our best results. And someone has to oversee the cooperation. In this instance it's me. If you have any bright ideas about what we should do, tell me about them so that I can consider them. If I make the wrong decision, shout at me until I make the right one. But don't just go ahead and make decisions on my behalf without asking me first.'

'Your point is understood,' said Polyaggle swiftly – rather too swiftly, Strider decided. 'I will not commit such a discourtesy again. I have much to learn about your mores.'

And that, thought Strider, *sounded like just about the most unconvincing climb-down I've ever heard.*

'Your apology is accepted,' she said formally. She turned her attention back to the Pocket in front of her. The *Santa Maria* continued to orbit the lifeless planet. There was no sign of any alien spacecraft in the vicinity, although Strider didn't know how she would be able to identify it if there were any. Using the tachyon drive, a hostile starship could be right beside the *Santa Maria* without any warning at all. She hoped that the Autarchy had decided the Humans were unimportant – that was the only explanation she could think of for why they had been allowed to flee from Spindrift's moon and why they had been thereafter unmolested.

'I wish to examine your Main Computer,' said Polyaggle.

Pinocchio had finished downloading. 'Feel free,' said Strider, concentrating on the Pocket.

She looked up just in time to see Polyaggle disintegrating into thousands – hundreds of thousands – of disparate parts. The pieces flew with a speed that baffled the eye to form a thin film all over the walls of the command deck: only the floor and the view-window were left uncovered. Then the fragments melted into the walls, so that it was as if Polyaggle had never been.

'Good trick if you can do it,' said Strider to Pinocchio with a shrug. She seemed to have lost the capacity for surprise – too many things had been happening, and too fast. Had Polyaggle proved capable of turning nearby stars into supernovae Strider might have raised an eyebrow. As it was, she just assumed the Spindrifter was some kind of colonial organism, and turned back to her task.

'I cannot,' said Pinocchio, taking the remark literally. 'Can you?'

Kaantalech had of course expected the Humans to run for cover, but also that she would be able to keep an eye on them. Instead it seemed that they had disappeared entirely from the face of The Wondervale. Perhaps they had gone home to wherever it was they had come from – or perhaps, after all, they'd gone on to their mysterious extra-galactic destination, Tau Ceti II. That wouldn't be a complete disaster, but it certainly wouldn't be as good as it could be. She *wanted* the Humans: more precisely, she wanted that technology.

The destruction of Spindrift had been very satisfying. The extirpation of the Spindrifters meant that there was one less species to attempt to counter her efforts once she had assumed the Autarchy. More to the point was the almost orgasmic joy she had experienced on sensing all those lives being extinguished. Even if the act had been unnecessary, it would have been worth it for those few moments.

'*Find them!*' she snapped at an aide, knowing even as she gave the order that it was worthless. The Humans had somehow managed to skip off the edges of the map, again. She wondered if they had had help. The aide gave a snort of salute, then rushed off to do his best to follow Kaantalech's command. There was the faintest of possibilities that he might be able to obey the instruction.

Kaantalech wondered when she should holo the Autarch with a progress report. He would be as delighted as she by the destruction of a supposedly minor world that had proved, instead, to be a technologically advanced potential hotbed of rebellion. On the other hand, he would probably want her to eradicate all the other seemingly insignificant worlds, on the basis that they, too, might one day be a threat to him. She wanted that threat to remain. Kaantalech knew better than the Autarch that many of the neutral worlds of The Wondervale were simply seeking an excuse to strike back against the tyranny. When the right time came – when she occupied the throne in Qitanefermeartha – she would issue orders for those worlds' destruction; she might even give herself the pleasure of leading some of the missions in person. But for the moment she had to play the game carefully.

There is no greater enjoyment than the anticipation of delight to come.

The first thing to do, though, was to find the Humans.

The left-hand communications Pocket surged into life. Pinocchio was nearer to it than Strider.

The creature displaying itself in the Pocket looked – Pinocchio checked his internal databanks – roughly like a terrestrial leech, but it had two blind heads and its slickly wet outer skin was covered with what seemed to be lesions; Pinocchio suspected these were sensory organs of some kind.

He looked over towards Strider. 'We have company.'

'Let me see,' she said.

The thing in the Pocket made a few noises that sounded to her ears like the farts you perform when you are absolutely certain there is no one within earshot. Then Ten Per Cent Extra Free cut in, and the farts became words.

'. . . communication from your Images. We are not seventeen parsecs from your current position, and like yourselves wish to see an end to the Autarchy.'

'Oh, yeah? Prove it.'

'Ask your Images.'

THE PERSON IN THE POCKET IS AN ACCREDITED SPEAKER FOR THE HELGIOLATH, said Ten Per Cent Extra Free. THEIR WORLD WAS TORCHED BY THE AUTARCHY ONE HUNDRED AND FORTY-TWO THOUSAND YEARS AGO, AND SINCE THEN THEY HAVE LIVED NOMADICALLY. YOU CAN TRUST THEM.

'How much?' Strider subvocalized.

IMPLICITLY.

'Do they all look as bad as this?'

YOU'RE ASKING ME TO MAKE A JUDGEMENT ABOUT THE BEAUTIES OF FLESHLY INDIVIDUALS, said Ten Per Cent Extra Free blandly. THE HELGIOLATH LOOK AS GOOD TO ME AS YOU DO YOURSELF, CAPTAIN LEONIE STRIDER.

'Not very, huh?'

I ADVISE YOU TO SPEAK WITH THE SPEAKER, WHOSE NAME IS ANRABH'IT RE'ETLIKA'N ARB'ORTHIA'BBA KORTLAND BUR'CRAN'SKEWGI'LL MEARA'SHEEM'A. HE WILL RESPOND TO THE NAME KORTLAND.

'Thank Umbel for that,' subvocalized Strider. Out loud she said: 'Our Images tell me that you are called Kortland.'

'It is part of my name. You may designate me thus. I would

prefer that you used my entire name, but I understand that it is difficult for your people to pronounce in full.'

'My name is Strider. That's not my full name either, but I'm content to be addressed by it.'

'We already know this. Your Images informed us. They also told us that you have a Spindrifter on board.'

'The last of the Spindrifters,' said Strider. She hated herself for having to say the words. 'The rest of her species is dead.'

'Yeah, I heard about that,' said Kortland easily. 'Ugly lot of buggers though, weren't they?'

'They were sentient beings,' said Strider. 'As you are. As we are.'

'True, there was that to be said for them.'

Strider thought for a moment. 'Just whose side are you on?' she said at last.

'Any side that will see the destruction of the Autarchy.'

'And after that?'

'Then we can go to the safety of the muds of some uncolonized planet. We Helgiolath never wanted to be a spacefaring species. It was something forced upon us.'

Strider wished she could conquer her revulsion and start to learn something of the Helgiolath's body language.

'Why do you think we can help you?' she said.

'We are not especially interested in you Humans, Strider,' said Kortland, 'but your Images could be of considerable assistance to us, as could the Spindrifter. As far as we are concerned, you are useful in that you offer them porterage.'

'That's frank,' said Strider.

'You mean?'

'Truthful. Honest.'

'We are an honest species.'

'Then let me be equally honest in return. I don't want your help under these circumstances.' She hoped that Ten Per Cent Extra Free wasn't transmitting too much of her underlying fury. It was probably a safe assumption. She was receiving no emotion whatsoever from the Helgiolath.

'What have you got to offer us?' said the alien with apparent disinterest.

'We saw off Maglittel.'

'That is exceptionally good news – although your Images told us that in fact it was them who killed it.'

Now Strider was beginning to pick up, through the translation, an emotion – impatience. 'They couldn't have done it without us,' she said.

'That is true.'

'So we're as much a part of the package as they are.'

The alien said nothing for a few seconds.

'That, too, is true,' he said eventually.

'Then hadn't you better stop being quite so frank?' said Strider. 'We may not be as advanced a species as the Helgiolath, but our Images wouldn't have adopted us had we been totally useless. Do me the favour of thinking about that – don't just dismiss the idea out of hand.'

Again there was a pause before the Helgiolath responded. 'I do not understand why we are arguing. You are a single ship, which we wish to aid. I am in command of a fleet of seven thousand six hundred and ninety-two warcruisers and ancillary vessels.'

'Ah,' said Strider.

'So if you would like to join us, you are welcome.'

'I must discuss this with my personnel.'

'That is understood. I shall contact you again shortly.' The communications Pocket went blank.

'What the hell does "shortly" mean?' Strider said to Pinocchio. 'A minute, an hour, a week, a month?'

'Who can tell?' said the bot.

'You're supposed to answer questions, not ask them,' she said.

'Am I?'

She laughed briefly, humourlessly. 'What do *you* think we should do?'

'I think we should join forces with the Helgiolath.'

'Why?'

'Alone, the *Santa Maria* can do nothing except run from the forces of the Autarchy. Sooner or later we'll be caught. But in the middle of the Helgiolath fleet we have a good chance of

211

survival – for statistical reasons if not for any other. And if Polyaggle succeeds in reconstituting enough of the Main Computer we may even be able to make our way back to the Solar System.'

'But can we trust them?' she said, more to herself than to the bot. 'For all we know, the Helgiolath might be just as bad as the Autarchy.'

'They know where we are,' observed Pinocchio. 'If they'd wanted to, they could have blown us out of space by now.'

Strider thought about this. The bot was right. If the *Santa Maria* was going to survive in The Wondervale she was going to have to make alliances. Part of Strider's reluctance to do so came about because of what had happened to the Spindrifters, but also, she recognized, there was more than a trace of xenophobia in her thinking. She knew it was illogical, but the fact that Kortland looked so hideous to human eyes made it difficult to trust the creature.

Not the 'creature'. The 'person'. She had to set herself straight on that. Members of any species capable of mounting a fleet of seven thousand six hundred and ninety-two starships were definitely 'people'. To date the human species had managed to launch exactly one, and in terms of the mission for which it had been designed it had not been exactly a dramatic success. The real question was whether the Helgiolath were good or bad people.

IF YOU DO NOT WISH TO JOIN THE HELGIOLATH, WE IMAGES WILL DO SO INDEPENDENTLY OF YOURSELVES, said Ten Per Cent Extra Free crisply.

The words jolted Strider. 'Can you run that past me again?' she said.

WAR IS NOT AESTHETIC, AND THIS GALAXY IS UNDERGOING A STATE OF PERPETUAL WAR. THIS IS A CONDITION WHICH WE IMAGES WOULD LIKE TO SEE ENDED. THE HELGIOLATH ARE MORE LIKELY TO BRING ABOUT THE DOWNFALL OF THE AUTARCHY THAN IS A SINGLE HUMAN SHIP COMMANDED BY SOMEONE WHO IS INEXPERIENCED IN THE CONDUCT OF SPACE WAR. IT THEREFORE MAKES MORE SENSE FOR US TO ALLY OURSELVES WITH THE HELGIOLATH.

212

'You'd desert us?'

THERE ARE FEWER THAN FIFTY BEINGS ABOARD THIS SHIP. BY ALLYING OURSELVES WITH THE HELGIOLATH WE MIGHT SAVE THE LIVES OF MILLIONS. IN OUR POSITION, WHICH CHOICE WOULD *YOU* MAKE?

'Yeah. OK.' She paced to the far end of the command deck, and then came back again. 'See if you can re-establish contact with Kortland.'

There was a subtle shifting of colours in the communications Pocket, and then she found herself facing the Helgiolath once again.

'You have consulted your people?' said the alien. Kortland seemed even uglier than before.

'No,' said Strider. 'I've consulted a bot and an Image. They've made a fairly convincing case.'

'You will join us?'

'You bet. Give me your co-ordinates.'

'Your Images already know them.'

The myriad entities that were also the single entity of Polyaggle wormed their way through the dead landscape that had once been the consciousness of the Main Computer. There were wastes that could, she knew, never be recovered: they appeared to her like cities that had been nuked, with buildings shattered and fallen and the tang of death in the air. But there were other areas where life clung on. Swarms of her gravitated towards each of them.

Here she infiltrated a subroutine and coaxed it back into some semblance of activity. She felt as if she were a nanobot penetrating the slightest neuron of an almost-dead brain. Elsewhere she was discovering all sorts of kinks in the puter's basic programming, and components of herself were reflexively straightening them out. It was obvious to Polyaggle that the Humans were hardly above basic grade in the construction of artificial intelligences. This largely dead machine had once had just about sufficient intelligence to start repairing the basic design flaws that had been built into it, but little more than that. It seemed to have developed a certain amount of curiosity – the

213

sign of a good puter – but to have been capable of little by way of creative thought. The millions of pieces that were Polyaggle sighed in unison as they worked their way through the turrets and sewers of the Main Computer's software.

Parts of her found a river that was frozen into immobility. On its silver surface there were small ripples with sharp edges. She skidded across the silent water, then nudged the first of the ripples into motion. The little wave broke, and in so doing caused others to break. Soon the river began to flow, albeit reluctantly: for a long time – milliseconds upon milliseconds – ice-floes bumped against the banks as the waters strove for motion. Somewhere far up ahead there was a waterfall that represented the start of a connective thought – a linkage between two remote parts of this thing that had once been a consciousness.

Somewhere else bits of Polyaggle encountered a sand desert that stretched for millions of square kilometres. They discovered that a weed was poking its pale green head through the surface. One of her touched the top of the weed while another blew up a wind, so that seeds were scattered all over the sandy surface. As much as a second was taken up while the weeds grew and died and grew again until a rainforest covered the land. Birds and bats flew between the sweaty trees, feeding on the humming insects. Polyaggle lost two of the particles of herself to the hungry creatures; each time she felt a small agony.

A highway on which the cars were still. Polyaggle touched them, and they began to move.

A nest of ants poised in motionlessness, one of the workers crushed almost flat by the weight of a crumb. A portion of Polyaggle buzzed against the nest and the ants lurched back into industry as if there had been no hiatus. The worker, the crumb on its shoulder, continued its relentless trek towards home.

A man in a laboratory was looking – had been looking forever – through an ultramicroscope at the colloidal solution on the bench in front of him. Suddenly sparks of light began to appear, moving in the drunkard's dance of Brownian motion.

The activity of the sparks brought the man to life. He stood up, punched a button, and watched as the colloid swelled until those dancing sparks were the size of his own eyes. Stripping himself naked, he plunged into the liquid, at last feeling the soft, fondling touch of what, for all his life, he had been able only to observe.

For eternity a woman who believed herself sterile had been watching the slick greenish head of an infant emerging from her vagina. She would have been overjoyed – had she been capable of thought. Now a fraction of Polyaggle touched her belly, urging on the process of creation. The baby shouldered its way through to complete the greatest quest of its life. Another followed. And another. And another. And then there were more. The woman rejoiced as the room filled with babies, piling ten and twelve deep, all screaming for her milk. Still she kept giving birth until the room was full and she was smothered to death by the mass of writhing, mucus-covered flesh.

You lose a few, thought Polyaggle.

The wind that came from out of the rainforest that had once been a desert brought with it locusts which died and fertilized the plains and then seeds which floated mistily down on to them. In pursuit came the birds, many of which also died through starvation and thirst. But other parts of Polyaggle, seeing that there were clouds in the world that was the Main Computer's residual consciousness, winged their way through them, causing raindrops to form. The second wave of birds found green pastures.

Little brown mammals followed.

Satisfied that she had begun a process of evolution within the Main Computer, Polyaggle withdrew.

'Are you there, Geena?' said Lan Yi once again to the empty elevator. He had deliberately stopped it midway between two levels of fields. He needed time to talk this over.

Once again there was no reply from her.

He couldn't believe she had just deserted him like this. Was she punishing him for the times he had wondered about the possibilities of bedding Strauss-Giolitto? No, surely it couldn't be that. Back in the time before she had killed herself she had watched his occasional infidelities with a benign smile.

Lan Yi knew there was something wrong with his thinking. Geena was dead – had been dead for years. Yet since the *Santa Maria* had arrived in The Wondervale his wife had been alive, although it was evident that he was the only person able to see her or hear her. She couldn't be alive: he had seen her corpse in its coffin, and then the cremation of the coffin. So much for logic: he had heard her voice and seen her face, and he had made love with her tenderly and sweetly last night.

Somewhere far beneath the surface his scientist self protested bitterly. Lan Yi ignored the dissident voice.

'Geena?' he said to the vacant elevator.

There was no response, just the emotionless whiteness of the lighting.

Suddenly Lan Yi became aware of how utterly lonely he was. A few metres away from the wall of this elevator was the hull of the ship, and beyond that there was vacuum that stretched out for ever. Somewhere in that vacuum, almost as isolated as he was, a small planet swam through its orbit around a small yellow star. He perceived the distance between them not just in terms of parsecs but in terms of years. He *knew*, too, that there were years and parsecs between himself and Geena. But, at the same time, she had been with him only a few hours ago.

He couldn't stay here for ever. Others would be wanting to use the elevator. Perhaps already there was a posse of techbots on its way to try to find out what had gone wrong with the mechanism. He had to press the release button soon. But he also had to say at least one last goodbye to Geena.

'Speak to me!' he begged, falling to his knees.

The lighting hummed faintly.

'Let's get this boat on the move, then,' said Strider to Ten Per Cent Extra Free.

Within the moment, it was as if all the surfaces of the command deck fell in towards each other in successive waves of coloured, feathery flakes. She put up her arms instinctively

216

to protect her face. Between the bright blue elbows of her jumpsuit she saw the tapestry of Polyaggle stitching itself back into existence. For an instant there was the sensation that iridescent wings filled all of the air; then the Spindrifter was standing in the centre of the command deck as if she had never been away. Her wings collapsed easily in to her sides.

'Nineteen point eight one three seven six recurring of your Main Computer is now functional,' said the Spindrifter, 'and that portion is sufficient to locate for you the wormhole that brought you here.'

'You mean we can get home?' said Strider.

'There is a chance. A good chance.'

Strider thought hard. 'Could you quantify your use of the word "good"?' she said at last.

'Travelling by wormhole is always a risky business because there is never a one hundred per cent certainty where or when you will arrive,' said Polyaggle as if speaking to a slightly backward child, 'but I and the Main Computer estimate that your chances of reaching the Solar System again by this means are in excess of ninety-nine per cent.'

'That sounds pretty good to me,' said Strider. She sat down slowly. 'When can we go?'

'There is one very grave problem.'

'Oh yeah?'

'You are well over a billion parsecs from your home. Establishing timescales over that sort of distance is very difficult.' Polyaggle paused. 'But as far as I can work it out, you seem to be several million years in your own future. The worlds you go back to may not be the ones you left.'

Strider shook her head wearily. 'I'm not sure I understand you.'

'If we successfully located this end of the wormhole, and travelled back through it, it is almost certain that you would discover your culture evolved several million years beyond the point where you left it. Your star would still be alive, of course. It is more questionable whether your culture would be.'

'The human species might be already dead,' said Pinocchio.

'It might indeed,' replied Polyaggle. 'The ancient species in

217

The Wondervale count their ages in billions of years, rather than millions, but our experience has been that the successor species last less long than that. Most destroy themselves within a millennium of achieving interstellar capability.'

'So there's no real way home?' said Strider.

'It depends what you think of as home.'

'We have a tachyonic drive,' said Pinocchio. 'Surely that could take us back.'

Polyaggle said nothing, and Strider immediately realized why. In order to get from place to place using the tachyonic drive you had to know where you were going. String on to that the fact that, apart from Polyaggle herself, the only ones aboard the *Santa Maria* who could operate the tachyonic drive were the Images, who presumably did not want to leave The Wondervale, and the problem became almost insuperable.

Besides, did Strider herself want to leave The Wondervale? Not long ago she had seen an entire species wiped out by the Autarchy. She didn't really understand the motivations that drove Polyaggle, and reckoned she would have had as much difficulty comprehending the imperatives of the Spindrifters as a whole – the Spindrifters had been alien and alien and *alien* – but the species had not set out to exterminate others. The Autarchy, by contrast, was only too happy to do so. There was a war between wrong and right to be fought within The Wondervale. The *Santa Maria* might be able to make only a very small contribution to the winning of that war, but it was a contribution nevertheless. Contrast that against the opportunity of going home . . . no, it wouldn't be going home, because home was not just a place but a time, and the time had seemingly slipped away.

Strider decided what she herself wanted to do: stay in The Wondervale and help the rebels. But it wasn't a decision she could take on her own – she had over forty people under her command, and a majority of them might want to make the break for Mars. She couldn't decide about their lives without asking them first.

'Can you make contact with Holmberg?' she said to Pinocchio.

'I've already done so. He's on his way to the command deck. He will be with us shortly.'

'Shift us to join the Helgiolath fleet,' Strider said to the Images.

Is THIS WISE? said Ten Per Cent Extra Free.

'I don't care if Holmberg wants to take the *Santa Maria* out from under me and try to get it home,' she said. 'I want to see this Autarchy driven from the face of The Wondervale.' She looked at Polyaggle. 'Even if I'm the only human taking part, I want to help avenge the death of the Spindrifters. This is a gamble I choose to take.'

Holmberg looked up through the view-window and felt himself to be a very small fish in a very large shoal. The star they were orbiting illuminated only a minor portion of the Helgiolath fleet, but even so there seemed to be an infinitude of spaceships out there. He knew there were only a few hundred that he could see; Strider had told him that in total there were nearly eight thousand.

'Most of the personnel want to try to get home,' he said a few hours later.

'And they want to take the *Santa Maria* with them?' said Strider.

'Is there any other way?'

'Not that I can think of.'

'I want to stay here,' said Strider. 'I think there are a few accounts that have to be settled.'

'I agree with you. I myself voted to stay in The Wondervale.'

She looked at him in amazement. 'I never thought of you as a natural-born revolutionary.'

'I've represented the personnel as well as I could. That doesn't mean I don't have opinions of my own. Perhaps we could help these people.'

'Who else wants to stay here?'

'Very few.'

'Any names?'

'You. Me. Lan Yi, for reasons I can't quite understand,

219

although he explained them to me in detail – the chance of carrying out a scientific investigation of the physiological construction of the Spindrifter appears to be a large part of it. Umbel Nelson. Maloron Leander. Maria Strauss-Giolitto, somewhat to my surprise. That's about the strength of your support, Captain Strider. Oh, yes, and the bot.'

'That's a very big "Oh, yes",' said Strider absently. 'He'll probably be more use to the Helgiolath than the rest of us put together.' She ran the fingers of one hand back through her hair. 'What do you think we should do?'

She found it odd talking with Holmberg this way. Ever since the *Santa Maria* had left Phobos the man had been her bane, except for that one moment when he had declared himself – improbably – to be her ally, and she had believed him. Now they were reclining naked in the bath in her cabin. His pink stomach protruded above the surface of the water. It was as good a place as any to discuss this. In a vague way she would have preferred him to have had an erection – as a sign of respect, as it were.

'You say that Polyaggle has reconstituted much of the Main Computer – enough that the *Santa Maria* might be able to find its way home,' he said.

'That's what she tells me. The Images agree.'

'I think we ought to let the *Santa Maria* go home,' said Holmberg. 'O'Sondheim could take over as captain, surely?'

'You mean I should desert my ship?'

Holmberg splashed his chest with water, then reached for the soap. 'One alternative is that you desert all the sentient species of The Wondervale. Another is that you get yourself and the ship back home but leave me and Nelson and the rest behind.'

'How safe do you think the *Santa Maria* would be?' she said. She pulled a knee up to her face for inspection. Dammit, somewhere along the line she'd picked up a bruise. She wondered when that had happened. 'I have a responsibility to my personnel, after all. A very heavy responsibility.'

'Can I be blunt?'

'You're normally more than that.'

Holmberg laughed. 'I'm not really qualified to judge, but I

think the *Santa Maria* has every bit as good a chance of making it home safely under O'Sondheim's captaincy as it would have under yours.'

She'd been long enough in the bath. The skin of her fingers was beginning to crinkle as the water cooled. She stood up, making waves that smacked Holmberg under the chin. Again she found herself slightly annoyed that her nakedness was having no effect on him. On the other hand, she suddenly reflected, *his* nakedness was having no particular effect on *her*. Even so, her confidence could have done with a dose of atavism right now.

'Oh, yeah,' said Holmberg, washing an armpit. 'I forgot to mention. There's a kid – a little boy – who wants to stay here as well.'

Towelling herself, she stared at him. 'We can't take a kid along. What about his mother?'

'She's dead. When you put five gees on the craft she was standing by her bunk. She fell and broke her neck on the edge of it. The medbots couldn't get there in time to help her.'

Oh great, thought Strider, *something else to be guilty about. I've created an orphan.* No matter how much she tried to rub herself dry, the area between her shoulderblades still stayed wet. She seemed to be on the verge of throwing away the chance of ever seeing Mars again. If what Holmberg had said was true, only a few of them would be joining the Helgiolath. Half a dozen human beings and a humanoid bot living in a community of beings that looked bad enough to make you want to turn away. Umbel alone knew how they smelt.

'I'd like to fight in this war,' she said, working the corner of the towel into her left ear. 'The funny thing is, I'd sort of assumed that you'd try to stop me.'

Holmberg seemed to have found something fascinating in his navel. He was picking at it with a fingernail. 'Why should you think that?'

'Well, you've been a bit of a difficult sod.'

'So have you.' Whatever it was that he'd been trying to scoop out now seemed at last to have come adrift. 'This is the

221

biggest adventure of my life. I don't want to go home now with my tail between my legs.'

Strider climbed into her jumpsuit. Her back still felt wet. 'You're not the man I thought you were, Marcial.'

'I know. I've spent several years living with your opinion of me, and it hasn't been the best of times.' He looked up at her with steady eyes. 'Ever since this mission started it's been my duty to represent the personnel whose opinions you've far too often ignored, Leonie. I've told you before, but you didn't properly listen. Now it's time I started to take a few decisions on my own behalf.'

She watched his bloated body as he sank himself further into the bathwater. 'You've been shamming.'

'Shamming about what?'

'About how things should be run aboard this ship.'

'To tell you the truth,' said Holmberg, 'I think most of the people on the *Santa Maria* should have been left back at home. Have you got any nail-scissors?'

'Why do you say that?'

'Because I want to cut my toenails.'

'No – I mean why do you say most of the personnel should have been left behind?'

'Because they're useless. If I'd been setting up this expedition for the SSIA I'd have made the crew no more than a dozen strong, and more likely half that.'

'Hardly enough to colonize a planet,' she said.

'My opinion, for what it's worth,' said Holmberg with exaggerated gravity, 'is that the first colony on any planet is doomed, no matter how many people are involved. There are going to be diseases – remember that killer diseases used to wipe out people by the hundreds of thousands? There are going to be creatures that want to eat us – not so much the big ones, which we can always laz if we're fast enough to see them coming, but the little ones, which we don't notice until it's too late.'

'So why,' said Strider, pausing by the door, 'did you come along?'

222

'Because I wanted to.' He smiled at her. 'The stars are the final frontier, aren't they?'

His smile faded.

'Look, Leonie, I don't care what the rest of you decide to do. I want to join the Helgiolath. I want to help this poor bloody galaxy get itself out of the mess it's got into. Like Lan Yi, I want to see what happens when Polyaggle gives birth to her new brood. I want to be there when the Autarchy commander who decided to destroy Spindrift is suddenly faced by a fleet a million strong.'

'Yeah, that's what I want to do as well. But . . .'

'But *what*? Let the *Santa Maria* go, Leonie, if that's what you really want to do. You've faced far more than you were ever expected to.'

She ran a finger down the side of her nose. 'So just the bunch of us stay here, huh? I dunno – just thinking about it makes me feel like I'm betraying the people under my command.'

'I don't think that's the way they'd see it.' Holmberg drew in his breath. 'When it comes down to it, Leonie, the blunt truth is that most of the people on board don't give a damn who's running the command deck so long as they're doing it efficiently and, above all, unobtrusively.'

Strider shrugged. 'I'm going to make my mind up later.' Once more she started to leave, then turned back. 'How come you're so keen for glory yourself, Marcial? You've never struck me as being that type.'

'I'm the last of a family of Reals. When I was fifteen we lived in Baghdad, where virtually everyone else was an Artif – hell, Leonie, we were unusual in being a family at all. One day my father got a bit stoned on ziprite and started telling all the people in the café he was in that Artiffing was immoral – that there was very good reason why we were all given just a single life. In the end they dragged him out into the street and drove a truck backwards and forwards over him.'

'I'm sorry. I didn't know that.'

'Then they came to our house and found my mother and my sister and did the same to them.' Holmberg began to climb out of the bath. 'It's OK to talk about it now. It was a long time ago, and most of the pain has gone. I was lucky – I was on the other side of town trying to make it with a girl whose name I can't now remember but who seemed very important at the time. What I *can* remember is getting home and discovering I didn't have a family any more. Toss over a towel, will you? Thanks. Polyaggle lost far more than a family on Spindrift. She doesn't seem to feel it the way you and I would, but I want to help right the wrong on her behalf, if I can. And there's not very much the good old human species – present company excepted, of course – has left to offer me. Any more explanations wanted?'

Despite his denial, she sensed that all this was a painful area for him. 'No. Thanks for – well, for opening yourself to me this way.'

'Even if I find I'm the only human being left in The Wondervale, I want to be here.' He grinned at her. 'I'm perfectly accustomed to loneliness.'

Looking at the Helgiolath was never going to be easy, Strider thought for what seemed like the thousandth time. The faces of Kortland – assuming they *were* actually faces – were in the communications Pocket now. Strider steeled herself not to turn her gaze off to the side.

'We've discovered how we might be able to get this ship home,' she said, 'but a few of us have decided we want to stay here in The Wondervale and help you people as best we can. Will you allow us to do that?'

Kortland didn't answer immediately. 'I think it may be possible,' he said after a while. 'There are difficulties.'

'Such as?'

'The air we breathe has less oxygen than you are accustomed to. If any of you want to live aboard one of our vessels, either you'll have to bring your own environment or you'll require surgical modification.'

Strider gulped. The thought of remaining suited up for the rest of her life was an unpleasant one. The thought of 'surgical modification' was not particularly attractive either. She didn't like the idea of Helgiolath surgeons poking around in her entrails.

224

'The modification would be neither painful nor gross,' Kortland was saying. 'It is a very common procedure. I have myself undergone it several times when it has been necessary to meet other species face to face.'

'What sort of modification are we talking about?' No way was Strider going to spend her remaining days looking like a Helgiolath.

'Your lungs would require alteration. The bacterial infrastructure of your body would need to be changed. The outer surfaces of your eyes would be toughened. There would need to be some minor brain surgery to alter a few of your sensory impressions, notably your sense of smell – and there'd almost certainly be a few trivial changes to your own bodily chemistry as well. Species of utterly different forms, as yours is to ours, normally stink intolerably to each other.'

Yeah. Strider could imagine that Kortland and his kind would stink. It hadn't occurred to her that the same might be true the other way round.

'This doesn't sound like minor surgery to me,' she said.

'The practices are well established,' said Kortland. Ten Per Cent Extra Free was introducing a touch of weariness to the alien's voice. 'We have machines that routinely perform such tasks.'

'I need to think about this. I need to talk it all over with the few of us who want to join you.'

'Please don't be too long.' She could sense that Kortland was becoming utterly exasperated with her. 'Your assistance is not very important to us. In fact, to be frank – to use your word again – your presence among us would be more of a nuisance than a help. But we're prepared to put up with that if we can have your Images and the Spindrifter as well.'

'I have a better idea,' said Strider. 'Give me a moment.'

'Granted.'

'Listen here, Ten Per Cent Extra Free,' she subvocalized.

I'M LISTENING. I COULD HARDLY BE DOING ANYTHING ELSE.

'You and the others have already done a lot to the *Santa Maria*. What more could you do to it?'

A GREAT DEAL.

225

'Could you turn it into the best fucking fighting vessel in The Wondervale?'

WE COULD MAKE IT A GOOD FIGHTING VESSEL. WE ARE UNABLE TO GIVE IT THE POWER OF PROCREATION.

'Then we stay here and fight. Damn what the personnel want to do. We can go home later.'

THIS WILL NOT BE A POPULAR MOVE.

'I don't care.'

VERY WELL.

'How long will it take?'

FOUR HOURS.

Strider put her forehead back into the communications Pocket. 'Within four hours you'll have an extra warcruiser,' she said to Kortland. 'Our Images will transform it within this time. Can you wait that long?'

'Possibly. Probably. Yes.'

IT WOULD BE BEST IF YOU AND YOUR PEOPLE WERE UNCONSCIOUS WHILE THE TRANSFORMATION IS BEING EFFECTED, said Ten Per Cent Extra Free.

'We make contact again in four hours,' Strider told Kortland.

'Agreed.'

The Helgiolath's semblance vanished from the communications Pocket.

'What do you want me to do?' Strider impatiently asked the Image. 'Go all over the ship knocking everyone over the head?'

THAT WILL NOT BE NECESSARY. I AM SPEAKING WITH PINOCCHIO AT THE SAME TIME AS SPEAKING WITH YOU AND EXPLAINING TO HIM WHAT WE ARE ABOUT TO DO. HE ALONE WILL BE AWARE OF IT ALL. AS FOR POLYAGGLE AND YOU HUMANS,

YOU HAVE BEEN UNCONSCIOUS FOR THREE HOURS AND FIFTY-THREE MINUTES.

Strider slumped by the communications Pocket. There had been no sensation of the passage of time at all, yet her mouth tasted the way it always did when she had just woken up from sleep. She rolled her tongue over her upper front teeth, feeling their griminess.

'That's it?' she said.

THE TASK HAS BEEN PERFORMED.

She moved to an adjacent Pocket and called up into it a representation of the *Santa Maria*.

'Oh hell,' she said.

The craft she was looking at was virtually unrecognizable. The *Santa Maria* had been designed for the mission it was intended to accomplish. It had not been pretty or sleek: it had been competent, if perhaps clumsily so. The Images had modified it so that it looked a little better and had been able to make planetfall, but still the *Santa Maria* had not been a truly elegant craft. Now it was an altogether different fish. It looked like a long dart, complete with tail feathers – in fact, it looked much like one of the Helgiolath warcruisers that formed the fleet among which the *Santa Maria* floated. It was visibly a creature designed purely for space: planetfall was no longer an option.

'What have you done?'

WHAT YOU ASKED US TO DO.

The command deck itself had changed. The Pockets were still there, but in front of each of them there was now an elaborate keyboard. She looked down at the one before her and realized that she could understand not just the conventional Argot symbols on the keys but also all of the others. This one here would open one or other of the blisters on the side of the *Santa Maria*, the blister concerned being determined by the use of other keys. Two of the blisters still contained shuttles; the others were each armed with twenty-three missiles of various types. Twenty-three seemed a perfectly natural number for the Images to have chosen, and then she remembered . . .

'It's not just the *Santa Maria* you've modified, is it?' she said. 'You've modified *us* as well.'

THAT WAS AN ESSENTIAL PART OF THE ALTERATION YOU ASKED US TO MAKE. YOU ARE COMPONENTS OF THE WARSHIP.

Strider could feel the difference. It was as if her blood were coursing more swiftly through her arteries. She drew herself up

227

to her full height, reached out her arms to either side and slowly clenched her fists. She felt *stronger*. And *faster*.

'These aren't just illusions I'm sensing, are they?' she said.

NO. WE'VE IMPROVED YOU. ALL OF YOU PEOPLE.

'Polyaggle? Pinocchio?'

WE'VE ADDED A LITTLE BULK TO POLYAGGLE'S BODY SO THAT SHE'S LESS FRAIL, BUT THERE WASN'T MUCH WE COULD DO WITHOUT TAKING AWAY HER ABILITY TO FLY. PINOCCHIO WE COULD NOT FURTHER ALTER USEFULLY. WE PROPOSED TO BUILD WEAPONS INTO HIM, BUT HE REFUSED US – WE WOULD HAVE VIOLATED ONE OF THE PRIME IMPERATIVES OF HIS SOFTWARE.

The communications Pocket lit up. Strider expected to see Kortland there, but instead there was an utterly different creature. This one looked somewhat like a tuskless woolly mammoth. 'Will you speak to me?' said the face.

'Who is this?' Strider subvocalized.

A SERVANT OF THE AUTARCH.

'My name is Kaantalech,' said the face in the Pocket.

GET RID OF HER!

'How?'

JUST WALK AWAY. YOU MUST CONTACT KORTLAND AT ONCE. IF KAANTALECH HAS TRACED YOU HERE THEN THE WHOLE OF THE FLEET IS IN DANGER.

It was difficult to imagine a fleet of seven thousand six hundred and ninety-two warcruisers – no, ninety-three, now that the *Santa Maria* was a part of it – being in any danger, but Strider took Ten Per Cent Extra Free's word for it.

IT WAS KAANTALECH WHO MURDERED SPINDRIFT.

'Then I wish to continue this conversation.' Strider subvocalized. To Kaantalech she said: 'What do you want of me?'

'Just a few moments. There are many ways in which we could help each other.'

'Name two.'

'I know where you are. I know that you are in the midst of a rebel force which the Autarchy will soon take pleasure in destroying. I could spare you and your people. I have that power.'

228

'That's one.' Strider spoke with deliberate flatness. This was the *thing* that had virtually wiped out the Spindrifters. It was difficult to know if one could actually be a friend of Polyaggle, but Strider felt that way towards her. The Spindrifters had done nothing to deserve to be wiped out. Leaning into the communications Pocket, she focused hatred on the creature.

'You yourself could be raised to a position of considerable eminence within the Autarchy,' said Kaantalech, clearly sensing nothing of Strider's feelings.

'I'm not interested.'

'It would seem such a waste to kill you all. Both the Autarch and I are eager to know where you have come from. We do not believe that you are from Heaven's Ancestor.'

'So that you can go and massacre the rest of my kind? So that you can conquer another galaxy?'

Kaantalech made a little pooting noise that Ten Per Cent Extra Free was unable to translate. 'You misjudge our motives. The Autarchy dominates The Wondervale because otherwise there would be anarchy and starvation.'

'The Spindrifters won't be starving to death,' said Strider drily.

'Precisely,' said Kaantalech, obviously missing the point.

SHE DOESN'T KNOW THAT POLYAGGLE IS HERE, said Ten Per Cent Extra Free. IF SHE DID SHE WOULD DESTROY THE *SANTA MARIA* WITHOUT A SECOND THOUGHT. KAANTALECH DOES NOTHING BY HALF MEASURES. CAPTAIN LEONIE STRIDER, I BEG THAT YOU DESIST FROM SPEAKING WITH HER. YOU NEED TO WARN KORTLAND.

'Can't Pinocchio do that?'

I HAVE ASKED PINOCCHIO TO COME TO THE COMMAND DECK FOR EXACTLY THIS PURPOSE. BUT THE WARNING SHOULD COME FROM YOU, YOURSELF – KORTLAND KNOWS WHO YOU ARE. HE DOES NOT KNOW PINOCCHIO.

'The only thing I would enjoy more than seeing you die,' said Strider to Kaantalech's semblance in the Pocket, 'would be seeing you die very slowly. Even better would be watching you rot in some dungeon somewhere. You murdered an entire species.'

229

'We put it out of its misery,' said Kaantalech.

'It *had* no misery, as far as I can gather.'

'If that is your feeling, I see little option but to put you Humans out of your misery as well, along with the Helgiolath foulness.'

Strider thought swiftly. Most of the people aboard the *Santa Maria* had not elected to stay here in The Wondervale. She had responsibilities towards them. She had very little doubt that Kaantalech could put most of her threats into effect, if the occasion arose – at least so far as the *Santa Maria* was concerned. Strider thought it less likely that the creature could so easily tackle the Helgiolath fleet – otherwise the Autarchy would presumably have done it long ago. However vast The Wondervale was and however adept the Helgiolath were at concealing their whereabouts, it was difficult to keep an armada of nearly eight thousand vessels secret.

'Don't ring me,' she said. 'I'll ring you.'

'You turn down my offer?'

'Too damn right.'

'I sorrow for you.'

'Sorrow away.'

Strider retreated from the communications Pocket and it faded into blankness. 'Where's Pinocchio?'

HE'S ON HIS WAY.

'Boot up the Pocket so that I can speak with Kortland.'

AS YOU WISH.

Strider didn't bother with any formalities. 'We're with you,' she said as soon as the leech-faces of the alien appeared in front of her. Quickly she told Kortland about the conversation with Kaantalech.

'We must move the fleet,' said Kortland promptly.

'That had occurred to me too, yeah.'

'Please load these co-ordinates into the remains of your Main Computer.' The alien gave a string of noises which were incomprehensible to Strider, but nevertheless she found her fingers were moving obediently across the keyboard in front of her. She felt a surge of energy far behind her in the *Santa Maria*.

And then everything changed.

Darkness, and the stench of decay. Loneliness. No stars in the sky, wherever the sky had gone to. She lifted her face above the surface of the rank sludge and tried to breathe, but all she did was drag some of the mud up her nostrils and into the back of her throat. She coughed for air, and at last her lungs were rewarded. Strider ran one hand down her own side. As far as she could tell she was entirely naked. She flexed her toes and felt the mud squidge between them.

She managed to get on to all fours just before a heavy foot came down with crushing force on her back, thrusting her face-first into the mud once more.

A moment later everything was different again.

She felt as if she were being turned inside out, so that her raw flesh was being exposed to the blaze of a million stars. She saw the brilliance of their light so vividly that she experienced it as pain, as if it were fire burning against her flesh. The radiance was bright enough that she was seeing it not only with her eyes but with the whole of her body. She had never known such agony. She would have preferred to have had her face stuck back into the inky darkness and the sludge.

And then again she was somewhere else, floating free in space, looking at the grey-white disc of a lifeless planet or moon. For a second or two she felt nothing but relief – weightless, painless, it seemed to her that she was dancing through the vacuum. Then she realized that she was still naked, and that her skin was peeling away in strips and her eyes were bulging as they struggled to escape from their sockets. The pain returned, this time like two blades of ice being thrust up through the soles of her feet to meet somewhere around her heart.

Yet again a shift of perception. Her hands and feet were tied together behind her back, and someone unseen was tightening the bonds. Her spine strained in the reverse curve, and she could feel the vertebrae pulling slowly but inexorably apart. There was a ripping sound as the skin of her belly rent itself asunder, setting her entrails free . . .

231

Crammed into a tight tin too small for her even to breathe. Nevertheless she dragged a breath, smelling her own sweat and the last piss she had had. The tin was getting smaller, crunching her shoulderblades, forcing her face into her knees.

And then freedom again. The atoms of her body were co-extant with the Universe. Her eyes were expanding gaseous nebulae left in the aftermath of supernovae. Her nipples were galactic clusters. The length of her body was the fabric of spacetime, all-encompassing and all-embracing. She was the goddess who was also all of eternity. Through her would be born every living thing that the Universe would ever see. She roared with triumph at each moment of parturition. She was the birthing of all things, way back when the Universe was nothing more than a thought written across emptiness and timelessness.

And then she was none of this. She was being very loudly and messily sick on the floor of the command deck of the *Santa Maria*.

She hauled herself up on to her haunches. A cleanerbot would sweep up the mess. Damn it, there *must* be a cleanerbot somewhere around. The stink of her own sick almost made her retch again, but there was nothing left to vomit.

She staggered to a Pocket and called up the representation of the *Santa Maria*'s position. The ship was still in the midst of the Helgiolath fleet. She looked up through the view-window and saw sparkles of confirmation swimming against the stars. Moving to a communications Pocket, she tried to contact Kortland, but it was impossible. The best part of eight thousand other ship commanders were presumably trying to do the same. Had they *all* gone through the nightmare she had just had? Maybe to a Helgiolath it wasn't a nightmare but a welcome temporary reminder of the glories of the mud.

She shivered. How had her personnel taken this? Had they shared the experience? She slipped a commlink into her mouth.

'We are perfectly safe . . .'

The sound of Maria Strauss-Giolitto screaming jarred Lan Yi from his sleep. He threw open the door of his own cabin and began to sprint towards hers.

He was halfway there when he realized that everything was utterly different. The shape of the space around him was all wrong. He paused, and looked upwards. Thirty or forty metres above him there was a shiny metal ceiling. The elevators were still there, but they were far nearer to him. The cabins themselves were much more closely clustered together than they had been. The air smelled of oil and electricity; before, it had smelled of the contents of the fields. The light was a slightly bluish glare.

Strauss-Giolitto was still screaming. There was no other sound.

He discovered that he was at the door of her cabin. The plastite looked less and less like wood as time wore on. Lan Yi tugged open the door and saw Strauss-Giolitto lying on her forcefield bed, her mouth in her hands. Her eyes were wide open but it was obvious that they saw nothing except the visions that her mind was creating.

He moved to her side and put his arm around her shoulders. They were slithery with cold sweat.

'Wake up,' he said. 'Wake up.'

Her shrieking became more muted, but would not stop. Her staring blue eyes turned briefly towards him and for a moment it seemed that she might have recognized him, but then all intelligence vanished from them. He stroked the soft fuzz of hair on her head, wishing that he could do more to help her than just mutter soothing nonsense words.

Her body suddenly twisted, as if she had been kicked in the back by some colossal force. The blow threw her at him so hard that he was smashed down on to the floor, with her on top of him. His head hit hard. The impact drove the breath out of his lungs, and for a moment he almost lost consciousness: intriguing lights and sounds, none of them making very much sense, filled his mind.

Reality returned. He pushed himself out from under Strauss-Giolitto. She was no longer screaming but weeping sound-lessly, as if in the extremes of pain. Snot was running from her nose; he wiped the clear liquid away with a finger. He looked at her body as it writhed on the floor, then at the forcefield bed. There was no possibility of his being able to lift her up there.

He slapped her face lightly, hoping to shock her out of whatever trance she was in. There was no response. He made to strike her again, then held back. She seemed to be suffering misery already: no need for him to add to it.

He became steadily more aware that there was no sound at all from any of the other cabins. Usually there would be something – the din of a holo or a musibot turned up too loud, the noise of voices raised in argument, a kid yelling about a stubbed toe.

Standing, he looked down at Strauss-Giolitto. There didn't seem to be anything he could do except wait for her to waken from her nightmare. Whether she would want him to be there when she did was a question he couldn't answer.

Lan Yi dithered. The fact that the *Santa Maria* had changed so dramatically was something he ought to investigate. He should also try to find out why it was that the other cabins were so oppressively silent. The life of a single person was of little significance if the whole of the ship were at risk.

Making a rapid decision, he left Strauss-Giolitto's cabin and walked quickly to the nearest elevator, glancing up frequently towards the new ceiling. The metal was reflective enough for him to see himself like a small rodent moving among the cabins. Why was no one else awake? Why had no one else responded to Strauss-Giolitto's screams?

The elevator was a long time in coming.

As he waited for it he wondered if he were the last person alive on the *Santa Maria*. Surely not: certainly Pinocchio would have survived. Or maybe not, because whatever had happened was just as likely to damage the bot's artificial brain as it was to throw Strauss-Giolitto into seeming madness.

Finally the elevator arrived. He pressed the pad for the command deck.

And found himself back in Strauss-Giolitto's cabin. She was stiller than she had been, but otherwise there was little change. For the first time since this had begun it occurred to him that he

234

was looking at an exceptionally attractive woman. He whipped the thought aside and once more headed for the elevator.

This time it came more quickly, but again he found himself back in Strauss-Giolitto's cabin the moment after he had pressed for the command deck.

Perhaps her need is the greater, he told himself.

Bending his knees, he grappled her shoulders and struggled to take her weight. The edge of the forcefield bed seemed an impossibly large distance above him. Somehow he got her into a sitting position. She was still sobbing silently, but the expression of agony had gone from her face. He waved a hand in front of those wide-open eyes but there was no sign of recognition. Moving around the other side of her forcefield bed, he hoisted her up by her armpits. Her body seemed to be glued firmly to the floor. He dragged again, and this time got at least her torso on to the bed. Straining himself until he thought he might pass out, he heaved once more, and this time her buttocks moved easily on to the softly glowing surface. One of her breasts brushed the inside of his elbow; it might have been erotic had she brushed it there herself, deliberately, but as it was he felt no more than slight exasperation – her impedimenta were getting in the way of what he was trying to do.

Moving again around the forcefield bed, he lifted her legs on to it. She was at a diagonal angle across the bed, her head hanging over the far edge. He did his best to try to straighten her body out. She must mass at least fifty per cent more than he did.

Her eyes closed. He hoped that this meant that she had fallen into real sleep, rather than whatever it was that she had been experiencing.

For a third time he ran to the elevator. Now it refused to respond to his call. He beat the side of his hand repeatedly against the pad, but nothing happened.

The elevator two hundred metres away likewise declined to appear for him. It didn't seem worth trying another.

He was increasingly unnerved by the almost-silence. There were still faint sounds from Strauss-Giolitto's cabin, but everywhere else there was nothing. He hadn't realized until now how much a part of the environment within the *Santa Maria* the insects and birds were. Yet again he looked up at the ceiling, seeing himself looking back.

He stopped at the next cabin he came to and nervously opened its door. All the holohorrors he had ever watched told him this was the wrong thing to do. When there's a preternatural silence you shouldn't be opening doors, because on the other side of them you'll inevitably find nasties. Much better to run like fuck.

Except that Lan Yi had nowhere very far to run.

The forcefield bed in the cabin had fallen to the floor. The glow of the forcefield was absent. There was dust everywhere, as if no one had been in here for a decade, or a century. Carefully moving his foot aside so that he did not step on the desiccated corpse of a spider, Lan Yi went through to the further rooms. He was less worried now about horrors, more concerned that he was trespassing – as if he were deliberately trampling on someone's grave.

The bathroom was empty, although the bath itself was full. He dipped his fingers into the water and found it hot. He flushed the lavatory, just to reassure himself that something around here still worked normally. He was back in the cabin's main room before it registered on him that yes, the damned gadget had done its stuff.

The little kitchen was likewise deserted. It was perfectly clean and dustless, as if its owner had scrubbed every surface carefully before departing.

This wasn't like the personnel aboard the *Santa Maria*. The joys of rediscovering plenteous clean water and safely edible food after a lifetime of Earth's pollution or Mars's shortages made most of them profligate with the stuff – had turned them into slobs. There should have been some scraps lying around, unless the cleanerbots had got here first. But if that had been the case the bots would have cleared all the dust out of the main room.

He checked the next cabin and found things very much the same, although the bath was empty. As he left the little building Lan Yi sang a few notes from Donizetti's *Maria Stuarda* just to

236

make himself feel that he wasn't the only person left alive. Then he remembered how Mary Stuart had come to her end and the song stilled in his throat.

Four more cabins went by. Could it be that Strider had called everyone up to the command deck? No – that didn't make any sense. If that had been the case there'd still have been junk left lying around – half-eaten meals or kids' toys or *anything*. Instead, everywhere he looked there was this bizarre mixture of utter cleanliness and a mess that betrayed all the signs of years having passed.

'Is there anyone there?' he yelled. The only replies were echoes.

Lan Yi squatted down on his lean haunches for thirty seconds or so and looked all around him. He knew this wasn't just a rotten dream – he was always aware of it when he was dreaming.

Just as he was getting to his feet again he heard a tiny sound. There was a whir as something rubbed against something else, and a small human grunt of effort. Infuriatingly, the noise stopped just before he could locate where it had come from.

Then he heard it again. It had come from one of the nearby cabins.

Hilary, playing with a spinning top, looked up as Lan Yi appeared in the doorway.

'Why didn't you answer when I called?' the out-of-Taiwanese asked, not sure if he was angry with the child or relieved that at last he'd found someone else alive. He softened his tone. 'Are you all right?'

'I'm perfectly fine,' said Hilary, 'except I can't get this bleeding top to stay upright, no matter how hard I try. Could you help me?'

Something drastic had happened to the *Santa Maria*, Lan Yi knew, but right now it seemed as if getting the kid's top to work was more important: big tragedies can be put out of your mind for a while, but small ones are more immediate.

He went down on his knees beside the boy. 'The trick is,' he said, 'to wind the cord very accurately and neatly around the

237

spindle. Oh,' he added, picking with his fingernails, 'and it's a good idea not to get knots in the string.'

'Where has everyone else gone?' said the boy. 'I'm getting hungry.'

'I'm not sure,' said Lan Yi. 'Apart from you and me, the only other person around seems to be your teacher.'

'Maria?'

'Yes.'

'Oh, that's OK then. I like *her*.' Hilary gave the cord a sharp tug and this time he got the top to spin rapidly. It waltzed away across the floor of the cabin, made an astonishing dart under the forcefield bed, and hit the far wall with a clatter. 'Could you wind it up again?'

'I think you had better come with me. I want to check up on Maria. She wasn't in very good shape when I left her. Bring the top with you if you want to.'

Hilary fetched the toy. It was obvious that Lan Yi was being boringly and disgustingly *adult*. Also, both he and Lan Yi had been here before: there had been some trouble, and Lan Yi had come along with Maria to rescue him from it. It had happened so long before that Hilary could remember it only as if it had been part of a dream. The child's face was telling Lan Yi that the best way of coping with a nightmare that keeps coming round and round again was to ignore it. One method of ignoring it was to perform displacement activity – like spinning a top. It was as good a way as any.

Was Lan Yi in Hilary's dream, or was Hilary in Lan Yi's?

Dream. Not-dream. It didn't matter. This was the reality with which Lan Yi was trying to grapple.

'You can play with the top in Maria's cabin, if you want to,' said Lan Yi as he took Hilary's hand. 'It might even help her. Even if it doesn't, I want the three of us to be close together.'

'Yeah, I guess that's OK,' said Hilary. His mother had kitted him out in a miniature replica of the standard-issue SSIA jumpsuit. Lan Yi wondered where Hilary's mother and her seamstress skills had gone to. He had a sudden vision of himself as a surrogate mother, and didn't like it at all. Geena would have been an excellent mother, but it had never happened; perhaps that was one of the reasons why she had died. 'When you have a cello, who needs a brat?' she had often said, and he'd believed her. 'They say that Kiliostrov's Second Concerto is more difficult than labour pains, particularly the pizzicato bits,' she'd said, 'but a lot more rewarding when you get it right.' He'd believed her then, as well. 'And a cello costs less,' she'd said one night in Algiers, 'except when an effing string breaks. Lan, there's this place down by the river that stays open late. Do you think you could . . . ?'

And he'd taken the money that had been going to be a bottle of rosehip juice and bought her a new string. Maybe that was something else that had turned her away from life – the lack of the rosehip juice one night. He'd never know.

Lan Yi deliberately walked at a child's pace as they went towards Strauss-Giolitto's cabin. His own mind was racing, trying to figure out various possibilities as to what might have happened, but he wanted to keep Hilary as calm as possible. Lan Yi still had to get Strauss-Giolitto out of whatever form of hysterical attack it was that she'd fallen into. The longer Hilary simply accepted that, you know, things were a bit odd but there wasn't much to worry about really, the easier Lan Yi's task would be.

When Hilary saw Strauss-Giolitto contorted on her force-field bed he let go of Lan Yi's hand and ran to her.

'She's ill!' he said. 'Maria's ill!'

'She will be all right soon,' said Lan Yi, following more slowly, wishing he was a bit more certain about what he'd just said. 'She is just having a tough dream. You must have had bad dreams in your time. Now it is her turn.'

Lan Yi sat down beside Strauss-Giolitto and put his palm on her forehead. It was much cooler than before. Her breathing seemed to be easier, and her eyes were still closed.

'She mending is,' said Lan Yi and was almost at once annoyed with himself for his lapse in basic Argot. 'She's mending,' he said.

As if on cue, Strauss-Giolitto opened her eyes. The madness had gone from them but it was plain that she was puzzled. 'Where are we?' she said.

'Where we've always been,' said Lan Yi. 'On board the *Santa Maria*. At least, that's where I think we are. The cabins are more or less the way they used to be, but the rest of the configuration of the ship seems to have altered. To have *been* altered.'

In her left hand she took one of his. In her right she accepted Hilary's small fingers, which were pursed tightly and only reluctantly eased open to curl round hers.

'I was somewhere else entirely,' she said, 'and it seemed to be forever. I was trapped in rotting mud, and then something stamped on me, and then I was being turned inside out, and then . . .'

'You were here on your bed,' said Lan Yi, and then realized how foolish the statement was. Her body had been here, but it had been all too obvious that her mind had not been. He was prepared to take her word for it that she had been suffering some quite different existence.

He said this.

'There were others there with me,' she said once he'd finished. 'I could sense them being there.'

'Others of the personnel?'

'I don't know,' she said. 'Just *others*. I think they weren't humans. It didn't *feel* as if they were.'

She sat up and wiped her eyes with her hand, getting rid of the tears. 'Why's Hilary here?'

'Because the three of us seem to be the only people left on this level of the *Santa Maria*,' said Lan Yi. 'I can't get the elevators to work. Everyone else seems to have vanished.'

He could see Strauss-Giolitto feeling around with her tongue for the commline that had been there throughout her adult life, then saw her disappointment. 'Yes, it is like that,' he said. 'I begin to wish that I had allowed myself more augmentation than just a secondary retinal screen – then perhaps I could try to communicate with any others who might have survived this . . . hazard.'

'What's so bad?' said Hilary. 'Maria's OK now.'

'Kid, where's your mother?' she snapped. Lan Yi thought she was being cruel, then realized she was giving Hilary the equivalent of a therapeutic slap across the face, much as Lan Yi himself had done to her a little while ago.

'I dunno,' said Hilary. 'She died a while ago. Maybe she'll be back in another while.'

'Let's hope it's not too long a while,' said Strauss-Giolitto, pulling herself into her jumpsuit. In other circumstances Lan Yi might have been sad to see her nakedness covered up. The child seemed not to have noticed. Lan Yi's mind was roaming around all the physics he knew, trying to figure out what had happened. Parallel universes – yes, the Images might have sucked away most of the *Santa Maria*'s personnel to their own reality for some reason of their own, but it seemed hardly likely. A reverse in the time flow, so that the *Santa Maria* had gone back to a time before any of the personnel were born – but then why would he and Strauss-Giolitto and Hilary have been exempted? Or were the three of them victims of some gross mental abnormality, so that their memories were misleading them?

None of it made sense.

'I think we should try the elevators again,' he said.

'Too right,' said Strauss-Giolitto, resuming the child's hand. 'Hilary, look, dammit, just leave that blasted top here. We can come back and get it later.'

'Aw, but I wanna . . .'

'Belt up,' said Lan Yi.

'Where'd you learn that?' said Strauss-Giolitto, looking across at him. For a second or so he thought she might smile, but there was still too much fear in her for that.

'From Strider,' he said. 'When she first told me to do that I started looking for a belt, assuming it was a safety instruction. It was very embarrassing for her to have to explain to me.'

This time Strauss-Giolitto did smile, albeit wanly. Lan Yi felt he had got rid of another obstacle. Strider had never in her life even dreamt of telling him to belt up, but the lie had served its purpose. There were now at least two adult human beings capable of dealing with the strange new environment this part of the *Santa Maria* had become. That was twice as many as there had been a couple of minutes ago.

'Hey, that's not a very kind thing to say to a . . .' the child began.

'The motion has been proposed and seconded, Hilary,' said Strauss-Giolitto.

Lan Yi took the boy's other hand. 'We must explore the *Santa Maria* and see if we can discover the root of this mystery,' he said, again aware that his Argot was slipping. 'This is a brave endeavour. We shall all gain great glory through it, not least yourself.'

'Oh yeah?'

'Yes,' said Strauss-Giolitto. 'Say, would you like us to swing you?'

'Spose so.'

After three swings between them, the third time doing an alarmingly dangerous-seeming backward somersault, the child was prepared to be cooperative. Strauss-Giolitto gave Lan Yi a glance over Hilary's head that said a lot. Lan Yi remembered what a pain in the butt he himself had been at this age and was able to give her back no more than a feeble grin. He reckoned that, on current showing, Hilary was in for a bright future. Although Lan Yi had no scientific evidence to back it up, he believed that the most intelligent people displayed a form of neoteny: they became mature long after they had reached physical adulthood. Before that they were insufferable. Hilary, who was about five – he had been one of the first born to the *Santa Maria*'s personnel – looked according to this theory as if he were going to be a genius in later life. At the same time, Lan Yi wished he could think of a good excuse for dumping the kid somewhere safe, secure and soundproofed.

The first elevator they tried was as unresponsive as the ones Lan Yi had stabbed at earlier. He insisted that all three of them press the pad – Hilary first, Strauss-Giolitto second and himself, as a last hope, third. Nothing happened at all. At least it was a relief that he didn't find himself transported back to Strauss-Giolitto's cabin again. He wasn't certain he could have stood that.

'I don't like the light out here,' said Strauss-Giolitto, looking backwards over her shoulder as if there might be somebody watching her. 'It's all wrong.'

'Everything's all wrong,' said Lan Yi, giving the pad a final press with the heel of his hand, knowing that it was useless.

'Are we actually still *on* the *Santa Maria*?' said Strauss-Giolitto.

'Better hope so,' was all Lan Yi could manage.

He wondered yet again if it were true.

'Let's try another elevator,' he said.

The third elevator obeyed Hilary's summons, its door sliding open in front of them as if there were absolutely nothing the matter, its bright light inviting them to enter. Lan Yi couldn't help but feel that they were walking into the jaws of a monster, but he ushered the other two in in front of him anyway.

'We have some progress,' he said. 'Hilary, will you kindly press for the command deck?'

'Yeah. Great. Oh, hang about – which button's that? I've never been up there.'

'It's the top button of the column,' said Strauss-Giolitto. 'If the elevator came when you asked it to, maybe it'll go where you tell it.'

She leaned over and scooped him up as the elevator door whished closed. Lan Yi wondered what they would do if the elevator refused to budge and the door refused to open again, but he said nothing.

'Here,' said Strauss-Giolitto to the child she was holding in her arms. 'Just go ahead and press that one.'

'OK.'

The elevator began to move towards the nose of the ship. Strauss-Giolitto put Hilary back down on the floor. Lan Yi watched the display above the door nervously. Of course, the display didn't mean much to him any more, but he was nevertheless keen to see the numbers ticking over towards the top. At the same time he was apprehensive: if they found the command deck as deserted as the lowest level, what could they do? He'd done it before so he knew it was easy enough to operate a Pocket – just stick your head in and *think* about what

243

you'd like to see – but he had no idea at all what he could do once he'd seen the display. Smile for the cameras, maybe. Strauss-Giolitto probably had even less of an idea than he did. Call the Helgiolath and ask them to talk him through it? Not much of an attraction the *Santa Maria* would be to the Helgiolath if they were going to have to spend days or weeks telling him how to pilot this strangely altered starship. Holmberg had told him the fleet they were joining was over seven and a half thousand strong. There'd be other things on the Helgiolath's minds: educating from scratch the crew of a single extra starship was not going to have a high priority.

'We're still going up,' said Strauss-Giolitto glumly. The vivacity she'd shown for a short while had leached out of her. She was able, though, to look down at Hilary and return his confident grin.

'You bet your bottom dollar on it,' said Lan Yi. 'We are going to make it – I feel certain.'

'What's a dollar?' said Hilary.

'Lan uses some expressions that're a bit unfamiliar to the rest of us,' said Strauss-Giolitto. 'Just kind of forget the words and listen to what he's saying. Most of the time – almost *all* of the time – it makes good sense.'

'A dollar is an old unit of money,' explained Lan Yi.

'What's money?'

'Something you can buy things with,' said Strauss-Giolitto.

'What do you mean, "buy"?'

'We are getting to the command deck,' said Lan Yi. He wished he felt a bit more confident they would actually reach it. Every moment he expected to find himself back in Strauss-Giolitto's cabin.

'Where's everyone else?' said Strauss-Giolitto.

'How do you mean?'

'We should have been stopped a few times by other people wanting to get on.'

'I think something very bad has happened. I do not wish to speculate further.'

'Cheery?' said Strauss-Giolitto.

'We seem still to be alive.'

' "Seem"?'

'That is as much as I can say. While you were unconscious there were some very strange things happening. There still are.' The indicator was one level short of the command deck. He put his arm on Hilary's shoulder, ready to stop the child from dashing out on to the deck. Lan Yi wanted to take a careful look at what they were getting into before they got into it. 'Have you tried to speak to the Images yet?'

'No.' Strauss-Giolitto looked puzzled. 'Where are they?'

'I do not know. That is one of the very many things that are concerning me.'

The elevator reached the level of the command deck.

The door opened.

The thing looking at them was barely recognizable as Strider. Her cheeks had fallen in on themselves. The array of darkly yellow teeth that showed between the leathery lips was an image of death. The eyes looked as if they had seen too much time evolve in front of them. She was crouched in front of one of the Pockets, but looking back towards the door through which they had just entered. Her hair was grey. But her SSIA jumpsuit was the regulation blue, as if she had put it on just a few moments ago.

'Who are you?' the thing that was still just identifiable as Strider hissed.

'Lan Yi. Maria Strauss-Giolitto. A kid. Looks like we're your crew,' said the tall woman.

Strider fell to all fours. She seemed to be growing older even as they watched. Lan Yi expected knuckle-bones to start showing through the flesh of her fingers.

'Everything's illusion,' Strider said.

'A philosophically interesting point perhaps, but . . .' Lan Yi began.

'I'm not talking about eternity,' said Strider. 'I'm talking about now.' She spat a decayed molar on to the floor in front of her, looked at it, picked it up, then put it back into her mouth and chewed it as if it were a toffee. 'Don't believe everything you see. Don't believe *anything* you see.'

Lan Yi took a couple of paces towards her.

'Don't come any closer.' There was a lethal quality in her whisper that stopped him in his tracks. 'I don't know who you are. You've told me names. I know the people whose names those are, but you don't look like them to me.'

'You look like Leonie Strider to me,' said Lan Yi, taking another pace forward.

'Bullshit to that,' said Strider. 'I no longer even look like Leonie Strider to *me*.' She spat out another tooth, then picked it up and swallowed it as before. 'What I see you as is walking mirrors, just reflections of real people. You could be anything.' She pushed her hand back through her hair, and most of it came away between her fingers. 'I don't know what the Helgiolath have done to us, but . . .'

'Were you in the place that was made up of mud?' said Strauss-Giolitto.

'Yes. I was there half a thousand years ago.'

'And something stomped on your back.'

'That was only a century later.'

'Yeah,' said Strauss-Giolitto. 'I was there as well. Then I saw what the stars are *really* like – they're not just pretty bright lights in the sky at all, are they?'

'No. They hate us.'

'That's taking it a bit far, Leonie.'

'I don't know. I think they probably do. Mind you, my perceptions may have been altered rather radically. I've stood guard here on the command deck for a hundred and fifty years, as far as I can estimate, without having even enough time off to eat or have a crap. The hunger isn't hard to cope with any longer; the constipation is.'

'You really *aren't* Strider, are you?' said Lan Yi. He pushed Hilary behind him.

'Of course I'm Strider.'

Lan Yi looked up at the view-window. There was nothing out there. Even if they'd shifted into intergalactic space there should have been some glimmer of light, somewhere.

'Go back to the elevator,' said Lan Yi softly to Strauss-Giolitto. 'Take the kid with you.'

'Don't talk shit,' said Strauss-Giolitto. 'I'm bigger and faster than you. And I'm more expendable. Remember, I was the one who got to go down to Spindrift.'

'OK, we'll both stay. Hilary, go to the elevator and take yourself somewhere very distant.'

'Aw, but . . .'

'Look,' said Strauss-Giolitto tautly, 'find yourself a black hole and fall into it. Don't pause at the event horizon.'

'Yeah, but . . .' said Hilary.

'Just for fuck's sake fuck off, fucking quick,' said Strauss-Giolitto.

'Oh, right, Maria. Why didn't you *explain* before?'

The two heard the noise of the elevator door behind them. Lan Yi reached out his right hand to touch the back of Strauss-Giolitto's left. For a split second he felt her reject the physical contact, but then she returned the gesture.

'Who or what are you?' he said to the thing that looked like an ancient Strider.

'I'm your captain.'

'I do not believe you. Just now you were telling us that we should not believe anything at all that we see. Now you are asking us to take it on credit that you are Leonie Strider.' He glanced sideways at Strauss-Giolitto; the woman was looking even paler than usual. 'Perhaps Pinocchio could judge.'

'The bot has long ago turned into a heap of rust.'

The thing that might or might not be Strider was crawling towards them. The movement seemed infinitely painful. What Lan Yi wanted to do was to step forward and pick her up in his arms. At the same time he knew that this was the very last thing he should do.

'I do not think that is so,' he said. 'Please start telling us the truth again. You did earlier when you said that everything around us at the moment is made up of illusion, and that we should not believe anything we saw. Now you are lying to us. I would be very grateful if you could stop lying.'

He touched the back of Strauss-Giolitto's hand again. Even the slight contact was enough to tell him how tensely held in place the woman's body was.

247

The light on the command deck began to dim. The dimming was so slow that Lan Yi hardly noticed it at first, and then he discovered that he was having to screw up his unscreened eye to see the face of the thing that he now knew was not Strider.

The thing's mouth opened, and teeth spilled from it, rattling on the command deck's floor. Behind those teeth appeared others that were much smaller but much more numerous and seemingly much sharper. The blue jumpsuit faded away from around the form of the creature, and Lan Yi wondered how he had ever been able to think of this as a human being, let alone the human being he knew as Strider. Six-legged and with what looked like feathers covering the parts of its body that the illusion of the jumpsuit had hidden, it was poised to spring at him.

Its mouth opened wider and wider – impossibly wider. There was very little he could see now but the interior of that mouth, which was darker even than the starless space he'd seen through the view-window. There was nightmare in the blackness of that maw, which had become as large as the command deck.

'Are you seeing what I'm seeing?' said Strauss-Giolitto.

'That is a difficult question to answer,' said Lan Yi primly. 'I very much hope that what you are seeing is less hideous than what I am seeing.'

'Couldn't be.'

The upper surface of the mouth had covered the view-window. The teeth of its lower jaw were slipping insidiously under their feet. They tried to move backwards, but the rear wall of the command deck stopped them.

The darkness inside the mouth of the Strider-thing was not absolute. There was a flipping black-yellow tongue several metres wide. Overhead, the teeth of the upper jaw were slowly lowering.

Lan Yi held his composure with great difficulty. His life had been a long one and it had been strewn with many griefs, most notably the way that Geena had so determinedly hurled herself out of it. He was not at all afraid of death, but he was certainly fearful of the pain that might attend his manner of dying. He wanted to bow down inside the mouth of the thing that had looked like Strider and beg for mercy, but he knew that he couldn't do that. He had to keep up the appearance of impassiveness for the sake of Strauss-Giolitto. Astonishingly, she was acting as calm as he was. Perhaps she was returning the compliment: keeping up appearances for *his* sake.

'Everything's illusion,' Strauss-Giolitto said. 'Just keep a hold of that. This isn't really happening.'

'It feels as if it is.'

She put her arm around his waist and hugged him to her. 'Let's go for a walk down the Yellow Brick Road, shall we?'

'That?' he said, looking at the serpent-like tongue.

'We can't go back, so we might as well go forward. Just at the moment, it looks as if we have a choice of being eaten or allowing ourselves to be eaten. I'd prefer the latter. It has a bit more dignity. Besides, sooner or later we're going to wake up.'

I woke her from a nightmare, Lan Yi thought. *That's why she's so insouciant about all this. She thinks it's just another bad dream. It hasn't occurred to her that even illusions can kill you.*

'Yes,' he said. 'Let's take that walk.'

Darkness was falling as the huge mouth closed.

The most difficult part was climbing on to the tongue. Its tip was moving from side to side in unpredictable flickers of motion. Lan Yi tried to grab it to hold it still, but the oily flesh kept slipping out of his hands.

Strauss-Giolitto hit the tip of the tongue hard with the side of her hand. For a moment it stilled.

'Climb on,' she said. '*Dive* on.'

She threw herself on to the tongue, losing her balance before she could rise to her knees and, somewhat shakily, her feet. She looked the way that Lan Yi had looked the first time he had tried water-skiing, over seventy years ago. There was so little light left that he couldn't see her face. This was probably a good thing. About three minutes into his first attempt at water-skiing he had been prolifically seasick. He took her hand, and she dragged him up on to the greasy surface of the tongue. It had started moving from side to side once more. She tried to pull him erect alongside her, but instead fell almost on top of him.

'Doesn't look as if we're exactly going to be dancing along like Dorothy and the Scarecrow,' she said into his ear.

'Let us keep going forward,' he said, resigning himself to death. *Better for her that she keeps thinking of all this as just a bad dream, something that will sooner or later be over.* 'Who knows what is at the end of the Yellow Brick Road?'

At the moment all that seemed to be at the end of the Yellow Brick Road was pitch blackness. The mouth of the Strider-thing had almost entirely closed. Lan Yi glanced behind him and saw just a strip of jagged-edged greenish light.

'Who goes first?' said Strauss-Giolitto.

'Whichever you prefer.'

'All right, I'll lead you. Take hold of my ankle and follow me.'

She crawled ahead of him. There was just enough light left for him to catch a glimpse of her foot, and he caught it in his hand. She gave a grunt of acknowledgement.

The jaws clenched tightly shut. There was nothing to see. The slippery tongue on which they were perched still moved erratically underneath them, so that even crawling was a delicate test of the ability to keep balance.

Lan Yi wondered how long he could keep going. Strauss-Giolitto had the fantasy that this wasn't really happening. He knew that it was. It might be an illusion, but so was the person on the other side of the mirror from yourself. If you ran to throw your arms around that mirror-person you could kill yourself just as easily as if you'd jumped off a tall building. He felt as if he were falling into Strauss-Giolitto's fantasy. Any minute now there would be the sound of breaking glass.

She was crawling ahead at such a speed that he found it difficult to keep up. Sometimes he found himself falling face-first into the accumulated mucus at the centre of the tongue. Still he clung on to her ankle. It seemed the one safe reference point in a universe that was currently nothing but darkness.

'We'll get there soon,' she said.

'Where?'

'At the end of the Yellow Brick Road there's always the Emerald City.'

There was a slight glimmer of light. It was dark red – not emerald green – and unreliable, but at least it was there. Strauss-Giolitto's boot, in Lan Yi's hand, looked black.

Then a new ripple was added to the tongue's movement.

'I think we've reached the back of the throat,' said Lan Yi, struggling for breath.

They were the last words he said before they found themselves sliding unstoppably downwards. The redness grew a little brighter.

Human stomachs are filled with acid. As he fell, releasing Strauss-Giolitto's foot at last, Lan Yi wondered what the stomach of the Strider-thing might be filled with. It seemed odd to be concerned about which particular fluid might be about to dissolve you, but Lan Yi couldn't help the curiosity.

But they weren't inside a stomach, he suddenly discovered: they were floating in free space, with the stars stretching out on every side as far as he could see. He stopped himself from screaming and looked at the figure of Strauss-Giolitto, tumbling out of control alongside him. Still she seemed unfazed by what they were going through – it was just another dream to her, maybe a dream she had already had. She was relaxing in the vacuum, stretching her arms out behind her as if she were luxuriating in a hot bath.

Lan Yi narrowed his eyes. The faintest points of light around them were swiftly winking out. He wondered why he was able to continue breathing in the vacuum: perhaps Strauss-Giolitto was right, and it really was some kind of dream. But it wasn't – he knew that. He'd experienced lucid dreams before, and this was identifiably not one of them. More of the stars were blinking into nonexistence. The whole of space around him and Strauss-Giolitto was beginning to glow softly. He reached out to take her hand. She smiled at him.

Almost all of the stars had gone now, and the glow of space was becoming dazzling. His body and Strauss-Giolitto's floated towards each other. He found himself wrapped tightly against her, so tightly that it was almost as if he might be absorbed into her. She had always been much larger than him; now she seemed to be twice his size. He wondered if she would next try to swallow him, in a recapitulation of what the Strider-thing had done to them.

Gravity returned suddenly, forcing them apart. They were lying on a hard surface of some kind which gleamed greenly.

'Ah, there you are,' said a huge voice.

Strider finally narrowed the focus of the Pocket so that she could see Lan Yi and Strauss-Giolitto. They were the last of her personnel that she and Ten Per Cent Extra Free had been able to identify.

'Ah, there you are,' she said, and reached into the Pocket to scoop them up. She held them carefully by the collars of their jumpsuits as she withdrew them from the Pocket's field. The first time she'd pulled someone out of the Pocket she'd held him on her upturned hand and then, when he was suddenly restored to his full size and mass, had been lucky to escape without broken bones.

'What an amazing imagination I have,' said Strauss-Giolitto, recovering her balance. 'Not that long ago I was being swallowed by you.'

'Really?' said Strider drily.

'This is actually happening to us, isn't it?' said Lan Yi.

'It has been,' said Strider. 'The worst of it seems to be over now.' She pointed upwards at the view-window. 'Unless reality has become a lot looser than anything we've all been through we're back in the middle of the Helgiolath fleet.'

'Have you any idea what happened?' said Lan Yi, obviously exerting considerable control over his body as he lowered himself into one of the command seats. He looked as if he were on the point of collapse. Strauss-Giolitto, by contrast, was pacing around the deck as if it were some new part of her dream, something that might reveal an interesting extra detail about her subconscious.

'The Helgiolath commander dictated to me how I was to shift the *Santa Maria* while still remaining a part of his fleet,' said Strider. 'Whatever's left of the Main Computer obeyed his orders. It's not something I'll let it do again.' She grinned without any humour. 'In future we'll just stick to the cosy old tachyonic drive, right? I don't think I could go through all that again.'

Lan Yi was breathing with great deliberation and his face was paler than she had ever seen it. 'One of these days we must compare nightmares,' he said heavily, 'but I would rather it were not soon. There is a lot I would like to forget. How, though, did Strauss-Giolitto and myself come to arrive in the Pocket?'

'As far as I can work it out,' said Strider, 'the Helgiolath make their ftl skips by thrusting themselves through different levels of reality – or different realities – before they reconstitute themselves somewhere else. Maybe they enjoy the experiences they undergo along the way. I didn't.'

'I echo your opinions entirely,' said Lan Yi.

'The Pockets seem to operate along the same principle,' said Strider. She sat down near him. 'I've spent the past four hours fishing people out of that damned Pocket. Two of them had been driven completely out of their minds by whatever it was they'd been through.' She flexed the knuckles of her right hand at him so that he could see the bruises. 'I had to hit both of them very hard to . . . sedate them. They're under the control of medbots now.'

Strauss-Giolitto wandered towards them. Her eyes were bright.

'Has the nightmare ended?' she said.

'Yes,' said Strider wearily. 'At least, as far as I can tell it has.'

Strauss-Giolitto looked disappointed.

'Are you all right?' said Lan Yi listlessly.

'Oh, I'm fine. Fine,' said Strauss-Giolitto.

To Strider it was obvious that the woman was a very long way from fine. She wished that she cared a little bit more.

'Could you look after her?' she said to Lan Yi.

'I seem to have been doing that ever since we came on board the *Santa Maria*,' he said with an air of resignation. 'Yes, of

253

course I shall.' He hauled himself to his feet. 'We must take the elevator back to our cabins,' he said to Strauss-Giolitto.

She gave him a confident smile. 'Want to screw me, is that it?'

'Not at this particular moment in time,' said Lan Yi. 'Please, just do what I ask.'

'Fancy your chances, do you?'

Strider had had enough. She applied the Strider Sedative with all the force she could muster, damaging her hand yet further. 'I'll get a bot to clear her away,' she said, looking down at the form of Strauss-Giolitto in front of her. 'I suppose I'm likely to be indicted because of this sort of stuff.' She looked at her hand, wondering if she had fractured her knuckles. 'I think I need a medbot pretty urgently.'

Then she saw the command deck twisting itself into curious patterns of bright colours, and fainted.

Lan Yi looked at the two unconscious women on the floor of the deck. His first instinct was to attend to them himself, but he knew that soon a medbot would arrive which would do the job much better than he could. Poor Strauss-Giolitto, in one sense. Poor Strider, in another. Both of them carried almost unbearable burdens.

'Where are you?' he said to the Images.

WE'RE HERE, said one of them.

'Who's speaking?'

TEN PER CENT EXTRA FREE.

'Is the *Santa Maria* safe?'

IT IS AT THE MOMENT.

'What do you suggest we do?'

THERE ARE IMAGES IN KORTLAND'S FLAGSHIP. WE HAVE ESTABLISHED CONTACT WITH THEM. WE HAVE EXPLAINED TO THEM THAT HUMAN BEINGS ARE NOT SUITED TO TRANSFERRING THEMSELVES BETWEEN REALITIES. THEY WILL PASS THIS INFORMATION TO KORTLAND.

'What would you advise?'

WE WOULD ADVISE THAT YOU DISTANCE YOURSELF FROM THE HELGIOLATH FLEET.

'But is it not our best defence?'

IT IS YOUR WORST ENEMY, AND PROBABLY YOU ARE THE WORST ENEMY OF THE HELGIOLATH.

'I don't understand.'

THE FLEET IS LARGE ENOUGH THAT THE AUTARCHY SHOULD HAVE DETECTED IT, DESPITE THE COMMUNICATIONS-DETECTION SHIELD IT HAS ERECTED AROUND ITSELF. WHY THE FLEET HAS NOT YET BEEN DESTROYED IS SOMETHING THAT WE DO NOT UNDERSTAND. AT THE SAME TIME, THE FORCES OF THE AUTARCHY SEEM ABLE TO DISCOVER THE *SANTA MARIA* WHER-EVER IT IS.

'Polyaggle said there was a way we could perhaps get back to the Solar System.'

THERE IS A CHANCE OF DOING THAT, YES.

'Why has Strider not instituted this?'

HER THOUGHTS TOLD US THAT SHE HAD DECIDED TO BE 'PHILANTHROPIC'.

Lan Yi thought about this for a few moments. He had no particular desire to return to the Solar System, where Geena had killed herself. When asked his opinions by Holmberg he had opted to stay in The Wondervale. But others – a majority of others – among the personnel had had different views. Why had Strider decided to ignore what they thought?

'Where's Pinocchio?' he said at last.

THE BOT IS APPROACHING THE COMMAND DECK. HE WILL BE WITH YOU IN TWENTY-TWO POINT ONE SIX SECONDS.

'And Polyaggle?'

SHE HAS YET TO RETURN FROM THE FRACTAL REALITIES.

The information made Lan Yi's face twist with pain. He and Strauss-Giolitto had experienced the nightmare of what Ten Per Cent Extra Free called the fractal realities.

'*Will* she return?' he said.

WE BELIEVE SO.

There was a mental silence. Lan Yi sensed that, whatever the Images had told them about Polyaggle, it was less than the full truth. But there was nothing he could do about it. Rubbing his hand tiredly across his forehead, he thought he saw one of the

Images – presumably Ten Per Cent Extra Free – in the side of his vision.

The left-hand communications Pocket sprang into life. There was a hideous double visage there. This must be Kortland. Holmberg had told him that the Helgiolath were far from pretty. At the time he had assumed that he was above any preconceptions as to what constituted prettiness: what counted were intelligence and motivations; they were the true beauties, rather than physical appearance. Now he knew what Holmberg had been talking about.

'Where is your captain?' said Kortland curtly.

'She is . . . unwell.'

Lan Yi heard Pinocchio entering the command deck behind him.

'There has been very great difficulty aboard this spaceship,' said Lan Yi. 'The shift you asked our Main Computer to perform caused much distress among our personnel.'

'I apologize for this,' said the two-headed leech-like thing. 'Had I realized, I would have—'

Lan Yi cut across him. 'We do not attach guilt to you, but at the same time I think it unwise that we remain a part of your fleet.'

'We wish to destroy the tyrant,' said Kortland. 'Is this not something you would wish to see? I had the impression from your captain that she wanted to experience the destruction of the Autarchy.'

'The Images aboard this vessel say that we would be better off without you, and that you would be better off without us.' Lan Yi peered at the alien. Biology was not his specialization, but he was beginning to perceive the elegances of Kortland's form. Where human beings had prehensile hands, the Helgiolath must use their mouths.

The Helgiolath appeared to be thinking; it was difficult to know.

'Are you our allies,' said Kortland eventually, 'or are you going to desert from our fleet?'

Ten Per Cent Extra Free managed to convey a sense of threat

in the translation. Lan Yi knew that he would have to speak very carefully in response.

Prompted by Ten Per Cent Extra Free, he said: 'We would like to assist you, but not as part of your fleet.'

'There is something you could do for us.'

'Tell me what it is. I am not the commander of this vessel, and so I cannot promise that we will obey your request.'

One of Kortland's heads turned away, but the other continued to look at Lan Yi. The seeming eyelessness of the alien's face was one of its most repulsive aspects, and yet at a different level Lan Yi found himself appreciating it. *Visible eyes are weaknesses*, he thought, *because if you can destroy a creature's sensory organs you can almost certainly, soon afterwards, move in for the kill. Sometime in the distant past the Helgiolath must have evolved away from having overt sensory organs in order better to protect themselves from predators. We human beings, on the other hand, not only have sensory organs plastered all over our faces but have even accentuated their obviousness by putting on secondary retinal screens. Before Strauss-Giolitto went through the Spindrifters' decontamination you could have blown every synapse in her brain by simply coughing loudly at her.*

'There is a planet that the Autarchy values above any other except Qitanefermeartha itself,' the Helgiolath said.

' "Qitanefermeartha"?'

'Qitanefermeartha is the planet at the very core of the Autarchy. It is not of current concern. It is so well defended that even this fleet might have no chance of succeeding against it. Perhaps in the future . . .'

The Helgiolath's second face turned back blindly towards Lan Yi. Did the aliens have two brains, one for each head? He was becoming much more interested in their physiology than he was in thoughts of fighting the Autarchy. The *Santa Maria* had been sent into space with the primary purpose of discovering a new world for humanity to colonize but with the secondary aim of studying alien lifeforms – not as lifeforms, exactly, but as representatives of other modes of evolution. Lan Yi had not been deeply involved in this part of the overall

257

project, but it had interested him nevertheless. If he were ever given the chance he wanted to investigate Polyaggle: she was clearly put together in some way that human biology had yet to encounter. Dissecting a Helgiolath could likewise add more to humanity's understanding of the workings of biology than all the thousands of years of research that had gone before . . .

'Please tell me what you would like us to do,' said Pinocchio.

Lan Yi started. He had almost forgotten that the bot was there on the command deck with him.

'I will give you the co-ordinates of this planet, which is called F-14,' said Kortland. There was a note of relief in the alien's translated voice, as if at last he were dealing with someone rational.

'Please do not do so as you did before,' said Pinocchio. 'We have lost several of our personnel to your mode of moving vessels through space.'

'You take this over,' said Lan Yi to the bot. He had become too intrigued by the Helgiolath to remember Strauss-Giolitto and Strider. A couple of medbots should have been here by now. Was his order of priorities Strauss-Giolitto and Strider or Strider and Strauss-Giolitto? This worried him as he turned away from the communications Pocket to look at the two women. Strauss-Giolitto was motionless except for the rise and fall of her chest as she breathed. It looked as if Strider had broken the woman's jaw, but this was nothing that a medbot couldn't deal with quickly. Strider, although her eyes were still closed, was mumbling some sort of gibberish. Spittle was leaking out of the side of her mouth.

'Translation?' Lan Yi said to Ten Per Cent Extra Free.

THERE ISN'T ANY.

'Is she all right?'

SHE WILL SOON RECOVER.

He knelt down beside Strider and took her head on to his knees, stroking her face.

'I have recorded those co-ordinates,' said Pinocchio behind him. 'You must tell us more about this planet.'

Strider was beginning to recover full consciousness. Her

eyes opened, staring into Lan Yi's, and then closed firmly again. 'The hill of unbelief is never the sight of seeing,' she said, very quietly.

'I do not understand you,' said Lan Yi.

Her eyes opened once more. This time she recognized him and put her arms up towards him, pulling his face down towards hers. He kissed her politely on the cheek. She responded by kissing him eagerly on the mouth. He was appalled. His mouth was Geena's territory, not Strider's.

'Stop, please,' he said, as her face moved briefly away from his.

He could see her eyes moving into focus.

She squirmed away from him across the floor of the command deck.

'It is undoubtedly very well protected,' Pinocchio said in the background.

The Images were no longer interacting with Lan Yi, so he had no idea what Kortland was saying from the communications Pocket; it sounded like an explosion of flatulence that he was pleased to discover was not coming from himself.

Strider was lugging herself to her feet. She seemed shaky, but the craziness had gone out of her eyes. Lan Yi saw her look towards Strauss-Giolitto, who was still unconscious, and then towards the back of Pinocchio, who was talking earnestly with the Helgiolath.

'I have now stored a back-up of the co-ordinates within myself,' the bot said, 'but until I have received human instructions I am unable to take further action.'

'Let me take over,' said Strider.

Her brusque brushing of Lan Yi out of the way as she moved towards the Pocket might have been offensive, but somehow it was not. The out-of-Taiwanese didn't even start to think about what Pinocchio felt as he was thrown aside as well. Instead he went to Strauss-Giolitto. Still no goddam medbots.

'Stop pissing about and give me some more fucking information,' said Strider into the communications Pocket.

Lan Yi hoped that Ten Per Cent Extra Free was performing adequate expurgation.

259

The flintreader in the eye of.

She.

Sun bright in the very high sky, then growing too much smaller. Feel of distance above ground. Wings flexing.

Dark sky now.

Thousands of children nudging uncertainly inside her. *This is not what we want, mother.* Most of them would die within moments of their birth, but enough of them would live.

The shape of creation was a rhombus. This had been known since time was very young.

Wings move, and then are torn from the back. Pain would be better than the sense of loss. The flintreader sees all, because he has become the too-small sun and the very dark sky. He is her magical incarnate lover and the one who surrounds her. She bites into him, feeling the warm succour of his fluids easing themselves as they should do into her mouth. The flintreader lets her take her fill and then releases her – thrusts her away from him.

This is not supposed to happen. The flintreader comes for a queen only in the moment of her death. It is not his role to mate with her through the feeding ritual, as he has just done.

Wingbrush. The flintreader once more?

No. Instead the Human-thing named Strauss-Giolitto. Hurtling towards the ground together with the human-thing, pulling her flesh away from her body in little pieces. No pain, but knowledge that the flesh would not return for a very long while.

Copulation with the Human-thing. Interesting but not greatly pleasurable. Try to make the bite, but this time pushed away even before the skin can be pierced.

Utter darkness, then brilliance.

The flintreader with her again as they fly, her wings restored, down topologically impossible corridors. Almost all of her dead, but almost all of her regrowing inside her.

Sharp blade descending. Flintreader gone from her side. Darkness brighter than the brilliance. Species-death descending with a loud shine. Descending towards her. Descending.

Blade, discovered from the Human-things, averted. She

260

wings in emptiness. Where the flintreader? Gone, as always is in life. First real hope she is alive. Thousand of lives inside her. Must be protected.

Fly on through emptiness.

No flintreader.

Human-things least bad option. Raise small ones until take back to Spindrift. Much flesh on Human-things. Birthing can be achieved.

Exchange flesh.

Blinding lights and once more the sensation of falling.

Exchange flesh, or feel the species slip away. The male and the female mate after the female is engorged with a litter and then the female sucks the flesh out of the male and plants her already sentient offspring into his shard. This is the way it has always been. This is rightness.

She is underwater, the worst of all places to be. The coldest of all water. Required: the warmth of the flintreader.

Now light again, and she can see bubbles of air drifting up swiftly from mouth. Wings start from back but are heavy with moisture. Dying here.

Back in air, but somewhere unknown – not Spindrift. Move wings, and now can fly. Air too thick for breathing. Gag as if trying to breathe water.

More pain.

But soon to reach the Human-things once more. Then to the birthing give and if only that forevermore the eleventh was the next number.

She.

Wanted to be.

Herself.

Again.

Flintreader holding her back.

Hitting him away.

Human-things excellent hosts for the brood. Better even than flintreader. More flesh.

In the end, Polyaggle spent a very long winter on a planet called Xr – where she was hunted through the snows by creatures that

looked like low walls but had gaping mouths in their centres –
before she was able to fight her way back through her
nightmares to one of the Pockets on the command deck of the
Santa Maria.

'You're the last to get here,' said Lan Yi, holding her in his
arms, although it was obvious to her that her bristles were
cutting painfully into him.

Did he have enough flesh?

There was a time when there had been a world called Preeat,
which had been inhabited by a pre-space people called the
Preeae, who looked rather like something you discovered
splattered on the windshield of a cabble. Now no one called the
planet Preeat any more, because it was much more conven-
iently referred to by the Autarchy as F-14. Of course, no one
called the dominant aboriginal species Preeae any more
because no one had seen any of them for a very long time. Two
thousand years ago the cleansing operation had taken the
Autarch Nalla about two seconds to conceive and about two
hours to watch being executed.

The Preeae had looked remarkably funny as they'd fried in
the Autarchy's beams: the spectacle had been well worth
watching.

The Autarch never did anything without reason, unless he
felt like it. The reason in this instance was that he needed an
unpopulated but hospitable planet so that his technicians could
develop and manufacture extra weaponry. The various species
of The Wondervale showed a remarkable amount of ingrati-
tude towards the Autarch, who spent much of his time – when
he remembered – keeping the galaxy in order. So it was
necessary to keep the forces of the Autarchy properly equipped
with weapons just so that they could enforce law and order
whenever they had to for the benefit of the people.

The Preeae, for example, were no longer unlawful or
disorderly.

The techs on the world that was now called F-14 had not
entirely been volunteers. To call them conscripts would have
been unfair, because most of them had been rather more

unwilling than that. Nonetheless they worked away faithfully producing the hardware for density rays, maxbeams, fudge-blasters and all the rest. Once every few planetary orbits a small armada of Autarchy warcruisers would descend to hoist skywards the products of the techs' endeavours. In the early days a few of the techs had passed loose comment about how they were less than totally happy with this business of manufacturing weapons of mass destruction. After those few had gone the way of the Preeae there was substantially less chitchat in the canteen of an evening.

F-14 was, naturally, well defended. For example, even a fleet of seven thousand six hundred and ninety-two warcruisers would have difficulty getting close enough to slide a missile through F-14's defensive shields. A single vessel that used cobbled-together technology that mixed the primitive with the best that the Images could produce . . .

'Is it really necessary?' said Strider.

'If this tyranny is to be ended,' said Kortland, 'we have to wreck its manufactory.'

'But what about all those people?'

'They are of not great importance. There are only a few hundred thousand of them. There are billions on billions of people in The Wondervale whose lives will be saved if the factories of the planet F-14 are destroyed.' Kortland paused. 'I once felt exactly as you do now. But do you kill a poisonous parasite before or after it kills a host of people?'

'I still don't like it,' said Strider.

'If it is something we can do and no one else can,' said Lan Yi, holding Polyaggle's claw, 'I think we should do it.'

Strider nodded to him. 'Yeah, better to kill people than to let billions of others be killed. Easy enough as a mathematical calculation. A bit more difficult in real life.'

'This is my reasoning,' said Lan Yi. 'I am pleased that the final decision will be yours.'

'Listen to your advisors,' said the translated voice of Kortland.

'I am. Pinocchio, cue in those co-ordinates.'

4

'Destroy, Destroy,' the Bellboy Said

F-14 didn't know what hit it until very much later. At one moment it was the most securely defended planet in The Wondervale with the exception of Qitanefermeartha itself and at the next a comparatively small warcruiser had somehow glided through the defences and was raining down a torrent of fire on to the surface. The enhanced *Santa Maria* now contained as much weaponry as the Helgiolath fleet had been able to give it. Here within the planetary atmosphere it was running on jets. What it couldn't maintain within the atmosphere was the full gamut of defensive shields: that was a cause of continuing worry to her.

Strider tapped away at her Pocket's keyboard, knowing that she was dealing out death but trying not to think too hard about the individual deaths. Pinocchio was alongside her, manning the next Pocket and operating even more ruthlessly than she was. He seemed to be treating it all like some kind of holo game. She was grateful to him, but was also aware that, every time she pressed a key and one of those little factory-blips on the ground blew into pieces, hundreds or perhaps thousands of sentient beings were losing their lives. It didn't make any difference that those beings had been constructing crueller weapons than even humanity had been able to devise. She fed in another co-ordinate at Pinocchio's instruction, watched another factory explode. She just hoped that everyone there had died instantly. The thought that some of them might live on for a few hours, a limb or two blown away, waiting for medical help that would never come, was more than she could bear.

Nevertheless, she hit another factory and gave another cry of triumph.

Between the factories there were constructions that she could recognize as residential complexes. Kortland had told her that she ought to target these as well, but she'd refused. This might be a necessary massacre, but there was no need to make it worse than it had to be. The children of the technicians might indeed grow up to be creators of weapons of mass destruction, but at the moment they had to be given the benefit of the doubt.

Small fighter craft began to rise from the planet's tormented surface. O'Sondheim, whose designated job this was, picked them off easily with phasers. There were no missiles or beams from the ground as yet: the people on F-14 were restrained by the fact that the *Santa Maria* was operating in the world's stratosphere, well beneath the defensive shield. Any missile or beam that failed to hit the warship might do damage to the shield, making the planet yet more vulnerable to attack.

Another factory erupted. This one must have contained particularly sophisticated weaponry, because the entire massif on which it had been built began to melt and then flowed like lava, albeit much more swiftly, down a long valley to engulf a residential complex. The *Santa Maria* was moving fast enough that all that Strider could see was the start of the carnage. She shut her eyes momentarily, trying not to imagine what was going on down there.

The *Santa Maria* jerked. The techs on F-14 had at last found some way to hit it. Nelson fell away from his Pocket and collapsed heavily to the floor, his hands over his face. Strider retained her balance with difficulty.

'What the hell was that?' she snarled at Pinocchio.

'I don't know. We have suffered no structural damage.' The bot was concentrating most of his attention on the destruction below.

'Yeah, but the next one could hurt us badly. Find out what it was.'

Her lover caused his torso to open so that a small metallic spine emerged, reaching its way unsteadily towards the glowing Pocket. The entire command deck lit up as the wire entered the Pocket. Pinocchio himself seemed to be jolted by the contact. Through the Pocket he was interfacing with the

Main Computer. The connection couldn't last long. If there was no response fairly soon . . .

Another shock ran the full length of the *Santa Maria*. This time the damage felt more serious. The Pocket in front of Strider began blinking away, every few seconds, from the scene on the ground to show the exterior of the ship. A big chunk had been taken out of one of its tail fins.

'The fighters are firing energy-seeking ballistics capable of – ' the bot began.

'Forget the command, Pinocchio,' Strider said. 'We're getting out of here.'

She leaned her head back into the Pocket and issued the necessary instructions.

The Pocket refused to respond. Instead, the 3D display vanished and she saw a graphic representation of a tract of landscape.

'What the—?'

'We're going down,' said Pinocchio.

'Who says?'

'The laws of physics. We've lost one of the jets.'

'Can't we just run on the other three?' She knew the question was stupid as soon as she asked it. With the latest redesign the Images had carried out, the *Santa Maria* was by no means an aerodynamic craft. It was supposed to be out in empty space, not dodging around in an atmosphere. The Helgiolath, when installing the weapons systems, had given the ship just enough jet propulsion to enable it to survive in such circumstances. As Kortland had made perfectly obvious, it wasn't particularly important to him whether or not the human beings aboard the *Santa Maria* survived this mission. There were thousands of spacefaring civilizations in The Wondervale: the disappearance of one, here or there, didn't make much difference.

'Are we going to be able to make a landing?' said Strider to both the bot and the Pocket. 'Or are we just going to make a crater?'

'Assuming we're not hit by another ballistic, we ought to be able to land, if we can find somewhere big enough and flat enough,' said Pinocchio.

Strider looked at the schematic display of landscape in her Pocket. There was a large expanse of desert right at its centre.

'I think the Images have taken over control of this part of the mission from us,' she said.

WE HAVE INDEED, said Ten Per Cent Extra Free.

'But can you get us off again?' Strider asked.

POSSIBLY. UNLIKELY. WE WILL ALMOST CERTAINLY REQUIRE HELP.

'Time until impact?'

FORTY-TWO POINT ONE THREE SECONDS.

'Everybody get down!' she screamed. 'Pinocchio, intercom and commline the rest of the personnel! Move it!'

The whole craft seemed to be trying to pull itself to pieces. Strider threw herself to the floor. It seemed odd that the view-window was ahead of her rather than above – one of these days she must instruct the Images to finalize their revampings of the *Santa Maria*. Assuming there *were* going to be any more days, of course. She could see a greyish sky streaked with even greyer clouds. There was a wallop of deceleration as the retro-jets cut in, and she felt as if she were likely to shoot straight out of the view-window to arc downwards on to the snow-covered peaks of a mountain range that appeared momentarily, dizzyingly, and then was gone. She could hear Pinocchio talking urgently into the intercom, making a loop chip, and then he was on the floor beside her. His face looked entirely tranquil. It was at times like these that one remembered most piquantly that he was not a human being, not a living creature at all. But he was a sentient one – that was the important thing.

THREE POINT SIX ONE SECONDS, said Ten Per Cent Extra Free. The Images would certainly get out of this alive, and Pinocchio almost certainly would. Strider was not so sure about the human beings, herself included, but with luck at least a few of them might . . .

For a split second Strider's stomach was at least fifty metres above her prone body. The *Santa Maria* bounced and rocked away over towards the right. Leander swore loudly as the crew on the command deck began sliding across the floor. Then the *Santa Maria* righted itself again, bounced again. Strider

267

wished she had something to hold on to. She felt as if she were a marionette under the control of some insane puppeteer who was taking sadistic pleasure in pulling all her strings at once. Her chin slapped the floor and she bit her tongue hard enough that she could taste the blood. The noise of the retro-jets was deafening, but at least the surface beneath her seemed to be more stable. She took a glance towards the view-window, but all she could see was the same grey, rain-heavy sky. There was a chance that the atmosphere of F-14 was poisonous to humans. What cocktail of chemicals would the rain in those distant clouds be composed of? At least the *Santa Maria* was headed for desert, where the rain wouldn't be an immediate problem. But what about the planet's micro-ecology? Ideally, she should keep everyone locked up in the *Santa Maria* until the Helgiolath or the Images or both engineered some way of getting the ship back up off this world, but she wasn't too certain that Kortland and his kind would make the effort and anyway the defence forces of F-14 were bound to get here first. No, the best thing to do was to get everyone out of the *Santa Maria* as quickly as possible and disperse them, hoping that there was nothing too lethal in the atmosphere. The Images could come along with Pinocchio; she would keep the bot beside her. Of course, a sand-desert wasn't going to offer too many hiding places, but . . .

Shit, that was the worst bounce yet, as if the *Santa Maria* were now beginning to think that it really *would* like to be shaken to bits, or, if not, would like to shake anyone inside it to bits. She chanced another look at the view-window and saw the desert vista wheeling at horrifying speed towards her. A sad thought occurred: presumably there were plants and animals which had somehow managed to eke out an existence in this waste, and now some shrieking behemoth from the skies had descended to shred them with the force of its impact or incinerate them with its retro-jets.

Hello, we're the human species. Don't you just like our funky sense of humour?

Pinocchio put a heavy hand on the back of her spine, pinning her to the floor. He was trying to say something to her but she couldn't hear it over the noise of the jets. There was nothing visible through the view-window now but a blizzard of orange-red sand. She wished the bot would take his damned hand off her, and wriggled her displeasure at him.

THOCK!

That was the worst bounce yet, but she sensed it might be the last. The racket of the jets was gradually declining, and there was the feeling that the *Santa Maria* was gradually slowing its erratic career across the desert surface. Once the people on F-14 got their fighters on to the job it wasn't going to take them very long to find the spaceship: the marks on the sand, observable out at least as far as geostationary orbit if some Autarchy minion wanted to be cutesy and shut off the defensive shield for a few moments, would tell them every-thing. Yeah, as soon as the boat stopped it was going to be a question of abandoning like there had never been an abandon-ment before. Everyone for herself or himself. With luck a few people could survive this disaster, so long as everyone went in different directions. Of course, everyone would be leaving tracks in the sand that would guide the searchers to their precise location. She wished, now, she'd countermanded the Images and told them to bring the *Santa Maria* down in water, but probably that would have vaporized an inland sea. With luck there might be a windstorm that erased their traces, but somehow she didn't think the possibilities were all that great.

The craft ceased shuddering. It had stopped its screaming skid.

Strider shook Pinocchio's hand away from between her shoulderblades.

'Right, everyone to the locks, quickest!' she yelled. 'We're a sitting target here. Pinocchio – tell everyone.'

HEARTFIRE AND ANGLER ARE TAKING ACTION TO SLOW DOWN THE SEARCH FOR US, said Ten Per Cent Extra Free. UNLESS THEY ARE UNSUCCESSFUL WE HAVE JUST OVER SEVENTY-ONE MINUTES BEFORE ANY OF THE F-14 FORCES WILL DISCOVER US.

'That's about three months too short a time for me,' said Strider breathlessly, hefting Leander on to her knees and then her feet. The woman's eyes were wild. Strider shoved her in the direction of where Pinocchio was at the intercom, indicating that he should take charge. O'Sondheim was all right, although like Strider he had bitten his tongue badly, but Nelson had at some stage dislocated his hip. Strider put her foot between his buttocks and yanked savagely. He gave a cry of agony, but she felt the joint jolt back into position.

'I love it when you treat me rough, babe,' he said as he failed to get up on to his hands and knees. His second attempt was more successful.

'Get to the locks!' she shouted. 'Suit up as you go.'

Evacuating the *Santa Maria* took less time than she had anticipated, even though four people who had been working in the fields had been smashed to death as the ship landed. Someone wanted to give the corpses a 'decent burial'; Strider ordered him to leave the bodies where they were, and backed up her argument with a wave of her lazgun.

The air of F-14 smelt like armpits – more accurately, Strider realized, it smelt like the armpits of the person who chooses to stand too close to you rather than one's own warm fust. It was presumably packed with organic chemicals of various possibly poisonous kinds, as she'd feared. She wondered how many of them she had breathed before she'd got the helmet of her suit on. Certainly enough to kill her if she was out of luck. The same was true for everyone except Pinocchio. She should have ordered that people suited up completely before they left the ship, but it had seemed like a better idea to get them out of it as soon as possible.

'Scatter,' she said through the suit radio. 'The further we are away from each other the more likely we all are to survive. Go in twos and threes.' She grabbed Pinocchio's hand. 'In five days' time I'll raise a commline conference if I can. If not, someone else can do it. It doesn't matter who. For now, what we have to do is get as far away from here as we can.'

The prospects weren't good. She'd scanned the horizon, and all she could see were dunes – except for the parts where there weren't even dunes. The F-14 techs were going to be able to blast the grounded *Santa Maria* to pieces without any difficulty and then simply follow the foot-trails of her people through the sands to whatever pathetic hiding places they'd managed to discover for themselves. Strider reckoned that the future of the human species in The Wondervale had about an hour to run.

'Time to go,' she said.

Strauss-Giolitto took Pinocchio's other hand.

'Lay off him,' said Strider.

'We're going in twos and threes, and this is a three. I want to survive. Pinocchio is my best probability of staying alive.'

Strider watched her personnel as they moved away across the desert. The surface offered at best a treacherous footing. A kid fell, making a fountain of sand. Two adults dragged it to its feet. The entire manoeuvre was so incompetent that Strider wouldn't have bet a penny on the family's chances of survival.

'How are we – how is anybody – going to find water or food?' she said as the three of them began to run. It was like wading through the shallows at the edge of the sea.

'Cut down your suit radio,' said Pinocchio. 'This is a question that is very soon going to occur to everyone else. They are less likely to survive if they worry about this than if they simply get as far away from the *Santa Maria* as they are possibly able.'

'None of us have much chance at all,' said Strauss-Giolitto.

'Things could be a whole lot worse,' said Strider.

'Tell me another one,' said Strauss-Giolitto as the three of them leapt cumbersomely over a . . .

'Stop,' said Strider. 'Have you just seen what I just saw?'

They hurried back to take a better look. The thing hovering centimetres above the surface of the sand was camouflaged, so that from even a few metres away it was hard to spot unless you knew it was there. About a metre square, it looked rather like a trapdoor – in fact, *very* like a trapdoor, with a hinged metal ring on it to aid opening. Strider nervously ran her glove just under its edge, making grooves in the sand there, to reassure herself that the artefact was indeed floating – that there was no mere optical illusion involved. Then, even more nervously, she hooked a finger of her glove through the metal ring, and pulled.

Pulled harder.

The trapdoor opened smoothly, although with some resistance, as if on hydraulics. Gazing down through the opening it revealed, the three of them could see what looked like nothing more exotic than a metal ladder, reaching far beneath them into darkness.

'Get working on the general suit-radio frequency, Pinocchio, and tell everyone to come over here. We're going down.'

'Is this wise?'

'It's got to be a better chance than milling around in the desert just waiting to be picked off before we die of thirst. Do the message on the commline as well, in case people have their suit radios switched off, or have moved on to personal frequencies.'

Strider looked at Strauss-Giolitto. Even through the slightly darkened glass of the tall woman's visor, Strider could see that she looked terrified. She reached out a gloved hand and Strauss-Giolitto clumsily took it, as if she were a young child needing reassurance from her mother.

Strider could see, in the distance, pairs and trios of suited figures turning towards them. A few, however, were still trudging resolutely in the other direction.

'Images,' she subvocalized, 'contact the rest. Then tell me what's actually at the bottom of that pit?'

A REASONABLE CHANCE OF ESCAPE, fluted the voice of Ten Per Cent Extra Free.

'Can you be a bit more precise than that?'

THE PREEAE.

'I thought they were extinct.'

EVERYBODY DOES. THAT'S WHY THEY'RE NOT. A FEW OF THEM SURVIVED THE TORCHING OF THEIR PLANET, AND THEY'VE BUILT UP AN UNDERGROUND CULTURE. WE'VE ALREADY STARTED SPEAKING WITH THEM ON YOUR BEHALF, BUT FOR REASONS THAT CAN BE IMAGINED THEY ARE VIRULENTLY XENOPHOBIC. IT IS HARD TO PERSUADE THEM THAT YOU ARE ALLIES, BUT IT SEEMS LIKELY THAT THEY WILL AFFORD YOU SAFE PASSAGE THROUGH THEIR TUNNELS.

'Where do the tunnels go to?'

THE NEAREST OTHER EXIT IS IN THE FOOTHILLS OF A

MOUNTAIN RANGE SOME FOUR HUNDRED AND FIFTY KILO-
METRES FROM HERE. I SHOULD ADD THAT THE PREEAE ARE NOT
BEST PLEASED BY THE FACT THAT YOU HAVE DRAWN ATTEN-
TION TO THIS INGRESS. AS SOON AS YOU ARE ALL THROUGH IT
THEY WILL HAVE TO MOVE IT, SO THAT THE AUTARCH'S
PEOPLE DO NOT DISCOVER IT. THIS WILL CAUSE THE PREEAE
LOGISTICAL DIFFICULTIES IN THE FUTURE, BECAUSE IT WAS
PLACED PRECISELY HERE FOR VERY GOOD REASONS.

'How much of this did you know before we crashlanded?'
The first pair of personnel were just arriving. They had
secondary retinal screens across both eyes, so it was impossible
for Strider to recognize them through their visors.

NOTHING. IF YOU HAD NOT DISCOVERED THIS ENTRANCE WE
MIGHT NEVER HAVE KNOWN ANYTHING ABOUT THE PREEAE'S
PRESENCE. THE NEURAL CAMOUFLAGE THEY HAVE ERECTED IS
VERY SOPHISTICATED INDEED. WE HAD NOT BEEN AWARE
THAT ANY CULTURE IN THE WONDERVALE WAS CAPABLE OF
CREATING THIS.

'Bit of a long shot that we discovered them, then, isn't it?'
said Strider, her eyes roaming across the wastes of sand around
them. The *Santa Maria* looked in a way like a grounded hawk.
It was the first time she had really seen the outside of her
redesigned vessel except through the Pockets, and it was also
the moment when she was abandoning it to whatever fate the
Autarchy's forces visited upon it. She did not consider herself a
sentimentalist, but a twinge of remorse passed through her, as
if she had just betrayed an old and trusted friend. A captain
should go down with her ship, and all that. No: she mustn't let
herself start thinking like that. The *Santa Maria* was a
collection of advanced technology, of bits of metal and
circuitry. It was just an object, not a personality.

WE EXPECT COINCIDENCES, said Ten Per Cent Extra Free.

'Run that past me again.'

OUR REALITY ONLY PARTIALLY OVERLAPS WITH YOURS.
THE NATURE OF THAT OVERLAP IS SUCH THAT 'LONG SHOTS',
AS YOU CALL THEM, HAPPEN VERY FREQUENTLY TO US WHEN
WE ARE IN THE WONDERVALE.

'Good thing we had you along, then.'

The Image quite clearly failed to recognize the tone of irony in her subvocalization. YOU WOULD ALL HAVE BEEN DEAD WITHIN HOURS OF ENTERING THE WONDERVALE HAD IT NOT BEEN FOR OUR INTERVENTION. MAGLITTEL WOULD HAVE BLASTED YOUR VESSEL TO SMALL PIECES.

'Four hundred and fifty kilometres is a very long way to walk. Our suits have air enough for only a couple of dozen hours.'

THE PREEAE HAVE A TRANSPORTATION SYSTEM, USING A NETWORK OF TUNNELS. BUT YES, SOONER OR LATER YOU'RE GOING TO HAVE TO ABANDON YOUR SUITS AND TAKE YOUR CHANCES. HEARTFIRE IS ALREADY DOING HIS BEST TO ANALYSE THE LOCAL MICRO-ECOLOGY TO TRY TO DETERMINE IF THERE ARE ANY MICROBES THAT MIGHT CAUSE YOU HARM. THIS WILL TAKE HIM SOME TIME, AND IT IS POSSIBLE THAT HIS RESULTS WILL NOT BE ENTIRELY ACCURATE. BUT HE WILL DO HIS BEST.

There was now a large cluster of suited personnel standing round the open trapdoor. Strider felt a pang as she saw the children among them. Children always looked so pathetic in spacesuits, as if the Universe should have been designed so that there was no need for such protections.

She explained the situation tersely.

'Pinocchio,' she said, 'tell me how many more people are still to get here.'

'There are three others. I am finding it impossible to contact them either by commline or by radio.'

'Is there any chance of your just physically going and getting them?' said Strider.

'Not in time.'

'Then we leave them.'

When the volume of the shouts of protest over her suit radio grew too oppressive she turned it off. She wasn't going to sacrifice forty-odd for the sake of three. Almost as important, she wasn't going to risk losing Pinocchio, whose abilities might quite possibly make the subtle difference between the survival and extinction of the rest of the party.

'Can you come with me inside my suit?' she said to Ten Per Cent Extra Free.

CERTAINLY. I ALREADY AM INSIDE YOUR SUIT.

'Good. I think I'm going to need you.'

SO DO I.

Once she sensed that the argument had died down she tongued her suit radio back on again.

'There will be no further debate about this matter,' she said curtly. 'I'll be the first to descend into the pit. You can decide among yourselves who is the next to follow me, but whoever it is must wait at least five minutes before they do so – got that? I'm going to leave an open line to First Officer O'Sondheim, and report to him exactly what I'm doing every step of the way. I don't want anyone intruding on that line – it's to be just him and me. If I meet a fatal reception you must disperse once more, under his general instructions. Clear?'

Heads nodded. Enough heads to assure Strider she didn't have a revolution on her hands.

'He and Pinocchio will be the last to follow down.'

She locked her radio on to O'Sondheim's.

'Got that, Danny?'

'Loud and clear.'

She fumbled her hand free of Strauss-Giolitto's and, not allowing herself too much time to think, dropped to her knees and hoisted herself in through the dark opening. She fastened the end of her belt-rope to the uppermost rung, though she didn't think the precaution would do her much good if she fell. It felt to her as if there were a very long drop beneath. She could hear the pulse in her temple beating more swiftly than it should be. What Ten Per Cent Extra Free had told her had been less than entirely reassuring. This might be a long climb down to disaster.

'How are things going with the Preeae?' she subvocalized to him.

THE NEGOTIATIONS ARE STILL . . . DELICATE.

'That bad, huh?'

THEY COULD BE VERY CONSIDERABLY WORSE.

'What do you think my chances are?' She was moving smoothly down the ladder now. After the first couple of dozen rungs it began to take on a helical form, which oddly enough

275

she found less vertiginous than if it had continued straight downwards. However different the Preeae might be physically from human beings, there was obviously some psychological similarity.

She tried to stop her breathing sounding so loud. Although O'Sondheim seemed to have discovered his own inner strength since the terror to which he'd succumbed when the *Santa Maria* had fallen through the wormhole, she still wasn't sure quite how reliable he would be under pressure. He had refused her orders when she'd told him they had to flee from Spindrift's outer moon. If he picked up from her breathing quite how frightened she was, he might be infected and spread the fear on to others. She wished she could have asked Nelson or Leander or Pinocchio to take on the task of ushering the personnel into the pit, but that would probably, besides destroying his belief in himself, have created even more panic among the personnel than anything O'Sondheim could do. With luck, Pinocchio would cope with any problems.

She looked up. The square of skylight above her seemed very small and a very long way away. She tongued on her suit lights, and kept going downwards. In front of her, between the rungs, the lights reflected off a slightly damp-seeming stone surface. The rungs themselves were rusted with age; she told herself not to think much about how fragile some of them might be.

Strider looked upwards again. Perhaps there was a mote of daylight visible above, perhaps not.

'I'm still going down,' she said. 'Nothing to worry about so far, Danny. The ladder starts twisting after a while, which might faze some people.'

'Message received and understood, Leonie,' said O'Sondheim's voice inside her suit. 'There aren't any signs yet of hostile forces. We're lucky. Keep your fingers crossed.'

'Ever tried crossing your fingers when you're climbing down a ladder in a spacesuit?' It was all right to breathe more loudly now; O'Sondheim would simply assume it was because of the physical exertion.

276

'Well, you could try crossing your eyes instead.' He was sounding perfectly confident. She hoped he stayed that way.

Strider became aware that there was a source of light beneath her. Pausing for a moment, she looked downwards and saw a yellow glow. It seemed improbably far away, as if she were crawling backwards down towards the core of the planet.

'Still there's been no contact,' she reported to O'Sondheim. 'The ladder has so far been in reasonably good repair, although the rungs are a bit rusty in places. Tell folk it might be wise not to try doing any acrobatics as they descend. Oh, yeah, and any kid big enough to climb down alone should do so rather than be carried. The less weight anyone puts on this ladder the better. But it seems OK to me.'

She briefly tongued off her suit radio.

'How much further am I going?' she said.

YOU WILL REACH THE BOTTOM WITHIN ABOUT FIVE MINUTES, AT YOUR CURRENT RATE OF PROGRESS, said Ten Per Cent Extra Free.

'I'm shit scared.'

THIS IS EVIDENT TO US FROM THE INCREASED RATE OF MUCH OF YOUR METABOLISM.

'I haven't had any ziprite in years, but I sure as hell could do with a jolt of it right now.'

She tongued the radio back on again. 'Ten Per Cent Extra Free thinks I should get to the foot of the ladder in a few minutes, Danny. Stop anyone else coming down until I get there.'

'Understood.'

She tried to increase the pace of her descent as much as she could without doing anything dangerous. The sooner she met with the Preeae and they either killed her or didn't kill her the happier she'd be. She couldn't imagine the state of a technology that could construct something as advanced as the trapdoor and at the same time relied on a simple ladder for the rest of the ingress. And yet, she reflected again, there was something pleasingly human about it – a neat mixture of the simple and the complicated. Over the centuries, humanity had made considerable technological changes in some areas but had wisely left other things alone, or reverted to the earlier models. For example, a door on hinges could be relied upon to open almost all of the time; a photosensitive door that nictated as people approached it was a pretty neat gadget, but if something should go wrong with it . . .

She was letting her mind wander.

'I've lost track of the time,' she said to O'Sondheim.

'It's three and a half minutes since last you spoke to me,' he said. 'We were beginning to get quite worried. At least we could hear you breathing.'

'Sorry about that.' She looked downwards. 'There's a very brightly lit area beneath me. I should be there very soon. Still no problems at all, except a touch of muscular fatigue. Send the fittest people down first. Yeah – send Polyaggle down first of all. Kids and fatties can follow later. I want to get the most possible people down here as soon as we can.'

'Present company excepted,' remarked O'Sondheim drily.

Despite her terror of what she was about to encounter, she managed a chuckle. 'Never been able to work out whether you're a kid or a fatty, Danny,' she said.

'Both,' he replied. 'But don't tell my girlfriend.'

'I didn't know you *had* a girlfriend. This should have been reported to me. *You* should have reported it.'

There was silence from the other end. Strider realized that O'Sondheim's remark hadn't been as flip as it had sounded, and wished she'd kept her mouth shut. After the first year out from Mars her First Officer had stopped making doe eyes at her, but he hadn't formed any kind of relationship with any of the other women on board, either. She'd seen the way that he'd tried to woo Strauss-Giolitto, and smiled; then had smiled with a bit less conviction once she'd deduced the kind of personal misery Strauss-Giolitto had taken on herself in order to be a part of the expedition. They were both very lonely people – lonelier than even she herself was. At least Strauss-Giolitto had Lan Yi's shoulder to weep on. As far as Strider could tell, O'Sondheim's mental maturity had never evolved beyond the idea that if you wept on a woman's shoulder you ended up screwing her and that if you wept on a man's you were betraying some obscure macho code.

She wasn't sure that her own solution – weeping on a bot's – was perfect, but it was obviously better than anything O'Sondheim had come up with.

She tongued off her suit lights. The yellowness beneath her was very close now. Glancing down yet again, she caught her first sight of the Preeae.

She took a sharp breath. The aliens were somewhat less aesthetically pleasing than the Images had described – not as bad as the Helgiolath but ... no, maybe they were worse, because they had a vaguely humanoid form. They looked as if they had somehow evolved to wear their more vulnerable bodily organs and their blood vessels on the outside, rather than sealed away carefully beneath decorous folds of flesh. They were bipedal, and had two arms, although from this lofty angle she couldn't work out their physical proportions.

Like the Spindrifters, they wore no clothing. All of the ones staring up at her as she descended, her hands and feet moving more uncertainly now, were, however, wearing things that looked suspiciously similar to lazguns slung around their necks.

'I'm about to make contact with the Preeae,' she said to O'Sondheim. 'Anyway, I hope I am.'

At least they had eyes that from this distance were fairly like human ones. It made the aliens a bit easier to contemplate. The trouble was, reflected Strider, that one gets so used to gauging people's reactions by their eyes that she could all too well completely misread what one of these Preeae was actually thinking.

She flipped off her suit radio.

'I'm going to need a lot of help here, Ten Per Cent Extra Free,' she said.

THEY ARE PREPARED TO TALK WITH YOU. THAT IS A GREAT ADVANCE ON THE SITUATION EARLIER. THE VERY WORST THEY WILL DO IS SEND YOU BACK UP TO THE SURFACE.

'Which is a long way away.' She was sweating unpleasantly in her suit just from the descent. What would she be like if she had to climb all the way back up to the top? Like a stranded whale floundering on the sand of the desert until the Autarch's people came along to put an end to her misery, that was what.

WE WILL ASSIST YOU AS FAR AS WE ARE ABLE. WE HAVE ALREADY BEEN ARGUING VERY HARD ON YOUR BEHALF.

'I'm switching back to general frequency now,' she said, tonguing the control as she did so. She wished her voice sounded less apprehensive.

IT SOUNDS FINE TO ME, said Ten Per Cent Extra Free.

Yes, thought Strider, *but you're not a rather vulnerable human being called O'Sondheim standing Umbel knows how many hundreds of metres above me wondering how long he's got to live. My voice might sound a bit grim to him, huh?*

The Image waited until her right boot was on the final rung of the ladder before it commented. WE WILL REMOVE ALL TRACE OF FEAR FROM YOUR VOICE AS WE INTERPRET BETWEEN YOURSELF AND THE PREEAE.

'Thanks,' she said, reeling in her belt-rope.

'For what?' said O'Sondheim anxiously.

'I was speaking to Ten Per Cent Extra Free,' she said. 'Now, Danny, keep listening in, but leave me alone to do one of the things I do best: act like a diplomat.'

He laughed.

'Thanks for the vote of confidence,' she said.

Several of the Preeae had drawn their weapons from their neck holsters – the aliens' arms were triple-jointed, Strider saw, so that it was as easy if not easier for them to reach to their necks as to their waists – and were directing them at her. She found the prospect of the weaponry less worrying than the physical appearance of the Preeae. She hoped that none of the personnel who with luck would be allowed down here to join her would do anything stupid – the children especially.

One of the Preeae took a step forwards. Presumably he was the leader of the contingent. Strider decided to address herself directly to him and leave the rest out of consideration.

'Look, dammit, let's get this straight: all we want to do is wipe out those bastards who very nearly fucking annihilated your entire species,' she said, hoping that she was hitting the right diplomatic note. 'That means we're on the same fucking side, so could you piss off with this super-defensiveness?'

The room around them was an empty box with various dark exits leading in various directions – some off to the side, a couple upwards, and quite a few downwards. Strider found it almost offensive that there were no technological artefacts on view – not even so much as a chair. This room was just a way-station into what she assumed was the system of tunnels Ten Per Cent Extra Free had told her about.

'We haven't got very long. There's going to be a few hundred Autarchy warships hitting the fucking desert above us pretty goddam soon.'

'We are aware of that,' said the Preeae. His voice sounded as though it tasted of metal. 'But we did not bring this antagonism down upon ourselves: it was you *things* that lured the Interlopers to this place. If you had left them alone they would have continued in ignorance of our existence.'

I SHOULD WARN YOU THAT WE ARE MAKING AMENDMENTS TO SOME OF YOUR REMARKS, CAPTAIN LEONIE STRIDER, said Ten Per Cent Extra Free.

'So your species could spend the rest of eternity living in hiding?' she said to the Preeae spokesperson.

'Living.' The single word made the point.

'Can I tell my people it's safe for them to come down here?' Much longer standing around like this and it'd be too late to get everyone in through the trapdoor. 'The Spindrifters thought it would be all right for them to carry on just living in quiet, but the Autarchy killed all of them except a friend of ours, who is here with us. You yourselves kept your heads down, but the Autarchy attempted to annihilate you. We human beings aren't any kind of saints, but we want to help stop these things happening.'

'And the Helgiolath?' said the Preeae.

'I'm not sure what their agenda is, but at this moment I think they're the best chance this part of The Wondervale has.'

'You will all need to be decontaminated,' said the Preeae.

Strider's heart leapt as she heard the translated word 'will'.

'You mean you'll allow my personnel to escape down here?' she said.

'For a short time only. Your Images have been very persuasive.'

'Start it off, Danny,' said Strider. 'We're provisionally welcome.'

'I was listening,' said the First Officer. 'Polyaggle's already on her way down, followed by a bundle of others. Still no signs of enemy action.'

'Good.'

Strider didn't know if Ten Per Cent Extra Free had interpreted any or all of this for the benefit of the Preeae. It seemed not, because the individual was still speaking.

'We will escort you to our nearest escape-way and release you back to the surface of Preeat. More than that we will not do. After that you will be on your own. We will be glad to be rid of you as soon as is possible. You have already seriously risked our security.'

'Nice to meet you as well.'

BE CAREFUL, CAPTAIN LEONIE STRIDER, urged Ten Per Cent Extra Free.

'Aw, fu—'

DO BE CAREFUL. YOU ARE NOT A MEMBER OF A SPECIES THAT HAS BEEN ALMOST ENTIRELY EXPUNGED. IF YOU DO NOT CHANGE YOUR TUNE IT MIGHT BE BETTER TO LET POLYAGGLE DO THE REST OF THE TALKING. SHE AT LEAST WILL BE ABLE TO IDENTIFY WITH THE PREEAE.

Strider took the point.

'Thank you very much for the assistance,' she said formally to the Preeae representative. 'We'll get ourselves out from under your noses just as soon as we can.'

' "Noses"?' said the Preeae.

After Kaantalech had finished eating one of her aides she wondered yet again if she should holo the Autarch to tell him the truth about the Humans having disappeared for the second time, and yet again she decided to procrastinate. All Nalla would do was get angry, then angrier. If he discovered that the

282

Humans were in the middle of a Helgiolath fleet he would become incandescent – which would be fun to watch but would probably be personally dangerous to her. If she just left it alone he would assume that the Humans had been vaporized along with the entire ecology of Spindrift above viral level – damned few viruses would be left, come to think of it, except those that were able to live in total vacuum. Big deal. Perhaps in a few billion years a bunch of them might drift panspermically across a few hundred parsecs and seed life on a virgin planet, and some new technological species would come screaming up into The Wondervale with a view to getting revenge. Kaantalech wasn't going to waste too much time worrying about the possibility: she would have been dead herself for almost all of those billions of years – so why should she care? – and anyway she was pretty certain that viruses had lousy memories.

Not only had the aide been heinously inefficient, he had been made of meat that was so stringy that most of her teeth were now singing out in protest because of the bits of flesh still jammed between them. He hadn't even tasted anything more than passable. It was so difficult getting the right quality of staff these days.

Spitting out a ball-and-socket joint, she turned to look at her surviving aides. Most of them had continued to work away at the puters they were wired into, guiding the remnants of the fleet back across The Wondervale towards Qitanefermeartha orbit, but a few had watched the butchery of the aide. They didn't realize it as yet, but they had thereby volunteered themselves to be next. If there was anything that Kaantalech particularly disliked it was disloyalty.

'I want a position on the Humans,' she said angrily. The aide really had tasted pretty poor: she hoped he hadn't been suffering from any infectious disease.

'We're doing our best, leader,' said one of the aides, not looking up from his puter, 'but they seem to have vanished from spacetime.'

'Keep looking.'

'Yes,' said several voices.

She waded splodgily through the thick coating of faeces and

283

other ordure that carpeted the floor of the *Blunt Instrument*'s command deck. Hers was not a tidy species – never had been. It always amused Kaantalech and her kind to see the way that other species were so prim about the products of their bodies' metabolism. Every now and then the *Blunt Instrument* was cleared out and the valuable nitrates extracted.

'I want a fast result,' she said, 'but I don't want it broadcast. The first person to track them down is to contact me and me only, understood? Of course, the rest of you will know what's going on, but I don't want a word spoken.' She snorted up what had once been a kneebone. 'Do I make myself clear?'

There was not a word of dissent.

Lan Yi spent not one moment regretting that they had lost the *Santa Maria*: it had been a spaceship, nothing more and nothing less. What was really upsetting him was that he had had to leave his musibot behind. He himself played only half a dozen musical instruments, and as far as he could work out he was by far the most technically talented of the few musicians who had been aboard the *Santa Maria*. Human music was one of the comparatively few things that the species could profitably have brought to The Wondervale. Music was a peacemaker, unlike all the other things that people called 'peacemakers'. It was very difficult to get two people to start fighting each other while they were listening to the divine cantatas of Pastredii or the songs of L5 or the mating music of hump-backed whales. If there was any sign of aggression afterwards you could always just recycle the chip. He supposed it was all a primitive form of brainwashing, but it was not one to which he objected.

He looked upwards, and his lights illuminated Strauss-Giolitto's suited bottom descending towards him.

Once upon a time . . . he thought, before a stirring of interest told him that he was lying to himself. *Yes, I'm being guilty of the most acute form of dishonesty: dishonesty of the self.* He smiled wearily at the way fate had treated him. First a wife who had strangled herself rather than continue the existence she shared with him. Now a woman who he was virtually certain

284

was not interested in him for the most fundamental reason of all. After Geena's death he had assumed there would be occasional – hell, after a while, frequent – sexual liaisons. The idea that bloody, nuisanceful, pestilential love might hit him was something that had never occurred to him. Now he found himself not only fonder of Strauss-Giolitto than he had been of anyone since Geena but also wanting to build a partnership with her. He had a couple of times lightly, as if joking, broached the notion to her, and each time she had taken it as the joke it wasn't.

He looked back at the slick stone surface behind the rungs. He was too old to be looking at women's rumps and thinking carnal thoughts.

No he wasn't. Never too old.

The thing he *was* was too old to do was go about falling in love with women who were a fraction of his age and who weren't remotely interested in him. Back in the Solar System, of course, he could have done something about it. He could have opted for the Artif way of life, taken up a female body, and then reintroduced himself – no, by that time *her*self – to Strauss-Giolitto, and waited to see what happened.

Except that the whole thing would have been a lie. Lan Yi loathed the notion of Artiffing. And he was a *man*, not some kind of sexless/sexed being. He wished the SSIA had chosen to board a load of sexbots, so that personnel like himself could at least try to fuck themselves into some kind of self-understanding; but the SSIA had been preoccupied with the notion of procreation. The idea of sharing a night with anyone other than Maria Strauss-Giolitto had become increasingly repugnant to him; although of course he would never say as much, the thought would be constantly in his head: *Second best. You're not the one I really want. Thanks for the mutual masturbation, but . . .*

With sexbots there was no need to pretend.

It was an odd time to be thinking about all this – or maybe it was the best time of all. Climbing downwards he was, for all he knew, likely to be dead within a few minutes. Perhaps there was nothing better to do in these putatively final few moments than to wonder why it was that the human species had since the very beginning of eternity managed to make a mess of things through confusing love, which was an emotion, with gender, which was a physiological fact.

He looked up once more – irritated to find himself feeling slightly guilty – at Strauss-Giolitto's buttocks. It wasn't particularly important to him whether or not he stuck a bit of himself into a bit of her for a while, although that could be a pleasurable conclusion to their lovemaking – if it would be pleasurable to her.

What he wanted to do was to make love with her, so that when they woke up together they could share a joke or give each other a massage or listen to some music or just lie there together, half asleep and half awake, enjoying the fact that they were in each other's arms.

It would take him an hour and a half to explain all this to Strauss-Giolitto, and even then she would probably either laugh it off or throw away his friendship, as if the latter had been polluted by the fact that he wanted to get that single stage closer to her. It was so much easier for most of the rest of the contingent that had come here on the *Santa Maria*: the normal conversation discussing such complexities consisted of 'Wanna fuck?' followed by 'Yes' or 'No' or 'If I can bring along a few friends'.

The light was growing brighter beneath him.

He'd lived a long time and solved quite a number of the mysteries of the Universe. Now, sadly, he faced the fact that he'd failed to solve some of his *own* mysteries.

What the hell?

He was probably going to be dead soon.

Among the Preeae, it was very evident, things habitually happened very quickly. Polyaggle spoke a spurt of noise through her suit radio that Strider could not understand and which Ten Per Cent Extra Free chose not to translate. At once the boxlike room filled with more Preeae, all armed with weapons that looked as if they could do substantially more damage than even a lazgun. The aliens lined the walls, their

286

weapons unwaveringly directed towards the humans. Strider made an instinctive move for her own lazgun, and then realized the stupidity of the action.

'What's happening?' she said to Polyaggle.

The Spindrifter looked at her in evident incomprehension. Then, a moment later, Ten Per Cent Extra Free performed the translation.

'They are escorting us to one of their underground shuttle-craft. This is not going to be a very pleasant journey, but most of us should survive. They want to get rid of us as soon as they can.'

'I don't much like the sound of "most of us",' said Strider. 'How many people are likely to die?'

'Two or three. Acceptable losses.'

'They're not acceptable to me.'

'You left three people out on the desert,' said Polyaggle.

'I had no option.'

'You don't have any option now. These people will help us if we move fast, but if we stand here bickering they're going to start having second thoughts about helping us at all.' Through the Spindrifter's visor Strider could see the tips of Polyaggle's wings briefly behind the tufted head as she touched her gloved claws together delicately. 'The Preeae's sign of acceptance is a stroke of one hand over one eye. I think you would be wise to perform that action now.'

Feeling that she was betraying something but not quite sure what that something was, Strider wiped a glove across her visor.

The gesture seemed to be enough. The Preeae gathered around the humans. Again Strider had to stop herself reaching for her lazgun. A triple-jointed arm, coloured green and red and yellow and one or two complicated colours whose names she could never remember, coiled around her waist. She forced herself to relax into the quasi-embrace.

'We'll be safe?' she subvocalized to Ten Per Cent Extra Free. 'Or should we start to fight it out right here and now?'

THE PREEAE WILL NOT HARM YOU. PROBABLY. WOULD YOU

The question was unanswerable.

The Preeae herded the humans towards a gaping hole in the room's floor. Strider shoved herself to the front, trailing behind her a clutching Preeae. A captain should lead her troops into each new hazard. 'Can you bring up the rear again, Pinocchio?' she asked the bot over her radio.

'I'll do my best,' the bot replied. The Preeae beside him looked at him sharply. Pinocchio had clearly not intended to speak out loud.

The Preeae which had its arm around Strider suddenly picked her bodily from the floor, swivelled her over its shoulder, and peremptorily threw her face-first into the hole.

Oh, well, this is it, thought Strider as the darkness closed around her. She felt like a pacifist torpedo: it was much against her will that she had been launched. She wouldn't explode, of course, when she hit her destination. Actually, come to think of it, she almost certainly *would* explode, but in a different sense of the word. The images in her mind weren't appealing.

And then she wasn't in darkness any more but in a wash of silvery light, as if the air were made of mercury. The visor of her suit automatically dimmed the glare, but did not change the colour. It seemed that she was floating down slowly, but she couldn't be sure because there wasn't any background against which she could measure her position. She floundered her limbs a few times and then realized the uselessness of the manoeuvre. *Better just to watch the pretty light, Leonie,* she thought, spreading her body into a star-shape, hoping she was right about which direction was down.

'Are any of you Images there?'

YES. YOU'RE PERFECTLY SAFE. Ten Per Cent Extra Free sounded more than usually supercilious.

'It might be a good idea if you told everyone else about this *before* they were flung down here.'

The silvery light abruptly vanished. Hundreds of metres beneath her she saw a hard stone surface rushing to meet her.

'I thought you said I was perf –' she began.

But she was flying. So this was what it must be like to be Polyaggle, except that she didn't have to make any physical effort at all to move herself from place to place. If she wanted to drift to the right then to the right she drifted. If she wanted to hover she hovered. It was the greatest freedom of movement she had ever known – better, far better, than free fall, where you always had to bear in mind that a minor motion here or there might have a major consequence later on. All she had to do was to *think* her position from one place to the next, and her spreadeagled body would take her there.

She was in a cavern, carved out of the rock, of such vastness that it was impossible to appreciate its size. All around her she could see yellowy brown stone walls, but they were too far away from her for her to be able to make out any details. She lazily turned herself over on to her back and saw that what she had been falling through earlier was a brightly white cloud. Another suited figure was just emerging from it.

She continued the rotation so that once more she was looking downwards. A ring of about a dozen Preeae were gazing up at her as she made her languorous descent. The trouble was that she wasn't sure how much she wanted to make that descent. If she'd had total freedom of choice she'd have opted to stay here for the rest of her life. She wished she weren't wearing her spacesuit – she wished she weren't wearing anything at all, so that she could feel the air moving against her skin and her hair.

It was her duty to be down there among the Preeae. She was the captain of the *Santa Maria* and she had to take command of matters on behalf of her personnel. But the temptation to stay here, wafting to and fro in the air, was almost irresistible . . .

She came to ground smoothly beside the group of Preeae and was immediately shoved a few metres to one side. What she hadn't noticed from aloft was that three of the aliens were pointing those ugly-looking weapons skywards.

'Tell everyone else they mustn't think of flying around too long,' she said urgently to Ten Per Cent Extra Free.

WE'VE ALREADY DONE SO.

'Thanks for telling *me*.'

289

The next person to arrive was Holmberg, followed rapidly by Senskatachowan – a bacteriologist from whom Strider had over the years done her best to conceal her dislike – and Hilary. Even through the spacesuit one could detect the child's sense of exhilaration. Strider grinned. She still felt that same exhilaration. If the Preeae suddenly changed their minds and decided to massacre the humans, she would thank them in her dying breath for the experience they had just given her.

More and more of her personnel glided into the ring of Preeae and were manhandled across to join her. A couple of them had obviously been terrified by their brief encounter with flying, and had to be supported by others.

She keened her eyes and looked around her. The cavern's walls were still impossibly distant: she could see only enough of them to know that they were there. No, that wasn't quite true. Here and there, in whichever direction she looked, there were circular or semicircular patches of darkness that were presumably the mouths of yet more tunnels leading to yet other parts of the Preeae's domain.

Once the last of the *Santa Maria*'s personnel had arrived – it was Pinocchio – the party was ushered unceremoniously across the floor of the huge cavern. The Preeae were not averse to using their weapons as goads with which to hurry the humans along. Some of the children began to shriek in fear, and most people switched off their suit radios and commlines.

Strider assumed that they were heading for one of those tunnel-openings, but suddenly the Preeae called a halt. One of the aliens moved ahead some fifty or sixty metres and made quick, complicated adjustments to the weapon he carried.

Oh, no, thought Strider. *It's going to be the firing squad for us.*

But instead the alien turned the modified weapon towards the ground. He did *something* to it, and then the floor just in front of him began to split open like the skin of an over-ripe fruit. The noise would have been deafening to the humans had it not been muffled by their suits. The vibrations underfoot were violent enough to make Strider stagger backwards and collide with Holmberg, who himself almost fell over from the impact. *This is what it must be like when an earthquake hits,* she thought. The jagged line of the split extended swiftly in either direction from them for almost a minute before the vibrations calmed down – for all Strider could tell, the opening ran the full width of the cavern. Then the noise started again, as the two puckered edges of the crack slowly pulled themselves apart.

The Preeae hustled the humans forwards.

As Strider looked down from the lip of the opening her first thought was that what she was seeing was a row of coffins.

'You're going to bury us alive,' she spat at the nearest Preeae guard.

He gave no reaction.

YOU ARE PERFECTLY SAFE, said Ten Per Cent Extra Free again. I TOLD YOU THAT THE PREEAE HAD A TRANSPORTATION SYSTEM. THIS IS IT.

'Why didn't that bastard hear me?'

WE DECIDED THAT IT WOULD BE MOST POLITIC IF WE TEMPORARILY CEASED DIRECTLY INTERPRETING YOUR CONVERSATION, CAPTAIN LEONIE STRIDER. FOR REASONS THAT MUST BE OBVIOUS.

'Whaddya mean, "obvious"?'

"THAT BASTARD."

'If someone's jabbing you around with a lethal weapon, what other term would you ascribe?'

IF SOMEONE'S SAVING YOUR LIFE, BUT MIGHT VERY WELL CHANGE THEIR MIND, WHAT TERM WOULD *YOU* ASCRIBE?

She decided not to answer the question, instead tonguing her suit radio on to the general frequency.

'I have consulted with the Images,' she said, hoping that her words could be heard over the din of wailing children – and a few adults, she was dismayed to realize. 'There is no cause for panic. We are not going to be harmed in any way.'

Strider realized that half her people probably still had their radios switched off. The others had probably heard her tell them not to panic just once too often.

'Can you give the same message directly to them?' she subvocalized to Ten Per Cent Extra Free.

I HAVE ALREADY DONE SO.

'Doesn't seem to have had much effect.'

The Preeae who had split open the floor of the cavern was gesturing to her that she should jump down into the coffin directly beneath her. Hoping that she was doing the right thing, she obeyed. The drop was less than a metre, but it seemed very much further. She lay down in the oblong box and resisted the temptation to cross her arms over her chest: her duty was to give her personnel an encouraging example.

The Preeae straddling the split directly above her made urgent gesticulations. It took her a moment to realize what he was trying to tell her, and then, clumsily, she got up on her hands and knees and turned herself around the other way. It made sense. If this conveyance system accelerated quickly up to any speed, it was best to travel head-first. She guessed that deceleration at the far end would be a bit more gradual. She hoped so.

She could see others of her personnel being urged into the coffins ahead of her. She assumed the same was happening behind, because every now and then the coffin in which she was lying rocked slightly. Some of her people were having to be forced pretty damned hard, despite the Images' reassurance. She repeated again and again over the general frequency that there was nothing to be worried about, all the time wishing that, as they'd dashed from the *Santa Maria*, she'd thought to jam a commlink into her mouth. Maybe she should have hooked up to the commline long ago, but she still disliked the thought of being invaded by technology, however useful that technology might be.

Couldn't someone get those bloody kids to shut up?

The same grinding, wrenching noise that had marked the opening of the split started up again, and the strip of light above began to narrow as the rocky edges moved towards each other. Now she started to feel real fear. She turned on her suit lights, and quickly issued an instruction to everyone else to do the same. She assumed Ten Per Cent Extra Free would repeat her instruction.

The split closed. She was staring straight upwards at what

looked like a rough-hewn granite surface, not fifty centimetres from her face. They say you can get used to anything, but Strider wasn't sure she was going to be able to get used to this. Again her pulse was pounding, and there wasn't anything she could do about it. How long was it going to take them to travel the four hundred and fifty kilometres? Would their suit air last out? The vision came into her mind of a string of what were now genuinely coffins arriving at the mountain terminus. She started doing some calculations before realizing that the Preeae's system would have to be exceptionally slow for that to be a concern. Besides, the Preeae must have aerated the whole system so that they, too, could survive it. What was more worrying was that, if she was as terrified as this, how would some of the others be reacting? Would any of the kids reach out an inquisitive hand to touch the moving surface as the coffins rattled along at a couple of hundred kilometres an hour, or whatever this apparatus was capable of?

Her last anxiety was removed when a metal lid suddenly appeared over the box in which she was lying. In a way, this was even worse.

With some difficulty she manoeuvred herself around until she was lying on her stomach, and tongued off her suit lights. Better to pretend that she was just lying on a bed.

But it wasn't like that at all. There was a jolt and then, for a long – a very long – moment, it felt as if she were standing vertically but pressing herself with all her force against a wall.

Then there was oblivion.

It took a long while for Commander Segrill's people to work out how to get the alien spaceship open, and more than once he was tempted to tell them to go at it with lazcutters. He restrained himself. The spaceship that had destroyed half the planet's manufactories and then come gracelessly to the ground here in the desert could contain much that was of interest, and could possibly be of great use in itself. Where the aliens had gone to was no great mystery to him: from the marks they had left in the sand – milling around for a while and then converging on a single point – it was obvious that they had discovered one of the Preeae's access points, which had since been removed. If the technology aboard the spaceship proved advanced enough, he would liaise as best he could with one of his Preeae contacts – negotiations were always tricky because of the Preeae's powerful xenophobia – to see if he could track the aliens down.

This attack could be the best thing that had ever happened during his stint in charge of security on F-14. The defensive shielding of the spaceship had been pretty sophisticated, so it was likely that the rest of the technology aboard would be of a similar standard.

He was one of four of the Autarchy's occupiers of F-14 that knew about the continued existence of the Preeae. As head of security it was his duty to exterminate those survivors. As someone who wished to see the end of the Autarchy sooner rather than later, he had kept very quiet about his knowledge, as had his three co-confidants. The Preeae presented no nuisance, and might one day be helpful.

It was easy to rise to a position of minor power within the Autarchy. All you had to do was say the right things and keep very quiet about what was actually going on. Gambling for higher stakes was a much more risky business: the Autarch became aware of your existence, which meant that there was the ever-present possibility that he would decide you were a threat. Within the Autarchy, possible threats didn't last long. But a mere commander of security was beneath the Autarch's notice.

The technicians on F-14 hated the fact that they were there. Most of the people within the Autarchy hated what they were doing, but they had very little choice about it: on the average planet even an ill timed fart could lead to a painful death. The power of the Autarch's forces was almost absolute, because it was built from the top downwards. Only a comparative few were loyal to the Autarchy itself, but those few had the power of life and death over those below them. The same principle applied all the way down, until finally the pyramid's base was formed by the vast mass of ordinary people, who didn't give much of a curse about the Autarchy but just wanted to live from day to day without the threat of being butchered.

Where the Autarchy had made its mistake was in gathering a very large group of such people on F-14. The technicians did what they did because they were forced to, and almost without exception they loathed the war machines they were having to create. For all they knew, that particular item of weaponry was going to be used to annihilate their own species.

Segrill had slowly, cautiously worked his way up through the system until he had been posted to F-14. If there was a single planet that could threaten the Autarchy, this was it.

There was a yell of triumph as someone managed to open the spacecraft's outer lock.

Maybe the aliens had booby-trapped their abandoned vessel. He had to take the chance that they hadn't.

Segrill, who was about the size of Strider's thumb, flew across the desert so that he could be the first to investigate.

Strider opened her eyes and switched on her suit lights. Directly beneath her face was a rather dirty metal surface; she was glad she was in her spacesuit because the surface looked as if it stank. She felt as if she had had a claustrophobic dream, then remembered that it had been really happening.

There was very little room in the coffin, but she was able to shuffle over on to her back.

'How long have I been out?' she subvocalized.

ABOUT TWO HOURS, said a voice which she recognized as Heartfire's. YOU WILL BE RELEASED FROM CONFINEMENT VERY SOON NOW.

'Where's Ten Per Cent Extra Free?'

CLOSE BY.

'How much are we at risk from contamination?' said Strider, wriggling to try to make herself more comfortable. Her back was aching. Ideally she would have liked to stand up and flex herself.

AS FAR AS I CAN ESTABLISH, NOT AT ALL.

'How far are we from the mountain escape-way?'

WE ARE THERE ALREADY. THE PREEAE ARE PREPARING TO RELEASE YOU ALL FROM YOUR CONTAINERS.

'How many of us are still alive?'

TWO ARE DEAD. ONE TORE HIS EYES OUT AND BLED TO DEATH INSIDE HIS SUIT. ANOTHER DIED WHEN THE MAJOR PUMPING ORGAN OF HIS CIRCULATORY SYSTEM CEASED TO OPERATE. IN EACH INSTANCE WE DID OUR BEST TO ASSIST THEM, BUT IT WAS BEYOND OUR CAPABILITIES.

'Who are the dead?'

THEY ARE NOBODY ANY LONGER.

Strider kept her anger under control. Over time she'd built up a relationship with Ten Per Cent Extra Free, so that he generally understood what she was saying rather than just the literal meaning of the words she spoke. Heartfire and Angler were rather more of a problem. She wondered how many basic errors there were in the interpretations they offered when translating between herself and other species.

'What were those dead people called?' she said.

THE PERSON WHO DIED THROUGH CIRCULATORY MALFUNC-TION WAS NAMED MARCIAL HOLMBERG.

Oh shit. A man whom she had begun to like.

THE PERSON WHO DIED BECAUSE HE RIPPED HIS EYES OUT WAS CALLED KHAN RAVI, AND WAS THREE YEARS OLD. ONLY A CHILD WOULD HAVE HAD ENOUGH ROOM IN HIS SPACESUIT TO REACH HIS EYES WITH HIS HANDS.

That was worse, a lot worse. Holmberg had led a reasonable adult life and then had experienced a few moments of agony before, boomf, he was gone. Young Ravi, by contrast, must have reached the outer extremities of terror and died in a loneliness that no one living could imagine.

She kept herself in check.

'How many of us are still sane?'

IT IS DIFFICULT FOR ME TO ASCERTAIN. WE IMAGES ARE NOT ENTIRELY CAPABLE OF TRACKING THE THOUGHT PROCESSES OF PEOPLE WITHIN THE WONDERVALE AND DECIDING WHETHER OR NOT THEY MAKE SENSE WITHIN YOUR OWN SPHERE OF REFERENCE.

'At a guess?'

MOST. PROBABLY ALL.

'You can't be more accurate than that?'

NO.

'What exactly did the Preeae do to us?'

THEY ACCELERATED YOU TO A VERY HIGH VELOCITY, AND
THEN THEY SHUT DOWN ALL YOUR HIGHER NEURAL FUNC-
TIONS. THEY WERE TRYING TO MAKE YOUR TRANSIT AS EASY AS
IT COULD POSSIBLY BE – IN THEIR TERMS.

'I'd rather have watched the rocks go by,' said Strider.

BUT A PREEAE WOULD NOT HAVE. AND NEITHER WOULD
MOST OF THE PERSONNEL YOU COMMAND. PLEASE DO NOT
OBJECT TOO LOUDLY, CAPTAIN LEONIE STRIDER. THE PREEAE
ARE DOING EVERYTHING THAT THEY CAN TO HELP YOU WITHIN
THE LIMITATIONS THEY EARLIER STATED.

'Yeah, I guess that's true,' she said after a second or two.

GLADNESS, said the Image.

The lid of her coffin swiftly withdrew. A ribbon of light
began to appear overhead.

She had spent almost all of the journey they had made in a
state of enforced sleep. Nevertheless, what she wanted to do
was to fall back into sleep. The option wasn't open to her.

A Preeae reached down, grabbed the front of her suit, lifted
her, and chucked her on to a hard stone floor.

Wherever it was they'd arrived, they'd arrived.

Strider was the first to remove her helmet. She wasn't sure it
was wise, and was slightly surprised – whatever Heartfire had
said – when she didn't drop dead immediately. On the other
hand, the alternative was that the small human party would
plough on through the foothills until, sooner or later, they
suffocated inside their spacesuits. With luck Kortland would
have kept an eye out for them and would send a rescue party . . .
but Strider reckoned there would have to be a hell of a lot of
luck involved. Maybe, maybe, they'd be rescued: much more
likely that they'd peter out, one by one, on the surface of F-14.
But, just in case, she wanted to conserve what was left of her
oxygen.

The air up here smelt good, unlike the fetid air of the desert:

the first deep breath she took tasted like cold water, even though the surroundings were surprisingly hot. Above them the slopes of the mountain seemed to reach upwards so far that they punctured the sky. There was some kind of springy blue-green vegetation underfoot, so that Strider felt as if she were lighter than usual. With the strap of her helmet looped over her left wrist, she drew her lazgun from her waist. She and her personnel weren't far from a glacial snowline, so water wouldn't be a problem – assuming there weren't things in the snow that'd kill them – but food was going to be more difficult.

The Preeae had dumped the humans out on the surface with very little ceremony. Last to be ejected had been the suited corpses of Holmberg and Ravi. The trapdoor, the same bluish-green as the vegetation, had hovered for a few moments longer and then reared into the air – and then vanished with such speed that, had Strider not been watching it, she would never have seen it go. There was a small cave near to where the trapdoor had been: after removing the oxygen tanks from the backs of the dead people's spacesuits, Strider and Pinocchio had stuffed the corpses into it. It wasn't much of a burial – in fact, it wasn't a burial at all, although Strider had said a few pious words – but it was as much as she could give them. She'd told Pinocchio to handle the body of the child: one look at the red-specked visor of the infant was enough to convince her that this was a job someone else should do.

'We might as well go all together,' she said blithely to the Images, feeling almost doped up by the air. 'Tell the rest of them to get their helmets off. Please.'

THIS WILL BE DONE, said Heartfire in his normal stilted fashion. She wished that Ten Per Cent Extra Free were back with her. BE CAREFUL WHAT YOU SHOOT FOR FOOD. NOT EVERYTHING HERE IS WHAT IT LOOKS. LET US GUIDE YOU.

'If it looks like food I'm goddam going to eat it. Have you guys ever known what it's like to be *hungry*?'

But at the moment she didn't feel hungry. What she felt as she loped along on the springy vegetation was pretty good. Sooner or later, though, she and her people were going to have to find something to eat. Maybe she'd have been better off going downhill rather than up – she could see there was prolific foliage of some kind down there – but she sensed that she'd made the right decision. Certainly the Images hadn't disagreed with her, and presumably they'd have kicked up a fuss if she'd been doing something stupid. Yeah: Heartfire was implying that there'd be food animals somewhere up ahead.

There was more oxygen in the atmosphere than she was accustomed to. On board the *Santa Maria* the oxygen level had been held somewhere between Mars-standard and Earth-standard, so that no one was too uncomfortable. Here the concentration was much higher than that, which was probably why she was feeling as if she'd just given herself a fix of ziprite.

The afternoon sun was very bright behind her as she climbed. She was not accustomed to seeing such a stark shadow ahead of herself. Far high in the sky small motes whirled: the planet had birds or bird-analogues.

The humans chattered as they went along, relieved to be released from the oppressiveness of the Preeae's underground realm. Strider realized that, for almost all of them, it was the first time they had been out in the open air for years – and that for the children it was the first time ever. Part of the reason for the incessant gossip might be that they were taking their minds off the fact that the open air might be killing them, even as they breathed it, but Strider thought not. This was the school outing.

A couple of hundred metres below the snowline there was a copse; Strider hadn't seen one since girlhood. They could hide in that for a while, leaving it only in ones and twos. Presumably the techs on F-14 had fairly sophisticated surveillance systems, so the less the cohort of humans was exposed on the hillside the better. If the copse was made up of anything remotely resembling trees, there would be food animals living within it. There might also be fruit – the Images would doubtless be able to analyse the vegetation to determine what was and what was not safe for the humans to eat. Berries. Nuts. Anything. She was beginning to come down off her oxygen high, and the prospect of eating something was becoming very appealing indeed.

They reached the copse and stumbled through the under-growth into the green-grey shade of what looked not unlike trees. Strider stripped off her spacesuit: there might be predators or stinging creatures around, but she was prepared to take the risk. Most of the other personnel did likewise; she insisted they each put their suit somewhere distinctive, so that they could find it again in a hurry. Because they were high up on the hillside she reckoned that, come nightfall, the current pleasant coolness of the air would turn into extreme cold: the suits would offer protection against that. Some of the people had been naked when the order to abandon the *Santa Maria* had come, and she issued orders that these people – except Polyaggle – should keep their suits on: there were no longer any medbots on hand to treat minor cuts and abrasions.

There was a sudden commotion within the undergrowth. Some largish animal was running away from them in panic.

FOOD, said Heartfire.

'Are there a lot of them in here?' she subvocalized. She wished she'd been able to see what the animal looked like.

ENOUGH FOR TEN OR FIFTEEN DAYS. ALSO, THE BARK OF SOME OF THE TREES IS EDIBLE AND NUTRITIOUS. THE FRUITS ARE NOT, ALTHOUGH THEY LOOK SO.

Strider barked out an order that no one was to eat anything until it had been verified by one of the Images. One of the kids – the one called Hilary – looked momentarily rebellious. She faced him down.

They had food. They could make fire. Water, in the form of snow, was only a few hundred metres away, although she guessed that this copse wouldn't have been here if there weren't running water somewhere around. Ten or fifteen days, Heartfire had said: with luck the Helgiolath would discover them before that. If not, there must be other places to go.

For the first time in a long while Strider began fully to relax.

A week later Strider was the chieftain of a tribe of naked primitives. Or, at least, that's what anyone would have thought had it not been for the way they used lazguns to shoot food and climbed into spacesuits every night. At the height of the day it was impossible to move around in your standard-issue SSIA jumpsuit, because you sweated so much from the heat – and anyway, after a couple of days, the garment stank not just of sweat but of quite a lot more, because the copse had turned out not to have running water after all. The best way of keeping clean was to have a snow-bath, though Strider allowed only two people at a time to do this. The process was reasonably effective but freezing: quite a lot of ribaldry was directed by the women at the men. The big animals in the copse turned out to look like mammalian seven-legged spiders on whose upper surface someone had mounted a rabbit's head; once you forgot about the appearance of the creatures – 'arachnibunnies', as someone had christened them – it was possible to enjoy their meat, which tasted like the very best textured soya protein you'd ever come across. Polyaggle – on the advice of the Images – stuck to the bark of the trees, which tasted like rotting maize if eaten raw and like barley if cooked. There seemed to be no bird-analogues dwelling among the trees, which puzzled Strider, because there were certainly bird-analogues flying high in the sky. Evolution, she reasoned, can play curious tricks.

One quarter of the copse was designated the latrine area, and by now people walked very cautiously there.

Strider was proud of her tribe. Whatever their living conditions might look like from the outside, they had accepted the rules she had imposed on them and were in fact a disciplined little community. The chores were shared around, and everybody did what they were supposed to do. Meals were eaten exclusively during daylight hours, because Strider reckoned that heat-seeking surveillance devices wouldn't spot the fires over which the meat was cooked when the rest of the landscape was so hot. If you got hungry at night . . . well, the taste of rotting maize went away after a while, or if you were very lucky there might be some cold arachnibunny left over from the afternoon.

She liked being a primitive. Her body was covered in scratches where she'd stumbled into thorny undergrowth, but once she'd learnt that the pain didn't hurt *that* much it didn't matter any more. The soles of her feet were quite another matter: after some experimentation she and everyone else kept their boots on.

Strider would have been happy to stay here for the rest of her life except for three facts. Sooner or later they were going to be discovered. The food supply was, as they'd known from the start, not infinite. And, by the law of averages, someone was almost certainly already pregnant: although there was a chance Pinocchio could perform the delivery safely, it wasn't something Strider wanted to prove empirically.

She was levelling her lazgun at an arachnibunny when the fighter craft arrived. At first she didn't pay attention to the faint whine, assuming that someone had disturbed a swarm of the little insect-analogues that plagued the copse and inflicted the occasional irritating bite. A single shot drilled through the arachnibunny's head and the creature slumped. She gave it another blast to be certain that it was dead, and was glad that she had done so because it gave a little reflexive kick of its legs.

The buzzing noise continued.

She moved forward to grab the arachnibunny by a leg, and then Ten Per Cent Extra Free spoke.

YOU ARE NEEDED ON THE FAR SIDE OF THE COPSE.

'Why?'

YOUR PEOPLE HAVE BEEN DISCOVERED BY THE FORCES OF F-14. THEY HAVE BROUGHT A FLEET OF FIGHTERS.

'Oh. Great.'

She looked at the dead animal. It could wait for a while.

Strider half-ran, half-tripped through the undergrowth. Now that haste was needed, being naked didn't seem to be such a good idea after all. Someone had had the sense to tell everyone else to shut up, because nobody – not even the kids – had started screaming. The whining sound decreased in volume. The Autarchy must have pretty goddam good technology if it could move heavy vehicles through the air with so little noise.

She tripped on a root and fell, knocking the wind out of herself. Some of the plants in this copse had stinging leaves, and one of them stung her just above the navel. It was exactly what she could have done without. She heaved herself to her feet and carried on, pushing away branches and tall, swaying plants with her hands.

This wasn't going to be the most elegant way to fight a battle, wearing boots and nothing else. With luck there wouldn't be too many war photographers around.

When she got to the end of the copse she threw herself down beside Pinocchio, who was lying flat on his stomach as he looked down the slope. His lazgun was in his hand, sweeping from side to side as if in search of something to shoot.

'The fighters are about a hundred metres downhill from us,' he said. 'There are approximately fourteen of them. I may have miscounted.'

Strider had difficulty controlling her breathing enough to be able to form words.

'I can't see anything.'

'They're small. The biggest of them is five metres across and about twenty-five centimetres high.' Pinocchio for once was sounding uncertain of himself – almost afraid, if that were possible. 'I think they must be remotes. What they likely want to do is blow away half the hillside and bury us in the rubble.'

'You'll probably be able to dig yourself out,' said Strider. The words were coming more easily now.

'Almost certainly,' said the bot. 'But only to find myself alone.'

WE HAVE MADE CONTACT WITH THE F-14 FORCES, said Ten Per Cent Extra Free.

'Good,' said Strider. 'Could you persuade a few of them to autodestruct?'

I THINK YOU MISPERCEIVE THE SITUATION.

The alien spaceship had been a fertile field. Segrill had expected that it would be fitted with the tachyonic drive, of course, but he had not expected the Pockets. He had wasted rather more time than he ought to have done playing with these, buzzing his head against each of them in turn and watching the wildest of his imaginings being brought into being. At last he had realized what the gadgets were *for*, and had called up a vision of the fleeing party of aliens. They were travelling on the

Preeae's transportation system, something that Segrill had experienced once and had vowed never to do again. They looked as if they were rigid with fear, which Segrill could understand. They were certainly rigid with something.

The nearest Preeae access point was about four hundred and fifty kilometres away. That was probably where the Humans were being taken. Speaking quickly into his kreebolly, he issued orders that twenty of the fighters should go to that point at once. The officer who took the instructions was obviously confused as to why he was being sent to this particular set of co-ordinates. Segrill decided not to explain. The fighters were to stay as high as possible and do nothing more than observe, because the Humans – if the technology aboard this spaceship was anything to go by – were probably equipped with pretty impressive weaponry.

The next few days were spent probing through the rest of the spaceship's appurtenances. Segrill watched entertainment holos which made very little sense to him as of course he couldn't understand a word of what the Humans were saying although he began to have a shrewd notion of their mating habits; he was less certain why sometimes two of the Humans would remove their clothing and roll around together. He accidentally fired off one of the *Santa Maria*'s missiles, and was thankful that they were in the middle of a desert: the resultant plume of sand was very impressive, and could probably have been seen five hundred kilometres away. Other items of technology were far more mysterious, having no apparent purpose that Segrill and his people could ascertain. There was a machine that emitted a roar of cacophonous noise when a button was pressed and then could only be turned off again with great ingenuity. Bots of various kinds crawled around the interior of the vessel, busily continuing to do whatever it was that they were supposed to do; some were clearly cultivating what Segrill recognized as tilled fields, but others had tasks that were quite inscrutable. There were also animals in forms that Segrill had never seen before, from small fluttering things not *totally* unlike himself to much larger quadrupedal creatures with nubby horns and the habit of excreting at unpredictable moments.

Through his kreebolly he called up data on the known life-forms of The Wondervale, ruthlessly narrowing down the scope of his search as he progressed. There was nothing the kreebolly could tell him about any of these creatures, nor about the dominant species: double-armed bipeds were prolific throughout the galaxy, of course, but none approximated to these except the Link–kreatzai, a barely sentient species (although Segrill had his doubts) that lived in conditions of astonishing filth on a world that closely orbited a red dwarf at the opposite extreme of The Wondervale. That the Humans were not the Runtuata was readily apparent from the debris they had left behind them. They were from a high-tech species.

Through his kreebolly he also recited a series of carefully constructed, carefully boring reports back to his deputy in Hallaroi. He had found an alien spacecraft, he said. The aliens had all died when the ship had crashlanded. There was little of technological interest here – that was probably why the craft had been able to slip through F-14's defences – but it was worth picking through what there was just in case something useful might be salvageable.

Segrill made sure that none of his people was within earshot whenever he made his reports, even though they were all utterly loyal to him . . . he was *almost* certain.

He had a sudden inspiration.

If the Pockets were capable of calling up anything he asked them for, presumably he could ask them to show him the surrounds of this ship as they had been a few days ago. That way he might be able to start guessing about where the aliens had come from.

Yes.

It worked.

He saw this ship in the middle of a sea of others. There were thousands of them there.

F-14 had several hundred warcruisers of its own, newly made and ready to be sent to various parts of the Autarchy. Segrill had, therefore, a personal space armada.

Joined to the vast fleet from which the Humans had come, it would be worth twice as much – no, far more than that, because on its own it would be next to useless against whatever the Autarch Nalla might think to put up, given time.

Segrill had never considered himself to be particularly philosophical or spiritual, but when he saw that fleet of alien starships he suddenly felt as if he were there at one of those infinitely rare moments when a corner of history was being turned.

Just as an experiment, he tried using the Pocket to look into the *Santa Maria*'s future.

It didn't work.

Strider didn't see the alien at first. It came hopping across the blue-green vegetation, winged itself into the air for a few metres, and then started hopping towards her again. She saw it out of the corner of her eye, but assumed that the local bird-analogue life had chosen a singularly inappropriate moment to display itself. She kept the downslope covered with her lazgun, moving it steadily one way and the other. The lazgun wasn't going to be a lot of use if those things out there were just remotes, but neither was anything else.

The little creature almost jumped on to her hand before she gave it proper attention. It had bird-like wings, but its body was more like that of a tailless mouse. Its head was vaguely reminiscent of that of a mouse as well, except that there were no visible ears.

THIS PERSON WISHES TO SPEAK WITH YOU, CAPTAIN LEONIE STRIDER, said Ten Per Cent Extra Free.

'Which person?'

THE ONE STANDING ALMOST DIRECTLY IN FRONT OF YOU. HIS NAME IS COMMANDER EBERRY SEGRILL. HE IS THE HEAD OF SECURITY ON THIS PLANET.

Strider focused on the small winged animal. She had been just about to bat it out of the way with the back of her hand.

'You mean he wants to kill us?'

I THINK YOU HAD BETTER SPEAK WITH HIM.

She looked more closely at the little creature, and then held out her hand. Without hesitation Segrill hopped on to her palm.

'We must talk to each other,' he said. Strider could hear both the piping noise he made and the words interpreted by Ten Per Cent Extra Free. The proposition seemed ludicrous on the face of it. If she clenched her hand tightly she could crush this tiny animal to a pulp. Yet Segrill was chief of what was presumably an efficient strike force and she was the leader of a band of primitives . . .

'Please explain,' she said.

'Not everyone who is in the thrall of the Autarchy wishes to see it persist,' said Segrill.

'How do I know I can trust a single word you say?'

'I will permit you to read my mind in its entirety,' said Segrill.

Strider didn't understand for a moment. Then realization struck her. The little alien assumed that the Images were an integral part of this particular small band of human beings. Why should he think anything different? Ten Per Cent Extra Free was currently operating out of Pinocchio, but of course Segrill couldn't see that. He must assume humans were telepathic. It might be wise to let him continue thinking that for a while.

'I've already done so,' she said. Because the alien was so close to her she couldn't even subvocalize. *Have you done a sweep of his mind?* she thought at Ten Per Cent Extra Free.

HE IS SINCERE, said the Image. I SHALL LET YOU KNOW IF HE STARTS TO LIE.

'And how can *I* know that I can trust *you*?' said Segrill.

'Because you're standing in the palm of my hand. More to the point, I'm metaphorically in the palm of yours. Each of us could destroy the other very easily.'

'That is true,' said Segrill. 'My people have lazcannon trained on you right at this minute.'

Strider hesitated. That was something more than she had anticipated. She had better get her mind together. If she continued to find it difficult to take this alien seriously she

307

might find herself and all the rest of her personnel dead very much more quickly than she expected.

'What can you offer us?' she said.

Segrill explained how the techs working on F-14 were, in effect, a legion of revolutionaries just waiting for the right moment to rise up. He had seen the huge fleet of Human warcruisers – it took Strider a further moment of thought to understand that what he had seen was the Helgiolath armada – and believed that he could add several hundred warcruisers to it, each crewed by dedicated warriors. The techs knew more about the Autarchy's weaponry – its strengths and weaknesses – than even the Autarch's military themselves, so that in effect he would be almost doubling the size of the 'Human' fleet. Although the Autarch, with warning, could set up a force much larger than the combined fleets, they would have the advantage of surprise – they might even be able to strike at Qitanefermear-tha itself before they were faced by any greater firepower.

Strider decided to put her cards on the table.

'Tell him what the true situation is,' she said to Ten Per Cent Extra Free.

'Are your friends the Helgiolath likely to accept us?' said Segrill after a short pause.

'If you're with us. If I'm able to talk to Kortland through a Pocket and persuade him that you're not snakes in the grass.'

This last metaphor clearly didn't translate too clearly. Strider had to explain it in two or three different versions before finally Ten Per Cent Extra Free hit on one that Segrill could understand.

'We must get you back to your spaceship,' said Segrill at length.

'How are you going to do that? I mean' – she waved with her free hand in the general direction of the hillside where the fighter craft lay squatly and small – 'you couldn't fit even half of one of us into your ships. By the way, just how *big* are these warcruisers you're offering?'

'Some of them are forty times the size of your own.'

'Um.'

'The techs vary in size between species very much smaller

308

than I am myself up to others that are nearly fifty metres tall. We all work together.'

'Are any of the cruisers as small as those fighters?' she said.

'Those fighters could very simply be converted into warcruisers, but you must understand that their firepower would not be great.'

'I think I just have the first glimmerings of an idea,' said Strider. 'I also think we have a partnership. I'd like to shake on it, except that probably you have some completely different method of signalling agreement and anyway I'm not sure I could do it without breaking your hand.'

SEGRILL'S SPECIES NORMALLY CONFIRM AN AGREEMENT BY HAVING SEXUAL INTERCOURSE, said Ten Per Cent Extra Free. WE THINK THAT IN THIS INSTANCE . . .

She stroked the top of Segrill's head, making sure that her touch was as gentle as possible.

'We're an alliance,' she said.

He leapt off her hand.

'Agreed.'

Then he was flying away across the hillside. He wheeled up into the sky for a moment, performing a complicated wing-movement that undoubtedly meant something to his troops – something like 'Don't shoot yet' – before she lost him from sight.

It was good to be back on board the *Santa Maria* again, and to be able to take a bath: that was just about the first thing most of the personnel had done.

Not Strider or her main officers, however: furtively hoping that they didn't smell as bad to other people as they did to themselves, they were trying to power the ship up, aided by the Images and by various of Segrill's techs. The difficulty was that, while the *Santa Maria* had been redesigned so that it could be operated in an atmosphere, it hadn't been adapted for landing or takeoff. It had jets that, with a little bit of cunning, could be used to lift it a few tens of metres off the ground, but thereafter its rocketry would be useful only for turning several

309

thousand square kilometres of desert, and whoever happened to be there, into glass.

Segrill had transported them from their leafy hideaway back to the desert by calling up one of the fighters under his command: this ship, crewed by the Bredai, who were rather larger than the average nightmare and required a methane atmosphere, had been almost of the same size as the *Santa Maria* itself. A human behavioural therapist, interested in the way these aliens interacted, had gone too close to one of them and been rendered, on the floor, as something quite disturbingly like a Preeae except for the bits and pieces of spacesuit scattered around the splotch. Strider didn't allow herself to spend too much time thinking about what had happened to the guy: someone had shovelled him up and they'd all given him a burial – a ceremony that had clearly baffled the aliens.

It had been a quick way to go. One moment you're conducting a piece of scientific observation, the next moment *splat*. One had to assume that, far in the past of every sentient species, there had been individuals who had made similar scientific discoveries. Let's try this nice new brightly shining fruit we haven't come across before. *Omnes:* Aargh.

Segrill had gone back to Hallaroi in hopes that the techs there would be able to solve the problem of getting the *Santa Maria* off the ground. Strider was in constant touch with him through the Images.

'This hasn't been the easiest of missions,' she said offhandedly to Nelson.

'I set off to Tau Ceti II and all I got was this lousy T-shirt,' he replied.

There was a beep from one of the communications Pockets. Strider moved to it and saw a semblance of Segrill: reproduced in the Pocket he seemed to be the same size as she was herself. The Images had clearly decided that she should speak to him face to face.

'There is a way,' he said, not concerned with any preliminaries.

'How?'

'We can *lift* you into space. A Bredai transport vessel is big

310

enough and powerful enough to haul you up into orbit. We're going to have to tamper with the size of the bay doors of the one that is just being completed in order to accommodate you, but this is not beyond our means.'

'Sounds good to me,' said Strider, although the prospect sounded terrifying. The immensities of what could go wrong filled her mind. Segrill assumed that the Bredai were his allies, but if they were in fact loyal to the Autarchy they could simply hoist the *Santa Maria* a few thousand metres in the air and *drop* it. Or, even with the best of intentions, they could allow an accident to occur which caused methane to flood into the *Santa Maria*.

'Go ahead,' she said.

5

My Fleet is Bigger than Yours

Kaantalech looked at her aide with what she knew was the
precisely proper expression of disdain. Not that the aide would
be able to pick it up, of course: any aide who grew clever
enough to be able to read her body language was dangerous,
and swiftly met the same fate as those who were too stupid. It
was a fine line you had to tread, being one of Kaantalech's
aides.

'You've found the Humans again, but they're in the middle
of an eight-thousand-strong fleet of warcruisers? That's worse
than it was before,' she repeated disbelievingly.

'That is what's happened,' said the aide tremulously. 'The
fleet has grown. Most of the ships are of the Helgiolath; the rest
we cannot as yet identify. And then there are the Humans.'

Kaantalech swore with elegant fluency. A fleet this size was
sufficient to inflict considerable damage on the Autarchy, at
least in the short term. She hadn't expected that other species
might start to add themselves to it.

Add a few hundred warcruisers and the fleet could . . .

Now *there* was an idea.

Add a few hundred warcruisers and you had a fleet big
enough to cause *permanent* damage to the current Autarchy.
Then there would be a hiatus while The Wondervale sorted
itself out, and *then* there would be the dawn of a new empire.
The future suddenly looked golden.

'I have spoken with the leader of the Human contingent
before,' she said. 'Establish contact again.'

'I'll do my best,' said the aide nervously.

Kaantalech hit him so hard that the sound of his bones
fracturing as his body shattered against the bulkhead remained

in the aural memories of her other aides for the rest of their lives.

'I want to speak with the Human-thing again,' she said. 'I need a volunteer to make the contact.'

Kortland made his decision. The raid he had mounted on F-14 had been, in the most unexpected of ways, a triumph. His fleet was now twice as strong – in effect if not numerically – as it had been before, and the Autarchy's main source of weaponry was hardly functioning at all. It wouldn't be long, though, before the Autarchy shipped out more techs to repair what farewell sabotage had done to the manufactories on F-14. He credited the Humans with their bravery and the ability they had shown to survive; had they not been so ugly he might have been prepared to award them the status of honorary Helgiolath. As it was, he was content enough to have their vessel as part of his armada.

The decision he made was simply enough expressed in a single word. He had thought this was an order that he himself would never be able to give – that it would be issued only by his successor, or by his successor's successor.

'Qitanefermeartha,' he said.

Polyaggle was attempting to establish contact with Kortland when a quite different face popped into existence in the communications Pocket. She recognized the species immediately: this was one of the Alhubra who had visited and attempted, from time to time over the years, to take over Spindrift and turn the planet to profit, and who had eventually destroyed her kind.

'You're not a Human,' said Kaantalech at once.

'I'm a Spindrifter.'

'There are no Spindrifters left alive.'

'I am.'

'I very much regretted the operational exercise which the Autarch forced me to perform. Please let me commiserate about the demise of your species.'

'Please let me commiserate about the demise of yours,' said

Polyaggle. She had never felt an emotion like this before – she guessed she must have picked it up from the Humans. It was vengefulness.

'My species is still alive and proliferating,' said Kaantalech.

'Not for long.' She didn't mean it. There were doubtless good Alhubra and bad Alhubra, just as there had been good Spindrifters and bad Spindrifters.

'I want to speak with your Human commander,' said Kaantalech.

'She may not want to speak with you.'

'Please ask her,' said Kaantalech. 'I am prepared to wait.' Drool was spilling out of the creature's mouth. Polyaggle, who did not salivate, was revolted.

She lifted her head from the Pocket and addressed Strider. 'There is a person here who believes it can do a deal of some kind with you.'

'Who is it?' said Strider, who was in the midst of trying to persuade the Images that perhaps they could resuscitate even more of the Main Computer than Polyaggle had been able to do, now that she had carried out the groundwork.

'It is a person from the Autarchy. It claims to have led the expedition that exterminated my species.'

'Tell it to fuck off, then.'

'It is most insistent. I believe it may have something to offer.' Polyaggle hated the words even as she spoke them. Were it not for the brood of new Spindrifters that was already forming within her she would have snapped off communications with the Alhubra-thing. But the Humans had befriended her, and one of them might form the nest for her brood. It was possible that the Alhubra could benefit the Humans, help them survive.

'OK, I'll speak with it,' said Strider.

Polyaggle stood aside to let Strider face the communications Pocket. In doing so she inadvertently brushed against Lan Yi, ripping his jumpsuit in several places with her bristles. He made the movement of his mouth which Polyaggle had come to realize was among the Humans a gesture of friendliness. She touched a claw to his hand by way of apology, and he made that

314

same gesture with his mouth again. She found it very difficult to like individual Humans, but this one seemed more amenable than most.

When her brood came to full ripeness, perhaps he would be the one.

'I have five hundred and twenty-two ships under my command, and I am prepared to join them to the Helgiolath fleet,' said Kaantalech to Strider as soon as she put her face into the communications Pocket.

'I don't think the Helgiolath will want you. You're the shit who destroyed the Spindrifters, aren't you? I thought I'd made my feelings plain enough before.'

'I was under orders.'

'Whose?'

'The Autarch Nalla's. He made me do it.'

'You could have refused.'

'If I had I would have been summarily executed.'

'So you thought it was worth annihilating an entire species just to save your own life?'

'This is irrelevant,' said Kaantalech. 'I can add considerable might to your fleet. I can also give much by way of information: I and my puters know more about the Autarchy's military secrets than you will ever learn.'

By your friends you are known, thought Strider. 'What you're trying to tell me,' she said, 'is that this could be a mutually profitable relationship?'

'It could indeed. I am as eager to see the end of the Autarchy as you are.' Kaantalech made a curious movement of her forelimbs which Strider couldn't interpret. 'I wish to see peace and harmony throughout The Wondervale.'

SHE'S LYING, said Ten Per Cent Extra Free.

'I knew that already,' Strider subvocalized.

'We have a common cause,' said Kaantalech.

'No, we don't. If I knew where you were right now I'd hit you with every beam and missile aboard this ship, and after I'd done that I'd get the entire Helgiolath fleet to do the same, and if that weren't enough I would chase you so far and so fast that you fell out of the side of the Universe. Is this clear?'

'We will talk about this again later,' Kaantalech said as her face vanished from the communications Pocket.

'Another nuisance commline call,' Strider explained sarcastically to O'Sondheim as she backed away from the Pocket. 'If only a few of them would start talking obscenely . . .'

Strauss-Giolitto woke to find there was a warm body beside her on the bed, and she snuggled affectionately against it. Then she woke again to discover that there wasn't anyone there.

Of all the recurring dreams she had, this was the cruellest.

Loneliness stretched out like a lake of unlit, unruffled water behind her. Ahead of her was the same black, still surface. She could speak openly to Pinocchio and with a certain modified frankness to Lan Yi, but otherwise there was no one on board the *Santa Maria* whom she could count as a friend. Yes, of course she missed sex, but what she missed far more than that was intimacy – the intimacy of whispering together in the moments before falling asleep, the intimacy of being in someone else's arms and holding them in her own, the intimacy of very slowly and softly licking a kneecap or a navel, the intimacy of waking together and both wanting a pee at the same time but neither of you willing to be the first to get up and go and have it. Masturbation could – and did – regularly relieve the sexual tension, but at the same time it made her all the more lonely.

She reached an arm across her forcefield bed, in the sleepy hope that for once her dream had not deceived her.

No. Still there was no one.

Strider and O'Sondheim were planning to pass over control to Leander and Nelson when the instruction from Kortland came through.

'Start with the big ones, eh?' said Strider to no one in particular. Flitting into the base of her Pocket were co-ordinates that she rapidly copied on her keyboard.

'What are we doing?' said Polyaggle.

'We're heading for Qitanefermeartha. The hub of the Autarchy.' Strider looked anxiously into her Pocket. She wished she could somehow divert the course of the *Santa Maria* so that she could take out Kaantalech, but she had no notion where Kaantalech was. In an intellectual way she knew that the Autarchy was committing crimes up to and including genocide all across The Wondervale, but that didn't match the emotions she had felt as she'd seen Spindrift die. Kortland was correct. While the time was right it was best to strike straight for the heart.

From all she had been told by Polyaggle and Segrill, the Autarch's fortress on Qitanefermeartha was impregnable. Assuming one could fight through the battalions of warcruisers there were still the forcefields to deal with. After that came the deadmetal. The alternative was to wipe out bits and pieces of the Autarchy, elsewhere in The Wondervale. Strider suspected this would involve crimes as great as the extermination of the Spindrifters. No, after all, diverting to discover Kaantalech and her fleet was not a good option.

Kaantalech could wait until later.

Strider pressed a final button, and everything in both the view-window and the Pocket changed. The vessels of the fleet were far more tightly bunched together now, so that it was possible to discern a few of the nearer ones as spacecraft rather than as just scintillating, moving pinpoints. In the Pocket itself Strider could see the overall configuration of the armada as it surrounded a small, undistinguished planet of a small, undistinguished star. In both the visual and the graphic displays of the Pocket it looked as if the fleet were forming an unbroken shell around this world, though she realized immediately that this was merely an illusion created by the Pocket's necessity to render eight thousand spacecraft as something larger than motes.

She squinted up at the view-window once again and speculated about which of the dots of the starry sky might be the planet they were surrounding. Somehow she had expected that it would be bright and awesome, as befitted its importance in The Wondervale, but of course she knew that from this

317

distance – they were half a light-hour out – it was possible that Qitanefermeartha was not even directly visible.

The first missile hit the *Santa Maria*'s defensive shields exactly seven minutes and thirty-three seconds afterwards.

'I would like to be able to study you. Would this be permitted?' said Lan Yi. There it was. At last he had been able to muster the nerve to put it directly to Polyaggle.

They were seated opposite each other with Lan Yi's chessboard between them. They were playing a variant of the four-handed version, each of them taking two teams; the objective was to obtain a misère, whereby you aimed to force your opponent into taking your pieces until finally only your two kings were left. He and Polyaggle had been contesting the game in various lengthy sessions ever since the *Santa Maria* had been lifted off F-14. They talked occasionally over the board; more usually they maintained silence, communicating through the moves they made – chess seemed to be not just an international but an inter-species language. The Spindrifter had taken to chess the moment Lan Yi had introduced her to the game, his underlying motive having been to lead up to the question he had just asked. Her only difficulty was in handling the pieces with her talons.

She looked at him blankly. Clearly what he had just said to her had been nothing more than a meaningless string of noise. She said something back to him, giving a little flutter of her wings as she did so. It was his turn to stare at her in incomprehension.

The Images were too busy elsewhere to be able to devote any part of their minds to interpreting between the two chess-players. This hardly ever happened. There must be some emergency brewing.

As there was absolutely nothing he could do about it, Lan Yi forced himself to relax. He shrugged at Polyaggle, returning the flick of the wings she had made towards him.

As he looked into her empty-seeming eyes, Lan Yi was hit yet again by the hugeness of the gulf that existed between them. They were learning the basics of each other's gestures, but

318

there was no question – possibly never *could* be a question – of their speaking directly to each other. The principles upon which the Spindrifter's language was constructed were entirely different from those that underpinned Argot. The two tongues had been born out of completely dissimilar species experiences and emotional states: although there were many areas of overlap – as evidenced by Polyaggle's seizing upon chess – Spindrifters and humans *thought* quite unlike each other. Lan Yi was amazed that the Images had been able to create communications between them at all.

That gulf – so vast. Presumably Polyaggle would feel closer to some of the ancient species, but otherwise she must be the loneliest being in all The Wondervale.

Are there degrees, however, of loneliness? thought Lan Yi, still looking into the vacuum of her eyes. *Isn't all loneliness the same? Is she any more lonely than . . . ?*

It came to him that, even more than the tachyonic drive, *loneliness* was what drove the *Santa Maria* through space. The ship itself was alone in The Wondervale, carrying as its cargo a few individuals who were in the wrong galaxy and the wrong time, an outcast even when it was acting in concert with other species, as now: only the Images could fully interact with the humans, but they were so different that they could hardly be counted as companions, or friends.

Even among the people aboard the *Santa Maria* there were great lonelinesses. Strider, forced to keep her emotional distance from her personnel and so able to find intimacy only with a bot. The bot himself, Pinocchio, who could form friendships with human beings – but how deep were those friendships compared with what he might achieve with another bot of his own calibre? Pinocchio, too, was communicating across what was in effect a species gulf. Strauss-Giolitto, whose lesbianism was now not just a suspicion but a certainty in Lan Yi's mind: her loneliness could be no less profound just because it had been self-imposed. O'Sondheim, who seemed on the outside to be so gregarious, yet was lost in a pit of solitude whose cause Lan Yi did not yet understand.

And then there was himself, who could look back over decades of loneliness.

He lowered his eyes and moved a rook.

Kortland's faces suddenly appeared in one of the communications Pockets.

Leander sprang to it.

'General announcement to the commanders of all vessels,' the Helgiolath said. 'There can be no interruption.'

Leander beckoned Strider, but Strider was lost in her own Pocket. Nelson, seeing the gesture, pulled at Strider's elbow. She moved rapidly across to join Leander.

'We have taken up formation around Qitanefermeartha, and its automated defences have been activated. Already we have sustained some casualties. It is vital that all craft maintain their shields at all times until we start to engage directly with the Autarch's warcruisers, which are now moving outwards towards us. Do not waste weaponry trying to destroy the automated ballistics: let the Autarchy waste these weapons. There will be fewer of them for us to deal with later.'

In order to launch a counterattack from a warcruiser, you had to drop your defensive shield for a tiny fraction of a second. That tiny fraction could be just enough time for a ballistic or a beam to sneak through and reduce your vessel to smithereens. This had been impressed upon Strider by an earlier general communiqué Kortland had issued, and she in turn had impressed it upon Leander and the others.

'All cruisers will now place themselves in direct communication with the central puter aboard this flagship,' the Helgiolath was saying. 'This instruction does not apply to those craft that are carrying back-ups of the central puter. The basic instructions are as follows . . .'

Not fully understanding what she was doing, Leander found her fingers dancing across the keyboard directly beneath her at the front of the Pocket. She knew that she was just a sentient channel through which the Helgiolath was feeding codes to the keyboard: the codes, like many of the keys, made no sense at all to her. What she was doing was unnecessary – the Images must be picking up all this stuff direct – but she found herself unable to stop obeying.

A second ballistic impacted against the *Santa Maria*'s defensive shields and exploded in a surge of fury and brilliance. Once again the craft itself was unaffected.

But there would have to come the time when the *Santa Maria* would be facing the might of the Autarchy head-on. A single ballistic penetrating through a momentarily dropped shield would rip the ship in half.

That time might not be long in coming.

Back on a hillside on F-14, when she had looked like nothing more than a naked savage as she and Segrill negotiated, Strider had had the beginnings of an idea. Later, after she'd established the *Santa Maria* in orbit, she'd explained it to him further.

Warcruisers are very large spacecraft – they have to be, because of all the weaponry they must carry, not to mention armoured shuttles for making planetfall, when that is necessary, and of course the troopers who will be going down in those shuttles. The average Autarchy warcruiser was home to upwards of a thousand personnel, and some of those were from species whose individuals were very large indeed – although few matched the Bredai for size. Most were on roughly the same scale as human beings. Very few sentient species were as small as Segrill's, the Trok.

Although warcruisers occasionally deployed fighters in combat, more usually they did not. The fate of a fighter when it came up against a defensive shield was much the same as that of a ballistic, but ballistics were significantly easier – and cheaper – to manufacture. Also, ballistics were a lot smaller than fighters and could move and manoeuvre much more swiftly, and so they presented a far more difficult target for the enemy to track and destroy – even despite the fact that the presence of sentient creatures aboard fighters made their trajectories much more unpredictable. Most of the time, therefore, warcruisers in battle were engaged in direct combat with each other: they were accustomed, in other words, to be fighting with objects that were as big as themselves.

Even a ballistic was quite large by comparison with a Trok fighter.

Of course, a Trok fighter couldn't carry the same firepower as one designed for a species built to the scale of, say, human beings. But that didn't matter too much. Its computers were every bit as skilful and speedy, and any missiles it launched could travel as swiftly as something far larger. A bigger missile could carry a bigger payload, certainly – one that could blow a warcruiser to pieces most impressively. But that was hardly necessary: in the hostile environment of the vacuum, a crippled warcruiser was a dead warcruiser. Though only a few metres across, the Trok's fighters were each capable of transporting – and directing – at least a couple of missiles which, assuming they penetrated the enemy's defensive shield, bore charges sufficient to do significant damage to a warcruiser's outer hull. And that was all that was needed.

Ever since the *Santa Maria* had rejoined the Helgiolath fleet she had been surrounded by a swarm of over a hundred Trok fighters under the overall command of Segrill. By comparison with the thousands of warcruisers amassed in the armada, the number was as trifling as the size of the vessels themselves, but Strider and Segrill were convinced they could do a disproportionate amount of damage to the Autarchy's forces.

WE ARE PICKING UP A NEW COMMUNICATION, said Ten Per Cent Extra Free.

'What is it?' said Strider. 'Put it on the communications Pocket.'

THE RELEVANT INDIVIDUAL DOES NOT WISH INITIALLY TO SPEAK WITH YOURSELF, CAPTAIN LEONIE STRIDER. WE COULD INTERPRET THE COMMUNICATION DIRECTLY TO THE PERSON INVOLVED ABOARD THIS SHIP, BUT WE BELIEVED THAT WE SHOULD ASK YOUR APPROVAL FIRST.

'Who do they want to speak to?' said Strider. It was unusual for the Images to consult her about very much. This must be something unusual.

POLYAGGLE, Ten Per Cent Extra Free replied.

Strider thought for a moment. She was fairly certain in her

322

own mind that the Spindrifter would do nothing to harm the *Santa Maria*, but she couldn't be a hundred per cent sure. Alien ways of thinking, as she kept telling herself, were radically different from human ones. Who could tell what was going on behind those impenetrably deep eyes?

'Can you ask Polyaggle to come to the command deck?' she said. 'She can speak via Pocket. I want to be able to see what's going on.'

WE CANNOT MONITOR THE POCKET AS SHE CONVERSES, said Ten Per Cent Extra Free reprovingly. IT WOULD BE AN INVASION OF PRIVACY.

Strider snorted. The Images had never been sticklers about her own privacy.

BESIDES, Ten Per Cent Extra Free added, BOTH BEINGS WOULD IMMEDIATELY RECOGNIZE OUR PRESENCE AND CEASE COMMUNICATION.

'Yeah,' she said. 'But I still want to be able at least to watch from outside the Pocket.'

WE HAVE REQUESTED HER PRESENCE, said the Image a moment later, AND SHE IS ALREADY MAKING HER WAY HERE.

Another ballistic impacted against the defensive shield as Strider waited. The effect inside the *Santa Maria* was as if everyone aboard had been brushed by a moth's wing. In the Pocket in front of her she could see, graphically represented, the Autarchy's warcruisers beginning to peel out of their orbits around Qitanefermeartha. The display told her that there were over four thousand of them. They were outnumbered nearly two to one, but there were still enough of them to ensure that this was going to be no walkover – especially since the Autarchy could count on the use of its ground-based ballistics as well.

The *Santa Maria*, too, was shifting its position under the commands of Kortland's central puter. Strider felt disempowered – hell, she *was* disempowered – by being able to do no more than watch her ship being navigated by remote control. One virtue the Helgiolath very clearly lacked was the art of public relations: it was all very well telling the individual commanders what was going on at the moment, but what they needed to know was *why* it was going on and, if all went according to plan, what was intended to happen next. As it was, Strider felt a seriously less useful component of the *Santa Maria* than her busted Main Computer.

Ten Per Cent Extra Free clearly picked up her thoughts.

KORTLAND IS INTRODUCING AN IMBALANCE TO THE ATTACKING SHELL AROUND QITANEFERMEARTHA, he said. HE IS AMASSING A FAR GREATER CONCENTRATION OF CRUISERS IN ONE AREA TO FORM, IN EFFECT, A SEPARATE FLEET THAT IS ABOUT THE SAME SIZE AS THE AUTARCH'S. CERTAINLY IT IS TOO LARGE FOR THE AUTARCH'S GENERALS TO IGNORE: THEY WILL HAVE TO DIRECT THE BULK OF THEIR FORCES TOWARDS IT. THE REST OF THE SHELL WILL BE MORE SPARSELY POPULATED BY CRUISERS – FOR A WHILE.

Strider nodded. The reasoning seemed sound.

ONCE BATTLE HAS BEEN JOINED, THE REMAINING HELGIO-LATH AND F-14 VESSELS WILL LIKEWISE COME TOGETHER, AND CONCENTRATE ON PIERCING STRAIGHT THROUGH THE RESID-UAL PLANETARY DEFENCES TO QITANEFERMEARTHA ITSELF.

'And in which bit of his armada has the mighty Kortland decided to put the *Santa Maria*?' said Strider, knowing the sarcasm would be picked up by Ten Per Cent Extra Free.

BECAUSE OF ITS ENTOURAGE OF TROK FIGHTERS, KORTLAND HAS DETERMINED THAT THE *SANTA MARIA* WILL BE PART OF THE FORCE THAT ATTACKS QITANEFERMEARTHA DIRECTLY.

'It would have been polite of him to mention it,' she said. The Image didn't bother to reply.

She continued to gaze into the Pocket. A few Helgiolath vessels had been eliminated, but so far the situation between the opposing forces had really not changed at all. They were like two people high on ziprite who had picked a fight with each other but were still at the stage of making aggressive punches into empty air. Whenever one of those punches chanced to land it did very little damage. Soon, however, the fight would be joined in earnest. And it would be to the death.

She turned to Pinocchio. 'Issue orders to everyone aboard – kids included – that they're to ensure they're properly kitted

324

out with fully charged lazguns. Tell them to check their suits, but not to suit up yet.' No need to get clumsy until you had to – and if the *Santa Maria* were badly damaged being in a spacesuit wasn't going to save anyone's life. 'I want twenty volunteers in case we're sent down to the surface to fight – if you can't get twenty, conscript a few. O'Sondheim is not to volunteer: he is to take over command from me in the event of my death. Neither are you – he'll need you. Understood?'

'Anything else?' said the bot.

'Yup. All volunteers, except those from the command deck, are to gather themselves in four of the shuttle bays. Organize them into suitable parties, Pinocchio. I'll lead one, Nelson another, Leander a third – I've just volunteered them for duty. We three will stay here until the time comes. Appoint someone else to head the fourth party and to be in overall charge of the rest until – if – we go down.'

The bot started working with his commline.

Behind Strider, the lock leading from the main part of the ship to the command deck soughed open. Polyaggle emerged, with Lan Yi following behind her. Strider scowled. She hadn't asked for the scientist to be here. Still, he would probably be of some use – especially if she and Leander and Nelson had to leave the deck under O'Sondheim's control.

'Pinocchio,' she said, indicating the newcomers, 'get some bot or other to fetch these two's suits.'

Polyaggle was moving straight towards the left-hand communications Pocket, which was automatically adjusting its height to welcome her. Strider felt a small shock of annoyance – as if the Spindrifter should have asked her permission first.

'We're beginning to pick up speed, oh darling of my dreams,' said Nelson.

He seemed to be a lot calmer than she was. His calmness was infectious.

'Keep your dreams to yourself!' she snapped, beginning to grin. 'And keep me posted.' She nodded towards Polyaggle, who had already immersed her face into the communications Pocket. 'I have other observation to do.'

Two ballistics hit the defensive shield almost simultaneously. Again the sensation of their explosions was hardly detectable aboard the *Santa Maria*.

Strider paced from side to side, her gaze fixed on Polyaggle's back. Reading the Spindrifter's face was impossible; reading her back was doubly so – or maybe it wasn't, because occasionally the wings would rise slightly from their sheaths.

She looked at Lan Yi. 'You know her better than I do. Any idea what's going on?'

He turned his hands outwards. 'Those movements of the wings are friendly gestures,' he said. 'Other than that I can't tell.'

Oh, shit! Most thoughts crossing Strider's mind weren't too great at the moment, but the one that had just done so was perhaps the worst of all. 'Ten Per Cent Extra Free,' she said urgently, 'I know you can't eavesdrop on what Polyaggle's saying, but can you reassure me of one thing? That's not Kaantalech she's speaking to, is it?'

IT IS NOT KAANTALECH. HAD IT BEEN SO WE WOULD HAVE INFORMED YOU, DESPITE THE VIOLATION OF PROPRIETY.

Then who the hell was it? She was still convinced the Spindrifter wouldn't knowingly betray the *Santa Maria*, but . . .

'May I evaluate our situation?' said Lan Yi politely beside her.

'Choose your Pocket,' she said, dredging up a smile from somewhere. It was nice to be looking at someone who wasn't bigger than her.

'Kortland's manoeuvre has been successful,' said Leander. 'The Autarch fleet seems to have decided it can pick the rest of us off later. A few warcruisers are still in Qitanefermeartha orbit, but the rest are heading towards the main fleet.'

'How certain are you of that?' said Strider absent-mindedly, still concentrating on Polyaggle's back.

'The Pocket . . .'

'Yeah. OK.' Maybe the Autarchy had technology capable of deceiving the Helgiolath's detectors; it was unlikely that they could delude the Pockets – or the Images. 'Keep watching.'

It was her enforced passivity that most rankled with Strider. Kortland was doing things. The Images were doing things. Polyaggle was doing things. All Strider and her personnel could do – at least for the while – was watch. Or, in Strider's case, watch and get angrier.

No, there was a bit more she could do.

'Pinocchio.'

'Yes.'

'Food. We need some food up here.' In a few hours' time they were likely to be fighting it out on Qitanefermeartha: it made little sense for them to be famished. 'And stuff to drink – it doesn't matter what. Get a bot on to it. Make sure the rest of the people in the shuttle parties get something to eat and drink as well.'

Practicalities, practicalities, she reminded herself. Sentient species throughout The Wondervale and the Milky Way and assumedly the rest of the Universe could devise the most elaborate philosophies and technologies, but all the time they had to eat and shit. Maybe the Images didn't have to – but they weren't really in the Universe so they didn't count. When the two great fleets finally joined battle there were bound to be thousands on either side who were stuck in the john doing whatever was their species' equivalent of pulling up their trousers. It didn't speak too much for the glories of sentience.

But then neither, more importantly, did warfare. Or tyranny. Or the way that some species – and she did not entirely except the Spindrifters and certainly not the Helgiolath – seemed to consider themselves superior to others.

Polyaggle's wings had stayed motionless for over thirty seconds now. Strider didn't know if this was a good or a bad sign.

'We have twenty-eight volunteers,' said Pinocchio quietly to her.

'Triage 'em down,' she said. 'I don't want any people going down on to Qitanefermeartha who aren't capable of handling a lazgun. If any of the kids have volunteered, tell them not to be foolish. Same goes for any of the elderly Reals who you don't think are up to it.'

327

'I have already done these things, Leonie.'

'Then just choose the best twenty.' What the *hell* was the Spindrifter up to? 'Be diplomatic, Pinocchio, like I would be.'

The bot made a curious strangled noise.

'You know what I mean,' she said.

At last Polyaggle eased her face out of the communications Pocket. Her wings were now moving agitatedly in and out of their sheaths. She looked directly towards Strider.

'I have been speaking with the Onurg of the Pridehouse,' she said immediately.

'That doesn't mean anything to me.'

'The Pridehouse are one of the ancient species of The Wondervale.' Polyaggle tapped her claws together hard enough that Strider could hear the click. 'One of the last things that Feefaar and Nerita did before our planet was disrupted was to send out a warning to all of the others of the ancient species.'

Strider waited for Polyaggle to continue. Lan Yi had emerged from the fascinations of his Pocket and moved to the Spindrifter's side.

'The Pridehouse detected my presence here on this starship,' said Polyaggle. 'Though they have maintained their neutrality over the millennia, they were' – the Images seemed to be searching for an accurate translation of the Spindrift word that Polyaggle must have used – 'they were *distressed* to hear of my species' demise. It may not be long before the Autarchy realizes that the ancient species still possess much of the technology they did before the secondary species arose, and then many more planets like Spindrift may be disintegrated.'

There was a short pause while the Images caught up their interpretation of what Polyaggle was saying.

'The Pridehouse have asked my consent to their sending a fleet to join us.' Again that click-*clack* of the claws. 'I told the Onurg that the decision was not mine but yours.'

Strider realized at once what a concession the Spindrifter had made. Humans were a raw species; the Spindrifters had been cruising the starways while Strider's ancestors had still been hunting in packs. When Polyaggle looked at the people aboard the *Santa Maria* she was looking down a staircase whose steps were billennia. Polyaggle was acknowledging the human species as equals. Strider had the embarrassing sensation that there was a tear forming at the corner of her eye.

'Kortland is the one who must settle this,' she said sharply. 'I'm just the captain of a vessel who isn't even allowed to make its own decisions any more.'

She turned to Leander. 'Raise Kortland in the other communications Pocket. Doubtless you'll have to struggle through about fifty thousand bureaucrats before you get to him, but make sure you do, OK?'

Leander nodded.

'It could give me no greater pride than to have the Pridehouse among us,' said Strider, keeping her words measured. 'I cannot imagine that Kortland will wish to turn them away . . . but you understand the protocols.'

A click together of the talons. Maybe the clicks were all subtly different from each other. Strider made the assumption that this one indicated assent.

'The Pridehouse are not the only ones,' added Polyaggle. 'There are also the Lingk-kreatzai, the Wreeps, the Semblances of the Eternal, the Fionnoids, the Janae and the We Are.'

Seven species willing to add their collective might to the forces of the rebels: it was an awesome thought.

'When can they be here?' she said.

'Not for some while.' Polyaggle shifted her wings. 'By the time they can resurrect their fleets the battle over Qitanefer-meartha will long ago have been won and lost, whichever way it goes. I have something to add, Captain Leonie Strider.'

'What?' So the intercession of the ancient races was, after all, just a sideshow, an irrelevance. There were going to be preconditions.

'These species do not wish to be under the command of Kortland. The Helgiolath can display a ruthlessness which is not to the taste of us ancients. The Onurg asked me if I would be the leader of their combined fleet.'

Oh, great, thought Strider. *Ousted out of the top job yet again.* 'Cancel that order, Leander,' she said.

It was a moment before she understood the meaning of the next few words Polyaggle spoke.

'But I told the Onurg that I owed my loyalty now to the Human species, and that you were my commander.' Click. Flutter. 'He has said that he will accept your leadership.'

'*What?*'

'The ancient species will pledge their fealty to you.'

'But I hardly know my way around this joint,' said Strider, waving a hand in the general direction of The Wondervale. 'I'm incompetent even to be a full part of the Helgiolath armada. I'm just a sort of very minor pawn in a chess-game whose board is too large for me to comprehend.'

'But this is what the Onurg and I agreed,' said Polyaggle. 'If you will consent to accept these ancient species.'

'How big is this fleet likely to be?' said Strider, asking the question more for the sake of saying something than for any other reason. Her mind was reeling.

'About forty-eight thousand craft, all told,' said Polyaggle. 'But only about ninety per cent of them are warcruisers,' she added apologetically.

Kaantalech, roused by one of her aides, looked to and fro among the array of monitors in front of her. In order to co-ordinate their attack on Qitanefermeartha, the Helgiolath had of necessity had to dispense with their communications shield, and for the first time she realized quite how huge a space-navy it was that the Humans had joined. She watched the way that the Helgiolath commander focused most of his firepower in one area, and put a forefoot to her proboscis in acknowledgement: this was exactly the tactic she would have used. The Autarch was too irremediably stupid to realize that the decoy could be larger than the killer force. His underlings would be too terrified of him to argue, because they knew that to do so meant a quick and certain death and their replacement by others more amenable to the Autarch's instructions, until at last, after some quick slaughter, the Autarch's fleet would be controlled by his catspaws. Better to take your chances in battle than to be killed out of hand by the Autarch. There was always just the chance that you might win.

Not this time, Kaantalech believed.

The Helgiolath had superiority not only in numbers but in intelligence and technology. If the battle started going against them they could flit themselves away singly to every corner of The Wondervale. The Autarch's warcruisers could follow them individually or severally, but in so doing would leave the home planet open to attack. Unless there was a lucky strike, those infuriatingly intractable Humans could harass the remaining Autarchy cruisers – and there were thousands of other Helgiolath vessels prepared to do the same.

No, Kaantalech reckoned, Qitanefermeartha was doomed.

Better for her and her fleet to stay out of it.

The holo to the side of her lit up, and she looked towards it with an appropriate expression of reverence and humility. There was, she supposed, just the most remote possibility that the Autarchy might defeat the rebels after all. A little token subservience could do no harm.

'Stars' Elect,' she said respectfully.

'I require your fleet to come to Qitanefermeartha immediately,' said the Autarch Nalla without preamble. Kaantalech could hardly believe it, but yet again he was taking part of his time out to copulate with one of his concubines. More than anything else, this persuaded her that she could find herself fighting on the wrong side of the war.

She gave a signal to an aide. Much as most of them loathed her, they loathed the Autarch more. Among the very first things they were trained to do was to recognize this rarely used signal.

What it meant was: *Interference of communications – and damn soon.*

The aide quickly obeyed, pressing his foot to a large square on the floor – a square that normally the aides made very sure they avoided.

The image of the Autarch in the holo began to disintegrate, shards of the colours that composed it starting to drift aimlessly towards the edges of the cubicle.

'I'm having difficulty making out what you're saying,' said

331

Kaantalech emolliently. 'Aide!' she cried off to one side. 'See if you can fix this thing.'

One of the aides started forward as if to obey, and she froze him with a glare.

Forming her words very carefully and clearly, Kaantalech said to the Autarch's dissolving likeness: 'I am trying to hear you, but we seem to be being jammed by Qitanefermeartha's defences. Which part of The Wondervale is it that you wish me to patrol?'

The holo of the Autarch faded into a nondescript miasma of brown-grey. On Qitanefermeartha he would be seeing Kaantalech's image doing exactly the same.

Once she had hoped he would turn his back towards her so that she could easily glide in the knife – twisting it as the whim took her. Now she was pleased that he had turned his back instead on the Helgiolath, and the Humans, and the F-14s and who knew how many other species. In tearing the Autarchy to pieces the rebels would be so reduced as to find themselves in a parlous state. The time would be right, then, for Kaantalech to ascend to the throne.

Autarch.

The Mighty One.

She gave her aides a few terse instructions, and her fleet began moving across the face of The Wondervale on what would seem like urgent business.

As if they were obeying Nalla's misunderstood orders.

Once the battle was joined in earnest things moved remarkably quickly. Strider, forcing to the rear of her mind the possibility that she might soon find herself at the head of an armada of nearly fifty thousand vessels (*How the hell are you going to cope with that, Leonie? Stop goddam* thinking, *brain: you'll almost certainly be dead before then*), applied herself to a Pocket. The Helgiolath's central puter was still enforcing its instructions on the *Santa Maria*'s Images, who were shifting the craft according to Kortland's dictates. The secondary fleet was beginning slowly to move together.

But it was what was happening to the main Helgiolath fleet

that held Strider's attention. The Pocket couldn't display the deaths of individual warcruisers: all it could show was statistics.

These started off depressingly – the Helgiolath were taking terrible punishment – but then became more reassuring as the rebels fought back ferociously. As she had when bombarding the manufactories on F-14, Strider found herself regretting the horrendous loss of life. Every Helgiolath warcruiser that died represented the lives of perhaps a thousand sentient beings. The same went for the Autarchy's vessels. All of these people were dying for something that wasn't even properly an ideal. They were being burnt alive or being spilt into space as if they were expendable – which was the way, Strider realized, that they *were* regarded. She had left three people behind on F-14 because they'd got lost, and she had realized fully the ruthlessness of that act – she still woke up, sometimes, from sleep in misery about it – but she'd never throw millions of people into the fray on the basis that more of them might survive than would of the enemy. Now she was facing herself honestly, what really started her from sleep was the question: *If I thought I had to,* would *I?*

Little sparkles of communication flashed in from other vessels of the secondary Helgiolath fleet. She assumed the Images were able to understand what they meant, and were operating themselves and the remnants of the Main Computer accordingly.

Polyaggle was still on the command deck, and clearly comprehended what was going on more than Strider did. Lan Yi was waiting around as if he wanted to be given a job to do, but at the moment Strider couldn't think of one to give him. She and the rest of her officers were too busy trying to stay on top of things as they and several thousand other vessels moved slowly, hopefully grouping not too obtrusively, towards Qitanefermeartha.

Abruptly their velocity picked up. However things were going for the bulk of the rebel fleet – the displays of that battle in the Pocket were now such a jumble of constantly changing statistics and graphic images that it was impossible to make

333

sense of them – Kortland must have decided that the Autarchy's defences were as fully engaged as they were going to get. Although she had no real religion, Strider found herself praying briefly to Umbel that the Autarch's cruisers were taking the brunt of the damage. The ancient species didn't like the Helgiolath very much, but she liked the Autarchy even less. Many of the Autarchy's people were probably conscripts – if not slaves – which meant that they, as individuals, hardly deserved to die; but then neither did the Helgiolath troopers. Every time one of the Autarch's warcruisers went down it was another step towards the end of the tyranny. Every time a Helgiolath warcruiser met its explosive end, by contrast, the more likely it was that the tyrannization would continue. The equation wasn't hard to solve. Even so, Strider found herself morally uneasy about the death that the rebels were dealing out.

Which she herself might soon be dealing out.

The *Santa Maria* found itself at the spearhead of the secondary attack – as always, Kortland was regarding the Humans as expendable. There was nothing Strider could do about it: the commands of his central puter were being obeyed to the letter by the Images.

Suddenly the situation went beyond some limit of her patience. To hell with just hanging around passively hoping for nothing better than to not get obliterated. She was fed up with the way Kortland was treating her and her personnel as expendable surrogate Helgiolath. She was in command of the entirety of one of The Wondervale's sentient species, just as Kortland was. It was time she started behaving accordingly – time to move from the passive to the active.

The volunteers for ground action were already in place.

Through a communications Pocket, she established contact with Segrill.

'Are you still with us?' she said.

The alien's voice, when he spoke, sounded puzzled. 'We surround your craft,' he said. 'Of course we are with you.'

'What I meant was, are you still prepared to act in concert with us?'

334

There was a note of relief in Segrill's reply. 'Yes. That has been agreed. We Trok keep to our agreements.'

'Then I think it's about time that I took the *Santa Maria* out from under Kortland's control.' *Assuming the Images will cooperate*, Strider added mentally.

WE ACCORD WITH YOUR ANALYSIS, said Ten Per Cent Extra Free.

'This is reasonable,' said Segrill.

'I want to go for it,' she said. 'I don't just want to be the cannon fodder up front. I want us to be the ones who lead the assault.'

'My species has little reason to love the Autarchy,' said Segrill. 'I will collaborate with you in any way you wish.'

'Then let's leave the rest of the pack behind.'

'This would please my people.'

'Ten Per Cent Extra Free,' said Strider, 'I want you to increase our acceleration even further.'

CERTAINLY.

She cut communications with Segrill and moved to another Pocket. In it she could see, almost immediately, the *Santa Maria* begin to move away from the rest of the wedge of warcruisers. Small darts of light around the image of her ship showed that the swarm of Trok fighters was doing likewise. This was probably the stupidest thing she had ever done in her life – and it might be the last thing – but she didn't regret it. Attack was the best form of defence. Or something.

'Shouldn't we have discussed this move?' said O'Sondheim from somewhere behind her.

'No,' she said.

She amplified the representation of Qitanefermeartha in her Pocket. Aside from the vast domed city, the planet looked much like Earth's Moon – although rather less hospitable. Behind the visual image, the Pocket was gabbling out data, the only important part of which, as far as Strider was concerned, was that there were only forty-nine warcruisers still waiting in orbit around the planet. Kortland's tactics had succeeded admirably. Hell, but right now she was in such a mood that she felt she could take out all forty-nine single-handed.

The speed with which the *Santa Maria* was moving ahead of the other rebel vessels had become giddying, even in the representation offered by the Pocket.

She sent a mental instruction to the Images, and Segrill's face appeared in her Pocket above the display of the *Santa Maria*'s position relative to the rest of the fleet.

'Once we're within a few light-seconds of those babies,' she said, 'they're going to start opening fire on us. They probably won't notice you. That's when I want you to strike.'

'This is understood.' The Trok was concentrating hard on something else – presumably the instrumentation of his fighter. 'If it were otherwise we wouldn't be here.'

'Gonna be a rocky ride,' said Strider.

'Too true,' said Segrill. 'Gonna be even rockier if you keep interrupting me.'

'Stay in contact.'

'Will do.'

She maintained the image of Segrill's face in the Pocket but focused on the graphic display at the base. The *Santa Maria* was now closer to Qitanefermeartha than it was to the Helgiolath vessels trailing behind it. Spots of light told her that the Autarchy had finally noticed her ship's approach and were sending out a further flotilla of ballistics. They didn't worry her. The *Santa Maria*'s defensive shield had soaked up the energies of all the impacting ballistics so far, and she was pretty certain it would continue to do so – the Images would have told her had it been otherwise.

More of a hazard were the forty-nine warcruisers.

She wanted to get this over with as soon as possible. Chances were that she and all her personnel would die, but that had been the case ever since they'd emerged into The Wondervale. This was probably their best shot to stay alive. She hoped so.

'Danny,' she said, 'here is what I want you to do.'

The disc of Qitanefermeartha more than filled the view-window now, but Strider didn't have the time to admire it. Face deep in her Pocket, she was busy watching the disposition of the guarding warcruisers. As yet they didn't seem to regard the solitary craft as much of a threat, and the longer they continued to feel that way the better it suited Strider. By now they must have spotted that there was a fleet of several thousand vessels behind her. One ship alone could do little damage to Qitanefermeartha, they must be reasoning: ground defences could repel it easily enough – if it was even worth their trying to do so. Better to concentrate on the imminent arrival of the main force.

Fingers crossed, Leonie.

'Segrill,' she said out loud into the Pocket.

The alien turned his attention towards her. Seeing just his face in the Pocket, it was hard to remember how tiny he actually was.

'Now is the time?' he said.

'Yes. One of my Images will enter your squadron and give you any navigational assistance you require.'

'We don't need any, Strider. You forget that we Trok have been a spacefaring species for several thousand years. We know what we are doing.'

There was no discourtesy in the response, but even so Strider felt rebuked. *Sizeist!* she said to herself.

'Good luck from here, Segrill.'

'See you downside if we both make it, Strider. If not . . .' The alien showed her his teeth in what she assumed was a smile.

Within seconds the Trok swarm was off. She imagined the little craft as being like stinging bees, and the Images therefore represented them in her Pocket as exactly that. The fighters spread out with astonishing rapidity towards Qitanefermeartha and then in both directions along the rough line of the planet's equator, the belt in which almost all of the warcruisers still orbited. She hoped the Autarchy wasn't able to monitor the course of the Trok fighters as clearly as she was: if so, they were dead before they even started.

There was a peculiar trace of guilt in her: the Trok craft were so small and the warcruisers were so large. Then she remembered what Segrill had just said about having been a spacefaring species for so many thousands of years. Yeah, it was a contest of equals.

Things became even more equal when the first warcruiser went up. Strider, fascinated despite herself, amplified the representation in the Pocket. The huge ship was peeling itself open as if someone were cutting it apart with a knife. When the knife got to the drive unit at the rear the effects were spectacular.

So you were worried about the Trok, Leonie? she thought.

'Any chances of one or more of you three going at these bastards, like you did around Spindrift?' she asked the Images.

IT WOULD BE MOST UNWISE. YOU NEED US AMONG YOU. It was Angler who was speaking this time. He was the Image whom she knew least well, if it could be said that she knew any of the Images at all. EVEN MORE SO IN A SHORT WHILE.

'How short a while?'

IF YOU WISH TO TAKE THE BEST ADVANTAGE OF THE CIRCUMSTANCES, WE WOULD SUGGEST THAT YOU DISENGAGE WITHIN THE NEXT TEN MINUTES.

Another Autarchy warcruiser seemed to be splitting itself open, almost as if it wanted to do so.

YOU MUST MOVE QUICKLY, BEFORE THE REST OF THE FLEET ARRIVES. AS SOON AS IT DOES, THE *SANTA MARIA* IS CERTAIN TO BECOME THE OBJECT OF ENEMY FIREPOWER.

'Who's staying with the *Santa Maria*?'

WE ARE, warbled Heartfire and Angler together.

'Look after Danny and the rest,' she said.

WE WILL.

'He's not that bad.'

UM.

'He's not.'

Silence.

She pulled herself away from the Pocket – possibly this was the final time she would ever do this – and barked to the command deck in general: 'Anyone who's volunteered for ground duty, it's time to move it.'

Nelson and Leander moved immediately towards the lockers along the wall. Lan Yi was already suited up except for his

338

helmet, which surprised Strider: she'd hardly thought of him as a warrior. Pinocchio was nowhere to be seen, which startled her even more: where the fuck had the bot got to? She didn't have time to worry about things like this if the urgency in the Images' paired voices were anything to go by. Polyaggle had vanished as well: the Spindrifter had probably separated up into her component bits again so that she could re-infest the remnants of the Main Computer. Strider herself jostled past Leander and dragged her suit from its locker.

The *Santa Maria* was going to be left with a skeleton crew, she thought dourly. Not the funniest of her jokes, in the circumstances.

Going down in the elevator she felt herself shaking all over. Way back when they'd been in orbit around Ganymede she'd done all the practices a shuttle pilot should do, but that had been several years ago. Before that she'd shuttled between Phobos and Mars, as part of her training. It seemed a very long time in the past. Did she still have the reflexive speed of reaction that she'd developed then?

There was only one way to find out.

First stop off: Nelson.

Second stop off: Leander.

Third stop off: Strider herself. She hoped Pinocchio had lined up someone good for the fourth shuttle.

Four suited figures turned to look at her as she burst through the lock into the bay where Shuttle A awaited her. Their visors masked their faces entirely, so that she could recognize none of them – except one, the alien design of whose suit betrayed her identity.

'*No*, Polyaggle!' yelled Strider as she raced across the floor of the blister towards the shuttle. 'If *you* die your whole goddam *species* dies.'

The Spindrifter made no sign of having heard her. Dammit – the Images seemed always to be deserting her at the wrong moments. What to do? Leave it – that was the best thing. If the bloody alien wanted to kill herself that was her own affair. At least she was wearing a lazgun, so maybe she could take out a few of the enemy before they got her.

339

'Into the shuttle!' Strider shouted unnecessarily. The four were already following her.

She waited impatiently while the shuttle's outer lock door operated. The Images had made modifications here as well, and the whole cycle was very much shorter than it had originally been, but it still seemed to her to be taking forever. She just hoped the modifications hadn't been so dramatic that she no longer knew how to fly the craft at all.

Finally the five of them were permitted by the automatics to enter the lock. There was barely enough room for Strider to fit on her helmet as they waited for the inner door.

Helmet on, she tongued her suit radio. Shit – she should have remembered to plug in a commlink. Too late now. There'd be some on the shuttle – probably in the first-aid box. *You're a creature of a different era, Leonie my gal, and sometimes you shouldn't be.*

'If you want to back out, this is your last opportunity,' she said.

There were assorted mumbles of dissent. No one was backing out. She felt atavistically proud of them.

The lock's inner door opened – at last.

The Images had made the interior of the shuttle roomier, but hadn't thought to add any extra seating. Strider threw herself into the pilot's chair and pointed Polyaggle towards the other. The remaining three personnel would have to fend for themselves as best they could in the space behind the seats.

She tongued her radio to the command deck's frequency, hoping O'Sondheim would have the sense to be listening in.

He had.

'Shuttle A is loaded and ready,' she told him as she strapped herself into her restrainer belt and surveyed the console in front of her. Not too much seemed to have changed except that, where before there had been an array of keyboards, there was now just a single, massively elaborate one. As when the keyboards had first been introduced to the Pockets, she found herself *recognizing* the symbols and functions on this. She wondered how many other minor alterations the Images had made to her . . .

'Shuttles B, C and D are likewise,' O'Sondheim responded. 'Who's piloting D?'

'Pinocchio.'

Strider would have surged up out of her seat had it not been for her restrainer belt.

'For fuck's sake! I explicitly told him he wasn't to . . .'

'It's a bit late now.' O'Sondheim sounded laconic. 'He's an independent-minded bot.'

'He's going to get an independent-minded hole lazzed right through his head next time I see him,' muttered Strider. Louder, she said: 'Better start counting us down, Danny.'

The blister portal directly in front of her slowly opened to reveal bleak space with just the thinnest of crescents of Qitanefermeartha cutting across the bottom left. Hearing O'Sondheim's countdown as just a reassuring drone in her earphones, she twisted around in her seat to see how the three people behind her were getting on. They'd moored themselves, using their belt-ropes, to the rears of the seating. Strider nodded. It was as good a way as any of keeping themselves secure.

She returned her attention to what O'Sondheim was saying just in the nick of time.

'. . . one . . . *now*!'

She pressed what she *knew* to be the right combination of two buttons on her keyboard and the shuttle shot forward. She was jammed back into her seat by the abrupt imposition of gees as the shuttle was suddenly on its own above the disc of the planet.

She tongued her suit radio.

'Status aboard Shuttle A?' she said.

There was a brief cacophony from Polyaggle, which presumably meant that the Spindrifter was all right. 'Uncomfortable,' said another voice, which Strider recognized as Strauss-Giolitto's; so now she knew who at least two of the personnel with her were. 'OK,' said a third voice: Strider couldn't immediately identify it.

There was no fourth voice.

'Can you two check . . . ?' began Strider. She didn't need to finish the question.

'It's Bartleby,' Strauss-Giolitto said a few seconds later. 'His neck's broken.'

So the arrangement with the belt-ropes hadn't been so good after all. Strider swore under her breath. There was nothing she could do to save the man – whom she recalled as a rather jovial, amiable ecologist.

The gees faded away as the shuttle ceased accelerating.

'Get the oxygen and recycling units off his suit, then,' she said. 'They might come in handy. And pass his lazgun forward to me.'

Before anyone could protest she had called up O'Sondheim. 'Patch me through to the other three shuttles, will you, Danny. We've had a casualty here – guy called Bartleby. Sam, I think his first name was. I want to get the status of the other crews.'

There had been no further casualties. Strider decided she would administer Pinocchio's rollicking later – there wasn't time right now for everything she wanted to say to him.

'How are the Trok making out, Danny?' she said.

'Better than you would ever believe.'

He began to cite figures, but just as he started she realized they were being displayed on one of the screens in front of her: what she had assumed was just some kind of interference pattern was in fact a perfectly comprehensible list of statistics. She glanced sideways at Polyaggle and saw that the Spindrifter was leaning forward, reading them intently. So the display worked in two entirely unrelated languages? Maybe the Images had been making a few minor adaptations to Polyaggle as well. Quite how much *had* they done to everyone?

Strider decided not to answer her own question in case she frightened herself.

She looked at the screen again. Somebody somewhere in The Wondervale had surely realized before that it could be a good idea to deploy the minuscule Trok fighters, but they must have forgotten. Segrill and his people had so far taken out twenty-seven of the defending warcruisers and themselves lost only three craft: if Kortland ever got to Qitanefermeartha he

342

was going to have to get a lot of extremely small medals made. Most of the Trok fighters had now divested themselves of their complement of missiles, and were beginning to move either towards space rendezvous with Strider or downwards to the planetary surface.

'Give me those co-ordinates, Danny,' she said.

He fed them direct into the four shuttles' puters.

'And now tell Ten Per Cent Extra Free that I want him here,' she said. 'Ask him nicely.'

A few moments later the familiar voice trilled in her ear. I AM ABOARD THE SHUTTLE, CAPTAIN LEONIE STRIDER.

She tongued off her radio. 'You know what I'm about to do, don't you?'

OF COURSE.

'You've said your goodbyes to Heartfire and Angler?'

BUT WE'RE NOT GOING TO BE SEPARATED, said Ten Per Cent Extra Free, EXCEPT IN THIS REALITY. IN OUR OWN WE ARE STILL INTERMINGLED, AS WE ALWAYS SHALL BE.

Strider abandoned the line of questioning. Later, maybe.

She tongued her radio back to the *Santa Maria*'s frequency once more.

''Bye, Danny,' she said. 'Get the *Santa Maria* the shit out of here as fast as you can. If you get back to the Solar System give it my love. Maybe I'll join you someday.'

A second later the monitors indicated to her that the *Santa Maria* had shifted away via tachyon drive – it could be anywhere in The Wondervale by now. But Strider didn't need the monitors to tell her this. She had *felt* her ship go.

Her ship.

The shuttles had been originally designed for landing on planets that had atmospheres: they had retro-jets and air-brakes to slow things down. The new-style, heavily armed versions the Images had tailored were a bit more versatile than that, but Strider was still virtually suicidal by the time the craft came to rest halfway up the side of a small crater.

'If I ever say anything bad about you again, Umbel,' she said raggedly, 'you have my permission to smite me.'

343

'Little lady, I wouldn't smite you unless you asked me real nice,' said a voice in her earphones.

Damned radios. No privacy.

'Umbel!' she said. 'You're down safely?'

'As safe as we can be,' said Nelson, 'in a shuttle that's never going to lift off this planet again unless you use a crane. That was . . . well, put it this way: they ought to fit out suits with dispose-alls.'

'Is there a problem?' Vomiting inside a suit could very easily be fatal.

'No, we all held it down. Or, rather, up. This here shuttle's lying on her back just at the moment. Only a few bruises are all we've got to worry about.' Nelson sounded relaxed – but then he usually did.

'Stop hogging the air, then,' said Strider. 'Leander? Pinocchio?'

'We have landed in perfect safety,' said the bot into her ear. 'Not the finest of lan –'

'Yeah, fine,' said Strider brusquely. *Bloody bot – too good at everything.* 'Leander?'

'Maloron Leander has broken her nose,' said Lan Yi's prim voice. 'Fortunately Shuttle C was not structurally damaged during the landing, so we have been able to remove her helmet and are now administering first aid.'

'How is she otherwise?'

'Swearing very considerably.'

Strider smiled. So Leander was all right.

'Rendezvous as you can,' she said. 'Shuttle D sounds as if it's best placed. Pinocchio, give us something we can triangulate on.'

Nelson's shuttle was certainly a write-off – Strider could see that as soon as she crested the rim of the crater – but the other three might one day be reclaimed. Who would do the reclaiming was a different issue. Probably not humans: the prospect of nineteen humans – no, there were only eighteen of them now – a Spindrifter and a bundle of Trok bringing down the might of the Autarchy seemed much more remote than it

344

had when she'd been up on the command deck of the *Santa Maria*, surrounded by the reassuring glow of her Pocket. Still, look what the Trok had managed to do to the Autarchy's warcruisers . . . Maybe small was beautiful after all.

The sky was beautiful as well, studded with more stars than it seemed could possibly exist. Here and there a sudden flare of light appeared – a new nova, as another warcruiser met its doom – and then very swiftly vanished. But nobody was paying any attention to the sky.

Their planned landing site had been some twenty kilometres towards the equator from the city of Qitanefermeartha, and despite the hazards they had all come down within no more than a few kilometres of each other. The only thing that anybody wanted to look at from here was the impossibly vast dome of the city. It seemed more like a landform – some inspiration that had occurred to plate tectonics on a day when it had nothing else to think about – than anything which had been *constructed*. It dwarfed any mountain range in the Solar System – even Mars's Olympus Mons would have looked merely plaintive beside it. The dome itself was difficult to discern clearly because of the motley of forcefields coruscating around it: it looked as if all the electrical storms in The Wondervale had come together for a convention.

It was little wonder that the Autarchy's defences had not been much concerned by the arrival of four shuttles; they probably hadn't even noticed the Trok fighters.

'This is going to be a tough nut to crack,' said Strauss-Giolitto.

'That's an understatement,' said Strider drily. Early in the mission she had been tempted to have the teacher bounced out of it, but something had happened to Strauss-Giolitto on Spindrift that had changed her. Quite what it had been Strider had never been able to discover, although she knew that Pinocchio had played a part in it. It hardly mattered. Now Strider found herself able to place her full trust in Strauss-Giolitto as a comrade in arms. It was a good feeling to know that the woman was here.

345

'Well,' said Strider after a few moments had gone by, 'shall we get going?'

The question was an order.

She began to leap forward. The surface gravity of Qitanefermeartha was about half Mars-standard, so progress was quick: twenty kilometres here was the equivalent of only a few kilometres at home. The little Trok spacecraft leapfrogged around the humans every once in a while, waiting like landmines on the dusty surface until the jumping, lumbering figures had passed them by before lifting briefly into the sky again.

Strider's plan had been to get down on to Qitanefermeartha and then attack. Her thinking had gone no further than this. Everything had gone fine so far, but now her head was empty of ideas. All she had was the conviction that the Helgiolath had got it wrong: Qitanefermeartha had been constructed to be able to repel huge space armadas rather than a few people in suits.

They skirted the edge of a small crater. Off to their left they could see a huge spaceport, although even this was dwarfed by the size of the domed city, which now seemed to crowd the sky. Still there had been no reaction from the city's defences. Strider felt as if they were a few ants crossing a floor: who bothers to stamp on the ants when someone is firing a lazgun in through the windows?

She called a halt a couple of kilometres short of the flickering forcefields. Even though running was comparatively easy on Qitanefermeartha, her own breath was coming in rough gusts, and the rest of the party, Polyaggle excepted, seemed similarly exhausted.

She tongued off her radio and said: 'I could do with a little inspiration here.'

DAWDLE, said Ten Per Cent Extra Free.

'Say again?'

DAWDLE.

'No, what I meant was that I'd be grateful if you could amplify on your advice.'

YOU WERE PERFECTLY CORRECT TO ASSUME THAT THE CITY'S DEFENCES ARE GEARED TO WATCHING OUT FOR BIG THINGS RATHER THAN SMALL THINGS, CAPTAIN LEONIE

346

STRIDER, JUST AS THE AUTARCHY'S WARCRUISERS WERE
INCAPABLE OF DEALING WITH THE TROK CRAFT. Ten Per Cent
Extra Free paused, then continued. QITANEFERMEARTHA'S
DEFENCES ALSO EXPECT ANY THREAT TO MOVE SWIFTLY – LIKE
A BALLISTIC OR A BEAM, OR POSSIBLY EVEN JUST A POWERED
VEHICLE. THEY WILL ALMOST CERTAINLY FAIL TO REGISTER
SOMETHING THAT IS MOVING SLOWLY. SO I SUGGEST THAT YOU
DAWDLE THE REST OF THE WAY. I SHALL ASK THE TROK TO DO
THE SAME.

'Strolling along isn't going to help us much when we hit
those forcefields,' she said.

NO. BUT I AM.

Reaching back through the layers of reality.

In the embrace of Heartfire and Angler.

Wrongness: Nightmirror missing. Not for ever. Knowledge
that Nightmirror will return.

Holding on to Heartfire and Angler. They the anchors that
moor Ten Per Cent Extra Free to The Truthfulness as he re-
enters The Wondervale.

Extending himself until he becomes the finest filament that
can connect universes.

Within the domed city of Qitanefermeartha. Some here can
see me. Pink, crystalline walls are safety. Shift electromagnetic
charge within one crystal and so spring to next. Becomes easier
very soon. Now at optimum rate down the tunnel of emf.
Spreading out, rippling through the structure until a mote of
oneself everywhere.

Become Qitanefermeartha.

Power centres. Some here, some there. Focus on the larger
power centres first. Some immediate allies: willingly accept
demise. Others reluctant: require debate. Radiant energy
absorbed as each dies, adding to strength, to bliss. Hard, now,
to retain oneself within walls – so much to *give* to the charged
molecules of Qitanefermeartha's atmosphere – but self *must*
restrain. One only power centre recalcitrant. Concentrate self
on it. Hold pattern around it. Very pretty pattern: surely power
centre want to be a part of it. Colours of life and of light.

347

Temptation.

Final and largest power centre submit, although only temporarily – not to die. Self agree it not die.

At last self is able to swallow forcefields and become so *mighty*. Too mighty for Wondervale. Release all into Truthfulness, where Heartfire and Angler receive it, and instantly begin to multiply.

Immediate glory.

Ten Per Cent Extra Free is the mighty father. Joy is throughout The Truthfulness.

Now smaller power centres. Nip one here, nip one there. Lasers die. Holos die. Cabbles die. All for the added greatness of The Truthfulness.

One day The Wondervale die . . . all for the added greatness of The Truthfulness.

No messenger was required to tell the Autarch Nalla that something . . . undesirable had happened. As soon as the lights dimmed he had called up a display of the status of Qitanefermeartha and seen that the screens were down. What had happened to make them so he did not know, and his interest was not great. Then the monitors themselves had died. The city seemed to have been drained of all power.

The most important thing for him now was self-preservation. It was the task of his guards and courtiers to defend the city. If they succeeded in doing so, he would return as their acknowledged ruler. If they did not – well, there was a galaxyful of replacements to draw upon.

Another Qitanefermeartha could be built, somewhere far across The Wondervale.

He lumbered from his throne-room through a concealed door and into a darkened corridor. The door slid shut behind him, but the lights did not come on, as they should have.

The Autarch paused momentarily. This was unexpected. His slow brain was always nonplussed by the unexpected, because it so rarely happened: the throngs around him relied for their lives on the fact that nothing should startle the Autarch.

He pushed on down the corridor nevertheless. It narrowed

348

progressively until its walls were almost brushing his shoulders as he forged ahead. Despite the darkness, Nalla had no fears. This passage had no branches: it led to one place alone.

His escape route.

A worrying thought began to trickle across his mind. If the lights refused to operate as they were supposed to, perhaps the escape hatch might prove equally recalcitrant?

No. Surely not. Back-ups backed up back-ups several times over to ensure that it would always function, no matter what happened to the rest of the city. An elevator would carry him hundreds of kilometres down towards the core of the planet, where there was a fully kitted bunker constructed out of deadmetal. Even if the world were blown apart he would be safe, for the bunker was rigged with full automatics and a tachyonic drive – it would take him across The Wondervale to safety without him having to lift so much as a suction-pad.

But, even so . . .

Agitated, he began to shuffle forwards even more quickly.

He discovered the doors of his escape route by the simple means of slamming his head against them. Let the might of the Autarchy curse this darkness! He reached with a forelimb up the side of the doors, seeking the sensor that would allow him ingress.

He found the sensor pad, and sucked at it with his paw.

Nothing happened.

Incredulous, he sucked at it again.

Still nothing.

He battered at the doors with his bony head, but they refused to yield.

He gave a loud trumpet of anguished frustration, and the noise echoed down the long dark corridor behind him.

The long dark *narrow* corridor.

He didn't have room to turn round.

In other circumstances the sight of a gang of Trok in spacesuits might have made Strider grin. Here, however, her first preoccupation – until the Trok and the humans started to keep a

349

respectful distance from each other – was to make sure she didn't stand on one of them.

'Have you succeeded?' she said to Ten Per Cent Extra Free as soon as the forcefields around the dome of the city ceased their glittering display.

YES. QITANEFERMEARTHA HAS BEEN LEACHED OF ITS POWER. ITS FORCEFIELDS ARE NO MORE, AND ITS DEFENSIVE WEAPONRY WILL NOT FUNCTION – I HAVE EVEN DRAINED INDIVIDUAL LAZGUNS.

'How many airlocks are there?' she said, staring at the blank door of the outermost.

SEVENTEEN.

'How are we going to get them open if there's no power?'

WHY DO WE NEED TO GET THEM OPEN? IF THERE IS NO POWER THE CITY OF QITANEFERMEARTHA IS SEALED OFF ENTIRELY, AND ITS INHABITANTS HAVE NO MEANS OF SETTING THEMSELVES FREE. IT IS ONLY A MATTER OF TIME – A SHORT TIME – BEFORE THE CITY WILL BE DEAD. ALREADY THE TEMPERATURE IN THERE IS BEGINNING TO DROP, ALTHOUGH AS YET ONLY BY A SMALL FRACTION OF A DEGREE.

'Fahrenheit or Kelvin?' said Strider.

EXPLAIN, PLEASE.

'Aw, forget it.'

She raised her glove towards her helmet, trying to push her hand back through her hair before she realized the futility of the movement. They were by now no more than a few hundred metres from the grim gateways into Qitanefermeartha, the Autarch's citadel. From here it was very difficult to see anything else but the dull surface of the deadmetal.

'Could you get those locks open if I asked you to?'

IT WOULD PRESENT NO GREAT PROBLEM. I CAN DRAW ENERGY BACK FROM MY REALITY INTO THIS ONE.

'And could you get them shut again?'

YES.

'Then I think our difficulties are over.'

She tongued her spacesuit radio to change frequencies.

'Pinocchio . . .' she began as the sky above her flared into implausible brightness.

350

Segrill thought quickly. After the destruction he and his Trok colleagues had wreaked, there were probably as few as twenty Autarchy warcruisers still in orbit around Qitanefermeartha, and even the smaller of the two rebel fleets was not going to take very long to account for them.

Although it was useless pouring firepower down on to a dome made of deadmetal, somebody was, sooner or later, going to try it.

This would have unpleasant consequences for anyone who happened to be standing, to seize a figure at random, a few hundred metres away from the main ingress to the city.

He tried to raise Strider on his suit emfer, but the humans were all operating in frequencies of the electromagnetic spectrum to which his own equipment did not have access. The more elaborate set-up back in his ship . . .

Yes. That was it. From there he could perhaps even be able to contact Kortland as well, which would be much more to the point.

How long would it take him to get there? The Trok had finally grounded their fleet only a kilometre or so back, but a kilometre was a long way for a Trok.

Half an hour, if he was lucky.

He set off, hopping along the barren, dusty surface.

The other Trok followed him.

'Half an hour, if I'm lucky,' said Pinocchio.

'Then get to it,' said Strider. 'I want to have this done by the time Kortland gets here. I want to show him we're not just some hick species from an out-of-town galaxy. I want to wipe that smug grin off his . . . well, you get my general meaning.'

The bot turned instantly and began to lope away across the breccia. Although many of the emotions he had observed in human beings were not as yet understandable to him, he was beginning to enlarge his range. He felt *something* towards Strider, while at the same time he was perplexed on the occasions when she acted quite unreasonably in the condition which she called 'angry'. He knew what 'physical passion' was, because he had observed hers at close quarters, but the

351

emotion itself was something fathomless to him. At this moment, however, he knew that what he was feeling was the thing called 'pleasure': he was moving at his own natural speed rather than at the speed even the most athletic of the humans could achieve; it was a *pleasure* to be able to do so after all this time.

Strider's shuttle was jammed midway up the inner side of a crater. Nelson's shuttle was lying on its broken back. But either Leander's or more likely Pinocchio's own . . . There was a chance, a good chance.

Just as he left, he noticed that the Trok were likewise departing. He could think of no reason why. Surely the Helgiolath would not be so illogical as to try to bring firepower to bear on the domed city: it was well known that bombarding deadmetal was simply a waste of energy.

'Look at him go,' said Strauss-Giolitto. She was leaning casually on Lan Yi's suited shoulder, her free hand holding one of her lazguns clear of her side. Although so much smaller than her, the out-of-Taiwanese seemed not to resent her weight. She was confused about her relationship with him. Had he been a woman, they would have been lovers by now – she was not unaware of the way that he felt towards her. In an ideal universe she would have been able to ignore how repugnant she found his body, but this was not an ideal universe. Once she had been in his cabin aboard the *Santa Maria* when he, unaware of her arrival, had emerged from the shower towelling his wet hair, a casual erection jutting towards his navel. She had laughed about the incident, as if it meant nothing to her, but the reminder of his masculinity had deeply distressed her.

Through the fabric of two spacesuits, however, she could tolerate some degree of physical intimacy with him.

Pinocchio she could hold close to her, but that was different. He could not threaten. He could not invade.

'Start moving away,' said Strider over the suit radios' general frequency. Everyone turned towards her except Poly-aggle, who seemed oblivious. Strider was gesticulating to them that they should move away around the edge of the domed city.

352

Strauss-Giolitto knew that the edge was curved, but this close it seemed straight. Easing her weight off Lan Yi's shoulder, she moved across to the Spindrifter and waved her glove in front of Polyaggle's visor. Inscrutable eyes looked back through the plastite at her. As always when as close to Polyaggle as this, Strauss-Giolitto felt a sudden arousal of sexual tension: intervening spacesuits didn't seem to make any difference. She pointed towards Strider, who was already beginning to move off. Polyaggle nodded – a gesture Strauss-Giolitto jealously knew the alien had learnt from Lan Yi – and made to follow.

Travelling across the ashen plain in the sort of slow lurching run that seemed best accommodated to the low gravity of Qitanefermeartha, Strauss-Giolitto saw that the Trok, like a small pack of lemmings, were slowly working their way in a different direction. What the hell were they up to? What the hell was *she* up to? She was following orders that had been issued perfunctorily by Strider, without having any notion of the reason why those orders had been given. She had no expectations that she would live out the hour: her anticipation had been that by now she would have gone out in a blaze of glory, wielding her lazgun like some old-fashioned pre-holo cowboy hero as she cut a swathe through alien monstrosities until in the end 'Oh, God, they got me. [Cough.] This is it, buddy. [A second and rather more anguished cough. A mixture of spittle and blood appears between the lips.] I only hope my death ain't been in [a long pause – a pause for which the word "pregnant" could have been coined] vain.' It would be the best way to go.

She had so little that she wanted to live for.

The craft which he had himself piloted had indeed made by far the better landing, concluded Pinocchio as he crested a low ridge to see shuttles C and D lying not very far away from each other on the rocky grey plain. For that reason it would be the more likely to be able to lift off again.

I AGREE WITH YOUR ANALYSIS, said Ten Per Cent Extra Free from somewhere inside him.

Not breaking stride, Pinocchio leapt towards Shuttle D.

There were further eruptions of light in the sky, but he paid them no attention. He cared very little which set of aliens killed which other set except insofar as the outcome accorded with the wishes of Leonie Strider.

The whole enterprise was going to require a remarkable degree of synchronization with the Image. Seated in front of the shuttle's main console, checking off the various systems to make sure that nothing of importance was malfunctioning, Pinocchio allowed Ten Per Cent Extra Free to infiltrate both himself and the shuttle's puter entirely. Within a small fraction of a second the three of them had become in effect a single machine, operating in perfect consonance. For Pinocchio the experience was unlike anything he'd known before – as if he were both more than himself and only a part of himself.

Half an hour, he'd said. He'd/they'd managed to do it all in just over twenty-five minutes. Five minutes to wait, in case Strider and the others were being laggardly.

A very long five minutes.

Segrill was first to reach his fighter and he virtually threw himself into the cockpit, flicking on its emfer as he did so. Luckily the instrument was still trained on Strider's frequency. Through his observation shield he could see that some of the other Trok had made almost as good time as himself.

'Strider!' said Segrill urgently.

There was no reply, although he could hear the sort of noises from her that he knew constituted a Human voice. Where was the Image? Ten Per Cent Extra Free wouldn't have deserted them, would he?

'Strider!' he bellowed with the full power of his lungs.

Still her voice went on. Perhaps she thought he was just static on the line.

He could see through his monitors the small party of suited figures. They were moving slowly away from the airlock doors – far too slowly. The first Helgiolath beam that hit those doors was going to render the Humans indistinguishable from the plain around them.

He jacked up the volume, and yelled again.

This time there was a reaction. Her voice ceased abruptly, and then after a short pause she said something – something utterly incomprehensible to him.

He swore bitterly. Was there nothing he could . . . ?

Wait a second – try the bot. If the Image was anywhere he was going to be with the bot.

But the bot no longer seemed to be with the Humans. Strider had now obviously called her party to a halt, and was staring towards the fleet of landed fighters. She'd at least worked out that the noise she'd picked up in her helmet had come from the Trok. With any luck she'd start moving in this direction – that would save time later.

She said something more. To him it sounded like 'Sheeeeeeaaagroooolllla'.

'Strider,' he said again to encourage her. He wondered what sort of bastardization his voice was making of her name.

The bot didn't respond either. Of course, it was somewhere out of the line of sight. Qitanefermeartha almost certainly didn't have much of an ionosphere. Segrill could try contacting the Helgiolath or the Bredai directly, but they were still busy finishing off the planet's defenders and would have other things on their minds than listening out for communications from the surface.

Nothing for it but to change the line of sight.

Segrill barked a general instruction to his personnel that they were to stay exactly where they were and then rapidly powered up his own fighter, cursing the fact that his spacesuited hands were so clumsy on the switches and buttons because he hadn't taken the time to reoxygenate the craft's interior.

The whole fighter seemed to screech as he cut in the upthrusters at twice the boost level he'd ever tried before. For a moment he thought the craft might actually shake itself to pieces. For a moment he thought the boost might actually shake *him* to pieces. He *forced* himself not to pass out as the light on the altimeter glowed red, then orange.

That should be enough – the bot could have got only so far in this time.

Off with the upthrusters. Slam on the downthrusters.

Shit! He hadn't belted himself in.

Again consciousness became something to be groped for as his helmet hammered against the cockpit's ceiling. Then he dropped like a stone, landing belly downwards spreadeagled across the control panel.

Keep a cool head, he told himself as reality ebbed and flowed.

Yes, but where *am I keeping it right at the moment? Somewhere in Heaven's Ancestor, it feels like.*

He threw himself off the console and scanned it rapidly through blurring eyes to ensure his fall hadn't done anything bizarre. Hit the wrong switch and you might be half a parsec away – or heading straight for the nearest disrupting warcruiser.

No. The worst that had happened was that the heating had been turned up.

Ship's radio on to broad-band. Get moving.

He had difficulty speaking. When he first tried to say the bot's name he discovered that there was a more particular pain mixed up in his general bodily agonies. If he hadn't broken his jaw he'd done something very like it. He moved his mouth experimentally. *Attempted* to move his mouth.

Other races had gods. He wished that the Trok did, so that he could call upon a few of them now.

No, his jaw wasn't broken. He wasn't going to *allow* it to be broken. He must just have jarred it numb when he'd crashed against the top of the cockpit.

Jaw, he thought, *if you've gone and broken yourself, after this is all over I'm going to break you again.*

He'd lost a few teeth. They'd grow back soon, but at the moment the bits were floating around disconcertingly between his eyes and his visor.

He made another attempt.

'Pinocchio.'

The bot came on-line instantly. 'Segrill.'

'Cannot speak Strider,' said the Trok laboriously, keeping the words down to a minimum and hoping the Image would be able to make sense of what he was saying.

And then Ten Per Cent Extra Free was in his mind.

THERE IS NO NEED FOR YOU TO TALK. JUST *THINK* AT ME.
PINOCCHIO WILL HEAR EVERYTHING THAT I HEAR.

Segrill obeyed, swiftly explaining what was very likely
about to happen and his madcap scheme for trying to prevent it.

YOU ARE CORRECT. THERE IS NO REAL ALTERNATIVE. I WILL
CONVEY ALL THIS TO CAPTAIN LEONIE STRIDER.

'That's insane!' yelped Strider out loud before she could stop
herself. The rest of the party stopped and turned to look at her –
all except Polyaggle, who continued trudging towards the Trok
fleet. The fighter that had rocketed skywards a short while
earlier was now returning more sedately to the ground.

'Nothing,' Strider said. She hoped she sounded adequately
reassuring. 'I'm just fixing something up with Ten Per Cent
Extra Free.'

She tongued off her suit radio.

'What do you think our chances are?'

BETTER THAN IF YOU STAY WHERE YOU ARE. THAT IS TO
SAY, CONSIDERABLY BETTER THAN ZERO. SEGRILL IS PER-
FECTLY CORRECT. IT WAS VERY STUPID OF ALL OF US NOT TO
HAVE THOUGHT OF THIS BEFORE, BUT IT WAS PARTICULARLY
STUPID OF *ME*. I PRESENT MY APOLOGIES.

Apologies from an Image? This was something Strider had
thought she would never hear.

'It's OK,' she said casually. 'Just don't do it again, huh?'

She wondered how she was going to persuade her personnel
to go through with this – persuading *herself* was going to be no
easy task. They must have reasoned it out by now that this was
likely to be a suicide mission all along, but there were better
ways and worse ways to go. Being flash-fried seemed one of
the better ways: one moment you were there and the next you
weren't. No pain, no hassle – no funeral expenses. Dropping
from a great height on to an airless planet struck Strider as
being one of the worse ways.

'What does Pinocchio think about it?'

HE IS IN TOTAL AGREEMENT WITH ME.

There was something vaguely chilling in the way that Ten

Per Cent Extra Free said this, but Strider didn't have time to think about it.

'All right. We'll do this. Can you hook me in with Polyaggle as well?'

CERTAINLY.

Diplomacy, thought Strider, *has always been my strongest suit – followed closely by tact, of course. I will handle this like the masterful politician I might have become had the romantic lure of starside – the glorious mysteries of the Universe – not been so great. I will cajole my people into accepting my point of view. I will use sweet reason and . . . aw, fuck it.*

Drawing a lazgun from her belt, she tongued her suit radio to the general frequency.

'Look, you bastards,' she said, 'here's what's going to happen. Anyone who objects' – she waved the lazgun – 'is going to be breathing vacuum about one split second from now. Got that?'

'You pilot this damned thing damned carefully now,' said Strider.

There was no reply. Ten Per Cent Extra Free had returned to more urgent duties with Pinocchio, promising her that he and the bot would give her people another half-hour to get clear. If the Trok pilot directly beneath her had heard what she had said at all it was obviously just gabble to him.

A Trok fighter is designed to carry a crew of between one and four Trok, who between them probably mass no more than a quarter of a kilogram, plus their personal equipment, food, essential supplies and so forth – perhaps another couple of kilograms. This is, in terms of the fighters' capabilities, the unimportant part of their payload. What they are designed to lift is an extra tonne of weaponry, including at least two ballistics that are rather larger and heavier than the fighter itself. The fighters on Qitanefermeartha no longer had to carry ballistics – they'd used them all to devastating effect against the Autarchy's warcruisers.

Trok fighters come in various shapes and sizes, but most of them have the approximate form of a domed lozenge some three metres long and some two metres wide. The only way a human being would be able to get inside one would be by transforming herself or himself into toothpaste. But the craft is easily capable of lifting and transporting the mass of a human being.

The rocketry is concentrated at what would be the corners if the fighter had been a rectangle rather than a lozenge. There are upthrusters there, and downthrusters; forward and retro-rockets. It doesn't really matter in this instance what the purpose of each of these rockets is in moving the spacecraft around: if you're in the direct line of fire of one of them you're very soon going to be toast. So attaching a belt-rope to the bottom of a Trok fighter and hoping to tag along behind is a very bad idea indeed, because sooner or later some part of your body is going to get burnt off. This would be painful. If you were lucky – or unlucky, depending on your personal tolerance of pain – the flare would fuse your spacesuit to the cauterized stump of your limb, so you might just survive.

Until the next time you flailed into the path of one of the rockets.

But there is one safe (*Safe? Hah!* thought Strider) way for a human being to be transported by a Trok fighter. Using your belt-rope, tie yourself tightly to the top of it, arms straight ahead and legs straight behind, tidily out of reach of all of the rocketry.

It's not pretty. It's not elegant. But it just might work.

Just might.

Strider had positioned herself so that she could see over the leading edge of the fighter to which Segrill had allocated her. If she and the Trok craft were going to end up screaming towards the surface of Qitanefermeartha at several hundred kilometres per hour she at least wanted to be able to watch – more accurately, she didn't want to spend the entire duration of the flight assuming this was exactly what was happening. As she fastened herself down she noticed that most of the rest of her party had chosen the same option – some of them, like Strauss-Giolitto, were tall enough to have very little alternative. Strider, her arms wrapped carefully around the front of the little

359

vessel, was currently looking at one of her own footprints in the dust, only half a metre away. In every sense, Polyaggle was the odd one out. Possessing no belt-rope, she seemed quite unconcerned – although it was difficult to tell – by the fact that she was perched in a sort of upright squatting position atop the fighter she had selected, firmly gripping items of its superstructure. The pilot of that particular craft had a tricky task ahead.

The first few laden Trok fighters were already gingerly lifting off, gaining good altitude before darting off towards the pole – northern or southern, Strider didn't know. As more and more people secured themselves, assisted by busily moving Trok, lift-offs became more frequent. Through Ten Per Cent Extra Free, Strider had told Segrill that she wanted to be last: it was her duty as captain to take the greatest risk. He had pointed out acidly that the people taking the greatest risk were in fact the pilots of the fighters who were *not* carrying burdens, because they would be the *very* last to leave.

She could feel the fighter beneath her powering up. Ahead of her she could see Polyaggle being cautiously lifted into the sky – how much strength could there be in those gloved claws? Strider abruptly suspected that the answer was: quite a lot. Her own pilot was using equal skill, cutting in his upthrusters very gradually so as to minimize the chance of her being affected by splashback. The noise inside her suit, transmitted via the frame of the fighter, was almost literally deafening; she raised her helmet slightly in the hope of cutting down the din, but the manoeuvre didn't seem to make much difference.

Slowly the footprint she had been watching – had become almost fond of – began to recede from her, and then it was erased entirely as the upthrusters threw the dust into turmoil. *I am never, ever going to travel this way again,* she told herself.

There was a spurt of altitude. As Segrill had warned all of them most forcefully, she looked neither to right nor to left in case a close-up glimpse of the upthrusters blinded her. On second thoughts, she closed her eyes and used her tongue to blacken out her visor: time enough to look at the scenery once the upthrusters had cut out. 'Above all else, keep absolutely still,' Segrill had said. Strider reckoned she could have given a marble statue close competition.

There was a lessening and a change in the nature of the racket filling her head. At the same time the pressure on her belly eased. Her pilot had switched off the upthrusters. She prepared herself for the inevitable backwards drag as the main rockets came on, and sure enough it came. She felt her belt-rope cutting into the underside of her buttocks, her groin, her shoulderblades . . . too many pains in too many parts of the body to be counted. It was half a minute before she plucked up the courage to clear her visor.

When she did so, she was entranced.

They were travelling only about ten kilometres up, at a guess – high enough to clear all but the highest of Qitanefermeartha's sharp mountains. A crater-strewn landscape was rapidly unfolding beneath her. Most of its variations in colour were created purely by shadows, but it was fascinating nevertheless. Whatever had happened during the planet's geological and meteorological past, various forces had conspired to produce every possible shape and form of pockmark, impact ray, lava spread and sinuous rille. She was reminded of the way the surface of Mars had looked before humans had got around to starting to terraform that planet, but all of this was on a smaller scale: it was a finely detailed miniature rather than a portrait that covered half the wall. She wished she could tell the pilot to go down a bit lower – although that would have meant she could make out less of the surface, because now they really were picking up speed.

Earlier she had promised herself she would never do this again. Now she wondered if she wasn't in at the birth of a great new leisure industry.

The chronometer display at the upper right of her visor told her that by this time Pinocchio and Ten Per Cent Extra Free must have launched the programmed shuttle. With luck the bot would for some while now have been legging it away from the city of Qitanefermeartha as fast as he could. Assuming the Helgiolath cruisers didn't start bombarding the city for another hour, he should be safely distant.

361

She tongued her suit radio to the general frequency. The static was abominable.

'Has anyone else survived this so far?' she said.

There was a confusion of voices.

'Quiet!' she shouted.

After a few moments the babble died down.

'I thought I might have been the only one,' she said into the comparative quiet. 'I guess we won't be able to count ourselves until we get to wherever it is the Trok are taking us. But, if you can all attain what is politely called radio silence, I want to check on one person.'

There was stillness.

It was impossible for her to mimic the notes of the Spindrifter language using the various tonalities available to Argot, but, very slowly and deliberately, she did her best.

'Poll. Eee. Aaag. Ull.'

Just above the static she could hear something that sounded halfway between a chirrup and a whisper. It didn't matter what the detail of the message was, as Polyaggle must have realized even as she spoke – because in a different sense the message had a very precise meaning.

Assuming their luck kept up, not just one but two of the species currently extant in The Wondervale had been saved by the Trok from possible extinction.

To hell with whether the Helgiolath got round to coining all those little medals: Strider was going to do it herself – with her bare teeth, if necessary.

From the outset Pinocchio had known that, whatever Strider might think, this was a venture from which he was not going to return; now that he was in virtual symbiosis with the Image, the knowledge was an integral part of his make-up. And Ten Per Cent Extra Free – or, rather, the part of the *Gestalt* that could be conceptually partitioned off as Ten Per Cent Extra Free – had conspired in keeping the truth from her. She might have done something foolish and typically human like countermand her earlier instructions to the bot. Pinocchio *could* disobey direct orders, especially if he believed that by doing so he was acting in Strider's best interests, whether she knew it or not – he wouldn't be down on Qitanefermeartha had that not been the case – but even then it was very difficult for him.

He watched, with Ten Per Cent Extra Free also watching through Pinocchio's photoreceptors, the ships of the little Trok fleet lift off one by one and then speed away overhead. From here even Pinocchio's acute vision could not make out anything more than the flares of the rockets. He wondered which of them bore Leonie – knowing her, it would be the last to leave. He felt something inside him which, after a millisecond's thought, he identified as sorrow. Farewell, Leonie. There was still that other of those things called emotions inside him – the one which as yet he had been unable to identify, though it had been increasingly affecting his behaviour in minor ways for some time.

The main body of the Trok fighters lifted off now, much more quickly, and streaked towards the pole.

He/they waited a further two minutes.

Time, he/they thought.

There is a limit to the accuracy with which a shuttle's course can be pre-programmed, especially a shuttle that is lifting itself from a slightly sloping, treacherously soft plain of dust: a tiny subsidence beneath it can throw all the calculations off by a crucial few metres. There is also a limit to the number of actions even an Image can manage to perform simultaneously.

Strider had imagined that the bot would be able to leave the shuttle before it flew on its final, deadly mission. In fact, his puter was required to assist the ship's own rudimentary puter make all the small adjustments that would be necessary during the flight. The Image would have been able to do this, of course, except for the fact that the Image was going to be otherwise employed.

I WILL REMAIN IN CONSTANT MENTAL CONTACT WITH YOU, said the Ten Per Cent Extra Free fragment of the *Gestalt*, BUT NOW I MUST RELOCATE TO THE INTERIOR OF THE CITY.

Pinocchio knew this, for the thought was in part his own. He nodded his head – a human reaction that had been written into his software. Perhaps it would be the last human reaction he would ever display. His inheritance.

He/they triggered the launching procedure, and rockets struggled to raise the vehicle off the plain. It weaved slightly as it ascended, and he/they reflexively made a trivial alteration to the programme. The dust roiled beneath the shuttle. The stars were very bright – they seemed brighter even than Qitanefer-meartha's dim red sun, which was lying just above the horizon. All were outshone by the occasional brief flares of destruction still continuing above him/them. The Autarchy's defenders were putting up a better fight than expected.

He/they primed every ballistic on the shuttle – every weapon down to the last spare lazgun – and then programmed the drive for auto-destruct. Finally he/they set the shuttle into full forward thrust, with an acceleration of over ten gees.

Low across the plain it sped as straight as a laser beam towards the city's gloomy deadmetal airlock doors.

The Ten Per Cent Extra Free part of the symbiosis drew back from The Truthfulness some of the energy he had earlier stolen from the city.

All seventeen of the airlocks suddenly opened just as the shuttle approached. Pinocchio hardly had time to register them as the shuttle, streaming vengeful fire, shot straight through them. They closed tidily behind it as swiftly as they had opened.

Beyond, further – less substantial – barriers awaited. They shattered under the colossal impact of the howling spacecraft. Even Pinocchio's night-vision could see nothing now – the plastite forescreen was completely obscured by debris. The *Gestalt* of himself and Ten Per Cent Extra Free had started to use senses that, mixing machine and Image perceptions, were utterly alien to the human experiential world. Nano-trickles of electrical current within Pinocchio's and the shuttle's puters interrelated with equally tiny pulses of trans-reality energy as the vessel ploughed through the flimsy walls and other structures of Qitanefermeartha, leaving thousands of dead and dying in the darkness of their wake.

The bot made a few more minuscule alterations. The impacts

kept inducing trivial deviations into the shuttle's trajectory. 2.339081 seconds to go. 2.339080. 2.339079 . . .

Pinocchio made a guess at the emotion his software had serendipitously developed towards Leonie.

Ten Per Cent Extra Free drew power from The Truthfulness, expanding his being until it contained almost as much energy as he had originally taken from the city.

And then he returned it to Qitanefermeartha's main power-generating station, a vast installation right at the hub of the city.

Priming it.

Everywhere – even in the tunnel where the Autarch Nalla struggled and cursed – the lights came on.

That was of only passing interest to Qitanefermeartha's citizens, however, because just under a quarter of a second later the powerful ballistic that the shuttle had become struck the very centre of the unstable bomb that the power-generating station had become.

A dome of deadmetal not only keeps things out: it keeps things *in*. There was nowhere for the fireball to go.

'At last, I've become a Real Boy,' thought Pinocchio in the instant that he, the shuttle, the central power-generating station and everything else for a hundred kilometres around were vaporized.

It took a little longer for the entire interior of the city to be sterilized.

Oh, *several* seconds.

6

Losses, Gains, Reload and Aim

From where Strider was sitting she could see the disc of Qitanefermeartha. She felt as if the planet should show some sign of the premeditated act of mass murder she had perpetrated upon it. Necessary murder, perhaps, but it seemed to her like murder nevertheless.

She shifted in her seat. Once they were safe at the pole – although two people had failed to make it – Segrill had communicated with his Bredai allies, and within the hour a Bredai shuttle had arrived to lift them off-planet: it had been about the size of the *Santa Maria*. By that time five of the humans had died of asphyxiation, and several others had required urgent treatment. Fortunately the air aboard both the shuttle and the mother ship to which they were boosted approximated to F-14's atmosphere, so with luck it didn't contain anything toxic. Even so, everyone was now following Polyaggle's example and as a precaution refusing to eat anything but textured vegetable protein; there was anyway little temptation to eat whatever it was that the vast, clumsy-seeming Bredai enthusiastically consumed in room-sized quantities.

There had been so many losses, mused Strider, aside from among her own personnel. The Helgiolath fleet had been reduced by over one-half, Kortland himself seemingly being among the casualties. Several of Segrill's fighters had simply vanished: just because the Trok were small didn't mean that their personal griefs were small. A few of Qitanefermeartha's defenders had fled into the wilds of The Wondervale, but the remainder had been destroyed in their entirety. The Autarchy had lost its Autarch, and its capital.

Everybody had lost something, it seemed.

She was annoyed with herself that only one loss seemed to count very much to her.

Pinocchio.

Lover, trusted friend, confidant, advisor. The person to whom she could confess her most intimate secrets, her most neurotic worries. The one member of her personnel whom she hadn't had to be captain of. The rock to which, in times of need, she could cling.

Bredai decontamination had made the Spindrifter version look positively subtle. Not only was Strider entirely hairless, she felt as if every follicle had been individually scoured out, and none too gently. The Bredai didn't have too much use for fabric, and so like everyone else she was naked – Umbel knew what they were going to do next time they needed to suit up. It was curiously reassuring that her physical nakedness matched her nakedness of spirit.

Pinocchio.

Which idiot back at the SSIA had thought to give the bot such an infantile, patronizing name? Again and again Pinocchio had proved himself to be at least the equal and usually the superior of the humans around him. She wished whoever it had been were in front of her, so that she could . . .

And then, as her blood cooled, she thought about the name a little further.

No, after all, the name had been perfectly apposite.

Odd how long it had taken her to realize that fact.

Danny O'Sondheim, leaning into the Pocket, felt as if the wormhole were actively pulling at him. He realized there was sweat on his forehead, but resisted the urge to wipe it away: to do so he would have had to pass his hand through the small green knot that the Images had created for him in the centre of the Pocket.

Dammit, but he missed the presence of Strider. Dammit, but at the same time he was glad she was gone: the *Santa Maria* was his. People didn't enlist in the SSIA to become seconds-in-command.

There was a strange taste in his mouth. He at last identified it as lime. That was the taste of the wormhole.

He pressed the button that the graphic display told him to press so that the tachyonic drive would cut in. He found himself grinning just before he pressed it. The drive itself was going to revolutionize humanity's physics. The ride back through the wormhole was going to be an exhilaration.

In point of fact, O'Sondheim first realized the *Santa Maria* had entered the wormhole when he found himself staring into a blackly cavernous maw, framed above and below by arrays of mauve and seemingly very sharp teeth. That the upper and lower jaws were currently several hundred kilometres apart did not reassure him at all.

It's all just an illusion, was his first thought. *Oh shit,* was his second.

Quite a lot had been gained, thought Lan Yi as he stroked the skin of his forearm, amazed yet again by its silky smoothness. Although the experience of decontamination itself had been unpleasant, he was captivated by the various sensations of its after-effects.

The destruction of the Autarch and of Qitanefermeartha was a first step towards, he hoped, The Wondervale's gaining some form of freedom as it struggled out from under the tyrant's boot. Of course, there would be another Autarch soon – as soon as various competing would-be heirs battled out the succession, wiping out a few worlds and species along the way. But the early days of a new tyranny are the time when it is at its most vulnerable: there was hope.

Alliances, too, were gains.

There was the alliance now of the humans with the Trok and the Bredai and the various other species who had thrown off the thraldom to which they had been subjected on F-14. The Helgiolath, the Onurg of the Pridehouse had explained, were not necessarily to be trusted for ever, but perhaps they could be trusted for now. And then there was the forthcoming alliance with the ancient species, something which Lan Yi eagerly anticipated. He still wanted to study Polyaggle, to find out how such a highly sophisticated colonial organism – if that was what she was – could have evolved. The prospect of discovering other, equally strange species stirred more than just his intellect. He was honest enough with himself to recognize that there was an emotional charge there as well. The appeal of scientific research can be described as the satisfaction of human inquisitiveness – which is a long phrase meaning 'the thrill'.

And there had also been a personal gain.

Lan Yi walked across the floor of the sparsely furnished common-room the Bredai had created for the humans and took Strauss-Giolitto's hand. She reached her head down towards him and they pecked each other chastely on the cheek. At some time or another as they'd separately careened over the barren plains of Qitanefermeartha they'd individually realized quite how much they meant to each other. Older brother, younger sister; big sister, little brother.

There were tears in Strauss-Giolitto's eyes.

'Shit,' she said, 'but I've been thinking about that damn bot again.'

It was several subjective days later when Strider felt the nudge of an Image into her mind. The probe seemed slightly clumsy and nervous, as if this were some kind of tyro. Was there such a thing as a newborn Image? She had come to the assumption that the beings were immortals.

LEONIE, said an unpractised voice.

Pinocchio's voice.

369